15 MINUTES

A Maizie Albright Star Detective Mystery

Larissa
REINHART

PASTPERFECTPRESS.COM

15 MINUTES
Maizie Albright Star Detective Series
Published by PAST PERFECT PRESS

Copyright © 2016 by Larissa Reinhart
Library of Congress Control No: 2016920746
ISBN: 978-0-9978853-2-3

Author Photograph by Scott Asano

Cover Design and Interior Format

PRAISE FOR THE MAIZIE ALBRIGHT
STAR DETECTIVE SERIES
15 MINUTES (#1)

"Hollywood glitz meets backwoods grit in this fast-paced ride on D-list celeb Maizie Albright's waning star—even as it's reborn in a spectacular collision with her nightmarish stage mother, her deer-pee-scented-apparel-inventing daddy...and a murderer. Sassy, sexy, and fun, **15 MINUTES** is hours of enjoyment—and a wonderful start to a fun new series from the charmingly Southern-fried Reinhart."
~ Phoebe Fox, author of THE BREAKUP DOCTOR series

"I was already a huge fan of Larissa Reinhart's "Cherry Tucker" series, but in her new mystery series, FIFTEEN MINUTES, she had me at the end of the first line: "Donuts." Maizie Albright is the kind of fresh, fun, and feisty "star detective" I love spending time with, a kind of Nancy Drew meets Lucy Ricardo. Move over, Janet Evanovich. Reinhart is my new "star mystery writer!"
~ Penny Warner, author of DEATH OF A CHOCOLATE CHEATER and THE CODE BUSTERS CLUB

"Armed with humor, charm, and stubborn determination, Maizie is a breath of fresh air. I adored every second of **15 MINUTES**. Viva la Maizie!"
~ Terri L. Austin, author of the ROSE STRICKLAND MYSTERIES and the NULL FOR HIRE series.

"Child star and hilarious hot mess Maizie Albright trades Hollywood for the backwoods of Georgia and pure delight ensues. Maizie's my new favorite escape from reality."
~ Gretchen Archer, *USA Today* bestselling author of the DAVIS WAY CRIME CAPER series

PRAISE FOR THE CHERRY TUCKER MYSTERY SERIES
A COMPOSITION IN MURDER (#6)

"Anytime artist Cherry Tucker has what she calls a Matlock moment, can investigating a murder be far behind? A COMPOSITION IN MURDER is a rollicking good time."
~Terrie Farley Moran, *Agatha* Award-Winning Author of READ TO DEATH

"Boasting a wonderful cast of characters, witty banter blooming with southern charm, this is a fantastic read and I especially love how this book ended with exciting new opportunities, making it one of the best book in this delightfully endearing series."
~Dru Ann Love, *Dru's Book Musings*

"This is a winning series that continues to grow stronger and never fails to entertain with laughs, a little snark, and a ton of heart."
~ *Kings River Life Magazine*

THE BODY IN THE LANDSCAPE (#5)

"Cherry Tucker is a strong, sassy, Southern sleuth who keeps you on the edge of your seat. She's back in action in THE BODY IN THE LANDSCAPE with witty banter, Southern charm, plenty of suspects, and dead bodies—you will not be disappointed!"
~ Tonya Kappes, *USA Today* Bestselling Author

"Anyone who likes humorous mysteries will also enjoy local author Larissa Reinhart, who captures small town Georgia in the laugh- out-loud escapades of struggling artist Cherry Tucker."
~ *Fayette Woman Magazine*

Portraits of freshly dead people turn up in strange places in Larissa Reinhart's mysteries, and her THE BODY IN THE LANDSCAPE is no exception. Because of Cherry's experiences, she knows that—Super

Swine notwithstanding—man has always been the most dangerous game, making her the perfect protagonist for this giggle-inducing, down-home fun.
~ Betty Webb, *Mystery Scene Magazine*

DEATH IN PERSPECTIVE (#4)

"One fasten-your-seatbelt, pedal-to-the-metal mystery, and Cherry Tucker is the perfect sleuth to have behind the wheel. Smart, feisty, as tough as she is tender, Cherry's got justice in her crosshairs."
~ Tina Whittle, Author of the TAI RANDOLPH MYSTERIES

"The perfect blend of funny, intriguing, and sexy! Another must-read masterpiece from the hilarious *Cherry Tucker Mystery Series*."
~ Ann Charles, *USA Today* Bestselling Author of the DEADWOOD and JACKRABBIT JUNCTION MYSTERY SERIES.

"Artist and accidental detective Cherry Tucker goes back to high school and finds plenty of trouble and skeletons...Reinhart's charming, sweet-tea flavored series keeps getting better!"
~ Gretchen Archer, *USA Today* Bestselling Author of the DAVIS WAY CRIME CAPER SERIES

HIJACK IN ABSTRACT (#3)

"The fast-paced plot careens through small-town politics and deadly rivalries, with zany side trips through art-world shenanigans and romantic hijinx. Like front-porch lemonade, Reinhart's cast of characters offer a perfect balance of tart and sweet."
~ Sophie Littlefield, Bestselling Author of A BAD DAY FOR SORRY

"Reinhart manages to braid a complicated plot into a tight and funny tale. The reader grows to love Cherry and her quirky worldview, her

sometimes misguided judgment, and the eccentric characters that populate the country of Hula, Georgia. Cozy fans will love this latest Cherry Tucker mystery."
~ Mary Marks, *New York Journal of Books*

"In HIJACK IN ABSTRACT, Cherry Tucker is back--tart-tongued and full of sass. With her paint-stained fingers in every pie, she's in for a truckload of trouble."
~ J.J. Murphy, Author of the ALGONQUIN ROUND TABLE MYSTERIES

STILL LIFE IN BRUNSWICK STEW (#2)

"Reinhart's country-fried mystery is as much fun as a ride on the tilt-a-whirl at a state fair. Her sleuth wields a paintbrush and unravels clues with equal skill and flair. Readers who like a little small-town charm with their mysteries will enjoy Reinhart's series."
~ Denise Swanson, *New York Times* Bestselling Author of the *Scumble River Mysteries*

"The hilariously droll Larissa Reinhart cooks up a quirky and entertaining page-turner! This charming mystery is delightfully Southern, surprisingly edgy, and deliciously unpredictable."
~ Hank Phillippi Ryan, *Agatha* Award-Winning Author of TRUTH BE TOLD

"This mystery keeps you laughing and guessing from the first page to the last. A whole-hearted five stars."
~ Denise Grover Swank, New York Times and *USA TODAY* bestselling author

PORTRAIT OF A DEAD GUY (#1)

"Portrait of a Dead Guy is an entertaining mystery full of quirky

characters and solid plotting...Highly recommended for anyone who likes their mysteries strong and their mint juleps stronger!"
~ Jennie Bentley, *New York Times* Bestselling Author of FLIPPED OUT

"Reinhart is a truly talented author and this book was one of the best

cozy mysteries we reviewed this year."
~ *Mystery Tribune*

"It takes a rare talent to successfully portray a beer-and-hormone-addled artist as a sympathetic and worthy heroine, but Reinhart pulls it off with tongue-in-cheek panache. Cherry is a lovable riot, whether drooling over the town's hunky males, defending her dysfunctional family's honor, or snooping around murder scenes."
~ *Mystery Scene Magazine*

OTHER BOOKS BY LARISSA REINHART

THE CHERRY TUCKER MYSTERY SERIES
Novels
PORTRAIT OF A DEAD GUY (#1)
STILL LIFE IN BRUNSWICK STEW (#2)
HIJACK IN ABSTRACT (#3)
DEATH IN PERSPECTIVE (#4)
THE BODY IN THE LANDSCAPE (#5)
A COMPOSITION IN MURDER (#6)

Novellas
QUICK SKETCH (prequel to PORTRAIT) in
HEARTACHE MOTEL
THE VIGILANTE VIGNETTE (#5.5) in
MIDNIGHT MYSTERIES

THE MAIZIE ALBRIGHT STAR DETECTIVE SERIES
15 MINUTES
16 MILLIMETERS
NC-17

To keep up with Larissa's latest releases, contests, and events,
please join her newsletter. The link to join can be found on her
website, www.larissareinhart.com

(Note: Larissa will not share your email address and you can
unsubscribe at any time.)

Thank you!

To Terri and Gretchen.
Thanks for waving those pom-pons, girls.

ACKNOWLEDGEMENTS

Ritter Ames, you're an incredible editor, book guru, and a great friend. Thank you for all the help and support. I bow to your genius and love of spreadsheets. Neither of which I don't think I'll ever attain.

The Mystery Minions, know that I'm thinking about y'all while I'm writing. You each represent the reason I burn the midnight oil. Thank you so much for your incredible support and friendship!

To my writing friends at Henery Press, my Georgia colleagues, and especially to Dru Ann Love, Phoebe Fox, Penny Warner, and Debby Guisti, thank you for your friendship and guidance. I love the encouragement and support of the writing community. It's a wonderful thing.

Claire Bamford, thank you for your wonderful friendship before, during, and after the HHI filming. You're an inspiration to me. Thanks for your words of TV related advice, answering my questions, and beta reading!

Risa, Robin, and Tomoo-san, thanks for answering all my questions during the HHI shoot. And for being a part of a book marketing campaign.

Thank you to The Killion Group for all their publishing services, particularly my fun cover. It's incredible to work with you and thanks for all your patience!

To the Funks, Reinharts, and Hoffmans, thanks always for all your love, support, and Facebook shoutouts. Also to my sweet friends (too numerous to name all of you) for your encouragement, especially the Metzler-Concepcions, Witzanys (thank you for letting me borrow Maizie's name), and the Benders. Love you! And to all the folks in Andover and surrounds, thank you for your hometown support!

Gina, Bill, Hailey, Lily, and Grandma Sally, thank you for beta reading, shipping books, receiving books, and generally putting up with me.

Peachtree City, Georgia, thanks for inviting Hollywood to town and giving me the inspiration for this series. And thanks for being such a wonderful place to live and raise my children.

And to Trey, Lu & So, you have my gratitude and my love always. xoxo

ONE

#donutdilemna #B-lister

OF COURSE, NASH SECURITY SOLUTIONS would be housed in a donut shop.

Time and the elements had nearly scrubbed the painted Dixie Kreme ad from the side of the old brick building and I'd almost missed it. But with my Jag's top down, the confectioned-carb aroma assaulted my senses. I pulled in a long, exhilarating breath, then pretended I couldn't taste that sweet mouthful of heaven.

My trainer, Jerry, would have accused me of manifesting donut reality through my sheer love of trans-fats. After all my years in LA, delectables like donuts should cause my brain to flash a warning with a similar intensity to the bright red neon "Fresh & Hot" sign hanging in this storefront window. However, my brain's warning was more of an appetizing apple red. As in Snow White's "One bite and all your dreams will come true" red.

My therapist has an opinion on that subject, something about denied sugar, both literal and metaphorical. Either way, donuts meant trouble.

I almost buckled to temptation. But I had a mission. I sucked down another mouthful of donut air, placed one Jimmy Choo in front of the other and moved through the front door of the Dixie Kreme Donut building. Then into a dim hall, up the stairs and into a dimmer hall. And stopped before the door with the words "Nash Security Solutions" painted on the frosted glass.

Not a modern glass door that swished when opened. An old wooden door. The whole building had that old-timey feel with the brass knobs and wood and the plaster-over-brick walls. Even the building's front door had a half moon, stained glass window. Those adorable antiquing couples in Pasadena would have loved the Dixie Kreme building.

For a long minute, I stood before that door inhaling *eau de donut* and evaluating my wardrobe choices. I wanted to look appropriate. This was my big break. Like a screen test, but better. My stylist might not have agreed on pairing the Jimmy Choos with a white, sleeveless Nina Ricci resort dress and my Chloé Clare bag. Sometimes my stylist went a little overboard. She would have gone with Louboutins and a Birkin. *Keeping Up with the Kardashians* and whatnot. Literally.

But this was Black Pine, Georgia, where Loubies and Birkins weren't fundamental. I grabbed the old-timey, brass knob of the Nash Security door and strode through with a "go get 'er" set to my features, ripping off my Barton Perreira Jet-Setters and shoving them into my bag like I was on an episode of *Miami Undercover*.

"Mr. Nash," I said with great authority. And then dropped my bag. Forgot to close my mouth. And I might have gasped.

From *Miami Undercover* to *I Love Lucy*.

Nash Security Solutions consisted of two rooms. The outer room had a battered corduroy recliner, a few metal file cabinets, and a frumpy couch. In this room, all was well, although run down and dusty. Unfortunately, the door to the second room stood open. I was unaware of the condition of that room because Mr. Nash of Nash Security Solutions was naked.

Well, not naked-naked. Half-naked. But he was a big guy. As in tall, solid wall of muscle. Movie star muscle. Like Mr. Nash had a personal trainer who specialized in tone and definition.

Except this was Black Pine, and I doubted Mr. Nash had ever hired a trainer to watch him sweat while screaming about the evils of trans-fats and the virtues of chili pepper colonics. Mr. Nash didn't look the type to put up with anyone yelling at him about anything.

He did seem a little slow, though. At my authoritative "Mr. Nash," he froze. With a t-shirt in one hand. And unbuckled jeans.

Giving me time to peel my ogle off all those muscles and the undone buckle and peruse his facial features. His head was shaved and his nose looked broken. A wicked scar curled from his chin to chiseled jaw.

But most astonishing, Mr. Nash's eyes were Paul Newman blue. Startling, intense, arctic blue.

He countered my ogle for a few long seconds, taking in my hidden curves, the reddish-blonde hair, sea glass green eyes, and a nice pair of legs. I get a lot of ogling. Vicki trained me to take ogles as a compliment. Should it bother me? Ask my therapist. She's got plenty to say on the subject, too.

Behind me, I heard the door open and close while Mr. Nash and I continued our stare-off.

"Didn't know you gave peep shows this early, Nash," said a deep, gravelly voice.

I jerked my eyes off the hard body and onto the older, African-American man dropping into the recliner. He wore a chef's apron over his t-shirt and jeans and smelled of donuts.

"Oh my God. I'm sorry," I said to all listening and glanced into the inner office where Mr. Nash fumbled with his belt buckle.

"Why should you be sorry?" said the man, throwing the lever on the recliner to prop up his feet. "Nash's the one raised in a barn."

"Morning, Lamar," drawled Nash, then addressed me. "Excuse me, ma'am. I'm sorry about this. Forgot to shut the door. And you are?"

I relaxed my face, which felt squinchy. My directors hated that look because it made me look constipated rather than astonished. Taking a deep breath, I said, "I'm Maizie Albright. I mean, Maizie Spayberry. Well, it was Spayberry, and I'm thinking about switching back permanently. Although I do like my other name. It has a better ring, which is why my manager changed it."

Nash nodded and focused on buttoning the shirt he'd slipped on, although he revealed a flash of what I like to call "WTH face."

"Spayberry. Which Spayberry?" said Lamar. "There's a ton around here. Unless you mean Boomer Spayberry? Of Deer-

Nose?"

"Yes, sir. Boomer is my father." DeerNose was big among those that shopped at Bass Pro and other hunting outfitters, but I didn't get recognized as a DeerNose daughter much in LA. It produced a feeling of pride and awkwardness. Among hunters, Daddy's considered the Michael Kors of clothing and accessories. He designs scented hunting apparel. The awkwardness comes with the scent. Deer pee. Big with hunters. Not so much with anyone else.

I glanced at Nash, who was now buttoning a white dress shirt over his muscles. An Armani. A bit old, but still sharp.

"I'm sorry, but aren't you expecting me?" I glanced at my watch. "I was told to come at this time."

"Told by who?" Nash paused the buttoning.

"A Jolene Sweeney. I didn't speak to her, my assistant set up the interview. Maybe our wires got crossed?" I raised my brows at the string of curses Mr. Nash uttered. "I'm sorry. Do I have the time wrong?"

Shooting a look of concern at Lamar, Nash pushed past me to flip the lock on the front door.

"So are you living over at the DeerNose cabin?" Lamar continued. "I heard it's pretty grand. Nice land Boomer's got, too."

"Yes, sir," I said, watching Mr. Nash pace before the locked door. "I haven't been in Black Pine for about six years. As a kid, I spent my summers here. Although I would've been better off moving back a long time ago. But you can't change the past. At least that's what Renata says."

"Who's Renata?" asked Lamar.

"Oh, my therapist. The last one." I bit my lip, realizing you shouldn't admit to numerous therapists in an interview. Or what should be an interview. "It's something we do in LA."

"Therapy?" asked Lamar.

"Rehab." Then bit my lip again.

Lamar smiled. He didn't seem to find Nash's pacing at all unnerving. "That's right. Boomer Spayberry's daughter is the TV kid. Maizie Albright. You were on that teen detective show, wasn't it?"

"Yes, sir. *Julia Pinkerton: Teen Detective.*" I grinned. "Before that was *Kung Fu Kate.* And a few pilots and TV movies. Julia's where my career really took off. And what inspired my new career."

"I don't watch much myself. Nash and I still prefer the radio for the Braves and Bulldogs."

"Because you're too cheap to pay for cable," said Nash.

"Don't need it," said Lamar. "You've got enough equipment, you could probably rig yourself some satellite TV."

"What did Jolene say?" asked Nash.

I looked from Nash to Lamar. He folded his arms behind his head.

"Miss Albright?" Nash's voice grew impatient.

"Me? Like I said, I didn't speak to Jolene. My assistant, Blake, did. Blake's gone now, or I would call her. I had to let all my people go. That was hard."

"The meeting, Miss Albright?"

"I'm sorry. It was about the apprentice position? I need two years training for private investigation and you need—"

"I need nothing." Nash swore using words not altogether familiar to me. And after living in LA, that's surprising. "Can you believe this?"

"Well," I slowed my speech. "I did believe it sounded legitimate. I mean, I haven't been in Black Pine for a while, but I assumed, or at least Blake assumed, everything was aboveboard. I think she checked your agency with Better Business or something—"

"I was talking to Lamar," sighed Nash. "Lamar, what do you make of this?"

"You know my feelings. But you could use help, Nash," said Lamar. "I'd ask about qualifications."

Nash turned from the door to look at me.

"Me?" I said. "I've been studying Criminal Justice at U Cal, Long Beach, while doing the show. But if you don't watch TV, you probably didn't know that. The producers liked the location shots on campus. I had to draw the line at them following me into class, because the professors got upset—"

"What show is that?" said Lamar. "One of them reality shows?"

«*All is Albright*. It got picked up after the first time I went to rehab. Vicki's idea to capitalize on my notoriety. Awkward, right? I was ready to be done with TV altogether, but it did pay for college. And all the legal fees. And my other bills—"

"Are you for real?" asked Nash. "Is this some kind of prank? *Candid Camera* type of thing?"

«*Candid Camera*? Like Betty White's show?" I shook my head. "I am entirely serious. Before I left California, I had Blake research private investigation agencies in Black Pine and yours was all she came up with. Is Jolene Sweeney your partner? Because I'm starting to wonder how Blake made the appointment—"

"Even I'm not old enough to remember *Candid Camera*, Nash," said Lamar. "I swear, you were born in the wrong century. Although, I'm not much for reality shows. Except *Cops*, I do like *Cops*.»

"Well, last season was a bit like *Cops*," I said. "That's when Oliver's non-profit was busted, unfortunately. Which led to my recent predicament. However, my therapist, Renata, and I do agree it all worked out for the best. I wanted out of LA. And this is a better way to fulfill my dream. A healthier alternative."

"Now that sounds interesting," said Lamar. "A bust as a healthier alternative. Not heard that view before."

"I think I've heard enough," said Nash.

The doorknob rattled, and we all hushed. Nash made the finger to the lips sign, and Lamar cut me a "can you believe this guy" type of look.

I wanted to giggle, but then a sharp knock sounded on the frosted glass, and my stomach sank somewhere beneath my knees. The donut smell and nudity should have given me fair warning. Vicki had told me moving here was a bad idea. She said I was too Beverly Hills for Black Pine.

I hoped I had enough Black Pine in me to make this work. Although it did seem, when I thought her wrong, Vicki usually proved me otherwise.

"I know you're in there, Wyatt Nash," said a female voice outside the door. "Open up."

Nash glowered at the door.

Lamar closed his eyes. A smile stretched across his face.

I clutched my Chloé bag to my chest, hoping I hadn't got locked in a room with two crazy men.

On the other hand, if the crazy was outside, I hoped the lock held.

The knocking commenced to pounding. "Very funny. Wyatt, honey. Open the door. I'm late for the meeting."

"I'm not your honey," said Nash. "And there's no meeting."

"Like I meant honey that way. Lord help me, Wyatt, just open the flippin' door."

"Jolene Sweeney, you have three seconds to leave the premises or I'm calling Black Pine PD and reporting a violation of your restraining order. I believe it said one hundred feet." Nash nodded his head and folded his arms.

My eyebrows shot up to my hairline.

Lamar sniggered.

"You dumbshit," said Jolene Sweeney. "I'm the one with the restraining order on you."

I edged toward the inner office door.

"Well then, I suggest you back down the hallway, and I'll just get out of here," said Nash. "I'm not even going to point out the fallacy of your logic in suggesting a meeting within one hundred feet of me."

I reached the inner office and checked that door for a lock.

"Lamar," said Jolene. "Are you in there?"

Lamar's eyelids drifted open. "Yes, ma'am."

"Just tell me this," said Jolene. "Did a girl show up?"

"There's one here now."

"Miss Albright," said Jolene. "Are you there? I'm so sorry about this."

"Ma'am?" I adopted my father's throatier, slower cadence, rather than my shriller, speedier California tongue. "Actually, my last name is Spayberry. There seems to be a mix-up. Mr. Nash, here, didn't expect me and doesn't need an assistant."

"Spayberry?" Jolene's knocking and rattling quieted.

Lamar and Nash glanced at me. I shrugged.

"I had thought..." Jolene paused. "I'm sorry, Miss Spayberry. Black Pine Group and I are expecting Maizie Albright from the *Julia Pinkerton: Teen Detective* show."

"So you don't need an assistant?"

"We thought if we sold to a national chain, Maizie might do endorsements. You know, grown up Julia recommending a real detective agency. Anyway, I think she's just looking to do research for a new show. You can go, Miss Spayberry. And no skin off your nose, Wyatt. When Miss Albright gets here, just let her follow you around for a few days."

Nash glared at the door. "Black Pine Group? That's who you've been talking to? Did you know I have a client there?"

"Wyatt, stop being so unreasonable," yelled Jolene. "I don't know what that local girl is doing there, but don't hire anyone. You can't afford it. We need to keep your overhead low. Get rid of her before Maizie Albright shows up."

"Are you just doing research for a new show?" Lamar asked me.

I shook my head and whispered. "I'm done with TV. I really do want to become a private investigator. I've had experience with them in the past. And I loved playing the part of a detective. That's why I majored in Criminal Justice. And then there's Judge Ellis's requirements. I need a job."

Nash gave the door a toothy smile and his cool blue eyes glinted. "Jolene, I will hire whoever the hell I want. This is still my business." He turned around and beamed the wicked blues on me. "You're hired."

Behind the door, Jolene hammered and swore.

"You're making my new assistant blush, Jolene."

"Please, Wyatt. If Maizie Albright shows up, don't offend her. Lord knows we could use the PR."

"When did I ever seem the type to let some TV personality follow me around? Now leave before I call the police and get myself removed from your presence."

"Go to hell," said Jolene.

"Probably," said Nash. "But later. I'm a little busy at the moment."

The door thudded and shook as if someone kicked it. Heels clicked down the hallway.

"Dammit." Nash punched the file cabinet. The bottom drawer slid open, revealing a mess of electrical cords. He kicked the drawer shut. "The Black Pine Group?"

I backed farther into the inner office, my hand on the door-knob. "What's going on here?"

"Do you know how to do billing?" asked Lamar. "Accounts receivable and payable? How to file receipts? What about surveil-lance? Due diligence research? Any experience there?"

"You're not really hired," said Nash. "I don't need an assistant."

"You can't live on spite, Nash," said Lamar. "I know for a fact your billings are a mess. You've probably got people who owe you money and you don't have time to chase them down."

"If I needed an assistant, I would have hired one myself."

"We've all needed someone to give us a break at one time or another," said Lamar. "And need I remind you, who gave you yours?"

"Who?" I said.

"None of your business," said Nash.

"Boomer Spayberry," said Lamar. "When Nash was setting up his office and struggling to make it a go, Boomer hired him to evaluate and recommend the security at DeerNose. Huge job. And it's not like Boomer wouldn't have gotten bids from bigger firms to get the best price."

"True," I said. "Daddy never met a dollar he liked to spend needlessly."

"I wasn't a charity case," said Nash.

"No," said Lamar, "but without a recommendation from some-one like Boomer Spayberry, you would have struggled to keep your business from going belly-up. I don't need to remind you what was going on at that point in your life."

"No, you don't," said Nash. "And I rather you keep it to your-self."

"Am I hired?" I squealed. "You don't know how relieved I am. Judge Ellis said I had ten days after reaching Black Pine to secure a job. You see—"

"First rule, Miss Albright," said Nash. "I don't want any details about your celebrity lifestyle."

"I don't mind hearing details," said Lamar.

"Do it on your own time." Nash turned back to me. "You're going to have to prove yourself. Because right now I don't see anything worth hiring. This is a serious business."

"Of course," I said. "I'm a quick learner. My directors all said so. Except one, but it was such a B movie, nobody tried very hard. Straight to video, you know. Even the Syfy channel rejected it."

"Do I need to remind you of rule one already, Miss Albright? Now, I've got some appointments to keep. I need to finish changing, so if you don't mind." Nash waved his hand.

"Time to make sure they're making the donuts downstairs." Lamar popped from his chair, grinning. "This is just what you needed, Nash."

"I need this like a hole in the head."

"I'm sure Jolene would love to arrange that for you."

TWO

#wannabedetective #LALooks

AFTER LAMAR LEFT, I WAITED in the outer office while Nash finished changing. With the door closed, thankfully. I took to fiddling with my sunglasses and wondering if this decision to apprentice Nash wasn't just a tiny bit rash. I've been known to do rash.

As I considered how to get Mr. Nash to write me a W-4 so I could get a copy to Judge Ellis, Nash's door swung open. A polished businessman in gray Armani slacks and Gucci loafers appeared.

I squinted at the Guccis. Perhaps I had been judging Black Pine fashion by DeerNose gear too long.

Nash glanced at his watch then pointedly at me. "I do have a meeting. So, see you.»

I nodded, then realized I was doing it again. Letting other people control the situation. Renata had lectured me on this. Although she mainly meant Vicki.

While I thought of a polite way to ask Mr. Nash to allow me in on a client discussion, a knock sounded on his door again. A normal knock this time.

Nash strode past me to usher in a middle-aged man, wearing khakis and a golf shirt.

The golf shirt insignia said "Black Pine Club." He also had the paunch, sunburned cheeks, and drawl of the Black Pine moneyed class. Mostly old money, although recently there'd been some new money with a resurgence of interest in the old resort town. A century ago, wealthy Georgians founded Black Pine Mountain Resort to escape the summer heat. During the Depression, muckity-mucks finagled a Works Project to dam a nearby river, thereby giving the mountain retreat waterfront property. From there, Black Pine Lake and Black Pine town emerged.

After the man had back-slapped Nash with a hearty "mornin'," he turned toward me for a quick perusal. "Now who's this ray of sunshine brightening your gloomy office, Nash?"

"David Waverly, this is..." Nash paused. He wasn't sure what to call me.

"I know who this is." David Waverly stepped forward to clasp my hand in his. "Maizie Albright. I heard you were in town. Jolene said you needed to follow Nash to research for a movie. This is a good sign."

"Now David," said Nash. "I don't know what you're talking about. This is Maizie Spayberry. She's just leaving. Come into my office so we can chat."

Waverly continued to pump my hand between his meaty paws. "Miss Maizie, I was a *Julia Pinkerton* fan. It is such an honor to meet you."

"Thank you," I said, unable pull my hand from his. "That's very nice of you to say."

"It was such a shame when Julia left for college and your sister, Amy, took over the detective business. Just wasn't the same. Why did you leave?"

How do I say, "Between seasons, puberty caught me and ended my career in teen television?" My look had gone from girl-next-door to *Playboy* centerfold overnight. I had spent my entire last season in Julia's cheer uniform, hugging books or hiding behind furniture to keep family-friendly ratings. Of course, that last season we did have a sudden spike in the middle-aged male demographic. Of which, it seemed, David Waverly was one.

I lifted a shoulder. "That's TV for you."

"How about an autograph?"

"I'll need my hand for that." I smiled and yanked my hand from his.

"Autographs later," said Nash and pointed toward the open

office door, gesturing for Waverly to enter. "We need to talk, David."

David Waverly ignored Nash. "I suspect my wife is having an affair."

"That's horrible," I said. "Why do you think that?"

"Sarah's been acting differently. She's quit her volunteer work, which doesn't make us look too good in the community. She denied an affair, of course."

"Do you have children?" I asked. "This will be very hard on your children."

Nash cleared his throat. "David, after a month of surveillance, her schedule is fairly routine. Sarah does go to the club every day. But she's not meeting anyone there. Sometimes she takes the boat out."

David Waverly leaned toward me. "We don't have children. She's not being open with me. She never understood me. I thought I should start collecting evidence to break the pre-nup. Just in case."

"Oh, my."

Nash dropped his hand. "Have you noticed anything new? Odd items in your home or car? Receipts? Strange credit card charges? Anything else I can investigate? I'm sorry, David, but I'm not seeing it."

"How long have you been married?" I didn't get a good vibe from David Waverly. Nash seemed eager to be rid of him as a client. Which also felt strange.

Nash's lips firmed, and he gave me a barely perceptible head shake.

I looked back at David Waverly, who counted on his fingers.

"Eleven years?" said David Waverly. "Sarah's number two."

Nash folded his arms. "Mr. Waverly, in these cases, fifty percent of the time a husband is not correct in his assumptions."

"Fifty percent." I turned to David Waverly. "Those are pretty good odds she isn't cheating. You must be happy to hear that."

David Waverly didn't look happy to hear his odds. "I'm sure I'm right. Why don't you see what Miss Albright can find? She's got experience."

"She played a character on TV," said Nash. "That's not experience. The show wasn't even believable."

"You watched *Julia Pinkerton*?»

Nash snapped a look at me, then addressed David Waverly. "I don't feel I can help you, David. Continuing with the investigation is a waste of your money and my time."

"I'm disappointed in you, Nash." A sly smile slid from Waverly's thin lips. "Is this about Black Pine Group selling your business? Don't worry about conflict of interest. Sweeney's handling it."

Nash's ears pinkened and a muscle flexed in his neck. "I'm not interested in selling. You've been talking to the wrong person. I'm dropping your case because I don't believe there is one, and it feels hinky to keep pursuing your wife while she golfs and shops for her lady things."

Maybe it was the mention of his wife's "lady things," but David Waverly's golf tan deepened in color. "I know my wife, and I know something's going on."

"Again, I'm sorry, David."

Waverly turned to me. "You need to help me. I'm sure you understand. Everyone knows what you went through with your husband. Maybe we need fresh eyes on Sarah. A woman's perspective."

"Oliver wasn't my husband. But I do understand feeling blindsided by someone close." I didn't like Waverly using my tabloid fodder for an appeal to make me discredit my almost-boss. But after all, Waverly must know his own wife better than Nash did. "Maybe Mr. Nash would let me practice surveillance on your wife?"

Too late, I saw Nash's clamped lip, bug-eyed head shake.

"How about just for a week?" I said. "And if I don't see anything odd, then you'll agree to let Mr. Nash drop the case?"

Behind Waverly, Nash rolled his eyes.

Waverly bobbed his head, the angry color fading from his cheeks. "Great idea."

"Alrighty," I said. "See you soon."

David Waverly rocked back on his heels. "I certainly hope so.

Come out to the club sometime. I'll take you out on my little boat."

I hadn't been gone from Black Pine so long that I didn't understand the euphemism. Little boats in Black Pine are not little. Just like Black Pine is not a little lake.

"That sounds lovely." Which is my euphemism for "not a chance in hell."

After a round of goodbyes and a firm closing of the office door, Nash set his blue laser beams upon me. "What in the hell was that? You can't offer your services to one of my clients. There's something hinky going on and you have no business getting involved. You're not even a real assistant. You're some crazy Hollywood detective wannabe. When you realize how dirty and sick this industry really is, you're going to wish you were back on TV."

"I thought maybe I could help you with an awkward situation? And at the same time, get a little field experience?"

"I tell you what's awkward. Having Maizie Albright in my office. It'll make a great bar story, but I wouldn't choose to have you meet someone like David Waverly."

"Why?"

"Look at the way he was slobbering all over you."

"That doesn't bother me, don't let it bother you. It's very gentlemanly of you, though. Thank you for your concern."

"You misunderstand me. I wasn't concerned for you. I'm sure you're used to men slobbering all over you. I couldn't get Waverly to pay attention because you were here. I need to remove myself from that job so I can focus on other assignments. Sarah Waverly is not having an affair."

"I suppose you do have a point there. I'll work on that."

He walked back to his desk and rooted through the folders stacked on his desk.

"So what's next?"

"What do you need me for?" Nash yanked on a folder and flipped it open. "Sounds like you're rounding up your own cases."

"I need to work under a private investigator. Two years, right? You're board certified with the Georgia Association of Professional Private Investigators. And you need office help."

"Leave GAPPI out of this."

"I just graduated," I pleaded. "I'm educated, Mr. Nash. I know what I need to do. Now it's training. It's only two years."

Nash's eyes flicked from the folder to me. "All right. I'll make you a deal. You successfully deliver this summons to the right person and I'll let you follow Sarah Waverly for a week." Then he cracked a smile.

A brilliant smile. With a dimple. Paired with those gleaming polar eyes, the broken nose and scar seemed to vanish.

I fell a teensy bit in love. But don't worry. I do that all the time. Hearts are made to be broken and so forth. Besides, I had a dream to fulfill. Maybe a naïve dream, but a dream nevertheless. I was on the road to becoming a real Julia Pinkerton.

WHILE I WAS CALIFORNICATING, BLACK Pine experienced an explosion of the economic and population variety. Besides the resort, vacation homes and private boat docks had always surrounded the lake. Those servicing the vacationers lived in Black Pine, once a town of about eight thousand. But in the last twenty years, the town had experienced steady growth. Partly in thanks to DeerNose apparel.

DeerNose had grown. Black Pine had grown. And about the time I got out of my first rehab stint—boom!—Black Pine quadrupled in commerce, population, and tourists. I didn't recognize the town anymore, except for the old square where Wyatt Nash had his donut scented private investigation office. And of course my daddy's land, which he'd protect with his guns and constitutional rights.

These days, Black Pine Mountain has real subdivisions. Gated. With those little security booths. And you can't throw a rock and not hit a strip mall. We're looking more like LA every day. I even found good sushi. In Black Pine, Georgia.

I know, right?

Following Wyatt Nash through town, I passed a Polaris ATV

shop and an Audi dealership. A live bait shop and a mega-Cabela's. A parking-lot-smoker-plastic-picnic-tabled barbecue joint next door to a gluten-free-vegan-organic cupcake shop.

You get the picture.

Nash's Silverado pickup hung a sharp right into a strip mall and then pulled before a hair salon. La Hair. Or LA Hair. The sign was in all caps, so hard to tell. I parked the Jag next to Wyatt Nash, hopped out of my car, and scrambled to meet him on the sidewalk.

"You know who we're looking for?"

"Tiffany Griffen." I shivered. From excitement or nerves, I wasn't sure. I'm supposed to inventory my emotions, but I tend to forget.

"I'll ask for her first. Give you an idea of what can happen." Turning on the heel of his Gucci loafer, Nash strode through the door of LA HAIR.

A tinkling bell announced my presence, quickly lost in the pumping rhythm of the top twenty hit playing from the speakers. The layered scent of acetate, ammonia, and Aveda gave me as warm a welcome as the chirping voices coming from the nail and hair stations. Behind a half wall, one stylist had a woman's head covered in foil. A nail girl chatted with a patron. I counted one more beautician, hands full of lather, soaping up a woman leaning back into a sink.

I smiled, wiggled my fingers, and strolled past the glass and metal shelves displaying hair product and junk jewelry. Leaving on my Jet Setters, I grabbed a *People* and relaxed into a molded plastic chair to watch Wyatt Nash in action.

He stood at the desk, waiting for the reception girl to unplug the phone from her ear. Rigid shoulders and stiff posture gave away his aggravation. Either with me or with standing in LA HAIR. Some guys can't relax in a salon. My daddy, for example. Probably hadn't seen the inside of a salon since he divorced my mother. Unfortunately, he could really use a trim. Particularly his beard.

The reception girl finished her call and gazed up at Nash.

"Would you like a cut?"

"Is Tiffany Griffen working?" asked Nash.

Five sets of eyes cut toward the manicurist, then to Nash. Everyone except for the woman bent backward over the sink. She had no idea that a hard-bodied giant with Paul Newman eyes stood in the beauty salon. Her stylist continued to massage shampoo into her scalp, her eyes on Nash.

The nail girl, a thin brunette with a pixie shag ombre dyed in electric blue, shook her head. "She ain't here."

"That's funny," said Nash. "Because when I called a few minutes ago, I was told Tiffany was working today."

"Sorry," said the brunette. "You were told wrong."

"Guess I'll wait until she shows."

"Guess you might be waiting a while, but suit yourself." The brunette turned back to her client and flipped on a small fan attached to the nail table. "Barb, you let these dry before you take off. I don't want to hear about touch ups."

With a scowl, Nash stalked to the line of plastic chairs and chose one near the reception desk, five chairs from me. Picking up a magazine from the table next to him, he glanced at it, looked at me, and threw the tabloid back on the table.

Time for Julia Pinkerton. I tossed the *People* onto a chair, rose, and strode past Nash to the desk. "I'd like to have my nails done."

"Mani/pedi?" asked the girl. Her dark, curly hair had been straightened and bobbed, setting off a snub nose, mocha skin, and chocolate eyes. Adorbs. Vicki would have told her to lose forty pounds, but I knew Spanx and the right jeans would have done her well enough without starving off the weight.

"Just a file and buff, I think." Pulling off my sunglasses, I slid them into my bag and smiled.

"You're M-m-maizie Albright," the girl stammered.

"What's your name?"

"Rhonda." She stuck out her hand and I shook it.

"Nice to meet you, Rhonda. How are you?"

In the salon area, the women had leaned forward, watching Rhonda and me. The stylist at the sink pulled a phone from her pocket.

"Just fine, ma'am." Rhonda still clutched my hand. "How are you?"

"I'm great, Rhonda. I've moved back home to Black Pine for good."

"Oh, that's nice," breathed Rhonda. "The locals will leave y'all alone if you want. We've gotten used to some celebrities coming up here."

"I am glad to hear that, Rhonda. I wasn't happy in Hollywood, you know?"

"You should hear what my husband calls Hollywood," said the foil lady. "Of course you can't be happy out there. This is your real home. It's right for you to come back to your daddy. We know all about what happened. Y'all ran around with the wrong sort."

"Would you sign me an autograph?" asked Rhonda. "And can we do a picture?"

"Sure, Rhonda." I reached over the reception desk, grabbed a pen, and signed my name in big, loopy letters on the schedule book.

Rhonda held out her phone, and I wrapped an arm around her neck and smiled for a selfie. Probably'd go viral, but I couldn't keep my debut in Black Pine under wraps for long. Besides, I felt bad for what was about to happen.

Returning Rhonda's phone, I glanced over my shoulder at Nash. He'd crease his Armani shirt if he didn't stop crossing his arms so tightly. And that scowl would cause crow's feet. I grinned at him. He looked at his watch.

"Now," I said, "how about that buff and file?"

"Yes, ma'am." Rhonda scurried from behind her desk, grasped my arm, and led me to the nail area.

Phones clicked photos as we trooped behind the half wall. I oohed and ahhed over the setup, glancing at the framed certificates in each station as I passed. Jenna. Shelly. Ashley. Ashley had a photo stuck to her mirror. Ashley wasn't working today.

Barb, the tiny woman with the wet nails, popped out of her seat. "I'm all done, Miss Albright." Grasping my hand in two of hers, Barb pumped my arm. "I am glad you have put that horrible business behind you. We here in Black Pine would love to welcome you back. As long as you don't do any of that funny stuff anymore."

"Thank you, Barb."

"Right?" said Rhonda. "They said in *Us Weekly*, you got a nice judge. He took it easy on you. Gave you probation and rehab and some fines."

I hated rehashing my former life. But I also hated how the tabloids always got the details wrong. It was a choice between allowing people to think the worst or coming off as defensive. A total lose-lose situation, as Vicki would say.

"I got lucky with Judge Ellis. And he agreed that moving to Black Pine and starting over was a healthy solution. I had to finish college and the 'minute I graduated' move back home and get a job. I have ten days to turn in a pay stub. Then another year of checking in to see that I stay on my feet."

"You need to speak to my church, Miss Maizie," said Barb, still pumping my hand.

"Barb, your nails," said the brunette with the blue ends.

Barb pulled her hands off mine and waved them in the air. "They're fine. Miss Albright, you go on and have a seat. I'll just sit over at the dryer table."

I slid into the seat before the brunette and studied the wall over her shoulder. No certificate. Brunette with the blue ombre dye must be Tiffany. When Nash had said her name, they had all shot her a look and Barb had quit talking, at least until I had introduced myself. Simple deduction, just like Julia Pinkerton would have done. My lips curled with excitement.

Leaning toward Barb, I winked. "I heard this was a good place to get a manicure."

Tiffany raised her brows. "People like you usually go to the shops over at the lake."

"Well, maybe I'm different." I smiled.

Brunette glanced at my Nina Ricci dress and snorted.

Ignoring the snort, I extended my fingers over the towel covered bump on her table. "So, Tiffany, how long have you lived in Black Pine?"

"Long enough."

Nash hopped to his feet. He clutched an envelope in his big hand.

I swiveled back to Tiffany. She narrowed her liquid-lined eyes, half stood, and drew an elbow back. I stared at the elbow, realized it was attached to a fist, and caught Tiffany's focused glare as her knuckle slammed into my nose.

My chair tipped back. My bag flew across the linoleum tiles. The Jimmy Choos shot into the air. And an intense, sharp pain ricocheted through my head.

I squeezed my eyes shut to the sound of more clicking phones.

THREE

#PunchintheDeerNose #ManiPediPow

I LOVED *JULIA PINKERTON: TEEN DETECTIVE.* Not because the show gave me international exposure. I worked with some great actors, both my regular cast and the guest stars. Real nice people who genuinely seemed to like me. Excellent crew and sweet craft folks. Treated me like a princess. On a long running show, they say your colleagues become family. That's true. But when a show ends, the family disperses.

And you don't always get a new family. Especially when you've outgrown your cheer uniform, but everyone still thinks of you as a cheerleader. And you weren't that great of an actress anyway.

Even in hindsight, I would have done the show all over again. But not for the reasons you might think. Julia was smart. Really clever, sometimes crafty, but still likable. The other characters underestimated her because she was a teenager, but Julia used it to her advantage. Her teenagerness was her disguise.

She began as a school narc in the first season, working with the local police department. But after falling in love with the high school basketball star/drug dealer—originally a redeemable character, but when his contract wasn't renewed, the writers had to flip him and kill him off—Julia lost confidence in the police and decided to strike out on her own. When you're a teen detective on TV, you can do that. It worked. For eight seasons.

That's like two millennia in TV years.

Plus, I met real police officers and real security agents. Advisors to the show. They took me for ride-alongs, got me into the Kids Police Academy, and let me hang out with them on set so I could listen to their stories. My agent and Vicki encouraged it, thinking it would help me develop Julia into a more convincing character, even though the advisors were actually hired to assist the writers and director.

Quick-witted and sharp, Julia could make the experts laugh. She asked provocative questions. Detective Earl King—guy with a permanent scowl and no neck—took me for ice cream every Friday.

Detective King said he wished he had a daughter as bright as Julia.

I'll tell you one thing. Julia Pinkerton would never have gotten socked in the nose by a nail esthetician.

I lay on the floor, holding my nose and tearing up. I was no Julia Pinkerton. I wasn't even a very good Maizie Albright. But I had succeeded in flushing out Tiffany for Wyatt Nash. Maybe he would still give me the job.

Mr. Nash handed Tiffany her papers, glanced down at me, and shook his head. "Guess I should have told you she has a record for assault. Didn't think she'd use it on you. They were all domestic disputes." After asking if I wanted to call the police, he offered me a hand up, steadied me on my Jimmy Choo wedges, and left.

Tiffany cursed him up one side and down the other as he walked away.

That girl has a mouth.

Blood dripped off the end of my nose and splattered my white dress. Grabbing the towel from the manicure table, I held it over my nose, inhaled acetate and ammonia, and almost blacked out.

"I'm so sorry." Rhonda righted the chair, grabbed my elbow and guided me to safety. "Thank you for not pressing charges. Tiff has some anger issues. And an itchy trigger fist. But only when it comes to subpoenas."

Barb, foil head, wet hair, and the two stylists stood watching us. While taking photos. Rhonda rushed back with a clean towel that smelled of Tide instead of OPI.

I gladly switched, handing off the nail towel with two fingers. If I had any blood left in my head, I would have blushed. The cloth looked like a prop from *Saw*.

Access Hollywood would've had a field day.

Tiffany glared at me from across our table. "Why in the hell would you go and give me away to that guy? Do you know what you've done?"

"Helped him serve you a subpoena." With my nose pinched, I sounded like one of Alvin's chipmunk brothers.

"To serve as a witness for my shithead ex-husband in his divorce proceedings to his third wife. You think I want to help that asshole?"

No wonder she was so upset. I tried to say, "Tell the judge you'll be a hostile witness," but it came out "Tedda dunge you'd be a hotel witna."

"You think you can interfere with people here in Black Pine?"

"No," I said. "Iba drying do gedda job ad a dedegib."

"I don't know what in the hell you're saying."

"I dink my node id boken."

Rhonda scurried back with a cup of ice, straw, and a Diet Coke.

"Dank you, Rhadda." I pulled off the clean towel and checked for fresh blood. "At least it stopped bleeding."

"I'll probably lose my job." Tiffany leaned back in her chair and crossed her arms. «And I guess you'll sue me now.»

"No." I felt the bridge of my nose. "Does it look swollen to you?"

"Yes. With my luck, you'll probably get two black eyes." Tiffany pulled out a pack of cigarettes from the drawer, tapped the pack on the table, and shook one out. "Listen, I don't have any money. Sue me all you want, but there's nothing to get. I rent, my vehicle ain't paid off, and there's nothing saved in the bank."

I smiled through the pain and accepted a sip of Diet Coke. "You think I'll really have two black eyes?"

Tiffany stuck the unlit cigarette in the corner of her lip. "Prob'ly."

"Oh my stars. You can't have black eyes. You're Maizie Albright." Rhonda slapped ice into the towel and slammed it across my nose. A new trickle of blood ran across the top of my lip.

Wincing, I handed back the Diet Coke so I could hold the new towel between my eyes.

"Honey, you keep ice on it now, then drink lots of coffee and do a mashed banana facial," said Barb. "The caffeine and bananas will make your capillaries shrink."

"I thought you were supposed to use raw steak," said Jenna.

"Not bananas. Pineapples," said Tin Foil.

"Good Lord," said the stylist Shelly to Tin Foil. "Look at the time. I've got to rinse off the solution before your hair falls out."

"Ice now. Warm compress in two days," said Wet Hair. "I was a nurse."

Thanking them, I scooted off my seat to scoop my spilled contents back into my Chloé bag. I examined the bent Jet-Setters and tossed them into Tiffany's trashcan.

Tiffany peered at me through half-slitted lids, her words working around the cigarette. "When can I expect the next subpoena?"

"I'm not going to sue you, Tiffany. I'll prove it to you. Let me buy you a drink tonight. Anywhere you want. In Black Pine," I added, unsure if Tiffany'd try to hustle me into a limo to Atlanta. Or a plane to Paris. That happened to me once before.

Rhonda clapped a hand over her mouth. "You're just like Oprah," she whispered.

"You can come, too, Rhonda," I said.

"Black Pine Resort," drawled Tiffany. "The Cove. How'd you feel about that?"

"That's fine."

"Might see some of your friends there." Tiffany yanked the cigarette out of her mouth. "You think you can handle hanging with me and Rhonda if your friends see us?"

"I don't have any friends in Black Pine. I haven't been home in six years." I made a quick inventory of people I knew in Black Pine who weren't family and weren't Tiffany and Rhonda. Wyatt Nash. David Waverly. Mr. Lamar. "I might ask about a case while I'm there, though. You won't mind, will you?"

"That'd be exciting." With her hands still clasped to her mouth, Rhonda's words were muffled.

I worked Julia Pinkerton's wry smile into her catch phrase. "I'll make it happen."

"Good Lord," said Tiffany. "You better be buying top shelf."

I FOLLOWED THE OLD BUSINESS HIGHWAY to Wyatt Nash's office, checking my swollen nose and darkening eyes at each stop light. I looked like Donatella Versace's plastic surgeon had given me a quickie nose job.

Thank God Vicki was back in Beverly Hills. If she'd seen me, she would have killed me. Just like when a club I'd been partying in was raided and a camera caught me after the sprinkler system went off. Although that soaked Isabel Marant dress did get me the *Maxim* cover. And the offer from *Playboy,* which I didn't do. You always do *Maxim,* if offered.

Really, Vicki should have thanked me. Instead of pointing out the effects of Patrón and Pinkberry on my hips. Easily seen through the wet Isabel Marant dress. But Renata the therapist helped me reconcile all that. No dwelling on the past. Although Patrón remained on the unimbibeable list. No more Patrón for Maizie Albright.

Oddly enough, my real problem was with Pinkberry.

I set that thought away and turned to my old standby: WWJPD, What Would Julia Pinkerton Do? Julia Pinkerton would solve Wyatt Nash's cases for him, thereby making it necessary for him to hire her. Though Wyatt Nash had made it clear he didn't want to hire Maizie Albright. He'd purposely set me up with a violent nail esthetician. But why wouldn't he want to work with Julia Pinkerton? Julia Pinkerton was a teenage detecting genius.

And Julia Pinkerton never let Patrón get in the way of a case. Mostly because she was underage. But still.

Considerably cheered, I pulled in front of the donut-scented building, next to Nash's Silverado. I sailed through the front door and up the stairs to the Nash Security Solutions door and, remembering my earlier mistake, rapped on the glass.

At Nash's, "Come on in," I grasped the old-timey knob and graced Wyatt Nash with Julia Pinkerton's presence.

Without the cheer ensemble. And I lost the teenage hip-pop, eye-roll attitude. I couldn't pull it off at twenty-five.

Nash looked up from his desk. "What are you doing here?"

"I am here to report my progress. Checking in."

Nash studied my face for a long second, then dropped his eyes to my blood splattered dress. "I suppose you're going to try to sue me, but I will take it to court. You brought this on yourself. I warned you. This is a dangerous business."

"Why does everyone think I'm going to sue them? Tiffany was so worried about it, I offered to buy her drinks tonight at the Cove."

"You. Offered to buy her drinks?" Wyatt Nash squinted at me. "What's wrong with you?"

"Nothing. A little swelling, but I think it's going to be okay." I patted the skin beneath my eyes. "I don't think they'll blacken, although Tiffany does. So, did I do good? You were able to serve Tiffany's papers pretty quickly. I feel sorry for her, having to testify for her ex-husband. That's got to suck. I called her boss and told her it was an accident. That should help."

"Are you nuts? She assaulted you. You could have googled her image on your phone in thirty seconds instead of pretending to get your nails done."

"But I helped you."

"Miss Albright," Nash's voice lowered and took on the cadence of one speaking to very young, intellectually challenged children. "Thank you for trying to help me, but just because you played a detective on TV doesn't mean you can be one in real life."

"We made a deal." I fought feelings of panic and septum pain and sought inner peace through Julia Pinkerton bossiness. "I'm going to start investigating Sarah Waverly tonight."

"Go home, Miss Albright." He slid a cool look over me. "Go put some ice on that precious nose before your pretty face really turns black and blue. Or you might think differently about suing everyone."

FOUR

#SueCity #DetectingFail

IT SEEMED BLACK PINE HAD turned sue-happy, which I had thought was a California thing. Once Nash knew I didn't blame him for my perhaps-broken nose, I hoped he'd feel differently.

After a cold compress, nap, and change at the DeerNose cabin, I, too, felt differently. Mainly less sore in the face. But also less distracted by the doubts and insecurity my therapist advised me to turn into something positive. "Because negative thinking creates negative actions. And haven't you had enough of those?"

So positive thinking told me buying drinks for Tiffany and Rhonda at the Cove could turn into the positive action of finding information about David Waverly's wife. Then I'd show Wyatt Nash I was more than an ex-teen star and together we could calm David Waverly's fears. I dressed for success and dashed to my little Jag.

Turning off the local highway, I followed the mountain road to Black Pine Yacht and Golf Club and Resort. Positioned between the club and guest buildings, the Cove featured a patio on the lake with docks for yacht members. I hadn't much experience with the Cove or the Club. I did know folks like David Waverly and Mrs. Waverly hung out there. Everybody with money, except Daddy, hung out there.

I left the Jag with the valet and entered the stacked stone and timber building. Very woodsy-resorty with giant walls of glass for lake viewing and French doors open to the patio. A massive stone fireplace divided the restaurant from the bar. I skipped the fireplace bar and headed to the patio, where the guests draped themselves around glass tables and lounge chairs. A handful of cigarette boats and even more cabin cruisers bobbed along the line of docks. Bartenders and servers, dressed in plaid vests, scurried to and fro with bourbons, scotches, and vast quantities of wine.

The Cove seemed more for those on a liquid diet. Hopefully, Black Pine could provide some sort of fatted calf for their prodigal actress. Renata the therapist wouldn't allow me bourbon, scotch, or wine. Veal was okay although she'd be happier if I were vegan.

Casual formal was the dress code for the Cove. Men had their Ralph Laurens and Brooks Brothers rolled to the elbow. Diamonds and designer maxi dresses adorned the women.

Tiffany and Rhonda were easy to spot at the bar. Rhonda in a cotton halter dress. Tiffany's sequined tank matched her blue-tipped hair. Tiffany had also added more eyeliner to her repertoire. Like Rhonda, I also wore a halter dress, but in a shimmery, dotted chiffon, with matching crisscross sash-wrapped jute wedges. Gucci. In honor of Wyatt Nash's loafers.

I hugged Rhonda, who enveloped me in a starchy-cotton, soft-bodied squeeze that left me a little dizzy. Partly because of her hugging strength. Partly because she had bathed in Vanilla Musk.

Rhonda peeled herself off me, rearranged her breasts, and turned to Tiffany. "I told you she'd come."

Tiffany did not hug me, but she unfolded her arms and uncocked her hip. I took it as a welcoming gesture.

"Did you order yet?" I asked.

Tiffany gave me a look that said, "Of course we didn't order. If you didn't show, we'd get stuck with the bill."

"Not yet," said Rhonda. "I'm wondering what to get. Maybe a mai tai. I'm feeling coconutty. You think they can make those?"

"I'll take a Jack and Coke," said Tiffany. "What're you having?"

"Seltzer with lime. And food, I hope." I raised a finger and a plaid vested bartender appeared to take my order. I skimmed the menu and turned back to Tiffany and Rhonda. "They have fried pickles."

Rhonda arched a brow that said, "Of course they have fried pickles." Rhonda and Tiffany spoke a lot without words.

"Your nose don't look too bad," said Rhonda. "But you need to chill on the concealer under your eyes. You come see me tomorrow and I'll fix you up. I do makeup."

"Thanks," I said. "Do you know anybody here? I need information on a Sarah Waverly."

Between my cold compress nap and shower, I had googled David Waverly. Waverly worked for a firm that bought and sold other firms. Although I didn't understand his LinkedIn description's catchphrases. His wife, Sarah, was on Facebook, but other than recipes and forwarded memes, she didn't share much. She had checked married for her relationship status. She and David belonged to the Black Pine Club and Black Pine Methodist Church. She didn't have photos of her tennis or golf pro. Or the pool boy. Or her pastor. Or any other men, for that matter.

That was about it for Sarah Waverly. If she was having an affair, she was having it offline. And according to Nash, invisibly.

Tiffany and Rhonda also pondered Sarah Waverly for a moment but came up empty. Sarah Waverly did not get her hair or nails done at LA HAIR.

"What do you need to know about her?" Tiffany leaned against the bar, making quick work of the Jack and Coke.

"If she's cheating on her husband."

Rhonda's brown eyes grew bigger and she refocused on sucking down her mai tai.

"Why do you care if Sarah Waverly is cheating on her husband?" asked Tiffany.

"I'm trying to get a job working for Wyatt Nash, the private investigator. When I quit acting, I went to college for criminal justice. I have a bachelor's degree."

"I thought you starred in that reality show, *All is Albright*," said Rhonda.

"My contract said it was supposed to be guest appearances. I did that while going to college. And when I graduated, I left."

"Why in the hell would you go to college if you could do reality shows?" Tiffany eyed me over her glass. "Is it because you're no longer an A-lister?"

My face heated. "Because I want to be a private investigator, not a TV personality."

"Like Julia Pinkerton?" asked Rhonda.

"Exactly."

"You do know Julia Pinkerton isn't real?" said Tiffany. "Being a detective ain't going to be anything like Julia Pinkerton. Especially if you work for that ass who busted me today. That's all you'll be doing. Serving papers to ex-wives of dumbasses."

"There's more to it than that. Like finding out if Sarah Waverly is cheating on her husband."

"Even better," muttered Tiffany. "You're crazy, throwing away a perfectly good reality show for some job spying on other people."

"Well, some people deserved to be spied on." I folded my arms. "And it wasn't a perfectly good reality show. *All is Albright* struggled in the ratings and was razzed by critics all the time. The word "inane" was used a lot. Besides, some of the nicest people I've ever met are detectives."

"I think being a detective is kind of exciting," said Rhonda. "You'd get the four-one-one on all sorts of juicy stuff. I love the low down. Especially on celebrities. Y'all are messed up worse than real people."

"There's also security," I said, deftly moving away from my celebrity messes. "Security is very important in LA."

"For security 'round here, you buy a deadbolt. Or a pit bull," said Tiffany.

"Not these people." Rhonda cut her eyes to the Cove regulars. "I bet none of these club people have a pit bull. They've got security issue needs. I bet you'd clean up on rich folks' security needs."

"Yep," I said. "And lots of secrets they want to be kept quiet. Believe me, I know. Although it's probably worse in LA than Black Pine. The secrets, I mean."

"If you were smart, don't tell anyone you want to be a detective. Nobody's going to share secrets with a snitch." Tiffany leaned against the bar, dangling her drink from glossy blue nails.

"Use Maizie Albright as a disguise? Good point. That's just what Julia Pinkerton did. Except her disguise was her high school cheer uniform." I turned to the bartender who offered me a square china plate. A handful of fried pickle chips had been arranged into an artful hill next to a squirt of white sauce shaped like Black Pine Lake. I breathed in the salty and tangy goodness, happy my trainer and nutritionist were two thousand miles away.

"That is the sorriest plate of fried pickles I've ever seen," said Rhonda. "They barely gave you any."

"She's right," said Tiffany. "The Cove is for steak, shrimp, and scotch. You want real food, we'll take you to town."

"I'd love that. But tonight, I need to do some business." I glanced around the patio at the Black Pine hobnobbers. "I figure I have two strategies. One is to speak to the staff privately. I'm sure they know Sarah Waverly, but they might not be allowed to share gossip without getting in trouble. I can also announce my presence as Maizie Albright, meet some club members, and try to pry information from them."

I reached for another pickle. The plate was already empty but for two swipes of sauce. That was the problem with fried pickles. "Okay, who should I try first?"

Tiffany pointed at a collection of servers hovering at the edge of the patio. "They're not doing anything."

I placed my pickle plate on the bar and sauntered to the cluster of servers. Three minutes later I sauntered back.

"What happened?" asked Rhonda.

"No go," I said. "I asked them if they knew Sarah Waverly. They said yes. I asked them if she was here tonight. They said no. Then I asked them if she came to the Cove without her husband. They said sometimes. Then I asked if she ever met anyone here. They said yes. I asked who and they all took off to their tables."

Tiffany shook her head. "You need to ask what they call leading questions. Those are yes/no questions."

"My last question was leading. I asked who Sarah Waverly met at the Cove. They refused to answer."

"Maybe their tables needed another round of drinks," said

Rhonda. "They are working, after all."

"Maybe they don't want to say who Sarah Waverly is meeting."

"Maybe they don't give a shit and wonder why you're being so damn nosy," said Tiffany. "Go ask someone else."

"Make your celebrity status work for you, girl." The purple orchid from Rhonda's mai tai was now tucked in her hair. "Make them want to tell you all about Sarah Waverly because you are flippin' Maizie flippin' Albright."

"Okay." I held up a finger.

The bartender materialized in front of me. His brown eyes smiled in appreciation. It was the Gucci. The dress looked like money. Or it was my boobs. The Gucci worked both like that.

"How do you get him to do that?" muttered Tiffany. "It takes a normal person years to get that guy for a refill."

"Hi," I said, using my Julia Pinkerton street-smart voice. "I bet you know Sarah Waverly. David Waverly's wife."

"If they're a member, I know them." The bartender waggled his brows. "But I don't know you. I'm Alex."

"I'm not a member," I said. "I just moved here."

Alex crossed his arms on the bar and leaned forward. "To Black Pine? You look familiar. Have you lived here before?"

"She's Maizie flippin' Albright," said Rhonda and pushed her empty mai tai glass forward. "We're partying with Maizie Albright. Up in the house."

I shot a look toward Rhonda. She had her hands raised and danced on her stool. She managed a good hip roll for a bar seat. "Cut back on the Bacardi for her," I whispered.

"No kidding?" said Alex. "I mean, you're really Maizie Albright?"

"Yes, but I'd really like to know about Sarah Waverly. I think she's seeing a friend of mine. On the side, you know? Like maybe you've seen her with someone?"

"Can I get your autograph?" He bent beneath the bar and came up with a stack of napkins and a pen. "Could you do a couple? My sister is a huge fan. So's my mom. And my memaw."

I signed three napkins. "Now can you tell me about Sarah Waverly?"

"Sorry." He shrugged. "David Waverly is here all the time. Don't really know her. I'll come back and talk later. I've got to take an order."

"Thanks anyway," I said.

"Damn," said Tiffany. "You sure you want to be a detective? You're too polite."

"I just need to work on my technique. Quickly. So I can impress Mr. Nash."

Tiffany shook her head. "I think you're better off going back on the reality show."

"Excuse me."

We turned from the bar to face a woman rocking an apricot maxi dress that clung to her tall, slender frame. Her sleek, auburn bob brushed her bare shoulders, drawing attention to a diamond pendant at her throat. Tiffany and Rhonda slouched back on their stools, while I felt myself straightening.

"I'm sorry to bother you." She held out her hand. "I'm Jolene Sweeney. Did I hear y'all say you're Maizie Albright? I'm glad I finally caught you. Sorry I couldn't meet you today. There was some kind of confusion. You're moving back to Black Pine?"

"Nice to meet you in person, Jolene." I winced at her iron grip. I still hadn't figured her for friend or foe, particularly as she wasn't the one who set me up for a sock in the nose. I decided to play it cool, waiting for the right moment to talk to her about the job.

"Are you looking to buy a house?" She pressed a card into my hand.

Sweeney Realty. "I thought you were with Nash Security?"

"Full disclosure. Nash Security is one of my businesses. I don't officially work there, but I'm part owner."

"Are you related to Mr. Nash?"

"Not related. Just a business relationship." An uneasy smile curled her lips. "Have you talked to Wyatt? Your assistant made it sound like you wanted an actual position. I thought maybe you wanted to do some character research. Or did you need security detail? Wyatt can certainly help you there."

"Actually, Jolene, tonight I'm trying to find Sarah Waverly."

"Sarah Waverly?" Jolene frowned. "David's wife? She doesn't spend much time at the Cove. I thought I saw her car, though. I can introduce you around, if you'd like. Fortunately, I know quite a few people here."

"That'd be really awesome. Maybe Sarah Waverly is here and you missed her." I slid off my stool and turned to Rhonda and Tiffany. "Did you hear that? Sarah's car is here. Are you coming?"

"We'll hang here a bit," said Rhonda.

Jolene tugged on my arm. "Come on, Maizie. Can I call you Maizie?"

"I'll see you girls in a little while?" I kept my eyes on Tiffany and Rhonda.

Tiffany shrugged. "Just don't forget the bill. I doubt Mr. Autograph'll let us leave without paying."

Jolene rolled her eyes. "Like Maizie Albright isn't good for a bar bill. Besides, once the whole crew of *All is Albright* gets here, they'll probably get a house tab going."

"Wait." I grabbed Jolene's hand. "What are you talking about? Why would the *Albright* team come to Black Pine?"

"I assumed everyone would come if they're going to film down here. They wouldn't hire a new crew, would they?" Jolene tucked my hand into her elbow and steered me toward the far side of the patio. "I was talking to Miss Vicki about it. She said the producers are real excited about an alternative location. Something about ratings."

"Vicki is here?" I clutched my Fendi Piccola pochette to my chest. The pickles flared into southern fried heartburn. "In Black Pine?"

"Not just Black Pine," said Jolene. "At the Cove. I figured y'all were here to meet each other, not Sarah Waverly."

"Oh. My. God." The crowd parted and I locked eyes with the woman leading court. Ironically, she also wore Gucci. Maybe not so ironic. She loved Gucci.

"I'm so excited y'all are doing your show here in Black Pine," squealed Jolene. "Your daddy must be thrilled."

"Oh. My. God." My father would kill me.

FIVE

#Poor&Famous #FabuNot

MY PLAN TO GAIN INFORMATION on Sarah Waverly had been crushed. For the moment. Vicki had a habit of crushing plans. Unless they were hers.

Vicki leaned forward for the double cheek kiss, careful not to touch for fear of smearing lipstick. Drawing back, she wrinkled her nose. "Have you been eating fried foods? Take some magnesium. Sweetheart, you know what it does to you."

"What are you doing here, Vicki?" I said, trying to keep hysteria from my tone. "I thought we had an understanding."

"They picked up *All is Albright* for another season. Surely Mickey called you. I never liked him as an agent."

"Mickey didn't call me because I fired him. And because I left my phone in LA."

"Thank God. You needed a new agent. And buy a new phone." Vicki gave Jolene a small push on her arm. "Get me a glass of pinot, honey."

I snagged Jolene's hand and clamped her to my side. "I don't need an agent anymore. I told you this before I left. I'm done. And I don't want a phone. It's part of the new me. Like no Twitter, texting, or email. Not even Instagram. I'm stepping away from everything."

"No phone?" Jolene blanched.

"You do know phones are also used for calling, Maizie? You sound like your father." Vicki tossed her platinum blonde waves behind her shoulders. "He probably doesn't have a cell phone, either."

"Who's your father?" asked Jolene.

"Boomer Spayberry," I mumbled, sure that Jolene could put two and two together and realize the Spayberry working for Nash was me. Proving me immature and reckless. Proving the same for Nash. But I had a feeling he and Jolene had already covered that ground.

"That makes you DeerNose royalty and a celebrity," said Jolene, seeming to have forgotten the addition of Nash's new Spayberry assistant.

Vicki rolled her eyes. "Figures. Douse a coverall in deer piss and become an overnight sensation. That's famous for Black Pine."

"Maizie's famous for Black Pine, too," said Jolene, overcome with a Realtor's hometown zeal. "And we have other celebrities, too. Mostly from Atlanta. We're now an 'it' location thanks to Maizie, DeerNose, and the fabulous surroundings of Black Pine Lake and Mountain. With the renovation and expansion of Black Pine Airport, the jet set can arrive by commercial flights as well as private aircraft. Luxury, beauty, and convenience in a remote mountain setting. Can't beat that with a stick."

"Spare me the hard sell. I know Black Pine well enough," snapped Vicki. "Where's my pinot?"

I raised a finger, commandeering a server with my Gucci curves. "She'll have a glass of wine," I nodded at Vicki. "And I would like another plate of fried pickles. Anything for you, Jolene?"

Jolene smiled. "Instead of pinot, why don't we order Champagne? Sounds like we have a lot to celebrate. I almost forgot you're another Black Pine star, Vicki."

I had to give props to Jolene. She had figured Vicki out quickly.

Vicki tried to raise her eyebrows, but botulism prevented much more than a twitch. "Cristal?"

The server nodded and disappeared in a burst of plaid. I glanced back at the bar and saw Tiffany and Rhonda watching me. I wasn't alone. I had friends. Sort of. I didn't need fried pickles. Although I still wanted fried pickles.

"Maizie."

I swiveled back to meet Vicki's glare.

"We need to discuss the new season. I assume you're staying with your father?"

"I fulfilled my contract, graduated from college, and now I'm getting a job. Per, you know, Judge Ellis's requirements? So no discussion is needed?"

Jolene shifted her look between us. "Job? Are you back to modeling? Black Pine is wonderful for location shoots. We've hosted a number of magazine and catalogs—"

"The state of Maizie's nose tells us her limited chances for any modeling jobs in the near future. And living in the land of saturated fats will end it all together." Vicki accepted a glass of Cristal from the server. "All her adult commercial shoots have been due to her fame, not her looks. She has me to thank for that."

Jolene grabbed a glass and clinked it with Vicki.

I recognized Jolene as those supercharged with the ability to assess a bread-and-butter situation and join the correct side. LA was chock full of people loaded with that skill.

"I meant my career as a private investigator. I'm on an assignment now, actually. I should be getting back to work." I hoped Jolene wouldn't begrudge me the chance to work at Nash Security.

With a quick pivot on my Gucci wedges, I trudged to the bathroom. Why did I even try to argue with Vicki? Vicki was the epitome of control. As Vicki became more powerful, my mess grew hotter. There was no defeating her, only escape. Evidently, two thousand miles wasn't far enough. I'd have to avoid her until she had no choice but return to LA to start the new season. Without me. Because I wasn't allowed back there.

Thank God for small favors like a judge's orders.

If only I were more like Julia Pinkerton. She would have stood up to Vicki a long time ago. Julia had that type of swagger. Whereas my swagger was the kind purchased at Barney's.

In the bathroom, the ladies' attendant noted my face, handed me a tissue, and opened a stall door. I'm not a good crier. I have pale skin, which morphs into a blotchy puff-fest within seconds of tears welling. Considering my nose was already three sizes too big, I didn't need more comments about my future in modeling.

Not that I wanted to model. You just don't want to hear your face might break a camera lens.

I commenced with the no-cry ritual. In the narrow stall, I pinched the skin between my thumb and pointer finger. Totally works. Learned it from a makeup artist. I pinched and breathed deeply. Sniffed a few times. And finished with three Tae Bo jab punches.

Back to work.

I left the stall tear free and returned the clean tissue with a twenty-dollar bill. "Hey, do you know Sarah Waverly?"

The attendant dropped the bill into a basket and leaned against the sinks. "Mebbe. But I cannot say."

The stall door behind us opened and a woman in another swishy maxi dress sashayed to the sink. She tossed her feathered blonde locks behind her shoulder and rinsed her hands in the running water that was cut on by the attendant. Leaning forward, the woman inspected her flawless makeup with a side glance to me.

"I know Sarah Waverly," she said to the mirror. "Who're you?"

"Maizie Spayberry," I said. "Who're you?"

"Amelia Brooks. Sarah and David go to my church." She shuffled in her Tory Burch clutch, pulled out lip gloss, and pouted her lips.

I watched her apply the gloss and thought about the thin ice I skated suggesting a church member might be having an affair. "Is Sarah doing okay?"

Amelia whirled around. Her gleaming lips curled. Excitement lit her eyes and boosted her voice. "What do you mean? What have you heard?"

"What have you heard?" I countered in a Julia Pinkerton tone. A bit high school-ish, but Amelia looked like she could relate. "Is Sarah having an affair?"

"I don't believe it. Although I totally would if I were in her shoes. Luckily, I have no need for that."

"Why would you have an affair if you were Sarah?"

"Turn around's fair play, am I right?" Amelia wiggled fingers heavy in karats. "What's good for the goose and all that? Why do you think so many girls around here get a little on the side? They're bored, lonely, and looking to get even."

My feelings for David Waverly took a nose dive. And they were already pretty low. "Does David know?"

"I tell you what, if David finds out Sarah's cheating, she's in some serious trouble."

The hairs on my neck rose. "Why? What would he do?"

Amelia pursed her shiny lips. "Toss her to the curb, for one thing. Without a penny. David's a good ol' boy. Butter doesn't melt in his mouth, cause he's cold as ice when it comes to business. And marriage to David Waverly is business. 'Course he's worth a lot. They have no children and David Waverly has made no bones about his feelings on that subject. He's positively feudal."

"How feudal?" I narrowed my eyes.

"Not medieval. Just feudal." Amelia shrugged. "Besides, I doubt Sarah's seeing anyone. She's too quiet. Although still waters run deep, as they say."

Poor Sarah Waverly. "I hope Sarah is okay. What does she do?"

Amelia tapped a finger on her chin. "She's treasurer of the Tuesday Tees, our ladies golf club. I haven't seen her in a while, but we group by skill level now. She was treasurer for the DeerNose Charity Ball, too."

That meant Daddy and Carol Lynn knew the Waverlys. I could find out more about Sarah and David Waverly at home.

"So where do I know you from?" Amelia cocked her head.

"She is Maizie Albright," said the attendant.

"I thought you said you were a Spayberry," said Amelia. "I'm sorry. You look different than Maizie Albright."

"It's the nose," I said. "It's a little swollen."

"No." Amelia tapped her chin. "You're bigger than I thought."

"Taller?"

"Just bigger." Amelia faked a smile. "But you look great. Really."

"Thanks." Amelia did not make me feel better about my future non-career in modeling. I pinched my thumb skin as I pushed through the bathroom door. By the time I got to the bar, I felt better.

"How'd it go?" asked Rhonda. "Did that skinny girl help you learn something about Sarah Waverly?"

"No," I said. "Another skinny girl did, though. I'm ready to go home."

"Are you okay? You're looking a little puny," asked Rhonda.

"Puny?" I said hopefully.

"Under the weather," said Tiffany.

"I'm fine." I handed Alex my Black card. "I've got some information about Sarah Waverly to report to Mr. Nash. He'll be impressed, right? And just as soon as he writes me that W-4, I'll feel even better. And in two years I'll have the necessary training and then I can open my own office and get licensed. I'll be on my own for the first time. No directors, producers, managers, agents, or bosses. Totally alone. That'll be really cool, right? Albright Investigations. Or Spayberry Investigations. I haven't decided yet."

My speech slid toward Valley as it sped up and tumbled from my lips. "I mean, it's not like I can't do this? My Crime Analysis professor said I was promising. And Detective Earl King said I was sharp. Well, he said Julia Pinkerton was sharp, but I've learned from her. I've been interested in private investigation work for a long time. Like ten years. I won the Kids Choice Awards two years in a row for *Julia Pinkerton*. That should count for something, right? I can do this, right? Become a detective like Julia?"

"Sure." Rhonda flashed Tiffany a look. A "Girl, this girl is crazier than you" look.

"Miss Albright?" The bartender leaned over the bar. "Do you have another card? Or cash?"

"Why?" My fingers felt icy as I dug into my Fendi pochette.

"This one's been declined. Actually canceled. I'm supposed to cut it up. Although, I can't since it's titanium."

"No. That can't be right."

"You can put her charges on my bill," said the honeyed voice cloaked in steel. "For tonight."

With my hand still inside my purse, I spun and faced Vicki. "Did you cancel my credit card?"

"The one I cosigned when you were a teenager? Yes, I did. You claimed you were ready for your independence. I assumed that meant in total."

"I don't have any income yet. I need that card."

"I guess you should have thought about that before you moved out. And it's not like you didn't earn anything from *All is Albright.*»

"I had to pay off my student loans. And those...other bills."

"Maybe you should talk to your father about extending you a loan. Or you can still sign on for Season Four. The producers agreed to help you with your," she mock quoted, "'other bills.'"

"You're one of the producers. You're doing this to try to get me back on the show."

Vicki shrugged. "By the way, because you have no phone, you haven't noticed the calls from the Jaguar credit people. They contacted me. And I told them where they could find you."

I gasped. "You sicced the repo guys on me? I need a car."

"Really, Maizie." Vicki sighed. "You've tried quitting before and didn't succeed. You need to work. I guess I should at least be thankful you're not partying this time. Or dating drug dealers." She studied the Gucci dress. "Although it seems you've transferred your addiction to a new substance. Keep it up and you're going to need a whole new wardrobe."

"Hey." Tiffany hopped off her stool. "Maizie's trying to work. She's got a whole plan figured out. She just needs a little time."

"And she didn't mean to eat all those fried pickles. That's what fried pickles do to you," said Rhonda.

Vicki's eyebrows strained. She flicked a glance off Tiffany and Rhonda and set me in her green crosshairs. "I see you're still picking up strays. At least in your last fit of rebellion, you chose Beverly Hills trash."

"Tiffany and Rhonda have been really nice to me."

"Can I get your autograph anyway?" Rhonda waved a napkin at Vicki. "I watch the show all the time."

"Who are you?" asked Tiffany. "I don't watch that show."

Our voices chimed in unison.

"Maizie's manager."

"My mother."

Vicki ripped me one last scathing look and stalked off.

SIX

#workworkout #supershizzles

I SAT IN MY ADORABLE BLUE Jag, pinching my thumb and breathing and doing my best to direct my thoughts toward positive affirmations. Wyatt Nash's dark building, odorizing the night with donuts, calmed me. Which was why I hadn't driven directly to the DeerNose cabin. My new life hadn't started off the way I'd thought. I knew I'd need a job, but now it also looked like I needed money.

I had lived a sheltered life. But frighteningly unsheltered in other ways. That's what Hollywood does to you.

A rumble penetrated the donut air. The Silverado pulled into the lot beside me. Nash clambered out of his truck and strode to my car.

I hopped out of my car, hoping Wyatt Nash was in a better mood than earlier.

"Do I need to file stalking charges, Miss Albright?"

He wasn't in a better mood.

"Mr. Nash." I smiled. "I wanted to tell you what I've learned about Sarah Waverly."

Nash halted a few paces from me. He had changed again. Back to the jeans and a black Guns N' Roses t-shirt that clung to his biceps and shoulders.

My trainer would be super impressed.

"What have you been doing?" he said.

"Hanging out at the Cove. I spoke to someone who knows Sarah Waverly. And also to some staff, but they wouldn't tell me anything."

"Why?"

"They probably worry about their jobs. If the members found out the employees gossip, they could complain and have them fired."

"Not why wouldn't the staff tell you anything. Why are you asking about Sarah Waverly at the Cove?"

"I wasn't going to take the night off just because I was meeting friends. That's how dedicated I am."

Nash looked toward the stars and muttered a few unpleasant phrases. He lowered his gaze back to me. "What did this person who knows Sarah Waverly say?"

"She couldn't believe Sarah would have an affair, although it sounds like David does. He's feudal and cold and planning to divorce her anyway. I'm really worried about Sarah Waverly."

"You don't know Sarah Waverly so there's no reason for you to be worried about her."

"I worry about a lot of people I don't know."

"I'm sure you do."

"Do you want me to type up what I heard for your report?"

"No. I want you to go home." He took a long step toward me, backing me into the Jag. "Are you in cahoots with Jolene? Why did you try to keep David Waverly on as a client when I told him I was done?"

"Cahoots?" I glanced at the building, noting the unfortunate absence of light in the neon "hot & fresh" sign. "Actually, this is very awkward. But I think Jolene's fallen into the Maizie-back-to-work-as-an-actress camp. Because she met Vicki. And Vicki is very persuasive. Now Miss Sweeney will most likely try to talk you out of hiring me. Please don't listen to them, Mr. Nash. You need an assistant. I need training."

He had opened his mouth at the mention of Jolene, then shut it. For a long moment, he didn't say anything. He stepped back and turned toward the building. "Good night, Miss Albright."

"Can I continue my surveillance of Mrs. Waverly for you?"

"Do what you like," he said, waving a hand behind him. "As long as you stay out of my hair. And keep your celebrity business to yourself."

I was officially on the case and out from under Vicki's thumb. Life couldn't get better. Except for the lack of money and repossession of my car. That kind of sucked. But silver linings and all that.

THE NEXT MORNING, I HEADED toward my first surveillance assignment. I left the top down on the Jag to better smile and wave good morning to the friendly Black Piners as I made my way toward Platinum Ridge, subdivision home of the Waverlys. Black Pine spread from the base of Black Pine Mountain, edged along Black Pine Lake, and trickled into the countryside.

On the far side of the lake, the DeerNose estate is hilly, mostly wooded terrain. Oodles of acres. From Daddy's dock, we have an excellent view of the mountain, which you can see on the DeerNose website. When I had bouts of homesickness, I used to Google DeerNose on the old MacBook and gaze at the majesty of Black Pine. Not that it's a big mountain. More like an oversized hill. But still pretty.

The security attendant, Hector, took down my license plate number and waved me through the gates of Platinum Ridge. The one-acre lot homes on Platinum Ridge tended toward large, multi-winged, multi-storied, stone and brick boxes. With lots of windows.

The Waverly house was no different. A long drive led toward a three-car garage attached to the stone house. Continuing down the street, I looked for an ideal stakeout spot. But the trees had been artfully arranged in the yards, leaving the street exposed. And this neighborhood wasn't one to have cars parked on the road without appearing obvious. No places to hide.

I parked down the street from the Waverly home, fitted myself with a ball cap and a pair of Tom Ford sunglasses, and walked. Two ladies in yoga outfits passed me, waving. I looped the cul-de-sac and walked back. The yoga ladies waved again, chatting as they walked by, not seeming to care I still stalked their street. Reaching my Jag, I turned and retraced my course. If anything, I was going to work off breakfast.

My trainer would be proud.

On my third loop, one garage door lifted, exposing the rear of a yellow Corvette Stingray. Mr. Waverly backed out, turned, and zoomed out the drive. Didn't even notice me.

I checked the time and figured Waverly for a nine-to-fiver. Two minutes later, the second Waverly garage door rose. I hurried back to my car. Sliding inside, I ducked as the silver Porsche Cayenne drove past, a woman at the wheel. Sarah Waverly, I assumed. Or they had help who owned Cayennes.

Exiting the Platinum Ridge gates, I saw the Cayenne in the distance, turning toward town. I followed until the Cayenne turned right, onto a side street. Sarah Waverly pulled into the lot of an office building and parked. With the stone facade, pitched roof and triangular windows, the building reminded me of something you'd see in the Rockies. Like in Sundance.

While I relived memories of Sundance, Sarah Waverly hustled from her car, a small bag in her hand, and entered the glass front doors. I parked and walked to the building. The sign read Black Pine Group. David Waverly's firm. I glanced around the parking lot but didn't see the Corvette.

Why would Sarah Waverly show up at her husband's office when he wasn't here? The bag she carried looked like one of those insulated lunch sacks. Was she bringing her husband lunch? At nine in the morning? Was this the behavior of a woman having an affair?

Maybe she felt guilty.

I strolled into the lobby and the young, pretty receptionist smiled. "Can I help you?"

"Is David Waverly in?" I asked.

She glanced at my chest straining the Stella McCartney Adidas stretch tee. Her upper lip twitched. "Mr. Waverly's not in now. Maybe he'd rather have you stop in later this afternoon?"

When you looked like me, you learned a thing or two about

men. And women. And expectations of people who looked like me. The receptionist thought I was David Waverly's current side of fries. And she wanted me gone before Mrs. Waverly walked out of her husband's office and noticed me. That the receptionist seemed unflustered by my presence meant this was not an unprecedented occurrence.

I did not like Mr. Waverly.

But he was Mr. Nash's client. Sort of. An unwanted client. But a client I could use to impress Mr. Nash.

"Okey-dokey," I said in my best bimbo voice. I leaned forward and whispered, "Did I just see Mrs. Waverly go inside?"

The receptionist lowered her eyes to the appointment book. "Dropping off his lunch. She's in his office now. But David's really not here. Call first?"

"Thanks." I sashayed from the lobby and out to the parking lot.

Five minutes later, Sarah Waverly hurried to her Porsche. She pulled out of the lot and turned right.

At the same time, I realized how stupid it was to drive around with the top down on my Jag. I made for a pretty obvious investigator. Or really dumb side of fries. In the time it took for the cover to latch and the windows to go up, Sarah Waverly had shot away.

So I was still learning.

AFTER DRIVING AROUND, THEN BACK to Platinum Ridge where I learned from Hector that Mrs. Waverly had not returned, I remembered Sarah Waverly went to the club most mornings. Nash had said so.

Feeling chock full of rational thinking and wise decision making, I went back to the club. Stopping behind a black Escalade, I sang along to a Top Twenty groove, while the vehicle waited—for no discernible reason—to pull into the drive.

As the song moved from the second stanza to a refrain, my fingers lost time with the bass line and began strumming the steering wheel to a more impatient beat. Luckily, I was in Black

Pine. If this was LA, someone would've climbed out of their car and pulled a road rage riot on the Escalade.

The Escalade's back door swung open. A woman—in black workout tights and a matching tank I recognized from the Splits 59 Noir de Sport line—hopped out and strode toward my car.

"Craptastic." I slid down in my seat.

Her blonde coif had been pulled up in a pert ponytail, but this was no cheerleader headed for pom practice. Any sideline cheers on Vicki's part required contracted fees against net profit percentages plus opening credit mentions.

In a preemptive strike, I zipped down my window and leaned out. "Can you tell your driver to let me pull in? I don't have time to talk—"

"This will only take a minute." Vicki's ponytail bounced as her slim hips made short work of the distance between the two vehicles.

"We're blocking the road."

Her exaggerated glance up and down the street agreed with my earlier assessment of Black Pine traffic. However, that agreement irritated more than consoled.

She stopped at my window. "Good morning, Maizie. I see you kept some good habits from your former career."

"I—" I clamped down on the words that might have tumbled forth without knowing the habits to which Vicki referred. She could be tricky like that. "What are you doing?"

"Obviously coming back from the gym. The resort is lacking proper equipment and a trainer. I had to get one from Atlanta."

"You shipped a gym here?"

"Really, Maizie." The ponytail twitched. "The Jaguar people need some confirmation you'll be paying them. Would you like their number?"

"I told you I don't have a phone." Or a paycheck, but I kept quiet on that one.

"They don't have a phone at that cabin? Please tell me your father hasn't resorted to living off the land again. Has he made good on his threat to teach you to hunt and clean your own dinner?"

I felt a shudder at that truism but caught myself before Vicki could see it. "Not recently."

"You know you can stay at the villa with me."

"Only if I agree to another season, right?"

"You like your comforts and the Spayberrys never cared about luxury. Speaking of luxury, I have a surprise waiting for you at the resort. It also arrived this morning."

I wished the surprise to be the title to my car, then repressed that thought. No need to further Vicki's opinion on my selfishness. "Thank you, but Daddy's house is just fine."

"Agreeing to another *Albright* season would be a nice thing to do for the parent you left behind. I can work things out with that judge if you'd let me."

Her maternal instinct to inflict guilt knew no bounds. "Judge Ellis was pretty clear about me not working in the industry—"

"This isn't about probation requirements." She crossed her arms. "This is about you hiding from your problems. Just like when you didn't make the cut for that Disney pilot. You ran here. And came right back to me when your father wouldn't let you audition for local theater. *The Sound of Music*, wasn't it?"

"I'm not hiding from problems." Sort of. "I'm not twelve." Physically. Although some (Renata) might question my emotional reactions to Vicki. "I am my own person and allowed to make decisions. Even if others disagree with those decisions."

"Which therapist taught you that?" Vicki arched a brow. "Your grandmother rarely said a kind word to me or anyone else and I never found rehab necessary. Your grandmother also didn't spend her best years fighting tooth and nail so her daughter could become a star."

"I didn't ask to become a star."

"How original." She narrowed her eyes. "Think about that response while you're with the family who ignored us when we were living in a one bedroom in the Valley. We didn't work this hard just for you to quit when the going gets tough, Maizie."

The ponytail whipped around and she stomped back to the

Escalade. Three seconds later, it zipped toward the villa entrance.

All I needed was a five-minute conversation with Vicki to doubt my every decision. I didn't want to be a star. Or did I? Was that why I offered my services to David Waverly even when my would-be boss told me no? For the attention?

"Am I a selfish, spoiled brat who doesn't deserve second chances?" I spoke aloud, hoping some note in my voice would settle my doubts.

The universe answered. A horn sounded. I turned in my seat to see an elderly man peeking above the wheel of a giant Buick. He shook a fist then accelerated around me.

I followed the Buick into the parking lot. Found a spot near the front door. Parked. Pinched my thumb. Then reminded myself why I was in the Black Pine Golf and Yacht Club parking lot in the first place.

I turned to the mirror where Vicki's green eyes stared back. Minus the chutzpah. "So Vicki spent her quality years working her tiny ass off to get you in the business. Remember, that was her prerogative. Now you're an adult. You have an obligation to follow David Waverly's wife. You can't chicken out just because Vicki scares you. You gave your word. Let's get to it."

Other than blink, I didn't move.

I tried again. "Would Julia Pinkerton sit in a car, staring at herself? No, she would not. She'd get out, find Sarah Waverly, and continue her surveillance. And still show up in time to cheer at Homecoming."

The sea glass greens narrowed. This time, Julia Pinkerton stared back at me. A snarky half-smile slid across my face. Reassured, I got out of the car and commenced my Sarah Waverly search.

I did a slow turn, spotted Sarah Waverly's Cayenne, and trotted to the Porsche to peek inside. Placing my forehead against the glass, I shielded my eyes. The front seat didn't have the normal debris my Jag had. Not even one of those little green Starbucks sticks. Even my assistant missed those when she cleaned out my car.

Poor Blake. Destined to clean out Starbucks' sticks for some other spoiled brat actress.

I circled to peer into the trunk. Saw Sarah Waverly's pink Callaway bag. Golf clubs. And what looked like an orange Prada handbag. I peeled my eyes off the Papaya Prada and thought hard. Sarah Waverly didn't bring her clubs inside. But why bother lugging clubs if she was meeting her lover? Proving David Waverly's theories correct and Mr. Nash wrong.

Shizzles.

Hang on. Why would you leave your handbag in the car with your clubs? Where would you go and not take your purse? I couldn't think of anywhere I wouldn't take my purse.

Troubled, I headed into the club pro office and toward the young man working the cash register, hoping Sarah was on the links. Without her clubs.

"Hey," I said. "I thought I saw my friend Sarah Waverly come in. She wouldn't mind if I joined her. When's her tee-off?"

The golf pro checked his computer. "She reserved a time starting ten minutes ago. Are you a member?" He cocked his head. "You look familiar, but I can't place you. Where do I know you from?"

I smiled. "I have one of those faces."

"No, not really." He gazed at me for a long second. "You look like somebody on TV."

"I get that a lot. Did Sarah come in here?"

"No, but she probably went in through the front doors. You can get to the locker rooms either way."

I spun toward the door and exited. I followed the sidewalk through the clubhouse front doors. The lobby had a great stone fireplace, a twin to the Cove's, and giant windowed views. A few members lounged on leather sofas and wingback chairs near the fireplace, taking no notice of me. Two halls split off the lobby. I turned right, toward the locker rooms and pro shop.

The locker room opened from the ladies', where an attendant sat on a small stool. She glanced up as I pushed through the door.

"Don't get up," I said, moving forward. "I'm looking for my friend, Sarah Waverly. Did she pass through here an hour or so ago? Short, chestnut brown hair and wearing white capri pants or maybe a golfing outfit?"

"No, ma'am."

"Did anyone pass through here?"

"No, ma'am. Are you a member?" she asked.

I pulled a Vicki and ignored her question, then entered the room. Wood-paneled lockers and cushioned benches lined the room.

No Sarah Waverly.

Two tennis-skirted women slung racket bags over their shoulders and strode to an outside door. I dipped my head into the dressing and shower area.

Empty.

Pushing open the outside door, I glanced out. A flagstone patio ran the length of the clubhouse. At the practice tees, just past the clubhouse, a man and an older couple chipped shots. The tennis ladies strolled off a set of stone steps, leading from the patio to a golf cart path. I followed the cart path to the first, second, and third tees. At the fifth green, I turned and headed back to the clubhouse.

Zipping through the locker room, I took the door leading to the pro shop. At the desk, I smiled at the cashier. "Hey, did Sarah Waverly check in with you? I couldn't catch her."

"No," said the clerk. "She's probably on the second or third hole now, though."

Which she wasn't.

Sarah Waverly had disappeared.

Fifty yards from where I had been arguing with my mother.

SEVEN

#LostHousewivesofBlackPine #Playbuoys

SARAH WAVERLY DID NOT MATERIALIZE in the club-house, but her Cayenne hadn't left the parking lot. Because there were two golf courses, lake view and mountain, I checked to see if she had gone to the wrong tee. Then checked the tennis and pool area. And every nook and cranny in the clubhouse. Other than randomly driving around the golf courses, I had explored all the options at the club.

Sucktastic. I'd lost Sarah Waverly.

Or she had lost me.

I stood on the patio and stared at the snack bar counter, long-ing for an unhealthy morsel or jolt of sugar. Anything that might make me feel better. I forced myself to look at the lake.

Mr. Nash was right. I couldn't be a real detective just because I played one on TV. I couldn't even find a woman on a golf course. My eyes edged back to the snack bar and I pinched my thumb skin hard.

This was why Vicki had returned to Black Pine. She knew I would fail.

Didn't take me long either.

Why couldn't I have kept my mouth shut instead of arguing with Vicki in the middle of the street? I might have seen Sarah Waverly leave her car or go into the club. If she had been picked up, I might have spotted them instead of focusing on Vicki.

Once again, I let my issues get in the way of a job. And this was a job I had fought for. And sort of scammed myself into.

"I'm such a loser." I had a college degree in Criminal Justice that was limited by my semi-criminal background. My real life skill set was meager. And now I had no money, was about to lose my car, and was restricted in my movements by a judge who found me a benign imbecile.

Maybe I should sign with Vicki, I thought. Let her work her magic with the judge. But I'd be stuck in reality show hell forever.

Once *All is Albright* lost momentum (because it would), I'd have to go on reality competition shows for B-list stars. I'd move on to the *Big Brother*-style shows where I'd be crammed into a house and forced to eat bugs with C- and D-list stars. Then I'd have another stint of *Celebrity Rehab*, followed by a *Celebrity Extreme Makeover*.

By then, TV might find it cheaper to go back to scripted drama programming, which would disappoint script writers who find reality TV more fun to write (or so I'm told). And reality stars who can't act—like me—would be out of a job.

In five minutes, I'd already talked myself out of two careers.

Vicki was right. When things got bad, I wanted to give up.

But I did follow direction well. I just needed training. Which meant I would have to fess up to Mr. Nash and beg him to train me.

Starting with, "How to Not Lose A Client's Wife."

I T'S VERY HARD TO FIND a pay phone. I had to borrow some- one's phone to google pay phone locations. Then drive to a gas station to use one of the two pay phones in Black Pine. Ironically, the other pay phone was in the Dixie Kreme Donut shop below Nash Security.

I dialed the Nash Security number while forcing my breaths from shallow to deep. "Mr. Nash, I need your help. I've lost her."

"Ma'am, I can help. Can I get your name?" answered Nash. "And who did you lose?"

"This is Maizie. And I lost Sarah Waverly."

"What?"

"I lost her at the club. She had a tee time. She parked at the club, but then she disappeared." While waiting for Nash to use less explicit words, I decided not to mention my Vicki detour. "I followed her from her home to Black Pine Group where she dropped off Mr. Waverly's lunch."

"Sarah Waverly does that every day. Then she goes to the club. You must have missed her. She's on the third hole, which can be tricky to find."

"No, she isn't." I pinched my thumb skin. "I don't think she kept her tee time. Mr. Nash, I've looked everywhere at the club and on the course. I can't find her."

A deep sigh resounded from the phone. "Did you check the docks? Sometimes she takes out their boat. Sarah's a good sailor. Just a minute." Papers shuffled in the background. "Dock B, slip four. The *Playbuoy*. It's a cabin cruiser. Stingray."

"Did you say *Playboy*?»

"Play-boo-ee. It's a pun, Miss Albright."

"Still," I said, "not very appropriate for a married couple, don't you think?"

"This coming from the girl caught on camera hauling off her panties?"

"They weren't panties. They were Spanx and I had been dancing all night and couldn't breathe. I didn't know the limo driver was going to open the door at that moment. Wait, a minute. How did you know that? I thought you weren't interested in celebrity news."

"No-Panties-Albright pictures were plastered over every tabloid cover in the nation for three weeks, Miss Albright. You stand in line to buy a six-pack and can't help but be confronted with your national exposure."

"I was—"

"I broke rule one, Miss Albright, and I apologize. Go check that dock."

"There's another thing," I hesitated. "Sarah Waverly left her purse in the Cayenne. A Prada. Actually, a papaya Prada."

"She didn't need it at the club, so she left it in the car."

"A woman does not leave her purse in the car when she's going to change into golf togs. Or yachting. She would leave it in her locker at the club or take it on the boat. Especially a Prada."

After a semi-long bout of silence, he said, "You have a point."

"Thanks." I brightened. "So are you coming?"

"Check the *Playbuoy* first. Then call me back."

"There's a slight problem."

A second sigh. Deeper than the first. "What is the slight problem?"

"I don't have a phone. I'm at a gas station. Could you possibly come to the club, just in case Mrs. Waverly isn't on the *Playbuoy*? And if she is, maybe you could point out some good surveillance techniques? As a certified trainer?"

"Miss Albright, if you lost your phone while partying at the Cove, get another one. I'm not rearranging my schedule to follow you around on the off chance you might want to speak to me."

"I didn't lose my phone. I don't own one anymore." I wanted to avoid Vicki in all ways possible, but I couldn't tell Nash I was afraid of my mother. As it was, she could still track me down. Not having a phone only hindered the inevitability.

An avalanche tumbled from my lips in my effort to explain. "I've been at everyone's beck and call for years. At first, it was a way for my manager and agent to keep track of me. Then directors and producers needed to keep tabs. I had one of the earliest smartphones, and they made me responsible for answering fan mail. As a teenager, I spent more time answering emails than on schoolwork. And social media. It was my job to Tweet and Instagram and Facebook and Vine and Snapchat and, like, Googlechat and whatever else my manager wanted me to do. Especially for spin control—"

"Rule one, Miss Albright." The expulsion of breath resonated in my ear. "Private investigators have phones. Most Americans have phones."

My face heated. "It got—"

"If you work for me, you will have a phone. If you really want to be a private investigator, the smarter the better."

"But—"

"Sarah Waverly is likely sunning herself on the boat. But I'll meet you at the club. Just in case."

BACK AT THE CLUB, I re-parked, re-checked the Cayenne, and re-entered the clubhouse. After a quick perusal, I shot out the back and onto a rubbery cart path leading away from the links and toward the Cove. A series of docks lined the lake and at letter B, I skipped up stairs and down the boardwalk, counting off slips until I reached number four.

No *Playbuoy*.

I ground my teeth, then stopped myself because I couldn't afford new caps. Nash had been correct and I had wasted his trip. I wished I could take back the phone call, but I wouldn't have known to investigate the docks.

Sighing, I squinted at the water, trying to catch sight of the Stingray, but most yachters headed away from the resort area and around the mountain to the far side of Black Pine Lake. Turning back, I eyed the Cove's patio and thought about asking if anyone had seen Sarah and the *Playbuoy*.

For my first surveillance, I had really screwed up. My therapist, Renata, would accuse me of transference, losing Sarah Waverly as the equivalent of losing track of my life. Particularly because I had allowed Vicki to divert me from achieving my goal.

Renata loved analogies.

The golf cart path continued toward the resort's villas and hotel rooms, but I stopped at the stone steps leading up to the restaurant. Perhaps someone had spotted Sarah with a man who was not David Waverly.

Maybe this would be the break in the surveillance case Nash had been doing for a month. David Waverly would be pleased that I had found his wife cheating. Maybe not pleased with his wife, but not so angry with Nash. That's a sort of win-win, right?

My Luluemon yoga pants and t-shirt felt too casual for Black Pine's premier dining experience, but I fluffed my hair and applied some lipstick, ready to bring Julia Pinkerton to the Cove. I swaggered up the steps and found myself on the patio.

Faces sunglassed in Ray-Ban and Westward Leaning dotted the tables along the patio wall. Most had silver coffee servers and dainty plates of fruit and yogurt. They looked a bit haggard and all too familiar. A few raised their coffee cups to me. Most seemed too tired to bother with a greeting.

The *All is Albright* crew. Holy shizzlations. These poor souls had been dragged through three time zones and tossed in what they would consider backcountry hell. Even with the fair-trade coffee, organic fruit, and natural Greek yogurt.

A camera shutter caught my open-mouthed astonishment. Al, the official *Albright* photographer, waved from a table. I waved back and he snapped another shot. I made a quick scan for Sarah Waverly, who was not breakfasting on the patio. However, my eyes locked on a particular Cove breakfaster, languidly sipping his espresso.

Double shizz.

Giulio Belloni. In Balenciaga. From the new summer collection. One of the few men I knew who could pull off skinny jeans and not look like an ass. He looked gorgeous. Like a dark-eyed, sensual Latin soap star. Which was his former gig.

Our eyes met. Mine had probably widened enough to swallow my face. His narrowed in heavy lidded triumph.

"Oh my God." I wished I'd entered the Cove from the front door. Or not entered at all. Or worn something other than a t-shirt that hinted at a muffin top.

Before I could escape, Giulio had paced the patio in long, quick strides. "Baby," he cried, loud enough for the *Albright* crew to hear. And probably pick up on their phones for a quick Instagram upload. "You left me in Beverly Hills. How could you?"

He captured my hands in his and drew me in for a soft, double cheek kiss that finished with a harder kiss on my lips. I always lost my lipstick around Giulio. I used to enjoy that until I realized Giulio only loved Giulio.

"I told you I was moving," I whispered. "I'm sorry about *All is Albright*, but the season was finished. You know I didn't renew my contract."

"Darling." Giulio ran his hands up my arms and grasped my shoulders, turning me slightly. "The season was finished, but what about us? We could never be finished."

Frigalicious, I thought, Giulio was probably Vicki's surprise luxury item. Giulio would never come to Georgia on his own. He also took direction well.

I glanced around the patio. Giulio had positioned us parallel to the camera crew. Al hopped up with a light meter to take a quick reading. Catching my eye, he smiled and gave me a thumbs up.

"What is going on?" I whispered.

"Darling." Giulio gave me a 90-watt smile and an Italian shrug. "Can I help it if the camera follows me around? You want to go back to my villa so we can talk privately?"

"No." I backed up, pulling Giulio with me. "I don't know what Vicki told you, but I'm done. I'm going to become a private investigator."

"That is cool, baby. I like it. Very sexy." Giulio gave my Adidas top a quick once over. "Listen, why don't you come back to my room anyway. I promise no cameras, no show. Just me and you and we'll have sex. I am so bored here."

"It's barely eleven in the morning. I've got to go. I'm working."

"But it's only eight in LA. I have the jet lag. Even in the studio jet, we do the red-eye. I am exhausted."

"Then get some sleep," I hissed. "I'm not having sex with you. We're not together. I have a new life here. You know what my therapist and the judge said. I can't be around anyone from my old life."

"I have no idea what you say, baby, but I'm sorry. I miss you. I miss..." Giulio thought hard. "I miss how we looked together."

He meant on camera. Giulio had been hired by the show's producers to create a romantic diversion after my breakup with Oliver.

Without telling me.

"An adult Maizie Albright is more interesting when the world thinks she's in love," Vicki had said after I accused her of manipulating my love life. «Whether you are or not."

By in love, she meant getting laid. Vicki still had enough Black Pine in her to use euphemisms for certain things better left unsaid. She also had enough LA in her to be pragmatic about certain things better left unsaid. Which is very confusing for an actress/daughter.

"Did Vicki bring you here to seduce me? She wants me to sign on for another season." I found it easier to be forthright with Giulio. His English wasn't good enough for euphemisms.

"No, darling. But she invites everyone from *Albright* to visit your hometown. I flew in with some camera guys and the hair and makeup." He stepped closer, skimming my arms to take my hands. "I am seducing you because I miss you. When we are together, I feel happy."

"Happy to be with me or happy to be in the show?"

"I don't know what you mean. I miss you so much." Giulio slipped his hands from mine to pin me against his chest. Lowering his head, he sequestered my lips for a long kiss.

I forgot to not enjoy myself for a few seconds, then pushed away. Glancing out at the patio, I got another thumbs up from Al.

Good thing I didn't do social media anymore, because that picture was likely to be Instagramed into oblivion.

"I have to go."

I pushed past Giulio and fled into the restaurant, hoping I'd find news of Sarah Waverly in the bathroom because that's where I headed. To not cry.

∞

THE RESTROOM ATTENDANT HAD NO Sarah Waverly news. The hostess, servers, and sous chef had not seen Sarah Waverly either. I left from the kitchen entrance, hugging the restaurant walls to avoid detection by the *Albright* crew. From the parking lot, I walked past the tennis courts and pool to get back to the club, where I would find Nash and deliver the news that Sarah Waverly had likely taken the boat out.

I slunk through the parking lot. Vicki Albright had invaded Black Pine and poised herself to reassume management of my life. For that, my father might kick me out for disobeying Judge Ellis's decree to avoid my old lifestyle. And I was about to confirm Nash's belief that I was an idiot for demanding he help me look for a woman who had taken a joy ride on her own boat. My emotional meter shot toward impending doom.

I stopped in front of a yellow Corvette and those thoughts disappeared.

David Waverly drove a yellow Stingray. I hadn't seen him in the Cove, and I'm sure he would have spotted me with all the fuss Giulio had made. Had he taken out the *Playbuoy* and not Sarah? Or had they taken it together?

I sprinted toward the club. At the entrance, I found Nash checking his watch and glaring at my approaching form.

"Someone took the *Playbuoy*," I said after apologizing. "But I don't know if it's Sarah or David or both. His car is at the Cove, but he's not in the restaurant."

Nash rubbed the bridge of his broken nose and trained his gaze on the Cayenne at the far end of the parking lot.

"Maybe your evidence made an impression on Mr. Waverly and he stopped believing his wife was cheating. Maybe he went home, made up to her, and they decided to spend a romantic day together on their boat. Maybe they'll decide to renew their vows and start over."

"You have imagination, I'll give you that."

"Thank you. What should I do now?"

"Do you have any equipment with you?" He held up his hand. "I don't want to rehash the phone conversation. You need a camera. With a good zoom and the ability to switch from video to stills. More than one, actually. Extra batteries and memory cards. And a telescoping monopod."

"Like a selfie stick?»

"An extension to keep your camera steady. You don't want to be embarrassed by your shaky video evidence in a courtroom," said Nash. "Didn't they teach you that in college?"

I felt my neck heat. "This is why we're supposed to have training. I have a GoPro somewhere. I got it in a gift bag from an awards show. Teen Choice Awards, I think. Or maybe it was the—" He raised a brow, and I stopped.

"Tell me exactly how you lost her."

I gave him the facts of my morning surveillance. Minus the Vicki part. "I don't think a two-timer brings lunches. I guess you thought the same. But Mr. Waverly is. Two-timing. I had my suspicions and they were confirmed by his receptionist when she saw me.»

"What?"

"The receptionist was not surprised to see me. She thought I was the other woman. And her non-surprise at seeing me for the first time means the other woman is changed out regularly."

"God Almighty."

"I know, right?" I crossed my arms.

His eyes cut to my arms crossed over my t-shirt then traveled over the yoga pants to my Golden Goose sneakers before centering back on my face. "Your nose looks better."

"Thanks." Before I could explain my anti-nose-swelling technique, Nash held up a hand.

"Let me think for a minute."

I quieted.

"I've always felt this case was hinky." He picked up a backpack and slung it over one shoulder. "We'll go to the lake and wait for the *Playbuoy* to dock."

"We? You're going with me? Like, to give me instruction? You're really going to train me?" I threw myself at him, squeezing him hard. "You won't be sorry."

He peeled me off his body. "No hugging either. That's rule two."

"Sorry."

"Try not to be so excited."

I couldn't help it. Finally, I was becoming the Julia Pinkerton I always wanted to be. Without the cheer skirt. And Clearasil contracts.

EIGHT

#MaximAttack #RepoMyDream

FOLLOWING THE CART PATH BACK to the lake, we found a bench across from Dock B and settled on it to wait on the *Playbuoy*'s arrival.

I tried not to smile or bounce. Or talk too much. Which was hard not to do when you're trying to impress your new boss. The more Nash didn't talk, the more I filled the void.

My therapist Renata said I'm uncomfortable with silence because I have deep-seated issues with social acceptance and belonging. I think it's because I spent so much time on noisy sets and shoots. All the action and off-camera chatting had given me an auditory attention issue. Also, I'm a curious person. Which is another reason I wanted to become a detective.

"When did you become a P.I.?" I kept the stream of questions moving, pausing only long enough for Nash to offer an answer.

Which he didn't.

"Did you always want to be one? Were you a cop before? Or in the military? How long have you had your office? I guess I should have asked you this yesterday during our interview, but I got sidetracked by Jolene and your meeting with David Waverly."

"It wasn't an interview," muttered Nash.

"And who is Jolene Sweeney? Why is she co-owner of a private investigation office when she's in real estate? Is she my boss, too? As in, can she fire me? Vicki will most likely talk her into firing me. I guess you'll have to make up your own mind about that, but I hope you judge me on performance. Except for this first assignment. Because I didn't know how to do proper surveillance."

Nash set down his binoculars to glare at me. "Jolene Sweeney is not your boss and don't let her try to convince you otherwise. Just simmer down."

I shut up for a good ten minutes.

An enticing aroma of grilled something floated from the Cove, setting off a din of hunger rattles from my stomach. I started another stream of chatter to cover the noise. "Does David Waverly often take the boat out during the week?"

"He doesn't, although sometimes he does business on the links. Sarah uses it more. Maybe my lack of finding any dirt on his wife led to a reconciliation. But..." His words drifted. Nash lifted the binoculars to squint through them again.

"To take the boat out during the day, even if he reconciled with his wife, doesn't fit his character, does it?"

Nash shook his head. "No, it does not."

Which confirmed the real reason Nash accompanied me to the dock. He was suspicious of David Waverly. "Why don't you like Waverly? Aside from the obvious philandering and animosity toward his wife, I mean."

"Didn't say I didn't like him."

I thought for a minute. "Didn't Jolene say Black Pine Group wanted to buy your business? Waverly didn't share that with you when he hired you to watch his wife. Is that what's bugging you?"

Nash kept the binoculars trained on the lake. "Yes. Among other things."

I smiled, pleased that we were having a sort-of-actual conversation. "Do you think he'd deliberately try to mess with your investigation? To encourage you to sell?"

Nash yanked off the binoculars to stare at me. The blue eyes appeared a bit dazed and confused. Or surprised at my utterance.

"Just an idea," I raised a shoulder. "That happened in *Julia Pinkerton*, Season 2, Episode 4. 'The Case of the Conglomerate Cover Up.' A corporation wanted the property where a popular teen club was located, so they tried to make the owner look bad by sending in kids to deal drugs."

Nash replaced the binoculars. "That's TV. And it's not the property location they're interested in. I rent from Lamar."

"Maybe they're actually after Lamar's donut recipes."

A smile snuck over Nash's lips.

I sucked in my breath. Thank God Nash didn't smile often or I'd be a gooey mess. I hopped to my feet to shake off my libido. "Why don't I get us lunch or something?"

"Hang on." Nash's hand landed on my elbow and he drew me back to the bench. "There's a cabin cruiser coming in now. Get the camera ready. If it's the *Playbuoy*, we'll slip over to the next dock and take some photos."

A moment later, he pulled off the binoculars. "It's the *Playbuoy*. It's slowing to idle in. Let's go."

We rushed to Dock A and huddled behind a big Chaparral speed boat. Truly a Julia Pinkerton moment.

Nash glanced around and pulled a ball cap from his backpack. "Put this on. You're going to pose like I'm taking your picture. Try to stand so you're not blocking the view of the *Playbuoy* but so it still looks like I'm taking your picture."

"I'll make it happen." I cocked a finger and shot him.

"What was that?"

"Julia Pinkerton's catch phrase."

He muttered something I didn't want to hear, so I sauntered up the dock to ready my position. I pulled on the Braves cap, placed a hand on my hip, and leaned forward, camera ready. Behind me, I heard more muttering. Whirling around, I encountered an older man, sitting on the bench of a Chris Craft launch, rooting through a large tackle box.

"Ahoy," I said. "Did you say something?"

"I said, you're blocking my light."

I looked up at the sky and noted the sun's position. Overhead. Which made sense for lunchtime. "I don't understand. I'm not that tall."

"Not the sun." He pointed across the dock to the Bayliner on the opposite side. On the bench, a woman in a bikini lay face down, sleeping. Her top was untied as to prevent tan lines. "The light bouncing off her Hawaiian Tropic oil." He grinned.

"We're just taking a picture." I edged toward the other side of the dock.

"Move the other way," called Nash, waving his hand toward the pervy fisherman's boat.

I stopped in the middle of the dock and posed again. This time, I leaned sideways to not block the Hawaiian Tropic light.

"What kind of pose is that?" called Nash. "I thought you modeled."

The fisherman peeled his eyes off Hawaiian Tropic. "What kind of modeling?"

"Mostly as a child. Later it's not really considered modeling. Just marketing. A few magazine spreads."

«*Sports Illustrated* swimsuit?" he asked hopefully.

"Not *SI* material, but thanks." I tilted my head, placed a hand on my hip, and bent my leg.

The *Playbuoy* was in view and a man was steering. I had yacht partied enough in Malibu to ascertain that cabin cruiser held a couple rooms below deck for comfortable overnight trips. Probably not necessary on a lake, but the *Playbuoy* looked impressive. And that's what counted on Black Pine Lake.

Nash swung the camera toward the docking boat, letting the shutter fly.

"I'm Hal, by the way," said the fisherman. "Now that I'm looking at you, I've seen you somewhere. *Playboy?*»

"Nope." I snuck closer to Hal's boat, trying to appear in the camera frame. I crossed my ankles and stuck my thumb in my yoga pants waistband.

"What do you call that pose?" asked Hal.

"Chillin' like a villain." I pretended to look into the distance, while watching the *Playbuoy* angle into dock. "Not appropriate for the red carpet, but good for Rodeo Drive shopping when you know the paparazzi are watching."

Hal stood, dumping his tackle box. "I do know you. You were in *Maxim's* "Hot 100" for five years. Number four, forty-two, seventeen, thirty-eight, and eighty-six. Respectively."

"Um," I twisted to glance at him over my shoulder. "That's a little weird. Only my manager remembers those kinds of numbers."

"Maizie Albright." He slapped his thigh. "Can I get an autograph?"

"We're a little busy. Taking pictures." Of a possible affair. Or marriage reconciliation.

I slid closer to the dock's edge, trying to see if the *Playbuoy*'s captain was David Waverly. I switched for a side pose, crossing my legs and bringing my hands up to my cap. Good for elongating the body and slimming your arms. Also good for watching a boat dock.

The captain was David Waverly.

Nash dropped to the dock, watching the cabin cruiser while slipping his camera in his backpack. He jerked his head at me and pointed down. I squatted next to the fishing boat and came face-to-face with Hal.

"How about an autograph now?" asked Hal.

I glanced at Nash, but he didn't show signs of hearing our conversation. He continued to pretend to mess with his backpack while watching the *Playbuoy*. David Waverly looped rope around the tie-off pilings, readying to drag the boat closer and fix the lines.

"I might have to leave in a minute," I whispered. "We'll have to do it fast."

"Is that your boyfriend?" asked Hal. "Kind of protective or something?"

"Kind-of-sort-of-not," I mumbled. "Just hurry and grab a pen, please."

Hal disappeared behind the captain's chair.

"We don't have time for you to make friends." Nash's whisper ended in a hiss.

"I'm not making friends. Hal keeps talking to me. And I'm trying to be inconspicuous, so I'm talking back."

"Talking about your *Maxim* model career is not being inconspicuous. It's conspicuous."

"I don't want to be rude."

Hal returned with a Sharpie and a life preserver. "How about signing this?"

"Sure," I grabbed the Sharpie and scribbled Maizie in big loopy letters.

"Don't you want to personalize it?" asked Hal.

All I knew of Hal was that he enjoyed scantily clad women. I wrote, "Hal, Take care."

Hal frowned. "That's disappointing. For a *Maxim* Hot 100, I thought you'd write something sexier.»

"I was an actress, not a writer." I grabbed the pen and wrote, "I'll make it happen" under my name. "That was my catch phrase. As Julia Pinkerton."

"Better, but still..." Hal shrugged.

"We need to go," said Nash.

I scurried after Nash. We stopped behind the speed boat, waiting while David Waverly traversed Dock B. He carried a gym bag and a cooler. At the dock steps, he turned onto the cart path toward the Cove.

"Follow him," Nash whispered. "But no more autographs. Just say no."

"Is that rule three?" I asked.

"Are you serious about investigation work or not? Get tough. Stop worrying about being rude."

"I don't know if I can do that." I paused and read Nash's face. "But I'll try."

"I'll hang back to see if Sarah Waverly is on the *Playbuoy.*"

"Are you sending me to the Cove to get rid of me?"

Nash raised an eyebrow. "Miss Albright, I've been trying to get rid of you since I met you. Now I'm asking you to do something useful."

"Oh, good." I beamed, but then sobered considering Sarah Waverly's disappearance. "If she's not on the boat, what will we do?"

"First I'll check the club's parking lot security footage." Nash shook his head. "If Sarah Waverly's really gone, that means someone picked her up. Could be innocent, but if she is having an affair, I somehow messed up the investigation. And in that case,

David Waverly is going to have my ass."

I contemplated that idea for a moment. I didn't like the thought of David Waverly taking Nash's ass. It might mean I wouldn't fulfill my dream of becoming a real Julia Pinkerton. But mostly, I felt worried about Nash's ass.

Well, you know what I mean.

L UCKILY, DAVID WAVERLY SKIRTED THE Cove and followed another cart path around the restaurant toward the parking lot. From a corner, I watched David Waverly toss the cooler and bag into his trunk. A moment later he had taken off in his Corvette.

I trotted back to the lake where I found Nash on the *Playbuoy*'s deck. I squatted on the dock and watched him root through the bench storage.

"He took off and I wasn't near my car to follow him," I whispered. "Aren't you worried about someone seeing you?"

"Hal's back to watching the sunbather and the boats on this dock are empty. I'm keeping a low profile." Nash opened another bench seat and peered inside. "The tackle is open and some of the fishing gear is dirty."

He dropped the bench's lid and tried the handle on the cabin door. "Locked."

"No Sarah?"

"She's probably been picked up at the club. I've not known Waverly to go fishing during the week, but it's not illegal. And it is Friday." Nash hopped onto the deck and we headed back to the club.

Black Pine Lake's beauty seemed spoiled by the sordid world of affairs and memorization of "*Maxim* Hot 100" numbers. I took comfort that my new career would make me known for my acumen and not my chest size or ability to chirp catch phrases on cue.

At the club, Nash and I parted. He to the security office to review video footage of the parking lot. I would make another search for Sarah.

An hour later, we met in the lobby.

"Did you see who Sarah left with?"

Nash shook his head. "Check this out."

He pushed through the club's front doors, and I followed him into the parking lot. We stood under the overhang that covered the drive before the front doors. Nash pointed at the camera perched on a beam facing the parking lot.

"One camera aimed at the entrance. It only catches the first couple rows of cars. Bullshit security."

"Did you recommend a multiple camera system with motion detectors and night vision?"

Nash gaped at me for a beat. "I left my card."

I nodded.

"Guess whose Cayenne is just outside the camera's lens?"

My eyes focused on the lot's far side, where the Cayenne was parked. "Wow, that's bad luck. You couldn't see who picked her up?"

"She didn't approach the club, but that's basically all the camera can catch. I couldn't see her leave. And I can't say if another vehicle pulled in and picked her up." Nash shoved his hands in his pockets. "I need to tell you something. Miss Albright, I have some bad news."

"About Sarah Waverly?" I feared the worst. She had been mugged in the parking lot, and I had not been there to prevent the crime. I might have even seen the perps if I hadn't been too busy bickering with Vicki.

Except the thieves left her purse in the Cayenne. And had not taken the Cayenne. What kind of muggers would not take a Prada or Cayenne? "Wait, what happened to Sarah?"

"This is not about Sarah Waverly." Nash stared at his boots. His jaw flexed, whitening the scar on his chin.

Oh hells, I thought. He's going to fire me over Hal's autograph. Or maybe he found out about the *Albright* crew coming to town. "I'm very serious about pursuing a career in private investigation, Mr. Nash. I'm sorry about giving Hal an autograph, but I was trying to get him to leave me alone. I have no interest in returning to TV."

"You've already told me that." Nash looked up. "I saw something else on the security footage. It's about your car."

"Did somebody hit my Jag? I knew I shouldn't have parked up front." I peered at the vehicles, but couldn't spot the blue convertible. "Where did I park?"

"It's been towed."

"Towed?" I sucked in a breath. "Vicki. She did sic the repo guys on me. Those bastards."

"Hold on. I do skip tracing all the time. It's not their fault."

My head drooped and my cheeks burned. "I am—"

"No need for details. Less is more when it comes to sharing personal business. I'll run you home so you can find out what happened to your car. Then I'll hightail it back here to watch the Cayenne."

"What are we going to do about Sarah Waverly?"

"I have to report this to David."

"Are you going to tell him we watched the *Playbuoy*?»

Nash's lips thinned. "I'll play that by ear. See if he tells me first."

"I should stay. I was supposed to be on Sarah Waverly duty this week. It's my fault I lost her."

"You're not any good without a vehicle," said Nash. "Get your act together and come back tomorrow."

IF I WERE WRITING A script, I would describe the ride to the DeerNose cabin as such: *Fade in. Interior old Silverado cab, early afternoon. Wyatt Nash, 30s with Paul Newman eyes, glowery and formidable. Speaking on cellphone while driving. Maizie Albright, 25 and hungry. Trying unsuccessfully not to bite nails or twist hair.*

I would've preferred to ride in uncomfortable silence than listen to the conversation Nash had with David Waverly. At one point, Nash had held the phone away from his ear rather than have his eardrum burst by the explosion of Waverly's anger. After a month of watching Sarah Waverly golf and shop, the first day

Nash took himself off the case, Sarah Waverly disappeared.

Nash described it as "hinky."

David Waverly described it as a "damned irresponsible, unpardonable, and incompetent blunder" and went on from there, adding curse words willy-nilly.

My name was not mentioned. I didn't know if I should thank Nash or worry it meant he no longer wanted me on the case. A case I created when I offered my services to a man for whom Nash didn't want to work. I wouldn't blame Nash for firing me. But I certainly did not want to be fired. I wanted to help Mr. Nash and undo my rash offer. I also had a Julia Pinkerton dream to fulfill. And there was the requirement to hold a steady job by terms of my probation. Plus, it would be nice to prove I could do this. That I didn't have to rely on Vicki for a career.

Maybe rub that in to Vicki, too. When she finally moved back to LA. Which would hopefully be soon.

But primarily, I needed to help Mr. Nash.

Nash hung up and tossed the phone into a cup holder. He stared into the windshield like he was counting every tree lining the long, wooded drive to the DeerNose cabin. "David Waverly could ruin me. He wants to ruin me. Will make it much easier to buy me out that way, I guess."

"What can I do?" I had not forgotten Jolene Sweeney wanted to sell Nash's business to the Black Pine Group. I'd screwed up Nash's life in more ways than one. My belly reminded me by recreating that feeling you get on Space Mountain at the peak of the last hill before you start spinning around the star room.

Nash sighed. "Nothing for now. I'm headed back to the club. Maybe someone saw her leave."

"Maybe a friend picked her up to go shopping." Without her purse.

"More likely she knew I was following her and arranged to meet her lover when she knew I wasn't watching." He parked and slammed his fist into the steering wheel. "Sumbitch."

I stayed quiet, watching a passel of Jack Russell terriers charge around the side of the cabin and dance across the driveway, yipping at Nash's Silverado.

Nash turned to me. "For a month, Sarah Waverly has not varied in her routine. Every morning she drops off a lunch at her husband's office before he arrives. Then she goes to the club, shopping, or back home. He goes to the gym first thing followed by a stop for breakfast. Every blasted day. And today? She takes off and he goes fishing."

"Hinky," I said, testing out Nash Security lingua franca. "She worked on the DeerNose Charity Ball. I'll ask Daddy what he knows about her while I see about getting a new set of wheels."

Nash sighed. "Don't know what good it will do, but might as well."

I chalked that statement up to "you're not fired." Yet.

NINE

#DeerNoseKing #TrustFundTurnOffs

MY FATHER, BOOMER SPAYBERRY—A.K.A. THE Deer-Nose King—married Carol Lynn—a.k.a. the sweetest woman in the world—midway through *Julia Pinkerton's* third season. We don't pretend Carol Lynn's my stepmom, although I had often wished for a stepmom, or any kind of mother, just like Carol Lynn. She had been raised with the strap, the Bible, and fried chicken. Carol Lynn cooked from scratch. She could also hunt and fish. And she never reads trades, tabloids, or even watches *E!* news. Or any *E!* at all.

Carol Lynn was the complete and total opposite of Vicki and my father loved her for it. He also loved their offspring—born before my first season of rehab—Remington Marie Spayberry. Named her after his favorite gun. Something Vicki would never have given him a chance in hell of doing.

Carol Lynn thought it cute, naming her daughter after a rifle. So was little Remi. Cute. And as fiery as her namesake.

Remi sat next to me at the wooden table carved from a great pine felled on my daddy's property. The entire house and furniture were created from those once living on Spayberry property.

And we're not talking a little cabin in the woods, as Vicki liked to pretend. We're talking five thousand square feet with nine-foot ceilings and a giant sun deck stretching across the back, with a view of Black Pine Lake through a mess of trees. The decor consisted of antlers, glass-eyed animal heads, and quilts. Made by Carol Lynn, naturally. The quilts, not the taxidermy.

When DeerNose started up and Daddy poured everything into

the business, he survived on local fishing and hunting. What is caught and hunted was still a culinary mainstay in the Spayberry house. "The Spayberrys have always lived off the land," Daddy had oft-quoted. Lucky for me, it's all lean meat. But even better, Carol Lynn cooks with real lard and butter.

Evidenced by my straining Gucci seams, as Vicki's discerning eye had noticed.

"What're you doing? Daddy says y'all's supposed to stay away from those social sites," said Remi, peering at my computer screen. She shook a lock of hair from her eyes and slid off her knee-sit to poke her head under the table. "Just a minute, girl."

"I know what Daddy and the judge said. I'm not doing social media. Haven't checked it since I left California. Not even Tumblr." I switched the screen from Sarah Waverly's Pinterest page to the Edgar report on the Black Pine Group.

A Jack Russell terrier, one of a half-dozen that roamed the property, had his paws on Remi's spindly thigh. His nose hovered below a spoonful of banana pudding Remi held above his mouth.

"Speak," said Remi.

The dog barked and received pudding. Remi stirred her bowl, took a bite, and fed another spoonful to the dog.

"That's really gross," I said.

"She's not the one who eats poo." Remi fed another heaping of pudding to the dog. "Her mouth's got less germs than people's. That's what Daddy says."

"Still gross. Your six-year-old butt is too skinny. You need to eat your own food. Besides, pudding is probably bad for dogs."

"She ate a bag of Hershey's kisses and that's supposed to be real bad for dogs. Banana pudding ain't going to do nothing to her." Remi scratched the dog's head. "Anyway, I'm not hungry. What're you doing?"

"Looking for a new car." I felt it prudent not to mention investigating a local man and his possibly philandering wife.

"Why? I liked your blue car."

"I couldn't afford it anymore."

"Are you broke because your momma stole your TV show?"

"Where'd you hear that?"

Remi shrugged.

"Actually Remi, the TV show is all hers. I only agreed to guest appearances to make Vicki happy. Even if she didn't appreciate my effort. Or understand I meant the appearances as more of a cameo role. Like the crew might catch me as I left the house. That sort of thing."

"Uncle Bud says Miss Vicki sold your soul to the devil and she kept all the money."

"Sounds like Uncle Bud is preaching again. Or drinking."

Remi held the spoon out for the dog to lick. "Is that why Daddy said you had to live with us? Because the devil's got your soul?"

"No, a judge said I had to live with my father until my probation ends." I considered her point. "Our daddy worries I might be a bad influence on you. But I'm good now. I've had lots of therapy. Tons."

"My kindergarten teacher had therapy when she hurt her knee."

"Is she better now?"

Remi nodded. "But she don't play Monkey in the Middle no more. That's how she hurt her knee. Slid out and fell when Carter tagged her."

"See, I'm like your teacher. And instead of Monkey in the Middle, I avoid LA to stay healthy."

"Remington Marie, you better not be feeding the dog again," thundered a deep voice behind us.

Remi dropped her spoon, and I slammed my laptop shut.

I spun in my seat to face Boomer Spayberry. The man stood six foot three, but in my eyes he was closer to seven. The only evidence of his aging in the last ten years was the accumulation of white in his nearly chest-length auburn beard. With his blue eyes and rounded cheeks, someday Boomer Spayberry would make an excellent Santa. He wore a sports coat with his jeans and boots. A sports coat of hand-painted camo and smelling like deer pee.

"Did you eat your lunch?"

"Yes, sir," I said. "Carol Lynn made pimento sandwiches, deviled eggs, and banana pudding for dessert. I was pretty hungry because

I skipped the biscuits and gravy this morning. I'm watching my carbs. Do you think she could do gluten free biscuits? You can do gluten free just about anything now. I don't want to bother Carol Lynn, but I think I've gained about five pounds in three days."

"I meant Remi." Boomer sighed. "I'm not worried about you skipping meals, hon'. Remi doesn't have your appetite."

I cut a glance toward Remi, but she had disappeared under the table. "Well, she'll appreciate that when she gets older. Daddy, do you remember a woman named Sarah Waverly? She worked on the DeerNose Charity Ball as treasurer."

Boomer stopped his stride toward the kitchen and dipped his hands into his coat pocket to pull out a phone. "Sarah Waverly? I don't rightly remember, but the charity committee ran that thing. I just rubber stamped most of their decisions." He thumbed through his contacts. "There she is. Do you need her number?"

"I was hoping you could tell me about her."

"Let's see." He scratched his beard. "Treasurer? All the reports were in good order. I don't really remember the woman, but I was impressed with her accounting. Sometimes these volunteers can barely add two and two. Made a decent profit on the ball for the children's hospital. DeerNose matched the funds and we cut them a pretty check. Yes, ma'am, that was a good fundraiser."

"Did you notice her cozying up to any men in her group? Did she leave the meetings early or come late? Did she," I paused, then rushed through the words, "come on to you? Like flirt or act suggestive?"

"Maizie Spayberry. God Almighty, why would you ask me such a thing?"

"It's nothing personal against you. I'm trying to learn more about Sarah Waverly's character. I'm working on a case."

"Are you now?" His smile shone through the beard. "There you go, getting on to honest work. I'm proud of you, girl. I was a little worried about you securing a position in ten days. I could get you something at the plant, but don't want to be accused of nepotism. You got the job, then?"

"Sort of." I gave him my *Seventeen* magazine cover smile and tried for a vague description. In my experience, particulars led Boomer toward statements such as, "people who act like idiots deserve to spend the night in the pokey without bail."

"Mr. Nash isn't entirely convinced yet of my abilities or qualifications. I kind of forced myself upon a case, and due to my involvement the investigation heated up. I hope to make things right and, in the end, keep the job."

"You keep at it, sugar. That's how I was able to make DeerNose the company she is today. Persistence and hard work. Didn't listen to the doubters or the disbelievers. Visited the bank every week until I finally secured my first loan, then personally hand-delivered the check that paid it off. You've got to believe in yourself and work your tail off to achieve your goals."

"I hope so. I'm worried I've screwed things up for Mr. Nash."

"You can't even think that way." Boomer shook his phone at me. "See, that's Hollywood talking. You don't believe in yourself because you've been living other people's dreams for too long. And look what they did to you. Turned my beautiful baby girl into some nut-cake living on bean sprouts and poison and running around with a bunch of fruit-loops. They made you into a lowlife criminal who can't even hold her head up around decent folks no more."

"I can't be around decent folks?"

"Probably shouldn't until this last TV show wears off. Thank the good Lord that's done. I've never been so glad as the day you came home and said that part of your life was all over. Even if it took a judge to do it."

I chewed on my nail and considered warning him about Vicki. But did it really matter if I wasn't going to do another season? Carol Lynn's cooking probably gave him enough high blood pressure. "I thought you might not approve of me becoming a private investigator."

"Shoot, I'd be just as happy if you got a job flipping burgers. As long as it's got nothing to do with those Hollywood people, you can do as you please." He glanced at my t-shirt. "'Cept stay off the poles, baby girl. Not that I think you would, but you do get talked into things."

"Daddy." I flashed another wholesome *Seventeen* pose, figuring we were on a good roll. "I was wondering if you had a car I could borrow. I no longer have my Jag and need something to get around town."

He narrowed his eyes. "What happened?"

«It was a lease. And it was collected, so to speak.»

Boomer shook his head. "That's why I pay for everything in cash. Took out one loan and personally—"

"I know, sir. You hand-delivered the check to pay it off as soon as you could. But I wasn't exactly raised that way."

His bright blue eyes pierced me. "It's time you learned, then, isn't it? I love you, Maizie, and that's why you need to tough it out. You're like those indigenous folks the missionaries talk about. The ones who have to be taught how to live in civilization. God bless them, they don't even know how to use a fork, much less get a job. And you were educated. Supposedly."

"Wha...? I had a tutor. And I went to college." I mentally shook off the analogy. I know he'd seen me use a fork. Plenty. "But Daddy, how can I persist and work my tail off without a car?"

"I bought you a vehicle for your fourteenth birthday. It's still in the barn where you left it."

"What vehicle?" My face squinched and I almost forgot to smooth out the wrinkles. "The dirt bike? I can't ride a dirt bike around town."

"Sure you can. The KLR's street legal. I've kept it maintained. Sometimes Carol Lynn rides it. May need to register it, but that's no big deal."

I shook my head. "I never learned how to drive it. It scared me."

"That's because you were fourteen and I got you 250 cc's. Too much power for a city girl. Should've started you at 125. My fault."

"I doubt I could drive it now. The only time I'm on a bike is for spin class. And those bikes don't have a motor. You have to pedal. Which is the point of spin. Pedaling and getting yelled at by the instructor."

Boomer folded his arms. "I don't know about spin, but I guess you better learn how to drive that dirt bike. And don't think about touching your trust fund or hitting up Carol Lynn for a vehicle."

"I'm twenty-five years old, Daddy. This is ridiculous."

"Your lifestyle was ridiculous, that's why I won't let you touch the DeerNose stocks until you prove your worth. I want you home again, but you've got to learn how to live like real folks."

I glanced around the palatial cabin and wondered how real was real. Daddy loved to make a point. Although sometimes it felt like I was punished for being raised by his ex-wife.

"How do I ride a dirt bike in a dress?"

"You don't. You need to stop dressing so fancy, anyhow. You don't see Carol Lynn prancing around in those see-it-all dresses."

Besides DeerNose-wear, Carol Lynn favored Carhartt, Simply Southern, and Dixie Outfitters. And Carol Lynn never pranced. At least I didn't think so. I wasn't even sure what that meant. And considering most women at the Cove did wear "see-it-all dresses," I felt Daddy a tad uninspired about my wardrobe.

"I guess I better learn how to ride the motorbike." I tuned my voice from glum to chipper, which made me sound like a sliding whistle. "I want to talk to the client on my own. See if I can do some damage control. My publicist taught me a few tricks."

Boomer brightened. "I'll get Carol Lynn to teach you how to ride. This weekend we can take the bikes and ATVs out on the trails. Remi will love it."

"Yay," I said in my most convincing "yay" voice. "Off-roading with the fams."

Good thing I was an actress. Because off-roading did not sound "yay." It sounded "boo." Maybe I was too Hollywood for Black Pine. Or too much Vicki's daughter.

With that disturbing thought, I set off, determined to learn how to ride a dirt bike to work.

Yay.

IT TOOK AN HOUR, BUT I finally got the hang of the dirt bike. Because it was kelly green and white—which showed dirt like crazy but maybe that was the point?—I named my bike Lucky. Like a four-leaf clover. And to maintain positive thoughts I wouldn't die driving the thing.

Remi loved the name Lucky. Said I needed it because I was "about the worst rider" she'd ever seen. Then she told me not to "kill myself" and laughed.

Carol Lynn gave me a tight smile, said I'd "do fine" and "remember to wear a helmet" and "don't forget about the clutch" and find "better shoes." She was right. My suede Rag & Bone ankle boots didn't go with kelly green and white. They also didn't go with dirt.

On shoulders of streets in almost-heart-attack-inducing traffic, I putted through town toward the Black Pine Group. On the quieter side streets, my anxiety lessened and I began to enjoy Lucky. Except for the deafening noise, bumps, jolts, and motorized friction that made my legs itchy, my butt hot, and my hands hurt.

Parking in front of the lodge-y office building, I fought the urge to shove my hands down my jeans and scratch my thighs. I wished I could have dressed nicer for this mission, but dirt bikes did not lend themselves to nicer. After a week of Carol Lynn's cooking, my Isabel Marant Étoile tee had shrunk. And my J Brand Minx jeans could not hide my love of biscuits. But as a fan of Julia Pinkerton's cheer ensemble, I figured David Waverly would not hold my wardrobe against me.

I planned to humble myself to save Nash's business. When I screwed up—or appeared I had screwed up—my publicist, Sherry, believed in an immediate public apology. In our culture of instantaneous news, a celebrity's speck of dirt morphs from meteor to asteroid in minutes. If not circumvented by a spaceship-sized apology, that chunk of dirt will create a *Deep Impact* crater in your career.

But I couldn't fool myself. It wasn't only self-sacrifice that led me to the Black Pine Group office. Besides an apology, I also hoped to learn more about the interest BPG had in buying Nash's business. And what was the deal with Sarah Waverly bringing her husband lunch every day?

As an ex-actress, I understood motivation. One may accuse TV of using too many stock characters, but there's a reason why they work. Mrs. Waverly's behavior didn't fit her character type.

I pushed through the glass door, into the airy lobby, and to the receptionist. She gave me an "I know you" look. Either she recognized Maizie Albright or remembered me as the bimbo in yoga pants from this morning. I decided to be neither and adopted my newest character, grown-up Julia Pinkerton.

"Is Mr. Waverly in?" I asked.

She looked at the appointment book, then the phone. Not that they told her anything. She needed time to think. Which meant she recognized me as the bimbo.

"It's business related."

"I'll see if he's available?" Her voice rose at the end as if she questioned my request as well as my integrity.

I strode to a modern black leather couch, dropped the Illesteva backpack that had to replace a purse for dirt bike driving, and gave a disgusted sigh at the financial magazines arranged on the glass coffee table. Not a single *InStyle* or *W* among them. Not that I wanted to check on news from home. I watched the receptionist pick up the phone, then set it down as an older man strode to the desk.

Not David Waverly. This man was tall and lean, with a thick shock of white hair and sun-browned, outdoorsy coloring.

He glanced in my direction and I detected a double take.

I smiled.

For a moment, he stood looking at me and strumming his fingers on the desk. Making up his mind, he strolled over. "Maizie Albright, right? I'm Ed Sweeney."

I shook his hand and noticed the absence of a ring from habit. "Any relation to Jolene?"

He gave me an aw-shucks grin and held up his hands. "My niece. I'm really not that old. Are you friends?"

I hesitated, wondering if I should reveal how I got my job with

Nash. "I met her last night at the Cove, and she's helping me with a few things. I moved back a few days ago. Staying with my father."

"Boomer? We'd love for DeerNose to go public."

"I'm not involved at all in DeerNose business."

Laughing, Ed stuck his hands in his pocket and rocked back on his heels. "You caught me. Talking to you is a pleasure, let's keep it that way. No business. What brings you to our firm?"

"I'm here to speak to Mr. Waverly. More personal than business. I owe him an apology."

"Really? I can't believe someone like you would ever need to apologize to David. What'd you do? Put a dent in his Vette?" Ed put his hand to his mouth and mock whispered. "I won't tell. Come back and have a drink with me instead."

"Now really, Mr. Sweeney," I said, knowing to play coy. Charming men were like bottled water in LA. Ubiquitous and obligatory. "It's not even five o'clock."

"Now really, Miss Albright. Maybe I meant coffee." His smile dimpled. "Call me Ed. Can I call you Maizie? Anyway, David's on a business call. It'll take some time."

I stood, swinging the backpack over one shoulder. "I'll take coffee. And some news. I heard you want to acquire Nash Security Solutions."

"We're not acquiring, we'll just broker the deal." He held out his hand, ushering me past reception and toward the back offices. "Jolene brought it up. She's part owner and wants out. Unfortunately, Wyatt Nash can't afford to buy her out. I'm looking into it as a favor for Jolene. It's one of the services we provide. Find a company interested in buying a smaller outfit to enlarge their hold in an industry."

"Nash's office would get bought out by a larger investigation company?"

"Sure. They might even keep him to man the office, but he'd most likely need to learn to play by corporate rules."

I couldn't see Nash playing by corporate rules. I doubted he paid much attention to any rules. Other than the ones he made for me. "I don't think he wants to sell."

"That's what I've heard. I promised Jolene to look into a buyer and all I can do is present the option to them." He held open the door to his office. A glass wall gave a view of the forested area behind the building. The other wood-paneled walls held framed photos of boat and island scenes.

I examined a two-foot model of a sailboat. "I guess you're a sailor?"

He chuckled. "Most in Black Pine claim to be."

"Do you sail on the lake?"

"Naw, I like the Caribbean. But then who doesn't?" He grinned. "I'll be back in a minute with your coffee. Don't go anywhere."

I dropped my backpack in a chair before circling the walls, studying the photos. A few showed candid shots of Ed Sweeney working the rigging on a large sailboat called *A Little Nauti*.

His desk didn't hold any personal photos. Only a laptop, a cup of pens, and a leather folder. A neat, orderly man. I thought of Nash's messy desk with folders spilling every which way, and file cabinets used for cord storage and who knew what else.

Ed returned with a coffee tray and more charm. "I should ask for an autograph, but I've never collected them. More fun to talk to celebrities in person. I heard you were going to film in Black Pine. Is that true?"

"No, I'm not on the show anymore." Hadn't Jolene mentioned me working for Nash? "You do know David Waverly hired Nash? Isn't that a conflict of interest?"

"Not now. Nash isn't on the case, right?" Ed paused to sip his coffee. "I wasn't thrilled when David told me he had hired Nash. He sold it to me as a trial run on Nash's detecting skills. I thought David meant using Nash for due diligence work, not investigating his wife. A little bird told me Nash wanted off the case because he couldn't find any dirt."

"Who's your little bird?"

Ed smiled. "Black Pine is growing but still talks like a small town. Anyway, if the investigation is done, that makes the conflict of interest less conflicted."

"What did Mr. Waverly hope to achieve in employing Mr. Nash?"

"As far as investigating his wife? Who knows? For the sale, good service would be in Nash's best interest. It's not like Nash Security Solutions has shareholder value or anything. We'd have to rely on personal testimony as well as his financial standing. It's a simple acquisition."

"And if Nash didn't do well? Would you drop the deal?"

"Ah. That's more complicated." Ed pursed his lips. "You didn't hear this from me, but you don't screw around with David. With all these questions, I assume you're friends with Wyatt Nash. I hope he did his best. Whether he wants to sell or not."

"What would Mr. Waverly do?" I pressed a thumb against my wrist, willing my heart rate to slow.

"Publicize the mess, blackball Nash, and force him to liquidate. David's specialty is takeovers. David's also got a temper fit to beat the band."

"Why are you telling me this?"

"I know Nash because of Jolene. Nash is stubborn as an old mule's mother. But if David suspected Sarah of anything..." Ed shook his head. "I never understood why she stays. David's an excellent partner in business, but I'd hate to be married to him."

TEN

#BlackPineBuyOut #ALittleNauti

A KNOCK ON THE DOORWAY STARTLED me. The receptionist poked her head in to announce David Waverly could see me.

"Miss Albright'll be with David in a minute, Elaine." Ed smiled and shooed her out with a flick of his hand. "Let me know if anything happens with Sarah, won't you? I worry about her. To be honest, I think it's pretty crappy to hire an investigator to watch your wife. Believe me, I once had a wife worth investigating."

"Mrs. Waverly brings her husband lunch every day. Do you know why?"

"Because that's the kind of gal she is." Ed stood, walked to the door, and opened it. "I'm sure her record is clean as a whistle."

"Quick question. Does Mr. Waverly often go fishing?»

"Fish? David?" Ed laughed. "He has the patience for golf and poker, but not for fishing. Fishing is not on David's agenda."

I almost asked Ed why David would have gone fishing on the *Playbuoy* that morning, but the pileup of coincidences put my stomach on edge.

"Nice to meet you, Maizie. I hope all this interest in Nash Security isn't because you're dating Nash." Ed clasped his hands to his chest. "You'll break my heart."

I shook my head and couldn't help but smile.

"Thank God. All better." He thumped his chest. "I had to ask. You're his type, but then I guess you're every man's type. Be careful with Nash."

My face heated, and I lost my Julia Pinkerton coolness. "Nash's type? Be careful? What do you mean?"

Ed winked. "Nash isn't tame. If he were a cat, I'd call him feral. He bites."

An extraordinary image flooded my mind, and I had to walk away from Ed Sweeney before embarrassing myself.

Don't even think about it, I told myself.

But there it was. Scenes of feral Nash and indecent biting filled my head when I needed to prepare myself for an epic apology to David Waverly. Bad enough my first impression of Nash had been seeing him half-naked.

I needed a brain detox. I found a ladies' room, locked myself in a stall, and did a deep breathing exercise. With my blood pumped, the images got better in a worse way. Exiting the stall, I pushed up into a Sun Salutation and dropped into Down Dog. Only the supreme ickiness of doing yoga on a bathroom floor helped to clear my mind off Nash's nakedness. And focus on germs.

My sympathy for Nash's situation had obviously warped my feelings for him. My therapist called it a version of the wounded bird syndrome. I wasn't always sure if I was the bird or the nurse, but in either case, I had a poor track record with dating. I was overdue for a therapy session. Just after I cleared up this problem for my little bird, Nash.

Which brought me back to Ed Sweeney's little bird who had told him Nash had dropped the Waverly case. It must have been David Waverly. But David Waverly knew I would be checking on his wife this week.

Weird.

The bathroom door opened and Elaine the receptionist walked in. "Oh my stars." She began to back out.

I popped up from Down Dog. "I'm ready to see Mr. Waverly."

ELAINE KNOCKED ON WAVERLY'S DOOR and held it open. Whereas Ed Sweeney had been into sailing, David Waverly stuck to generic art prints. He rose from behind his gigantic desk. The kind with carving and lots of polished swirls in the wood. One more cluttered than Ed Sweeney's, but more orderly than Nash's.

"I wasn't expecting you, Maizie." Waverly flashed me a guarded smile. "I hope Nash didn't send you."

"He doesn't know I'm here." I shook his hand, remembering to slip mine out before he tightened his grip.

His sweaty palms helped.

"I know you're upset over today's news about Mrs. Waverly. Have you heard from her?"

"No." Waverly's lips thinned. He waved a hand toward a chair before his desk. "I knew it was just a matter of time. Nash shouldn't have been so quick to make up his mind."

I dropped my backpack on the floor and lowered myself into the chair. "Is Nash still watching the Cayenne, then?"

"No. I fired him."

I almost shot out a "How can you fire somebody who quit" but caught myself. "I don't understand. Nothing happened for a month and now that something's happened, you give up? I know you're angry at Nash—"

"I have my evidence and no longer need his services." The broken capillaries in his nose darkened.

"But evidence of what? You don't even know what happened."

"Here's what I'd like to know. I'd like to know how many times she's slipped away in the last month without Nash knowing. You got lucky." He emphasized the "you" with a point.

I didn't feel lucky. "I missed her by minutes. You didn't happen to see her at the club, did you?"

"No."

"When was the last time you saw her?"

His nose burned brighter. "Just what are you insinuating?"

"I'm only trying to understand what happened."

"Miss Albright, you don't need to understand. My wife left with another man. It's not your business anymore. You can't play detective because I fired your associate. It's done." He stood and walked to the door.

"Wait. What about Nash? You can't hold him responsible. He

did his job, whether you want to use him or not."

"He did a poor job." Waverly's eyes narrowed. "You tell Nash if he mentions a word about my wife around town, I will bury him. I don't care if Ed Sweeney is brokering a deal or not."

I stalked to the door. "Nash isn't like that. He's not going to air your dirty laundry just because you fired him."

Waverly kept his hand on the lever, preventing my escape. "Why do you think you know Nash so well? You've figured him out in what, a day? You think people are honest with you because you're a famous celebrity? I tell you what, Miss Albright. We enjoyed seeing you play detective on TV, but entertainment news reveals your actual exploits. We know all about you. But you don't know anything about us."

I HAD A LOT OF QUESTIONS and an uncomfortable feeling David Waverly was right. I didn't know anybody in Black Pine except family. Because a continent separated us for most of my life, I didn't even know them well.

At the receptionist desk, Elaine gave me a placid smile that kept her true feelings behind her teeth. Probably wondering why I visited Ed Sweeney and David Waverly. And if I truly were a side of fries. Or maybe still wondering why I did yoga in public bathrooms.

"I thought Sarah Waverly was going to the club this morning," I said. "I couldn't find her. Did she mention where she went after she dropped off Mr. Waverly's lunch?"

"You should ask David, not me." Her tone made it clear she had not been impressed with my yoga moves.

"I don't think he knows."

She gave me a condescending "you look dumb which makes me feel smart" smile. "When Sarah walked through the lobby this morning, she was talking on the phone. Not that I was listening, but she was loud. I heard her say, 'we'll talk about it at the club.' So before you start asking other people, ask her husband."

"She met her husband before he went fishing this morning?"

"Fishing?" She laughed. "I don't think so. He often breakfasts at the club with business associates. He probably met his wife for breakfast and you missed her."

"Probably," I said aloud, but thought, not likely. And by the way, not only was he fishing, he had sweaty palms and a bad case of irrational anger. Like he's guilty of something.

I didn't know Waverly well, but I knew plenty of moody folks. David Waverly did moodiness better than actors. Perhaps thinking his wife had snuck off for a canoodle gave him sweaty palms and irrational anger toward Nash.

Maybe Waverly thought Sarah had been canoodling with Nash all along. That would give Waverly cause to "ruin" him.

Just like the "Criss Cross Double Cross" episode in *Kung Fu Kate,* Season Two. Except for the "canoodling." No one canoodled on *Kung Fu Kate.*

Maybe Sarah disappeared on the very day I began watching her because she had run off with Nash. And they both knew I'd suck at surveillance. A great opportunity to sneak away. Nash would give the appearance of searching for her until the coast was clear for him to join Sarah.

I didn't like that idea.

"Insecure much, Maizie?" said my inner Julia. No way was he canoodling with Mrs. Waverly. She wasn't even his type.

I was. According to Ed Sweeney.

Renata the therapist would have a field day with those shallow thoughts. Not to mention the split-personality slippage.

I scooted out the BPG glass doors and found Lucky resting on her kickstand. Just hours ago, Lucky had been a blue convertible. I consoled myself that I had enough Spayberry in me to learn to like Lucky. Besides dirt bikes burned more calories than convertibles.

Tossing on my backpack and helmet, I aimed Lucky toward the old business highway and teetered toward the Nash Security Office, hoping to get more questions answered.

Or if nothing else, grab a donut from Lamar's shop.

At the old Dixie Kreme building, I inhaled the alluring aroma of glazed goodness, but my mission sent me zipping up the stairs past the siren call of donuts. I knocked on Nash's door and slipped inside at the holler to "come on in."

I found Lamar sacked out in the recliner and Nash pacing from inner to outer office. His earlier polo and slacks had disappeared. Now a faded Scorpions concert t-shirt clung to his biceps and frayed jeans hugged his thighs.

Did I say hugged? I meant covered. Modestly.

"I just came from the Black Pine Group. David Waverly said he fired you." I shoved thoughts of Nash's possible affair with Sarah Waverly to the back of my mind. But studied his reactions. Just in case.

"Don't get him started," said Lamar. "I told him firing is better than the other possibilities David Waverly could deliver."

"What were you doing at the Black Pine Group?" Nash stopped pacing.

"I thought I'd apologize to David Waverly for losing my tail on his wife."

"That's nice," said Lamar. "You hear that, Nash?"

"My hearing is excellent, Lamar. Why in the sam hell would you do something like that?" He folded his arms over the winged skull logo.

"I was worried about you. You said David Waverly was going to ruin you."

"Isn't that nice?" said Lamar. "She's worried about you."

"That's none of your business." Nash pointed a finger in my direction. "Your job does not include worrying about me."

"He threatened you, if you don't keep quiet about his wife leaving." So pleased with the "your job" phrase, I refrained from pointing out that if David Waverly ruined Nash I would be out of a job. "The truth is I didn't actually apologize. I had planned on it, but then forgot after hearing he fired you. He was rather rude."

Nash waved a hand, dismissing Waverly's rudeness.

"Did you find out anything more about Sarah and where she went?" I sat on the couch.

"Nope." Nash turned his back on me to pace. "Waverly had the

Cayenne towed to a local garage. Seems like he's done with his wife. If Sarah returns, she'll be forced to call a cab or hitch a ride home."

"I'm worried."

"I told you not to worry about me. I'm moving on."

"Not about you." I set aside his "moving on" for later analysis. "Waverly doesn't fish. Like at all."

Nash stopped pacing and turned. "Say that again."

"Two different people couldn't believe Waverly would spend the morning fishing. And Waverly and his wife were supposed to meet at the club this morning."

Nash looked at Lamar. "Damn hinky business."

Lamar opened one eye to fix on Nash. "Be careful."

Nash walked to a filing cabinet, opened a drawer, and pulled out a small duffel bag. Slinging it over his back, he looked at me. "You coming?"

"Where are we going?"

"The Waverly home."

"What if Sarah Waverly is there?"

"Then we say, 'so glad you made it home safely without your car. Your husband is a supreme asshole. Have a nice day.'"

"What if she's not home?"

"I want proof that she really left her husband. I'm rigging a camera so I can see if Sarah Waverly does get home safely."

"You're very concerned about Sarah Waverly."

"You're the one who told me she left her papaya purse in the car and a woman always carries her purse."

Lamar smiled. "Well, then."

"Enough with the 'well thens.' I don't need any thinly veiled told-you-so's, Lamar." Nash jerked his chin to the door. "Let's get going. Keep your ears open, Lamar."

ELEVEN

#NoFishing #VetteMan

WE RODE IN NASH'S SILVERADO, which I appreciated as my thighs couldn't take another crosstown trip on Lucky. At the entrance to Platinum Ridge, Nash signed us in for a "security evaluation" at the Waverly residence. He pointed at the dashboard clock, waiting for the gate to lift.

"We don't have much time." He drove past the guardhouse. "Waverly might swing by here after work. I never saw him come home before seven, but today's been odd all the way around."

"I thought we were checking to see if Sarah came home and installing a camera?"

"Yep."

His "yep" didn't instill much confidence. Particularly when we parked in the cul-de-sac, two houses away from the Waverly home. I hopped out and trudged after Nash.

At the Waverly mailbox, Nash opened his duffel bag and pulled out a small lawn service sign. He planted the sign in the mailbox garden and dusted his hands.

I pointed to the sign. "Does the camera have a DVR? Must be pretty small."

He shot me a look of surprise, then nodded. "Only a quarter-inch thick. And motion sensitive. I'll check on it in the morning. If she's home, I'll grab it on our way out."

"Cool. We only had props for Julia Pinkerton, but Detective Earl King showed me his covert surveillance gadgets. He had a button camera—"

"Less is more, Miss Albright." Nash slipped the duffel over his shoulder and began walking up the drive. "Let's see if anyone is home."

I hurried to catch him. "We're just ringing the bell and leaving if no one is home, right?"

Nash glanced at me over his shoulder. "Do you think I'd condone breaking and entering?"

"Of course not." I blushed. "You belong to a professional association with a code of ethics to uphold the law."

"Damn right," he said. "But I also have David Waverly's security codes and permission to enter his house."

"He fired you."

"We haven't met yet to formally break the contract. And he's making this personal. The way I see it, if the codes are changed, I won't override them and enter. But if he hasn't changed the codes, then I can still enter. I want to know what's going on."

He hopped up the brick steps to ring the bell.

I stopped on the second step and watched from behind a potted topiary. No one appeared behind the front door's frosted glass window.

Nash spun around and sped down the steps, following the slate slabs back to the drive. At the garage, he entered a series of numbers. The left garage door rose. "You coming in? Because I'm putting the door back down."

I glanced at the neighbors' homes, checking windows for Nosy Nellies. "You see, there's this thing."

"Come on. We don't have all day."

"I really can't violate any laws. Look, I'm on probation and—"

"Suit yourself." Nash disappeared inside the garage.

Down the street, I heard the rumble of another garage door opening. I scurried down the steps and across the lawn to the garage, slipping inside before the door reached the midway point. The door jerked to a stop, half-closed. I flattened myself against the far wall.

On the landing before the back entrance, Nash smacked the button to start the motor again. "I thought you were afraid of violating the law."

"I was worried someone would see me standing on the porch. I'll wait in the garage."

"Your logic doesn't compute, but fine." Nash turned the handle on the door.

I looked around the garage and realized there was no place to hide if Mr. Waverly returned.

"Wait," I called, running across the garage. I charged up the stairs and through the open entrance door into a mud room. Jackets hung on hooks below nameplates. Labeled shelves held accessories and shoes. Considering only two people lived in the house, Mrs. Waverly seemed overly addicted to her label maker.

Nash stood before another security pad. He tapped in the code and shut the back door. "Are you going to hide in here or are you going to help me?"

"Help," I whispered. "Although maybe I should be the lookout. From here."

"I figured you had experience from your TV show. TV detectives B-and-E all the time."

"I thought we weren't breaking and entering. You have the security codes."

"Relax, Miss Albright. Take a deep breath or something. You look like you're going to pass out."

I dropped to the floor into Down Dog and tried to center my chi.

"Lord help me." From between my legs, I watched Nash (upside down) stride from the mud room and into a small hallway.

Nash was right. Julia Pinkerton snuck into houses, offices, and schools all the time with no real consequence. Which was not true life, I know, but I needed a good dose of Julia before I had an anxiety attack and blacked out in the mudroom. Where someone would definitely find me.

"Wait." I scrambled to my feet and ran after him.

I found Nash in a large, sunny kitchen full of mahogany cabinets and dark granite. He stood over a desk built into the cabinetry, flipping through an agenda.

"You've been here before." For surveillance or hanky panky?

"Yep." He opened the top drawer and slid it shut. "Didn't find anything then, neither. Sarah Waverly's the most organized subject I've ever investigated. Look at this drawer."

I looked. Caddies held each item, including one for used twist ties.

Disturbing.

"Can I see Mrs. Waverly's closet?" I asked.

"Why?"

"If she's this organized, I'll figure out the clothes she took with her. If she really did leave, it would tell me something about where she went and the type of person she left with."

"Miss Albright, once again you surprise me." Nash shut the drawer and crossed the kitchen.

I followed him down another hall, past an open great room and three closed doors. Persian rugs, potted plants, and mahogany tables abounded. Lifestyles of the rich and suburban. Nash stopped before each door to glance inside. At the foyer, an elegant staircase led to the second floor.

"I saw a stairway in the kitchen." I didn't like walking through more of the house than needed.

"Just checking for bodies on the way."

At my gasp, he grinned. The dimple almost melted my anxiety. Almost.

We mounted the stairs, then traipsed down a longish hall. Nash nosed behind each door before swinging a right into the master. A sitting room led into a spacious bedroom done in chocolate and aqua with more mahogany pieces.

I followed Nash into the large master bath. Glancing in the mirror, I saw my freckles stand out against my more-than-usual pale skin. I wondered if LA HAIR did spray tans.

"Housekeeping comes on Mondays." Nash's voice emerged from the toilet stall.

"What?" I said, smoothing my hair from Lucky's helmet head.

"Trash has been emptied, but it's Friday." Nash flicked a finger over a toothbrush and looked at me. "Miss Albright, can I tear you away from your reflection to search Sarah's closet before David comes home?"

I watched flames lick my neck and cheeks. My eyes met his in the mirror. "Of course."

Nash strode across the bathroom, swung open the closet door, and held it. I pulled in a deep breath of cedar, leather, and fabric softener. The room had been lined with racks and shelves. I missed my walk-in system. I glanced longingly at Sarah Waverly's color coded and seasonally organized clothes and shoes, but I pointed at a tall, narrow dresser.

"Lingerie?"

Nash shrugged.

I moved to the dresser and began opening the drawers. Each one had been sectioned with a frame. And as many women do, the undergarments were organized by style. Less desirable pieces were found in the back. Everyday and more delicate items in the front. Gaps on both sides of the divider showed missing pieces.

"Dirty laundry?"

Nash found a hamper by the door. He popped the lid to glance inside. "Empty."

"You said housekeeping comes on Monday?"

"That was the schedule the past month."

We retreated down the back stairs in silence. After a brief stop to look at the kitchen trash, we continued into the laundry room. I spied the dainties hanging from a tiny clothesline over the sink. Four pairs of undies. Still damp. They'd been washed today. More clothes had been washed and folded, waiting in laundry baskets.

"Housekeeping did come today unless David Waverly has a side hobby of washing his wife's delicates."

Nash studied the door jamb, refusing to look at the hanging panties.

I eyed him with a hearty bout of suspicion. "Are you embarrassed to look at Sarah's undies? You don't seem like the modest type."

"This is the trouble with a girl assistant. Finding problems where there aren't any." He turned into the hallway. "I'm going outside to check their garbage."

I followed him into the hallway. "I'm not a girl. I'm twenty-five. How old are you?"

"Thirty-two." His voice was gruffer than usual.

"Thirty-two's not that old."

"A lot older than twenty-five."

"My ex-boyfriend Oliver Fraser was thirty-five."

"Before or after he went to prison?"

"What do you know about that? I thought you didn't care about celebrity news."

"I can't miss your face plastered all over the tabloids in the grocery store."

"I can't help that." I took a deep breath. "Besides, I have put all that behind me."

"See that you do, Miss Albright. Here's an investigator training tip. It's a little hard to do undercover surveillance when the investigator is front page news." He shoved through the mud room door, leaving me in the hall.

I hoped that didn't mean I was about to be fired. Even if Nash were guilty of canoodling, I had to keep my job or face legal consequences. Unless I took up Vicki's offer of help.

A craving for sugary trans fats flashed through me.

I stared at the kitchen, jonesing for something unhealthy. Nash was busy with the trash. Maybe I could find a clue to Sarah's whereabouts in the kitchen. Like the pantry. Or the fridge.

At the bottom of the pantry, I found the cooler David Waverly had been carrying from the *Playbuoy*. It had been wiped clean, the interior still damp and shiny, and smelled like bleach. I resisted the snack bags of Dixie Cakes and left the pantry to find Nash. In the mud room, I heard the garage door rumble. Thinking Nash must be ready to leave, I opened the door.

No Nash.

Instead, a yellow Corvette rolled into the garage.

TWELVE

#FallenAndCanGetUp #HeilCujo

I SHUT THE DOOR AND THREW my back against it. This is where it ended. David Waverly was about to catch me snooping around his house and would have me arrested. Judge Ellis would tell the local D.A. to throw the book at me. I probably couldn't buy a cushy jail cell in Georgia like I could in the overcrowded California prisons.

Who was I kidding? I had no money for a pay-to-stay. I spent everything on legal fees and celebrity lifestyling in California. I'd share a cell with a toothless meth user who would shiv me with a spork when I refused to act out scenes from *Kung Fu Kate*. Was it despair or pride that kept me from the prison talent show? Shiv or no shiv, I just couldn't hop like a show biz monkey anymore. Besides, I was way too pale to wear orange. They probably didn't allow self-tanner in prison. My roommate might try to siphon the chemicals to get high.

"Snap out of it," said an internal Julia Pinkerton voice. "And get out of the mud room."

The threat of prison had split my personalities.

The Corvette's growl echoed, then cut off. I dashed into the kitchen. The mud room door opened. Fingers tapped the keys on the security pad.

David Waverly was in the house.

I opened the French door and prayed the porch had another exit. Hiding behind a glass door would not work.

Behind a fern, I found a screen door and steps leading to a flagstone patio. I was outside. And still visible if David Waverly happened to look out a window. A six-foot metal fence topped with spikes enclosed the yard.

Where was I? Compton?

Wait. The back wall must have been fenced by a neighbor. A six-foot brick wall concealed behind a row of magnolias. With no spikes.

Much better.

Afraid to look behind me and see David Waverly standing before one of his many windows, I sprinted for the brick wall, passing a kidney-shaped pool with a waterfall. Behind the pool house, I paused to rest my elbows on my thighs and pant. Jerry, my trainer, would be disappointed. He'd insist on intensifying my cardio work.

I supposed Jerry was correct.

Keeping the pool house at my back, I approached the magnolias. Smooth cement capped the brick wall about six inches above my head. Not an easy climb, but better than six feet of iron with poky things at the top.

However, I would have liked a chain link. For some reason, every *Julia Pinkerton* city chase scene had a tall chain link fence blocking her escape.

In the distance, a frenzy of barking began. Tuning my focus to the wall, I scanned for footholds between the bricks. Standing on my toes, I hooked my arms over the wall cap and pushed my feet against the magnolia behind me. Working my feet up the magnolia, I hugged the cement top and heaved my torso to meet my arms. With a fair amount of wiggling, my legs met my upper body and I found myself on top of the wall, staring into another backyard. Near the neighbor's house, I spied a wooden gate covered with some flowering vine. Below me, a border of azaleas grew in a pine straw bed.

I jumped, aiming for the pine straw, and fell into an azalea. Unhurt, I popped up and began walking toward the gate.

The barking intensified.

I paused, swung my gaze away from the lovely flowered gate, and noted a German shepherd standing some fifty yards away.

Then saw the doggy door cut into the basement door. The barking had been Mr. German Shepherd giving me fair warning from his inside digs. And now he was outside.

"Oh no," I whispered. "Oh, please no."

The German shepherd pricked his ears forward.

My eyes swept to the gate and back to the dog.

He flicked his ears back and bared his teeth, uttering a low growl.

I looked over my shoulder, toward the Waverly wall. I could not climb an azalea to scale that wall. I needed a tree for a boost. At the side wall closest to me, a leafy, low-branched cherry tree stood in the corner. Better than an azalea, but not close enough for comfort.

On *Julia Pinkerton,* I had worked with a German shepherd during an episode where Julia had befriended a K9 officer. The officer had a daughter in a wheelchair and Julia used the dog to stand up against the daughter's high school bullies. That particular episode had been after-school-special-ish, but I had learned a few things about attack dogs from the animal handler. Happy, the K9 actor, had been Schutzhund trained. German shepherd's and the like had three drives: prey, defense, and social.

If I ran, this dog would go into prey mode. He would chase me, pull me down, and eat me.

My heart beat in my throat. I needed to stay calm. I had to pee in the worst way. Where was Wyatt Nash when you needed him? Hiding in the Waverly garbage can?

The dog began barking again. Warning me to leave.

I couldn't cross his territory. I glanced back at the tree. Only twenty feet away. I'd already climbed a brick wall. I could do it again.

The barking grew louder.

I took a deep breath and lunged toward the cherry tree.

Behind me, the dog galloped, ready to drive me from his property. Or kill me. Probably the most excitement he'd had in ages.

The cherry tree trunk was too far from the wall for my tested scaling approach. I grabbed the thickest branch overhead and walked my feet up the bricks. Grabbing for a higher branch, I swung my right leg on top of the wall.

Below me, the dog snapped and snarled.

I flung my left leg onto the cement cap. I now hung lengthwise over my attacker, my heels caught on the smooth cement wall. My butt dangled above a dog with serious teeth.

The dog jumped. His wet nose grazed the exposed small of my back. The teeth snapped, but didn't catch.

Biting my lip to keep from crying, I stared at the branches above me. How long could I hang like this? Would the dog's owner eventually come out to examine the kind of squirrel her pet had treed?

I hoped the owner was a *Julia Pinkerton* fan.

"Nice doggie," I called in the calmest, happiest voice I could muster. Which was neither calm nor happy. I wished I knew German. *Kung Fu Kate* had encountered an evil German scientist once, but because that show was meant for the six to twelve demographic, we'd only used fake German accents.

I summoned my best German. "Halt. Wiener schnitzel. Heil."

Why were there no Spanish attack dogs? I knew enough Spanish to get around LA.

The dog growled and barked. He leapt and caught the hem of my shirt in its teeth.

At the rip, I jerked my body north, snatching another tree limb. I had managed to move from straight line to acute angle but lost a chunk off the back of my Isabel Marant Étoile tee. A two hundred dollar doggy dinner.

Panting, I turned my head to catch a glimpse of the shepherd. He sat with his head cocked, studying me. The strip of cloth had caught on one incisor. It hung from his mouth like a long tongue. His ears lay flat. Our eyes met. His lip curled back, exposing his teeth. The cloth dropped to the pine straw.

I almost peed my pants. Almost.

"Help," I whispered. "Mr. Nash. Please help."

The cherry branches were not strong enough. The one I currently grasped thinned as it grew from the trunk. No hand-over-hand push toward the wall would work. My thighs burned with the effort to keep my heels on top the wall.

"Okay, Maizie," I said to myself. And to Rin Tin Tin, who was also listening. "What would Julia do?"

As a tumbler, Julia would have used her core ab strength (and a stunt double) to fling herself on top the wall. My core abs had had more workout with fried chicken than Pilates lately, but somewhere beneath the layer of donuts and pickles, there had to be a muscle or two left from my trainer's whip cracking.

Stretching toward a higher branch, I wiggled forward until the branch bent.

I really hoped I didn't fall on top of the dog. I didn't want to hurt him.

Or get eaten.

Pushing my knees out, I rocked onto my toes. I ducked my head, grunted, and thrust forward, letting go of the branch. My hands windmilled, slashing at the branches and leaves.

I was on top of the wall.

And over.

I couldn't stop. A flower bed rose to meet me. I tucked, slamming into the ground. I continued to roll down a slight incline and stopped in a tangle of sticky shrubbery that left a pleasant, sharp scent in my wake.

Rosemary.

I lay for a long minute, panting and accessing bodily damage. Nothing broken. Thank God for tumbling muscle memory.

Julia Pinkerton's cheerleading had saved my life.

I dragged myself upright, scratched and bruised, but unbroken.

From a trampoline, a group of kids watched me, their jaws disengaged from their mouths. This house didn't match Platinum Ridge's glitz. I had landed in the backyard of a neighboring subdivision.

At my feet were a trampled rosemary bush and a lot of crushed parsley and thyme. I brushed off the herbs, climbed out of the flower bed, and ran for the street.

MY WALK THROUGH THE NEIGHBORING subdivision, along the main road, and back to Platinum Ridge was fraught with musings.

And repeated horn honking. My shirt was ripped and I had accumulated enough foliage on my person to fill a small botanical garden.

I tried not to think about my evident failures but focused my concentration on the case at hand. Where was Sarah Waverly? Did she run off with the milkman? Or with Nash? Perhaps she was kidnapped. Or maybe Waverly had snapped. Lured her on the boat and threw her overboard.

David Waverly's house had been cleaned on the wrong day. Which could mean...his housekeeper needed Monday off. His cooler had been cleaned with bleach. Which could mean...he'd caught a bunch of smelly fish.

Or had gotten rid of smelly evidence.

I jumped to conclusions too easily. Most likely, Sarah Waverly would return with a reasonable explanation for her disappearance. Her friend had grabbed her and they had driven two hours to Atlanta for a big sale at Saks. In her excitement, Sarah had forgotten her purse.

Yeah, right. I sighed. Who forgets their purse when they're going to Saks?

I trudged to Platinum Ridge's adorable guard box, got in line, and sucked in a Lincoln's exhaust fumes before approaching the guard. I recognized Hector from my failed bout of surveillance earlier that morning. Hector didn't care about celebrity autographs. However, personal security detail was something Hector had been familiar with in his country of origin. That Mr. Waverly wanted someone keeping tabs on his wife did not ruffle Hector's wavy hair in the least.

"Hey Hector. I need back in."

Hector's eyebrows nearly hit his hairline. "What happened to you?"

"Your community is well protected," I said. "No need to test the walls. Listen, has Mr. Waverly talked to you about Mrs. Waverly today?"

"Not following, Maizie. Mr. Waverly hasn't talked to me about anything today. What's going on? Anything I should know?" He paused, narrowing chocolate brown eyes. "As one security person to another?"

I'll admit that gave me a thrill. "Remember when I was tasked with keeping an eye on Mrs. Waverly's movements?"

"You mean your surveillance duty this morning?" He smirked. "You lost her."

"I know where her car is."

Hector shook his head. "If you were in my country and you lost the boss's wife, the boss would have cut off at least one of your fingers. Maybe cut your throat, depending on how much he liked his wife."

I fingered my throat. "When you say boss, are you talking boss of a company or more of a cartel?"

Hector rolled his eyes. "So what're you gonna do?"

"Keep your eyes and ears open, Hector. I'll keep you posted. Right now, I've got to walk back to the Waverly house."

"Mr. Waverly is there now."

I nodded. "Please tell me a Silverado truck has not exited. If Mr. Nash left, I'm just warning you that I will most likely cry and I get very blotchy."

"He hasn't left. Probably still talking to Mr. Waverly." Hector pressed the buzzer for the gate lift.

Obviously, the sacking of Nash hadn't been discussed with Hector. "Thanks Hector," I said and jogged through the gate.

"Hey Maizie," Hector called after me, "nice bra."

I looked like I just climbed a tree, was attacked by a dog, fell off a wall, and rolled down a hill into an herb garden. And still the focus was on my boobs. So Hollywood of Hector.

After sweating up the massive hill to Granite Drive, I found Nash's truck parked in Waverly's driveway. I stood next to the truck considering reasons why Nash would move his truck to the conspicuous driveway setting. Giving up, I approached the door. Nash must have gone back inside in a less sneaky, more invited capacity. However, I couldn't bring myself to ring the bell. My tee hung lopsided in two big flaps, and at my attempt to feel my back I realized the tear had rent to the collar. My black La Perla bra was available for the world to see.

Hector wasn't as pervy as I thought.

I raised my knuckles for a gentle rap and saw a figure shimmer behind the frosted glass. With a quick prayer that anyone other than David Waverly would answer the door, I shrunk behind the topiary.

The front door swung open. Nash stood on the threshold in his Scorpions t-shirt and huggy jeans. His eyes narrowed then widened.

"What in the hell happened to you?" he whispered.

"I don't want to talk about it." I felt a tear form and pinched my thumb so hard I cried out.

"Are you okay?" Nash stepped out the door. "Holy hell, you look like crap."

"What are you doing in there?"

"I thought you were trapped inside, so I drove up and asked Waverly if I could speak to him. Criminy, it's been almost an hour. I was headed out, thinking I'd have to get back in later tonight to look for you." Nash studied me, then wiped his thumb across my cheek. "Dammit, you're bleeding. First you get socked in the nose and now this. I don't think you're cut out for this business."

I jerked back a sob and shoved it in my "cry later" repository. "I'm totally cut out for this. I escaped out back, but landed in the next subdivision, Echo Ridge. Only a mishap."

"Mishap? You look like you tussled with a cement truck." He placed a hand on my elbow and led me down the steps to the truck.

"Where's Mr. Waverly?"

"Hopefully not calling the police." Nash opened the passenger door and pulled my elbow toward the cab. "Get in the truck. Please. And hurry."

I scrambled into the cab and waited for Nash to climb in and back out the driveway. "What happened?"

"Look, I don't think it's a good idea for you to be involved anymore. Especially after I had you watch Sarah Waverly when the case, for all intents and purposes, was complete. This could get ugly."

"But I'm already involved." My panic-stricken words slew forth faster than a Ventura County mudslide. I couldn't be taken off the case now, not with Sarah Waverly's life at stake and Vicki circling my career carcass. "I was almost eaten by a dog today. Not to mention my nails." I flashed the jagged, dirty bits of keratin that were once long, polished finger accessories.

"Miss Albright." Nash held up a hand.

"I know. TMI. But I've already plunged in. You can't yank me off the case now."

"I can do what I damn well please. The shop is still mostly mine. For now."

"What happened?"

Nash sighed. "I tried to explain what happened this morning but things heated quickly. He accused me of something and I accused him of something."

"Did he accuse you of having an affair with his wife when you were supposed to be watching her?"

"Dammit." Nash punched the steering wheel. "I did no such thing."

"Fine," I said. "What did you accuse him of? Murdering his wife?"

He turned to glare at me. "Not in so many words. But I did suggest he might have chased her off. You know what he said? Last night, he told Sarah about hiring and firing me. Thinking she might confess something."

"He didn't fire you, you quit. And I thought we had agreed I would be doing surveillance this week."

"He might have been trying to get a rise out of me. But if Sarah was waiting for an opportunity to leave, she might have thought she was in the clear."

"Or they got in a big fight in the parking lot and something happened. When she was at Black Pine Group, she was overheard telling David they'd talk at the club."

We quieted for a moment, our thoughts picking over possibilities.

«Are you going to tell me why you were in such a hurry to leave?" I asked.

"I told you our conversation heated up."

«How?»

Nash sighed. "He made an ungentlemanly remark."

"About Sarah?" I watched his reaction, wondering if Nash had really gotten involved with Sarah.

"About you."

"Oh." I switched my gaze to the road to hide my blush. "What did he say?"

"Let's just put this in the TMI box, Miss Albright. I'll pick up your bike and take you home."

"What are you going to do?"

"My name and reputation are on the line now. I have to know what happened to Sarah Waverly." Nash glared at the windshield. "Maybe she ran. Maybe he did something to her. I've got to know."

As did I. And not just because my future was tied to Nash's office and private investigation's license. But because that papaya Prada purse made me fear the worse. I'd lost a woman.

Nash could take me home, but I wasn't taking myself off the case.

THIRTEEN

#BurlesqueMama #LikeABoss

AFTER PICKING UP LUCKY AND tossing her in the back of the Silverado, Nash jerked to a stop before the DeerNose cabin, chucked Lucky and me to the gravel, and took off before the Jack Russells had a chance to nip his tires.

Remi watched the proceedings from the porch. She jumped off a rocker, leaving it to lurch and crash against the pine wall, and scuttled into the drive to check my newest fashion creation.

"You missed dinner," she said. "Daddy caught some bass. I hid mine in a napkin for you and left it on your bed."

I winced. "I appreciate the thought, but the fridge would have worked."

"Daddy ain't going to like this." She fingered my rent t-shirt. "He said there's a reason why drawers are called 'underwear.' You should've heard what he said about that one dress you wore out in Cal-i-for-nia. Every time we went to the store, Daddy'd see your picture on a magazine cover and he'd turn purple. He looked just like a muscadine."

"You can't see my drawers. That's my bra. And people show those all the time. It's practically an accessory. Besides, I didn't rip it on purpose. A dog did that."

"Well, that's different. What kind of dog?"

"A big one with big teeth."

"Your life is so exciting." She ran a hand over Lucky's kelly green seat. "I wish you'd take me on a stakeout."

"When you're bigger." I ran my hand through her scruffy brown locks and admired the natural golden highlights glinting in the setting sun. "When I finally get my own private investigator office, I'll contract you for surveillance duties."

She beamed a gap-toothed smile at me. "Can I ride Lucky, too?"

"Remi, I would love to give you Lucky. As soon as I get on my feet, I'm going to get a new car. Another convertible. Maybe even a green one." I spoke with confidence to convince myself. Power of positive thinking and all that. "Riding Lucky through town is not as much fun as you'd think. She makes my butt burn. But for now, I'll make do. I need to shower and change my clothes, then I'm taking Lucky out again."

"If you don't like riding Lucky, why don't you get that Mr. Nash to drive you around some more?"

"No can do, Remisita."

"Don't you like Mr. Nash?"

"This has nothing to do with whether I like Mr. Nash or not."

"Then why do you get that funny smile when I say his name?"

"I don't have a funny smile." I folded my arms at Remi's bouncy yes-you-do nod. "Anyway, I don't want him to know I'm going out tonight to continue my investigation.»

"You're fibbing to Mr. Nash."

"Not exactly fibbing," I said. "I messed up and now I've got to fix something. I'll tell him after it's fixed."

Remi slid me a cool look. "When I do that, I usually get in more trouble."

A S I EXFOLIATED OFF THE garden dirt and dog drool, I tried not to dwell on Remi's parting shot and turned my thoughts toward the investigation. David Waverly looked suspicious, but suspicious meant nothing without evidence. Upon learning David fired Nash, Sarah could have made a break for it. Nash looked a teeny bit suspicious, too. Or tenderhearted, which seemed very un-Nash-like, but what did I really know about the man?

Maybe I needed to know more about the man.

I thought about all the ways I might like to know him, then

sluiced cold water over my body.

While I glossed my lips with NARS in Super Orgasm—after all, it was Friday night—I decided on a plan of action. Nash would focus his attention on Sarah Waverly tonight, probably interrogating the maid service and scouring her credit card and phone records again. I wanted to do something. Maybe canvass the neighbors. Which would be difficult for a Friday night in LA, but this was Georgia. Daddy and Carol Lynn stayed home on Friday nights and got up early on Saturday mornings to shoot things or fish or drive their ATVs.

I know. Weird.

I donned another t-shirt and jeans ensemble. At this rate, my Black Pine wardrobe changes were rivaling *Kung Fu Kate*'s.

HECTOR WAS NOT WORKING THE Platinum Ridge guard house. Tonight's Guardian of the Platinum Gates was an elderly man who studied Lucky before examining me.

"Mr. Deevers," I said, reading his name off his badge. "How are you?"

"I heard Maizie Albright was riding around on a motorcycle. That's not a motorcycle."

"No, this would be Lucky, the dirt bike." I offered him my Whitening Strips smile. "I guess you recognized me."

He held up the *Black Pine Gazette*. My eyes dropped to the picture below the banner. Giulio and I playing tongue tag at the Cove. The caption read, "Hollywood Returns to Black Pine: Maizie Albright Back to Business?"

"Oh boy," I said, "I don't remember Giulio's hand on my butt. It looks bad, doesn't it?"

"The article says you drive a motorcycle. That's not a motorcycle."

"I'm sorry to tell you the media often gets the story wrong." I paused, waiting for the scathing remark about my public indecency.

Which didn't come.

Either Black Pine was full of creepers or Deevers had an obsession with Kawasaki's. "So, can I go in?"

"Where you headed?" Deevers shook off the bike drama and picked up his clipboard. "It's pretty late."

"For a Friday? It's not even eleven." Having done my homework, I gave him Bethann Bergh's name. The one Granite Curve neighbor who was home on a Friday night and willing to talk to me.

"It's late for any night." Deevers penned my name and Lucky's tiny license plate number on his clipboard. "But suit yourself."

"Mr. Deevers, that list shows the time and vehicle whenever someone goes into Platinum Ridge, right?"

He nodded.

"Can I see the list?"

"I can show you when you came in." He thumbed through the papers. "You've been here a lot today. Different vehicles, too. Are you sure you don't have a motorcycle?"

"I know when I came in. I want to see who else drove in earlier today. Starting around nine-thirty in the morning."

If someone had picked up Sarah Waverly, they might have brought her home for her things, thereby explaining the Prada bag in the car. Perhaps she didn't like the Prada and wanted to exchange it. Can't account for tastes.

Deevers shook his head. "I can't show you the list. There's video, too. But only Mark Jacobs can give you permission."

"Marc Jacobs?" I blinked. "The designer?"

"Mark Jacobs at Community Management. He's head of security for all their properties. I'd need permission from him."

I briefly wondered if Mark Jacobs of Community Management also liked bags—he'd probably understand my dismay over the Prada—then got on with the task of keeping Lucky upright while moving.

At Bethann Bergh's house, I parked in the driveway but sat for a long minute to study the house across the street. The exterior lighting bathed the Waverly house in a golden glow. If David Waverly was home, he kept the lights low. Maybe Sarah came home and they were having a sexy reunion.

Or David was slouched in bed with a gin and tonic, watching his wedding video and mourning the should-have-dones and why-didn't-I's.

Or maybe David Waverly was getting rid of evidence. Or a body.

I shivered and honed in on the itty-bitty camera planted by the Waverly mailbox. If David left or Sarah showed, Nash would see it. I hopped from Lucky and sped to the house, eager to talk to Bethann. I leaned on the bell. The locks on the door tumbled.

An older woman in a flowing, filmy nightgown and matching red robe opened the door. Her blonde hair was teased and piled behind a delicate tiara that didn't go with her jet chandelier earrings. The red kitten heel slippers had fuzzy, fake fur trim. She pinched a martini glass between two fingers.

I had wandered into the set of *Valley of the Dolls*. Or possibly *Peyton's Place*.

"Bethann Bergh?"

"Maizie Albright," she shrieked. "Come in, girl." She waved me inside. A fur-lined handcuff dangled from the non-martini wrist.

I eyeballed that handcuff and shuffled a step back.

The person attached to the handcuff was the only neighbor willing to talk to me. I needed something to bring to Nash. Any little tidbit that might persuade him to keep me on the investigation.

The hells.

Mincing over the threshold, I stopped at the entrance to her living room. Her decorator had made an interesting choice with the whole "*Pretty Little Liars* meets *Vampire Diaries*." Velvet curtains pooled under the tall, Georgian windows. Candles flickered from all flat surfaces, including the fireplace mantle. A round divan had been covered in black satin with electric purple pillows.

She pointed to the divan.

I chose a wooden chair with a red velvet cushion.

"Can I offer you a cocktail?" Bethann swept her hand toward a cart packed with decanters and a silver ice bucket. The little cuff swung back and smacked her wrist. She dropped her arm, wiggling her fingers.

"No, thank you." I smiled. "I just wanted to ask you about your neigh—"

"Let's get started." Bethann circled the divan, then attempted to crawl on top of it. She held out her martini glass. "Do you mind setting this down?"

I stared for a good three seconds, considered bailing, then stood to retrieve her glass and placed it on the cart.

"How would you like me?" She growled and pawed the air, then sat up on her knees. "I can do kinky. Or play it safe with plain old sexy." Dropping a shoulder, she wiggled until the robe slid down her arm. She arched an eyebrow and pouted.

I had to remind myself to blink.

"Maybe you like crazy?" She hopped to her feet and shimmied while belting out the chorus to *Viva Las Vegas*.

«Definitely don't like crazy," I interrupted.

"Gotcha." The shimmy halted. "Just tell me what you want. I can do something else."

"I think I've got the wrong house." God, I thought, LA had enough freaks. Who knew Georgia was chock full of sex maniacs?

"Wait," she said. "Let me try something else."

"Please don't." I backed toward the door, hoping I could unlock it.

"Is it my age?" She gripped her throat. "I don't mind the face nip and tucks, but I don't know how to get rid of the neck lines. Do you know somebody who does that? I'll fly to California."

"What? No. Listen, there's some kind of miscommunication here. I wanted to talk to you about the Waverlys."

She cocked her head. "The Waverlys? Are they doing this, too?"

"Dear God, I hope not." I held up my hands. "I don't know what you're doing, but let's not involve anyone else."

"Just give me some direction. I'll do whatever you say. I've been in the Piners for years."

I curled my lip at the name of her sex club. "I'm sure you have. There's been some confusion. I know you hear a lot of things about Hollywood, but I'm not into this." I kept my hands up as I edged toward the front door. "Not judging."

"But I want you to judge."

"Oh, please no. I'm going now."

"I'm sorry." She rushed to the door and threw herself against it, raising her arm. The cuff dangled over her head. "I overplayed the kinky. When I heard you wanted the sexy neighbor, I just thought I'd go for it. I don't have to do kinky."

"Why would I want a sexy neighbor? I live with my father." Realization struck me like a riding crop smacking a naughty bottom. "Wait. Who told you I needed a sexy neighbor?"

Bethann dropped her arm and leaned against the door. "It's advertised in *Atlanta Extras*, but I heard about it through my theater group, The Piners. They're looking for 'original, quirky locals' to give the reality show some authenticity."

"Dammit. Vicki," I mumbled, then gave Bethann an apologetic smile. "Sorry, I'm not doing *All is Albright*. And I have no control over casting anyway."

"Do you want my headshot? Even if you don't do casting, maybe you could slip it to a producer?"

I reached for the doorknob.

"What if I tell you about the Waverlys?"

I thought about the wasted night, poor Sarah Waverly, and my boss having his ass served on an expensive platter by David Waverly. And Vicki auditioning sexy neighbors for my return to the small screen. How did she keep inserting herself in my investigations? "You tell me everything you know about the Waverlys. And I will give Vicki your headshot."

Bethann skipped down the hall, her kitten heels pattering like machine gun fire on the tile. Before she flew through the door at the end, she turned. "Are you coming? I'll make us a pot of tea and some cheese straws while I dish on the Waverlys."

At the mention of cheese straws, I hurried after her.

TWO HOURS LATER, I STUMBLED out Bethann's front door, clutching her head shot. For once, I felt glad to drive

Lucky, only for the night air smacking my face on the ride home. Bethann didn't give me much information, but "not much was better than nothing" as the director of *Hell is for Children* (a straight-to-video comedy-horror), loved to remind me. When my feet hit Bethann's driveway, I rubbed my eyes, checked the dim drive again, and glanced around the dark street.

Hells to the shizzle.

Someone had stolen Lucky. I plunked my hands on my hips and marched down the driveway. What was wrong with Black Pine, Georgia?

At the end of the block, a pickup cranked its engine, circled the cul-de-sac, and drove to stop in front of Bethann's house. The Silverado's window zipped down. I couldn't see the man inside, but I certainly felt the pissiness emanating from the truck.

"You stole my bike?" I folded my arms over my chest. "What are you doing here?"

"Funny, I was wondering the same about you." The driver door popped and a moment later, Nash stood, towering over me. "I distinctly remember telling you to stay off this case. I thought you said you took direction well."

"I'm improvising."

"Get in the truck. I'm taking you home."

I tilted my chin and smiled to counteract his glare. "I have my own transportation. I was going to visit you in the morning and deliver notes on my interview with Bethann Bergh. You don't need to babysit me."

"That scooter is not transportation. It's one in the morning. I'm taking you home." His jaw popped with the grind of his teeth. "I'd hate to think of tomorrow's picture in the paper. Not that your splatter outline on Highway 16 would be any less grisly than that picture of you groping Giulio Belloni."

I sucked in my breath. "I wasn't groping Giulio. If anything, he was groping me."

"My apologies, Miss Albright. The angle of the picture didn't reveal your hands, only your ass. The part not covered by Belloni's hand, that is."

I was glad the dark hid my flushed cheeks. "Did you spend a lot of time studying that picture? You seem to know the hand placement pretty well. For a guy who doesn't like entertainment news, you seem really up on your stuff."

"The front page of the local paper is hardly entertainment news. Get in the truck."

"I will see you in the morning with Bethann's report." I widened my eyes and used my *Cosmo Girl* smile. "My bike, please."

Nash pulled in a deep breath and closed his eyes. "Miss Albright, it would comfort me greatly if I could drive you home."

I hastily recovered from my jaw drop. I didn't know Nash could do Southern Gentleman.

"If you put it that way..." I climbed into the truck. Then flinched at the bang of Nash's door slamming shut.

He jammed his key into the ignition. "I bet you still don't have a phone."

"Why do I need a phone?"

"To call a cab instead of driving that piece of shit bike? Or to call an ambulance when you get hit by a truck?"

I thumbed the edge of the head shot. "To be fair, I don't have money for a cab. And if I got hit by a truck, an ambulance wouldn't do me much good."

I don't think my words comforted Nash. The glow of the dashboard light highlighted the bulging vein in his neck. Bulging veins didn't promise me jobs. I knew that from experience. Producers were famous for their throbbing veins.

I switched topics. "Bethann Bergh had some interesting things to say about the Waverlys. First off, she's never seen nor heard of Sarah with another man in the time they've been neighbors, which has been about eight years. However, there's an old rumor. Ten years ago, Sarah left David for another guy but came back. They went through marriage counseling. Bethann's not sure if that rumor is true, but might account for David's paranoia."

Nash's grip on the steering wheel relaxed.

"On the other hand, David is a well-known Mack Daddy. Bethann thinks it's the money that attracts the women, but he's pretty bold. He's hit on Bethann at parties. Get a couple scotches in good ol' David and his horny meter shoots through the roof. Bethann blames this on Sarah. Says she's a cold fish. But this is coming from a woman who likes to pair handcuffs with her vajazzle."

Nash cut me a side glance.

"Yeah, she flashed me. There are some things I will never get out of my head."

"Good Lord," he muttered.

"Here's the thing about the boat. David joined Ed Sweeney and the Black Pine Group because he and Sarah knew Ed from some racing club out on the coast. David sold their sailboat for the *Playbuoy* when they moved to Black Pine. Guess what David uses the *Playbuoy* for now?"

"Not fishing?" Nash slipped a hand to the seat console, rolled his shoulders, and eased his back against the seat.

"Yep. Hooking up." I shook my head. "If the woman also has a boat, they meet in some notorious cove on the lake to cover their tracks. Isn't that disgusting? If David's going fishing, he's using his junk as a pole."

"I'll tell you what's disgusting. Hearing those words come out of that mouth."

"I'm sorry. Growing up in Hollywood, I spent a lot of time with adults who didn't filter."

He cast me a long look.

"I know, rule number one. So, if David was acting suspiciously today, he might have been cheating on the boat."

"And Sarah might have bolted."

"Except she left her purse. Did you talk to the house cleaning service?"

"A man did ask them to come on Friday, but they couldn't say if it was David Waverly. He left a message without his name." Nash drummed his fingers against the cup holder. "But the housekeeper said a suitcase was missing along with some of Sarah's clothes."

"Did she say what kind of clothes?"

"Nothing special. As a matter of fact, the clothes missing were actually ones Sarah had set aside for charity. The housekeeper only noticed because she'd planned on taking them today."

"That makes absolutely no sense." I curled the headshot in my fist and banged it against my knee.

"Why?"

"If you're running off with a man, you'd take your best, not your worst. Who starts day one of your new life in Goodwill clothes?" I thought of his old Armani. "I'm speaking from a woman's perspective."

"So we're back to David as a suspect. He could have gotten rid of any evidence and then had the maid come in for double duty. I wonder what he did with that suitcase."

We had reached the entrance to the DeerNose cabin. I pulled a remote from my backpack and the gates swung open. We fell into silence as the Silverado bumped along the wooded drive. No golden glow of decorative lighting on the Lincoln Log Mansion. Security lights flared at our entrance, flooding the drive and house in their harsh light.

Nash squinted at the house. "Did you recommend those surveillance cameras? Those are new."

"I thought they needed some updating. I recommended a varifocal lens with night vision and 1080p HD."

"I did the original security installation." Nash paused. "But that was a while back. When I first opened Nash Security Solutions."

"With Jolene," I prompted, but Nash didn't take the bait. Instead, he opened his door and walked around to pull Lucky from the bed. I grabbed my backpack, slid out the door, and met him at the tailgate.

"Am I still on the job?" I clutched my backpack and the head shot but leaned against his tailgate with all the nonchalance I could muster.

Nash turned from Lucky to face me. "This again? I appreciate you spending your Friday night gossiping with Bethann Bergh, but you need to extricate yourself from the Waverly mess."

"I didn't just gossip with Bethann. I sat through an audition that would have made adult entertainment history."

"I can't even promise I'll be in business next week. You know

David Waverly is gunning for me. Jolene will do whatever she can to proceed with the buyout. Maybe Sarah didn't run. Maybe she and David planned this together to make me look bad. Did you think about that?"

I shook my head. I had higher hopes for the poor, beleaguered wife of philandering David Waverly. To think she'd help her husband dupe the private investigator who had been following her? That's worse than hating on the homewrecker instead of your cheating boyfriend.

"I want to help you."

Nash pinched the bridge of his nose, then strode forward, forcing me to straighten against the truck. "Miss Albright. Do you have no instinct for self-preservation? I am royally screwed." He laid a big palm on the tailgate and leaned in.

His aftershave's spicy scent wafted toward me, making me melt just a tiddle. I'd always been a sucker for bergamot.

"You need to find another job. You shouldn't be associated with me. Waverly could make you look bad. I'm trying very hard to be a nice guy."

"Are you kidding? Bad press should be my middle name. Why would that stop me?" The headshot curled in my hand reminded me what I had at stake. Gathering my best Maizie Albright grit, I pushed forward until I hovered just below his icy blue gaze. "I'm not giving up. I want to help you. And I really need to know what happened to Sarah Waverly."

We eyed each other, neither backing off.

In the shadows, the hollows of his chiseled jaw and cheekbones deepened, making Nash look swarthy and dangerous.

My heart pounded and my throat felt dry. A similar feeling to when I confront Vicki about ramrodding my career. Or taking the majority of my salary. Or scripting my love life. In those circumstances, I usually gave up. But this time, desperation kept me from ducking my head and bowing out of our standoff. I lifted my chin and added my best J.P. smirk.

Nash's scar flexed with the tightening of his jaw.

I felt a sudden urge to tinkle.

A night breeze blew a tendril of hair across my face and with it the scent of the surrounding pines and Nash's spicy aftershave. I closed my eyes to inhale a calming breath and when I opened them, my body had shifted closer to Nash. Or his had inclined toward me. I jerked and we nearly bumped chins. We were within kissing distance.

And he did not back off an inch.

Holy Frigalicious.

I let my gaze travel from his scar to the crystal blue residing beneath his lowered brows. His nostrils quivered, but his eyes locked on mine. Almost like eye sex. But scarier. And hotter.

I bit my lip and tasted NARS Super Orgasm. Which smacked of inappropriateness.

Or hopefulness.

In the motion-sensor floodlights' harsh glare, Nash's features softened. The substantial shoulders relaxed and the scarred scowl faded.

I hiked in another deep breath and caught his eyes dropping to my chest then flitting back to my face.

My pulse quickened. The loose lock skipped across my cheek, tickling my nose. I blew it away and sensed Nash's body tense. The wisp blew across my face again and my nose wriggled. I reached to brush the hair aside just as Nash's hand lifted to my cheek.

I dropped my hand and held my breath, pretty sure that otherwise, my heart would explode.

Sweeping the tendril off my cheek, he tucked it behind my ear. Then glared at the tendril as if it had forced his hand to move it. "You're a real pain in the ass, Miss Albright."

My stomach did a flip worthy of *Kung Fu Kate*. That powerful finger had danced across my skin with the tenderness of fairy wings. I kept my thoughts from straying toward fantasies about Nash using those fingers to dance across other parts of my body. Never mind the whole "pain in the ass" thing. In LA, PITA clauses were a daily life mantra. Everybody and everything were some sort of pain in the keister.

"I am sorry you feel that way, Mr. Nash. Does that mean I can continue with the investigation?"

"Christ Almighty, I feel powerless to do anything to stop you anyway. You always get your own way, don't you?"

I still reeled from the whole delicious hair tucking when his "get my own way" slapped me in the face. I stepped back and felt the Silverado's bumper dig into the back of my thighs. The NARS lip gloss left a bitter taste in my mouth. "I guess you'd like to think that wouldn't you? Most do."

He jerked his chin toward the Lincoln Log Mansion. "If you're not born into the lifestyles of the rich and famous, you've got to shove your way through the door somehow."

Summoning my Maizie Albright brave face, the one used in the constant reign of catastrophes that was my life, I said, "I suppose that's true. I'll see you tomorrow morning."

I sidled out from under his arm and forced my legs to walk when they really wanted to run. Once inside the cabin, I snuck to a window to watch the Silverado tear out of the drive, almost hitting Lucky in his effort to get away.

A Jack Russell darted into the room and leapt against my legs to greet me.

«At least I haven't lost my job yet." I knelt to pet the little dog intent on battering my thighs with his paws. "My therapist, Renata, always said I've got to make my own happiness, not expect others to give it to me. Find one thing out of my day that made me happy and focus on it."

I glanced at the headshot I had promised to give to Vicki. Which meant I had to see Vicki. Which equaled being chased up a tree and almost eaten by a dog. Or withstanding a surprise burlesque performance by a 55-year-old woman.

Although, not quite as bad as losing a client's wife and helping my new boss to possibly lose his company.

"I'm having trouble finding my happy." I gulped and pinched my thumb skin. Unfortunately, the best moment I'd felt in a long time had occurred right before Wyatt Nash told me he thought I was a spoiled brat.

Right about the time when he wanted to kiss me.

There was my happy.
And now it was gone.

FOURTEEN

#CheeseGrits&LALooks #BillingsBust

WHEN MY LIFE HITS THE skids, I find comfort in two things: Ben & Jerry's Chubby Hubby and the salon. Vicki always said, "You've got to look great to do great things." That was one axiom that proved its worth in Hollywood. I was betting on it for Black Pine, where women still wore hats to church and lipstick to the Piggly Wiggly.

I woke before the sun—a habit born from my days on set which started hours before any filming—hurried through my morning routine, and ate a quick breakfast of Carol Lynn's cheddar cheese grits casserole with a side of bacon.

All the Spayberrys were dressed in DeerNose this morning, ready for their early fishing expedition. The scent of deer pee almost put me off the cheese grits casserole. But not quite.

"Good luck, girl," said Boomer. "We Spayberrys know the early bird gets the worm. Guess you get that from me."

So happy for Daddy's approval, I didn't mention my pre-dawn habit had been formed on the West Coast. "Actually, I'm going to hit the salon first. Look what Lucky is doing to my nails." I wiggled my fingers at Carol Lynn, who acknowledged my misfortune by dropping another spoonful of grits on my plate.

Daddy sighed and looked to his youngest for support. From beneath the brim of her pink and green camo hat, Remi gave him a gap-tooth grin while hiding a spoonful of grits for the Jack Russells to lick. He turned to Carol Lynn. "Sugar, have you seen the paper?"

She shook her head.

"That's two days now the paperboy's missed our stop. I'm going to have to call the delivery service."

"I'll do it, Daddy." I grabbed my empty breakfast plate and hopped to my feet. I wasn't about to tell him I had hidden the papers to prevent him from viewing the "Maizie Does Black Pine" chronicles.

Although if he got a lucky cast, he might catch the Saturday edition in the lake.

I MET RHONDA AT THE DOOR as she flipped the sign from "Y'all Come Back" to "Y'all Come In." A beaming smile dimpled her plump cheeks and she quickly unlocked the door.

"Hey there, Miss Maizie." Rhonda grabbed me for another hug of goodness, white musk, and light.

I felt one thousand percent better.

With the overhead fluorescents highlighting her blue ends, Tiffany stood with her back to the door, stocking the polish shelves. At my hello, she dropped the China Glaze bottle she held. "What are you doing here?"

"My dirt bike's ruining my nails." I glanced at the mirror behind the counter. "And my hair."

"At least your nose looks better," said Rhonda. "And the ice must have worked because the bruises under your eyes almost don't show."

"Thanks. I needed to hear that." I threw myself at Rhonda, eager for another hug. "Yesterday was a long day. Totally rank."

"Are you still working for that detective?" Rhonda released me from our hugfest to grab a drink from their tiny fridge. "What'd you find out about that Sarah Waverly?"

"She kind of disappeared. While I was watching her."

"Oh my stars," said Rhonda. "That is not good."

"It pretty much sucks. Especially since Mr. Nash didn't know his partner had hired David Waverly's firm to buy out his business. So, I screwed that pooch. And I'm really worried about Sarah. Her husband disturbs me."

"You disturb me," said Tiffany. "Cut out this job like a bad weave. Sounds like you're going to lose it either way. From cable star to unemployed. I will never understand you. Put me on that stupid reality show. I'd put up with Vicki's shit for that kind of life."

"Me, too," said Rhonda. "I can sit around and talk about nothing for days. And look fabulous. If they're going to film in Black Pine, you think you can get us an audition?"

"Believe me, you don't want to work on *All is Albright*." I accepted the Diet Coke Rhonda handed me, then held out my hand for a straw. "You're much better off."

"Like hell," said Tiffany. "You just think you want to live like 'real people.' Nobody in your family lives like real people, not even your dad. Just wait. Two weeks of working for Nash Security and you'll be begging Vicki to let you back on that show."

My throat tightened and Diet Coke fizzed up my nose.

"Anyway," I said after Rhonda pounded on my back and gave me a tissue, "I don't have a choice. I'm supposed to keep consistent employment."

"What do you mean you have to keep consistent employment?"

"It's probably part of her probation," said Rhonda.

"That means you've got a parole officer in Black Pine," said Tiffany. "Which one? You don't want the one I had. She's a psychopath. What'd you do?"

Now I had a new anxiety for my non-therapist. Psychopathic probation officers.

"The charge was aiding and abetting." I chewed my lip. "My boyfriend."

"Oh my Lord." Rhonda's hands rose in the air and she danced in a circle. "I know all about it. Her boyfriend was this club owner. And he got Maizie to hold her AA meetings at the club. Where he sold Oxy to the alcoholics. He also had a senior citizen prostitution ring going."

"Oliver owned a non-profit community center, not a club," I said. "He didn't know about the seniors hiring prostitutes. He thought the girl doing massage was legit."

"What about selling Oxy at the AA meetings?" asked Tiffany.

"True." I winced. "Oliver seemed like a nice guy. He was very committed to providing community services."

"Like hookers for grandpas." Rhonda's body quaked with laughter.

"Holy hell, Maizie," said Tiffany. "How do you expect to become a detective if you can't even figure out your boyfriend is a dealer?"

I raised my chin. "Things are a bit obscured in Hollyweird. Oliver was well respected. He's from a prominent Beverly Hills family. It was a surprise to everyone."

"Sure, baby." Rhonda gave me a small push. "Go on, get your nails done."

With my cheeks burning, I grabbed a bottle of RGB "Toast," to match my mood, and followed Tiffany to her station. Dropping into the chair, I laid my hands on the folded towel on her table. "I can't believe how bad my nails look. Vicki would be appalled. I've done weekly manis since I was four."

"At least she taught you something." Tiffany kept her eyes on my fingers splayed over the towel. "Don't take this the wrong way, but did you bring cash?"

I stalked back to the reception area to dig in my backpack to find my Coach wallet and returned to Tiffany. I swallowed hard, knowing further humiliation headed my way. "How much is a manicure?"

Tiffany stared at me. "How much do you think a manicure costs?"

"I've always put everything on my card and let Vicki pay it off." Tears welled in my eyes and I pinched my thumb skin. "I feel like an idiot. I don't even have a car anymore. I'm riding the dirt bike I got when I turned fourteen."

"Oh my stars." Rhonda clapped a hand over her mouth.

"Unbelievable. It's like you're from another planet." Tiffany pointed to the chair and I sat. "You've been in two hit TV shows, a crap reality show, some shitty movies, and your face has been plastered all over the place. You must have a ton of money."

I shrugged.

"Unless..." Tiffany leaned back and crossed her arms. "What the hell, Maizie. Your mother is a piece of work. Get a friggin' clue."

"I cannot be a victim to my learned behavior. I can only unlearn it and begin fresh."

"What in the hell does that mean?" Tiffany picked up my hand and began rubbing remover on my nails. "Why are you defending her?"

"I'm not defending Vicki. My therapist told me it means I've got to move on. That's what I'm doing."

"Yet, she still controls your wallet. And your life."

"Not if I can keep my job. And not as long as I can dodge her until they return to LA for the new season."

"Your plan is to live on minimum wage and hide from your mother? You're in serious need of a reality check."

"You already gave her that, Tiffany," said Rhonda. "Her face is still recovering."

Tiffany shook her head while she lathered my hands in pink lotion and shoved them in warming gloves. "Girl, you are one hot mess. But I'll give you this. You certainly have a good attitude. I'd have gone postal by now."

I beamed. "Thank you, Tiffany."

"So what are you going to do about Sarah Waverly?"

"I'm headed to Nash Security Solutions after this. We'll probably talk to more neighbors, check the surrounding hospitals and transportation services. Maybe she got a ride to the airport." I left off the part about Sarah leaving her purse in the car. Staying positive and whatnot.

"You sound like you know what you're doing," said Rhonda. "I'd love to hang out with you while you're playing Julia Pinkerton."

"Maybe you can," I said. "Let me find out what Nash wants me to do and I'll give you a call."

NASH'S PLAN WASN'T EXACTLY WHAT I had in mind. In fact, Nash wasn't even at his office to deliver his plan. Instead, Lamar clarified Nash's plan. Which consisted of me answering the phone and updating his accounts receivable.

Not exactly the *Sherlock* scenario I had in mind.

"Maizie, are you paying attention?" asked Lamar.

I nodded, pretending Morgan Freeman explained billing invoice software because I found it more comforting than knowing Nash had tasked poor Lamar with that job. There was something about the smell of donuts and Morgan Freeman's voice that felt like the equivalent of homemade mac and cheese. "Got it. Customizable invoices. Check."

"You really will be helping Nash by taking over his billing and answering the phone." Morgan Freeman's voice softened. "It's a good place to start. You should never have been tasked with surveillance on your first day."

"Yep," I said. "Total FUBAR. But that's my own fault."

"I've got to go downstairs and keep an eye on my own minions." Lamar chuckled. "If you're a good girl, I'll bring you a box of day-olds."

I hugged Lamar, glad he didn't keep to the same no-hugging rules as Nash. In fact, Lamar seemed to enjoy it. I gave him an extra squeeze for the donuts.

Because my new tasks still provided me with a W-4 and experience in a private investigations office, I decided to make billings part of my "making Maizie Albright an integral cog in the Nash Security machinery" scheme. At the same time, I learned more about Lamar and his Dixie Kreme staff. Lamar refused to tell me anything about Nash, but he did expound on his family donut business. Lamar's grandfather was one of the early African American business owners in Black Pine. Lamar had begun working in the bakery at twelve, then at eighteen had joined the army where he served as an MP and later went into law enforcement. After his father died, Lamar moved back to Black Pine and Dixie Kreme Donuts.

Turns out Lamar loves cop and donut jokes, too.

Without telling me this, I deduced Lamar had known Nash for a long time. Probably since Lamar had returned to baking and Nash was a kid who liked donuts. Then Nash got interested in security, possibly because of his friendship with an ex-cop baker.

All weekend, I worked billing but had only seen Lamar. Wyatt Nash might've been on the trail to Sarah Waverly, but he was also avoiding me.

B Y MONDAY, SARAH WAVERLY'S DISAPPEARANCE had made the news. Evidently, Nash had found something during his Maizie-avoidance to offer the police. And as I was benched, I had to read it in the paper like every other Black Piner. At least the reporters had found better news than me for their headlines. In the case of his missing wife, David Waverly had made a big splash in a bad way.

The paperboy lived to see another day.

However, Nash had landed in deeper shizzle. According to the *Black Pine Gazette's* exclusive interview with David Waverly, he swore to ruin Nash Security Solutions for bungling the investigation and for bringing this "sham of lies, deception, and transference" on his head. No real concern whatsoever about finding his wife. At least, in my opinion.

Hinky. As Nash would say.

After reading the exposé, I tore out of the DeerNose abode for Nash Security. Didn't even wait for breakfast. And Carol Lynn had made pecan pancakes.

At the Dixie Kreme building, I tripped over myself flying up the stairs and through the door. Nash sat at his desk with the paper, reading the interview to Lamar. I restrained from giving Nash a hug, which I thought he probably needed.

Did I say restrained? I meant refrained.

Nash paused at my party crash, rattled the paper, and continued his delivery, ending the story with a deep snort.

"You best watch your back, Nash," called Lamar from the recliner. "I heard Waverly was not satisfied with the interview done by the *Gazette*. He called WBP-TV and the *AJC* for a press conference today. Maybe he'll drum up some other Atlanta media while he's at it."

Nash shot up, ramming his chair into the back wall. "What the hell for? He believes Sarah ran away with her boyfriend. A boyfriend who, in my opinion, does not exist."

"But now David's saying he thinks Sarah was taken." Lamar's eyes remained closed. "Story suits your findings."

"Where'd you hear all this?" asked Nash.

"That's the talk early this morning in the shop. David's going to offer a reward." Lamar cranked the chair into an upright position. "You should be worried, too, Maizie. The news people will find fascination with Maizie Albright working at Nash Security if they don't already know."

They knew. DeerNose cabin had been besieged with calls from various news organizations and social media crackpots. Most believed I was using my experience at Nash Security to prepare for a comeback role. *Julia Pinkerton Redux*. Rumors flew around Hollywood, particularly when my ex-agent or any production company refused to claim me. Because the *Albright* camera crew had holed up in Black Pine, speculation of a new TV series had grown. Social media meant gossip traveled at the speed of light, evolving and expanding. Like a shooting star catching space dust and ice crystals.

In other words, a gigantic ball of dirt and gas.

When I had left home, I spotted Daddy walking the fence line with his new Browning 725 Citori. When I had asked him if he'd shoot trespassing reporters, he said, "It's a sporting gun, baby girl." Then laughed. "But they don't know that."

I guess shooting reporters wasn't sport. Boomer Spayberry would consider it a survival strategy.

I didn't mention any of this, knowing how Nash felt about Hollywood rumors. However, I did have a problem where I could use his expertise.

"I think someone's following me," I said. "In a van. All weekend and again this morning."

"A van? The street is clogged with vehicles. There's a bunch of them taking pictures of the building." Nash paced to the window and peered out.

"That's good business for me," said Lamar, rising from the lounge chair. "I better check on the shop. Nash, you best find solid evidence that David Waverly has done away with his wife or you'll be facing a slander and defamation suit. Especially if a body doesn't show up."

Nash kept his eyes on the window but waved him off. "I'm working on it."

"You be careful, too, Maizie," said Lamar. "What'd that van look like? I'll keep my eye out."

"A tall, black Mercedes. Hard to miss. I don't think it's paparazzi, though."

Nash turned from the window. "Sounds like a Mercedes Sprinter."

Lamar pointed at Nash. "Waverly or his lawyer might have hired another private investigator to watch you."

I had a bad feeling about that van. A Vicki feeling.

Waving goodbye to Lamar, I perched on the La-Z-Boy to resume watching Nash pace. "What did you tell the police about David Waverly? You must have found something."

"I talked with a buddy on Black Pine PD. It isn't illegal for an adult to go missing. But the police can enter the missing person in the FBI's NCIC database, so it goes on record and law enforcement can put eyes on the case. If she turns up, they'll document it."

"How did David Waverly find out?"

Nash grimaced. "Most likely when the police showed up at his house, naming him a person of interest."

"Person of interest? Doesn't that mean they have some evidence?"

"I tracked Sarah's phone to Black Pine Lake."

"What do you mean? She left it in the Porsche at the club?"

"Nope." Nash stopped before the La-Z-Boy and rested his hands on his hips. "I mean the actual lake. And that's where I'm guessing we'll also find her suitcase."

"O.M.G."

"Right." Nash held out his hand. "Miss Albright, would you like to accompany me to the lake to watch the police dredge it?"

I contained my gasp and stopped my head from bobbing like a jackhammer. Grasping his hand, I allowed him to pull me up, exhilarating in the strength of his long fingers. Then tried to play it cool by smoothing my Topshop A-Line tank. While really making sure they hid the unbuttoned state of my R13 skinny jeans.

"And Miss Albright?"

"Yes, Mr. Nash?" I held my breath, wondering what miracle would come next. A proclamation of his gratitude? Fill out my W-4? Give me a holla?

"Try not to look so excited."

FIFTEEN

#DeepShizzle #CelebSellOut

THE PARKING LOT OF BLACK Pine Golf and Yacht Club and Resort (what a mouthful) teemed with vehicles and rubberneckers. Nash found one empty slot on the grass strip near the road and we hiked across the lot to the nearest building, the Cove.

"We'll cut through to the patio and take the stairs down to the docks," said Nash.

I dug the heels of my Fendi Goldmine boots into the black-top as best I could and shook my head. The cast and crew of *Albright* most likely breakfasted on the patio. The Cove abounded in bad Maizie juju. No way did I want to promenade through that restaurant with Nash watching. That patio held more traps and obstacles than the "Perilous Swamp of Torturous Terror" (*Kung Fu Kate*: Season One, Episode Five).

Let me clarify. No way did I want to take a chance on Vicki meeting Nash.

"Let's cut around the building instead. It's a beautiful day," I said. "Except for the whole looking for a body in the lake thing. But why not enjoy the sunshine while we can?"

"It'll take twice as long. And I can grab a coffee on my way." Nash quickened his pace to rush up the steps to the restaurant. "You're going to get plenty of sunshine all summer, Miss Albright. This is Georgia."

He bounded through the door, while I squirmed on the pavement.

Come on Maizie, I thought, what's the worst that can happen?

Would Julia Pinkerton bail on her boss and possible love interest—unrequited love interests still counted in TV scripts—just to avoid seeing her mother?

Considering Julia's veterinarian mother had died in a tragic fire while rescuing guinea pigs from Drusilla DeVilla (who reappeared in Season Six to operate an illegal underground lab for testing lipstick on spider monkeys), no.

Nevertheless, Julia would never allow the potential for great humiliation and possible firing to stop her.

I adjusted my Stella McCartney shades, cocked a hip, and marched through the door, hoping the stunnas and swag would distract from the fact that I wore black leather boots in June.

The doors to the restaurant side had been closed. I passed the empty fireplace bar, spotted Nash slipping through the patio door, and halted in the doorway to scope the scene. A mix of locals and crew breakfasted on the patio. Several waved. I returned their wave and strode through the door, heartened by the absence of Vicki's entourage.

However, Alex, bartender and cutter of my Black Card, flagged me before I had completed my beeline. Figuring he wanted more napkin autographs, I called out to Nash that I'd grab coffee for us and scooted to the bar.

"Hey, Miss Maizie," Alex said, readying two mugs for coffee. "I've seen your pictures online all week. I'm really happy to see you this morning."

"Thanks. I need these coffees to go if you don't mind."

"Look." He pulled out his phone. "I've been following you with Google Alerts. A few days ago, this popped up on Twitter. 'Maizie Albright on Black Pine Mountain. Hit and Run?' Dude, you got twelve thousand retweets with that picture."

"It wasn't a hit-and-run." Glancing at the photo, I recognized the stretch of road between Echo Ridge and Platinum Ridge. Also, the ripped Isabel Marant Étoile that flashed my back muffin. My heart thawed toward the social media blitzkrieg I had been ducking. The blitzkrieg was fueled by fans, after all. And some fans actually cared about me. "That's kind of sweet they're so worried.»

"*E! News* did a short interview with Vicki Albright and Giulio last night. Vicki said you're taking your sabbatical seriously and working hard at getting yourself back on track. And Giulio said he's living in Black Pine to show his support."

"Sabbatical? Good grief." I shoved my heart back in the media freezer. "Don't believe a word of it. It's all PR for the show."

Alex fiddled with my bar napkin. "Uh, Maizie. Someone wants to take your picture. Is that okay?"

"I'm a little busy." I hesitated, returning my thoughts to the adoring fans who had retweeted my injuries. Didn't I owe them something for their concern? "Okay, I'll do it."

I fluffed my hair and turned, wishing for the millionth time in the past week that I'd worn something that wasn't going to put me on the year's "Worst Dressed" page. As I searched the patio of brunchers for the photographer, an unpleasant warmth crept up my spine to flush my neck. The feeling that occurs just before the realization you've done something asinine. Not a new feeling in the Maizie Albright repertoire, but all the same, an unpleasant one.

"I don't see the photographer." To make up for my wardrobe, I had my knee popped, my hand on my hip, and my chin lowered, ready for the picture.

"Over here, Maizie." Alex had gone around the bar to swing open a set of French doors. Photographers and reporters spilled onto the Cove patio. I watched, open-mouthed, as someone slipped Alex a wad of folded bills.

"Alex." I couldn't believe he'd do this. But then, I could. Happened plenty of times by people who knew me better than Alex.

He shrugged, pocketing the money, and walked off the patio toward the servers' kitchen entrance.

"Maizie," a reporter called. "Is it true you moved back to Georgia to avoid facing a trial? How's Oliver Fraser? Have you spoken to him since he was sentenced?"

"Maizie," another called. "Can you tell us about your recent accident? Were you really hit by a car on Black Pine Mountain?"

"Maizie, can you tell us about the new season of *All is Albright*?

And is it true you're reprising your role as Julia Pinkerton?"

"Is Giulio living at your father's house?"

"Your father is the CEO of DeerNose. Do you support the murdering of animals for sport?"

"Are you really working at Nash Security Solutions to prepare for a Julia Pinkerton movie?"

"Does living in Black Pine mean you've reconciled with your estranged father? Is it true that he refused to let you see your sister unless you quit the show?"

"Maizie. Are you still with Giulio? Are you pregnant with his baby?"

They all spoke at once, holding recorders and microphones, rattling off questions faster than I could process the words. Cameras clicked and two crews took video footage.

At the last question, I glanced at the flare in my Topshop tank covering the low-rise skinny jeans I'd fastened with a looped rubber band. Now Hollywood would believe I had snuck home to have Giulio's secret love child.

Jerry the trainer had been right about carbs kicking my ass.

I looked up and sucked in my breath.

Vicki approached in a black, floaty crepe jumpsuit with crisscross straps that accentuated her slim shoulders. She peeled off her oversized Oliver Peoples sunglasses, so the cameras could catch the Albright green eyes. Her Dior red lips pursed as she stepped in front of me.

"Vicki Albright! How do you feel about your daughter's accident/animal murder/rehab/sentencing/pregnancy? Is it true, she has to audition for the new Julia Pinkerton movie? What does it mean for the show?"

From behind me, I sensed another presence. I looked over my shoulder to see Giulio stride in and slide his hand over my biscuit bump.

While I stared dumbfounded, he smiled and leaned over to kiss my forehead.

The camera shutters whirred like artillery fire.

Vicki set me up. She probably slipped Alex a Benji to text her my arrival. How would I get out of this? Daddy would kill me, then kick me out. Nash would fire me, just to protect my pretend-unborn baby. Then Vicki would swoop in for the checkmate, creating a contract that would bind me to Albright Productions forever. I was a hair short of losing all self-respect.

Was God punishing me for all those years of taking the money and privileges for granted when I didn't want to work for them?

I sent a thought to the universe, promising to do better. Then grabbed Giulio's hand and jerked it off my stomach, careful to not let the press see me bend back his pinky.

While Vicki fielded questions about the show, Giulio brayed with pretend mirth at my touchiness. His fingers slipped around my wrist and jerked me to my toes to face him.

"Maizie," he whispered. "You are causing my feelings to hurt. And my finger. Kiss me now."

"Giulio, let go." I pulled, but he held tight. "I don't want to kiss you. This is a sham. I'm not having your baby and I'm not doing the show. I'm trying to work, for God's sake."

"I support this detective career as long as it doesn't interfere with the raising of the baby. You are glowing, so beautiful."

"Are you insane? I'm glowing because it's Georgia in June and I'm wearing black leather knee boots. There is no baby," I said. Loudly. Compounded with a shove. That knocked Giulio against the bar.

Giulio gasped. His eyes brimmed with unshedable tears. He was a much better actor than everyone gave him credit.

Perez Hilton was going to love this.

Vicki spun around and grabbed my forearm, pressing her thumb into the crevice of my elbow. The effect caused a simultaneous buckling of my knees and contracting of my bladder.

It is my belief that Vicki took that Jujitsu class just for these opportunities.

"Maizie," she muttered. "Wave, smile and walk away. Do it for me."

Giulio was an actor with an agent. He could get another part that wasn't Maizie Albright's baby daddy.

But Vicki was my mother.

I wanted to believe I had just been a gullible idiot and not a malicious brat who took advantage of her status to get away with breaking the law. But maybe I was a brat, who'd taken advantage of the mother who fought Hollywood for me and the father who disapproved of what I'd become.

And now I took advantage of poor Nash, whose whole livelihood was poised on the brink of ruin. Because I had wasted precious time battling with Vicki instead of watching a woman who was now missing.

Why did I think I deserved this new career? I'd already proven I was no Julia Pinkerton.

Actually I was no better than Vicki, scrambling for the life she'd thought she missed out on. At least there hadn't been any dragging of lakes on Vicki's watch.

I waved. Smiled. Walked away.

SIXTEEN

#SpinCity #LastKnown

BEHIND ME, I COULD HEAR the press shouting Giulio's name and briefly wondered how Vicki would spin my escape. The trick was in neither confirming nor denying anything. Speculation fed more stories. More stories kept careers alive.

Which was very frustrating when one wanted that career to die.

Nash waited for me. I had no choice but to move on. Near the pier, a Lake Patrol boat idled. On the docks, men and women in various uniforms clustered. Another boat trolled farther out on the lake. Squinting, I could make out the brown Park Ranger stripes. My gaze swept from the lake and docks to the cart path where Nash watched privately, binoculars trained on the boat.

I quick-stepped to Nash's side. He let the binoculars drop around his neck, then jerked his head toward the Cove patio.

"Where's the coffee?"

"Alex didn't have to-go cups. Sorry."

"Maybe they ran out. The Cove's pretty crowded today."

I quickly segued. "What's going on in the lake? Did they find Sarah Waverly's body?"

He shook his head. "The police and rangers are using sonar. They've got divers on standby. If that doesn't work, then they'll have to drag. Time-consuming, dangerous stuff."

I shivered. "Did they arrest David Waverly?"

"Nope. Nothing to arrest him on. Yet."

"Aren't they looking anywhere else?"

"A forensic unit searched his house. Police are knocking on Platinum Ridge doors." Nash grabbed the binoculars. "The phone is the biggest lead."

"When did you find the phone?" He wasn't looking at the lake, but staring at the cluster of people on the dock.

"A few days ago. Friday, maybe?"

"You found evidence on the boat three days ago and didn't tell me? You know I care what happened to Sarah." I whirled in front of his binoculars. "You should have told me."

"You're blocking my view." Nash lowered the binoculars to glare when I didn't move. "This is not some stupid TV show where the mystery's wrapped up in fifty minutes. These are real people."

"I know that." I squeezed my thumb skin and tried not to blink. "I want to help. For real."

Nash jerked his thumb at the Cove. "See what you drag around with you?"

"Is that why you're so angry? I can explain." I glanced up at the patio, where the camera crews had grouped on the edge to film the Lake Patrol boats. Reporters filed down the stone steps. "It's not my fault. I don't want them. I didn't ask for this."

"Guess what? I didn't ask to be stuck with you either." His cool blue eyes bored into me. "When you get tired of playing detective, you can go back to lifestyles of the rich and famous. I'll be lucky to work at McDonalds."

"But..." I glanced over my shoulder and saw the press swarming toward us.

"Dammit." Nash grabbed my arm, pulled me behind him, and edged backward down the path, away from the docks.

David Waverly and Ed Sweeney broke off from the law enforcement huddle to stride down the dock toward the growing group of reporters eclipsing the lake edge. A uniformed policeman pushed past them to bar the press from accessing the dock.

At the edge of the steps, Waverly halted, gazing down at the legion of reporters. A smile grew and faltered. "Thanks for coming."

The questions started immediately.

"So the reporters had come for a press conference?" I said.

"Waverly called them here?"

"Did you think they just hung around here, hoping you'd show up?"

Obviously, Nash didn't understand paparazzi. Or maybe he didn't yet realize the entire *Albright* crew stayed at the club villas. "I can't hear what they're saying."

When I tried to squirm around Nash, he held out an arm to block me. "Just hush. Don't let them see you."

With Ed Sweeney looking on, Waverly held a hand up to the body of press, indicating he would speak.

"The police are searching every possible avenue for my wife, including the lake." Waverly's voice carried over the rustling of the crowd. "I'm offering a reward for any information about Sarah Waverly's disappearance. I'll also offer private interviews to legitimate representatives of the press."

"I don't get it," I whispered to Nash. "If he thought Sarah had run off with someone, why is he now acting like he thinks she's been taken against her will?"

"Because Waverly knows he looks suspicious. Her phone is somewhere in that lake. He's desperate for anything to nose the police away from himself as the prime suspect.»

The buzz of reporters died down.

"Come on. Let's cut out," said Nash.

Waverly's voice called over the crowd. "There's the man who should be held responsible. For a month, he stalked my wife. Yes, I hired him for surveillance because I thought Sarah was having an affair. The day after he quit, she disappeared. Likely coincidence. Now I realize that I had sent a wolf to watch over my poor Sarah. That man is the real suspect."

"Sumbitch." Nash halted our walk and turned around.

The reporters whirled. Photographers snapped shots of Nash.

Waverly hopped from the dock steps, pushing his way through the crowd toward us.

Nash pressed his back against me, trying to block me from the press's view.

However, if I knew anything, it was dealing with the press. Particularly bad press. This was the moment where I'd redeem the mess I'd made. I moved around him.

He growled and tried to pull me back.

The crush hurried toward us, responding to the bigger story.

"Long time, no see." I smiled, while automatically adjusting myself for the best camera angles. "Sorry about earlier. I was really taken by surprise. As you can see, I'm not dressed for speaking to the press. The news of Sarah Waverly's disappearance has upset all of Black Pine."

I leaned forward, allowing for a conspiratorial sharing with the camera shutters. "Vicki and Giulio don't even realize this breaking local news. I'm sure they wouldn't have called you to discuss a TV show when this tragedy is happening in our midst."

"Unbelievable," muttered Nash.

"Hey," called David Waverly, moving forward. "What are you saying? This is my press conference."

I ignored Waverly to point at Nash. "This man, Wyatt Nash of Nash Security Solutions, has been working tirelessly to learn what happened to Sarah Waverly. He won't rest until the truth is discovered. Nash Security Solutions brought her disappearance to the attention of local law enforcement."

"Is it true you're studying for a new Julia Pinkerton movie?" called a reporter.

"Should that matter when a woman's life may be at stake?" I asked. "What matters is that Wyatt Nash will not cease until he uncovers the truth."

"Brother." Wyatt rubbed his brow.

I drew the cameras away from the unflattering shot of Nash's face covered by his hand.

They focused back on Waverly. "What can you tell us of your wife's disappearance?"

"I can tell you this," said Waverly, turning to the cameras. "Wyatt Nash watched Sarah for a month. The day she vanished, Wyatt Nash sent an actress to follow my wife. Maizie Albright was the last person to see my wife alive."

My smile melted.

Behind me, I heard a string of expletives. Before me, I watched fingers tap David Waverly's quote on various devices.

David Waverly may have wanted his fifteen minutes of fame, but it only took fifteen seconds for my failure to be broadcasted to the world.

SEVENTEEN

#NoDonutsForYou #DebutanteDistress

A S A REWARD FOR BEING the last known witness of a missing woman, Black Pine police offered Nash and me a ride in a golf cart. To a waiting patrol car. We then drove to the Black Pine Police Department where we had separate detainment rooms and answered questions about the Sarah Waverly surveillance. For many, many hours. With bad coffee. And no donuts.

More reporters waited for our exit of the pokey. It seemed all too familiar. Flashbacks of the indictment against Oliver played in my head.

And later on *E! News.*

Walking from the police station, I couldn't look at Nash. Partly due to my embarrassment. Partly because I couldn't take my eyes off the Escalade parked before the police station. I couldn't see her, but I could feel her eyes boring through the tinted window.

Like a nightmare, her presence seemed to pull me through the crowd. While my mind shouted "Stop," "Run Away," and "Find a crucifix," my legs carried me straight to the waiting car.

The door opened and she dipped her Oliver Peoples so I could catch her once over. "Really, Maizie. How hard is it to smile, wave, and walk away?"

I found myself climbing in the Escalade. I turned toward the back window as we pulled away.

Nash stood on the sidewalk, ignoring the reporters, and watched our departure. His expression remained shuttered, but I could feel contempt rolling off him, like a simmering volcano spewing clouds of disgust.

I spun in my seat and fixed my attention on the back of the driver's head.

This felt much worse than Oliver's indictment. That had been a knee-buckling shock, but I had been innocent in that scandal, no matter how it looked. This scandal? Not innocent. And pretty much all my fault. I flashed a look at Vicki. Sort of her fault, too, if she hadn't blocked traffic with this stupid Escalade.

"Really Maizie," said Vicki.

I flinched. Had she read my mind?

"As I taught you to always do your best, I assume you gave this job your best shot." She patted my knee. "It's not the end of the world."

"A woman is missing, Vicki."

"Of course you didn't do anything criminal. They could argue negligence, maybe, but these suspect charges won't stick. I'll get my people on it."

"I don't want your people on it." When would I stop sounding like a whiny teenager? I was twenty-five already. "I'm going to handle it myself."

"Right." She slipped off her sunglasses, pulled out her phone, and began thumbing through her emails.

"How do you not see this is important to me? To do something on my own? To clean up my own messes? To live the life I want?"

"Who lives the life they want?" Vicki rolled her eyes. "You have obligations. Responsibilities you left behind when you ran back to daddy. You want to clean up your own messes? Start with those."

"I can't go back to LA even if I wanted to, Vicki. Judge Ellis—"

"Judge Ellis gave you an excuse to run away. You have created another fantasy world for yourself. Except this time, you're not getting paid to play a detective." The green eyes bored into me. "Am I right?"

I sucked in my upper lip to prevent any whimpering.

Vicki sighed. "I'm your mother, Maizie. I know you better than anyone. And I want what's best for you. Let me help you. You want to play a detective again? I'll get you a new agent and we'll start fielding scripts. But in the meantime, I need you for the show. As much as I'd like to star in *All Is Albright*, the audience wants you. You're the draw. How can you turn your back on me now?"

I closed my eyes to stop the Space Mountain star room feeling. How long before I broke down again and bowed to her bidding? Now that the police were involved, my probation was really on the line. Letting Vicki solve these problems would make my life easier, even if it wasn't the life I wanted.

And it would make Nash's life easier. But it would also prove him right about me. I was a spoiled twenty-five-year-old brat who needed her parents to bail her out.

Although Renata would say my relationship with Vicki was more codependent than parental.

The Escalade stopped. I glanced out the window. We were in front of the DeerNose gates.

"I don't want to prove him right about me. I want to prove him wrong," I said, thinking of Nash.

"Of course," said Vicki, her eyes back on her phone.

"You don't even know what I'm talking about."

Vicki leaned across me to open the door. "I'll contact you when the new contract's ready."

"I can't do the show."

"Don't be an idiot. The way things are looking, you're about to find yourself in front of that judge one way or another. You're going to need my attorney." She gave me a sharp look. "And she doesn't come free."

I climbed out and entered Daddy's security code. The Escalade pulled away and the gate swung open. A small figure surrounded by a pack of smaller figures hurtled down the drive. Reaching me, Remi stomped her scooter's back brake. It sparked and jerked to a stop. The Jack Russells continued to the gate, barking at the retreating Escalade.

Remi peered around me. "Who was that?"

"Vicki."

"She didn't want to come in?"

I shook my head.

"Is that why you're sad?"

"No, it's because I've let a lot of people down. And every time I try to fix things, I make them worse. It's so bad I might have to move back to Hollywood."

"I thought you weren't allowed to go back there."

"I'm not. That's how much I've screwed up. Bad enough to go to jail. Or let Vicki put me back on the TV show. Which is only slightly better than prison."

Remi squinted at me. "How's that?"

"If Vicki owns me again, I have to do what she says all the time. Which is like jail. Except she'd probably let me go to Barney's by myself. Which is better than prison."

"Can I visit you in the Vicki jail?"

I swallowed the lump forming in my throat. "Daddy wouldn't want you to visit me in Vicki's jail. He thinks LA's not a good place for kids."

"Then you shouldn't go there."

"You're right." I pinched my thumb, sniffed, then forced a smile. "Julia Pinkerton never let her sister Amy down. I'll have to figure something out."

"Start with saying you're sorry. Grownups like that."

"My publicist would agree." I grimaced. "Let's hope Nash counts as a grownup."

THE NEXT MORNING, I WANTED to hide in the DeerNose guest room. Or a spa. Instead, I donned a pair of J Brand cropped leather pants, sleeked my strawberry blondes into a tight French braid, and powdered my freckles. That black leather would roast my legs to fricassee in the Georgia June heat, but I could not face another day in my usual Lucky-riding attire.

If I was going down, I was going down looking good.

Plus, the sweating I was about to commence might melt off some pounds. Therefore, I sought out Carol Lynn's breakfast victuals in the DeerNose kitchen. I would need all the comfort sustenance I could get before attacking the day.

Upon seeing my ass-kicking apparel, Remi snorted, inhaling the eggs she had spooned into her mouth.

While Carol Lynn pounded on her back, Daddy looked up from his coffee and paper.

"Your probation officer called," he said. "You going to fix this before they throw your butt in the can?"

"Yes, sir," I said. "I never should have tried to talk to the press in the first place. But I thought I could help Mr. Nash."

"The longer you wait to gut this thing, the bigger the mess and smell."

"Um, okay." Daddy's hunting analogies didn't always translate. But I got the gist. Still. Eww.

After biscuits, bacon, and two sunny side ups, I had some issues getting my left leg over Lucky. An issue with leather I had overlooked. But I would not be deterred. Maybe I did have too much Vicki in me, but Julia Pinkerton would have applauded my can-do-ism. I hoped Nash did as well.

The sleazier entertainment reporters hung by the DeerNose gates. More credible journalists stalked Nash Security. I kept my helmet on and swished through the door, past the bustling Dixie Kreme Donuts, and up the stairs to Nash Security Solutions. Lamar looked up from the recliner. Nash's inner sanctum door remained closed.

"Hello, Lamar." I pulled off my helmet and held it against my hip. It helped to draw attention away from the rim of belly that had squeezed out of the leather waistband.

"Well, now," said Lamar. "Playing *Charlie's Angels* today?"

"I need to apologize to Mr. Nash." I jerked my head toward his door. "Is he in?"

"Jolene's in there with him."

I sucked in a breath. "If she wants Black Pine Group to sell Nash Security Solutions, how does the David Waverly business affect that sale? Help or hurt?"

"I doubt Black Pine Group would touch him now. Even if Ed still pushed it for Jolene's sake."

"That's what I thought. But that's good, right? Nash didn't want to sell."

"But the other half does. He's losing clients over this mess. She may end up buying him out."

"Jolene would be Nash's boss?"

"She'd sell it under a new name. Nash would never work for Jolene. Bad enough partnering with her." Lamar cranked the chair up to sitting. "I told that kid not to marry her, but he was in dumbstruck love. At the time, he was hungry for something like her. He learned the hard way."

Marry Jolene? My wounded bird syndrome struck a record high. I was dying to get details on their ruined marriage—what was "something like her" anyway?—but I refrained. For now. Poor, poor broken-hearted Nash. "I need to help him."

"Then what're you doing standing around here? Apologies ain't going to help Nash. Get to it, girl."

"But the police said we aren't allowed to do anything with this case. We're suspects. And they could arrest us for obstruction."

"I doubt that stops Nash. He's on a mission to find the truth. This isn't just about saving his name and business. A woman disappeared on his watch and he can't live with that."

"But I'm on probation." The excuse sounded lame in the face of Nash's mission.

"I suppose you need to decide how much you want to help Nash. He sure wouldn't want you to jeopardize your probation."

"Don't tell him. I'm going for it." I turned toward the door, then looked back at Lamar. "Actually, I've got no idea what to do. That's why I need training. I don't have any equipment either."

"You don't need equipment. I know you've got a brain. I keep reminding Nash there's no body. Yet."

"You think Sarah's not in the lake?"

"Hard to say. Pretty foxy of David Waverly to throw off a murder by having Nash follow her in the first place."

"Hinky," I said. Then blushed at the look Lamar gave me. I guess we weren't allowed to share catch phrases. "So maybe I should try to figure out if David Waverly is capable of that level of malevolence. Or maybe Sarah really was abducted. Maybe David Waverly had an enemy. Who, for some reason, has chosen not to reveal themselves yet."

"There you go," said Lamar. "You already studied the victim a good bit. Now learn more about the main suspect."

"Tell Mr. Nash I'm on it." I shot him with my finger, Julia Pinkerton-style. "I'll make it happen."

I will not explain the look Lamar gave me.

I HONED MY DAVID WAVERLY FOCUS on his golf buddies, which meant a return to the Black Pine Club, fast becoming a hotspot for a non-member like myself. Today I would banish Maizie Albright to the wings and stay in character. Full-on Julia Pinkerton. Before entering the club, I did some quick acting warmups to grab the essence of Julia. A few yodels, ten deep breaths, and five squats. With some difficulty in the leather pants.

Feeling better, I breezed into the clubhouse. Ignoring the "Members Only" sign, I pushed through the lounge's heavy door. Wood paneling, overstuffed leather sofas, and polished stone and granite topped coffee tables packed the room, all backdropped by two-story windows that overlooked the lake.

Behind the bar, a handsome Latino man nodded. I gave him a cool, Julia half-smile and checked out the room. Two elderly gents in plaid pants and pastel polos sat in club chairs, holding the Atlanta paper within squinting view. Even at this distance, I could see the headline, "ALBRIGHT PRODUCTION TALKS WITH BLACK PINE CITY." Even better, the upper fold photo featured a grainy shot of Giulio and I in another clincher.

"Frigatastic," I said, faltering back to Maizie. Daddy wouldn't miss that one. He had the *AJC* delivered to the office.

While I reeled from headline shock, the lounge door opened, producing a burst of Chanel No. 5. My olfactory behavioral conditioning immediately sent my stomach rolling. Sweat broke out on my neck. A certain sphincter tightened. A half-second later, I once again faced Vicki.

"There you are," she said.

"How did you know I was here?" I sucked in a breath. "Did you microchip me during my last teeth whitening treatment?"

"Really, Maizie." She patted her Saint Laurent Sac de Jour bag. "I have the new contract."

"I'm sort of working now? I'll get back to you?"

Vicki glanced at the golfers, took in the *AJC* headline, and looked back at me. A half-smile curled her Dior Diablotine lips. "Oh, my. Front page. How did I miss that?"

Vicki missed nothing.

"I suppose that won't help your case much." She sighed and smoothed the nonexistent wrinkles on her Diane von Furstenberg sheath. "I meant your probation case. Not your detective case."

My mouth dropped open.

"Flies, Maizie." Vicki checked her polish—Also Dior. Victoire red.—then blasted me with her sea glass greens. "Now, about the contract."

"How can you be so underhanded?"

"You can't expect a press conference to not make the paper."

"That picture's not from the press conference." I lowered my voice. "That was taken at my college graduation party. The one I wasn't allowed to have due to my probation requirements. But you threw anyway."

She shrugged. "We were competing with *Billionaire Kids of Chicago.*"

"I'm trying to investigate a missing woman. I don't have time for your publicity stunts. Shouldn't a possible murder take precedent over a reality show?"

Her brows flickered. "If only you could have applied such dramatic flair to the movie, *Her Last Prom.* Maybe it would have done better in ratings."

"You said nothing would have helped that movie."

"I was speaking as your manager." The cat grin dissolved into a pout. "I'm speaking as your mother."

I felt my face get squinchy and adjusted before she could comment.

She flipped her wrist and examined her Rolex. "I'm late for a meeting. The contract?"

"No." I crossed my arms over my chest.

"Don't do that unless your biceps are toned."

I dropped my arms.

Also my dignity.

"Maizie, things *can* get worse." She spun toward the door. "Get a phone. Then call me."

O.M.G. She had shifted tactics. Was she threatening me? As my manager? Or my mother?

Which was worse?

While I chewed my lip, the bartender approached with a "May I help you?" and an "Are you a member?"

I said something about needing a drink. And fried pickles. Then amended my request to coffee and a paper.

I needed Julia back, but Maizie had really thrown me off.

I followed him to the bar, slid on a barstool, and flipped through the *Atlanta Journal Constitution* to the lifestyles section. I sipped the coffee and scanned the article. Which didn't report much more than the headline. Except for getting the dates of my last rehab stint and Oliver's parole hearing wrong.

"Is that you?" The bartender pointed to the photo.

I sighed and nodded.

The bartender smiled. "I'm Ramón. You want a splash of whiskey in your coffee? That's what those two are doing." He nudged his chin toward the men who had dropped their papers to watch us.

"Better not, but thank you." I pushed the newspaper away. "Do you always work in the lounge?"

"No, I float. Sometimes I wait tables here and at the Cove. I think I've seen you there."

"I can't seem to avoid the Cove. Do you know David Waverly?"

"Sure, he's here a lot."

"What do you think of his wife disappearing?"

"Maybe she took off. I can't imagine someone kidnapping her. That kind of thing doesn't happen in Black Pine." Ramón shrugged. "They seem wealthy, though. Was there a ransom note?"

"Not that I've heard. You don't think David could have done it?" I trailed off, hoping Ramón would follow.

He didn't follow.

"Did you see David Waverly last weekend?"

"Let me think." Ramón tapped his fingers, his gaze searching the ceiling. "Saturday night, I worked the Cove. Patio. Waverly had dinner outside but went into the fireplace bar later. Had someone with him."

"A woman or a man?"

"Woman. They played it cool at the bar, sat in a corner so it wouldn't appear they were together, but still..." He smirked. "However, we're not supposed to talk about guests."

"Of course. Wouldn't be prudent to spread the hanky panky." I winked, while internally I seethed. How dare David Waverly publicly drink with his side piece when his wife had gone missing? He zipped to the top of my main suspect list. Not that I had any other suspects. Yet.

"I think they were doing business. Your mind matches your picture, you know? Looks a little dirty." Ramón laughed. "They were having a drink and chatting, but probably didn't want anyone to know. It happens enough here."

"You don't want to tell me who he met?" Julia had returned and had tipped her head back to meet Ramón's gaze. "You know my secrets now."

"I don't know all your secrets. Only the ones I read in the headlines." His smile turned saucy. "And from that photo, it looks like you've got some good ones."

I dialed Julia back a notch. "Who does David Waverly hang out with here?"

"Can't say, but he always plays Texas hold 'em on Sundays with his buddies. The hospitality office likes to take pictures of that kind of thing to put in the newsletter." He winked. "Catch my drift?"

"Caught it." I shot him my coquettish *Vogue* smile. "Thanks."

"Good luck with Hospitality. How about a picture together?

Like the one in the paper?" Ramón laughed at my reaction. "Just kidding."

I left the lounge feeling good about my detecting skills and headed toward the hospitality office. Behind the hospitality counter, a woman in an aqua Black Pine Club blazer tried to calm a knot of arguing retirement-aged women dressed in golf togs. The woman in the blazer had a cat pin and red readers hanging around her neck. She was not in Julia's demographic. Her shoulder length bob looked rumpled, like she had dragged her hands through her hair too many times that morning. Judging by the argument among the ladies' golf group, she'd probably been massaging a growing headache.

"Can I help you?" she asked, approaching the counter.

"Hi, I'm Maizie Albright," I said. "I heard the club has poker games every Sunday. Does someone in hospitality take pictures?"

When she nodded, I asked if I could see them.

"Are you a member?"

"Not exactly." I offered my *Tiger Beat* smile. Winsome, wholesome.

She wasn't impressed. "Club pictures are for private use of our members."

"I'm not going to use the pictures. I want to see who's in them."

She shook her head.

Behind her, the argument grew louder. A woman wearing diamonds on much of her person grabbed an armful of aqua blazer. "Christine, this is ludicrous. Grace always does the Tuesday Tees write-up. Tell Harriet she's being ridiculous."

«Grace got my group's score wrong and she misquoted Janet," said Harriet.

Christine forced a smile. "Just a moment, ladies." She turned back to me. "Anything else?"

I spoke past Christine to Harriet and Diamonds. "Tuesday Tees? Wasn't Sarah Waverly in your group? Wasn't she treasurer at one time?"

"Yes." Diamonds' brows rose fractionally and she dropped Christine's arm. "Do you know Sarah? You probably haven't heard what's happened to her."

"Unfortunately, I read about it in the paper. Why did Sarah drop out of your group?"

Harriet rolled her eyes. "She said she was too busy. Doing what, I don't know. We could've used her help. Our new treasurer has made a mess of the accounting. Can't seem to find enough to cover the banquet costs, so we're going to have to charge this year."

"That's too bad," I said. "When was the last time you saw Sarah?"

Harriet looked at Diamonds. "Didn't we see her last week?"

A voice piped up behind Christine. "We saw her about a week ago. We were on the lake course's eighth green. She was on the *Playbuoy*."

"Was she fishing?" I asked.

"No. On her laptop." A shrunken woman who had survived a number of eye lifts and a lip injection pushed her way to the counter. "And she didn't wave."

"Maybe she didn't see you."

"Nothing should impede a wave. It's a simple gesture. And polite. There are rules."

"Politeness is very important," I said, unsure about the rules of waving. "Did you happen to see her on Friday? She arrived at the club around nine thirty in the morning, but I'm not sure what happened to her after that."

"No. And if I do see her again, I do not plan to say hello. And who might you be?"

"Maizie Albright."

"I know you," said Harriet. "Aside from your Hollywood she-nanigans, I mean. Your father is a Spayberry and your mother was Miss Black Pine some thirty years ago."

"Yes, ma'am. In 1985, I believe."

"She tried to compete twice. Which isn't done."

"I remember that," said Diamonds. "After she didn't win Miss Georgia. We sponsored her. The Black Pine Club, I mean. When she competed for Miss Georgia."

"I'm sorry about the divorce," said Harriet. "It's a shame she didn't let you come home for the season."

"Season?"

"Cotillion, dear. You could have used the lessons with that parentage. But as your mother was a former Miss Black Pine, you would have been guaranteed an invite."

"I think I was doing *Kung Fu Kate* at the time," I said.

"Why doesn't your daddy join the club?" asked Eye Lifts, spinning us away from Vicki's dubious parenting. Or was it parentage?

"He's not a club type of person."

"Nonsense. It's about supporting the town."

"I think he feels he's supporting the town by supplying jobs at DeerNose. Ma'am."

"That boy had a lot of potential," said Diamonds. I assumed it had been a while since she saw Boomer Spayberry, who looked no more a boy than I did. "All-State in football. Georgia Bulldog. He had hustle. Especially for a little backwoods Spayberry."

"Yes, ma'am." Daddy was still backwoods, but he was also CEO of a company regularly seen in *Forbes*. Which, I suppose, didn't mean much if you didn't belong to the club.

"Are you going to join the club?" asked Harriet.

"Right now, I'm just looking for Sarah Waverly." Then realized in a sudden burst of inspiration that Maizie Albright might have some leverage with her odd parentage. "Although I'd love to see some club activities. How about showing me pictures from yesterday's Texas hold 'em?»

"Christine," snapped Diamonds. "Pull up the pictures on your computer."

"But," said Christine, "the rules..."

"She said she's going to become a member," said Eye Lifts. "Let her look. Maizie Spayberry is Boomer Spayberry's and a former Miss Black Pine's daughter."

Christine ran her hands through her hair to squeeze the back of her neck.

"You need shiatsu," I said. "Works wonders. And if you have a cocktail first, you'll be really relaxed."

We settled in front of Christine's computer, the elder debs and

I, and paged through photo after photo of mostly men sitting around green cloth tables, smoking cigars, and drinking from cut glass tumblers. Ramón wasn't kidding when he said they took pictures. The club was snap happy at commemorating their members' activities. I learned this as I sat through fifty-three photos of the Tuesday Tees and the Ladies' Tennis before I could look at the Sunday night poker game.

If you were wondering, poker photos are not very interesting. But I had evidence that David Waverly did indeed play poker. Interestingly enough, so did Ed Sweeney. And Jolene Sweeney.

"These are all club members?" I pointed to the men and Jolene sitting with David Waverly. "Do you know them?"

"Of course," said Diamonds. "That's William Dixon, David Waverly, and Ed Sweeney. The Dixons owned the first mercantile store in the county. Now, Ed Sweeney—his family is not from this county. I believe they are from Augusta. He works with David Waverly and Bill Dixon. The Waverlys are also not from Black Pine originally. We're getting more and more of those."

In California, people spoke in similar tones about the immigrant communities. However, instead of chafing about the Guatemalan yard guy, these women were talking about some rich, white dudes from Augusta living on Platinum Ridge. I couldn't wrap my brain around it.

"Do you know Jolene Sweeney?" Just out of curiosity and not because any five degrees of separation from Wyatt Nash fascinated me.

Which it did.

Diamonds and Harriet exchanged a thoughtful gaze, trying to place Jolene Sweeney.

Eye Lift spoke first. "The real estate girl. Always at the Cove. She doesn't play league golf."

"Of course," said Diamonds. "Pretty, young redhead. Moved up from Atlanta, I believe. Although she was raised here. Miss Black Pine 2007, but we did not sponsor her."

"Don't y'all have a tee time?" asked Christine, who had been slugging coffee in the corner. She looked in desperate need of some peace. And a massage. Possibly a Xanax.

I recognized the cue to leave. I had gotten what I needed. A new name to interview. And an ex-wife of Nash's to interrogate. I mean question. "Christine, I need to make a call. Is there a phone I could use?"

"You're not a member, so I can't let you use my office phone." She paused, clearly torn between getting rid of me and breaking rules. "But there's a privacy box for cell phones in the lobby. You can take my cell phone in there. Return it when you're done."

"Thank you, Christine." I lifted the hinged section in the counter and scooted into the hall. "And thank you, ladies. Nice to meet you."

Eye Lift waved. I made sure to wave back.

IN THE LOBBY, I FOUND the privacy box, which looked like it had once been an actual phone booth. From back in the day, when rich golfers needed hand-carved wooden booths with stained glass windows. Shaking off the feelings one acquired when entering a tiny room with opaque windows and coffin-like walls, I dropped on a plush bench. I left the door open, dialed Nash's number, and announced myself.

"Where are you?" he barked. "Lamar said something about you doing investigative work. What hell have you unleashed on me now?"

"No hell," I said quickly. "I'm checking David Waverly's alibis. He had dinner at the Cove on Saturday and spoke with a woman at the bar. Which is tacky, but not damning if he believed Sarah left him. Do you still think David Waverly could have done something to his wife? What does Jolene think? Did you ask her?"

"I'm not really sure about any of this," he said, deftly skipping over my mention of Jolene. "Sarah could have been picked up without anybody noticing. The media loves the idea of her kidnapped. But why wouldn't the kidnapper carjack the Porsche while they're at it?"

"A random kidnapping makes no sense. Unless a ransom comes

later." My focus turned inward, thinking of possible ransom screw ups. "Maybe they are taking too long cutting out individual letters from newspapers and magazines. Or they mailed the ransom letter and it got lost in the mail. Or they stuck it on the Porsche with tape and it fell off. I think the quality of tape has really gone downhill, don't you? If there's even a little bit of dirt on the tape, it won't stick—"

"Or Sarah Waverly left willingly with someone but didn't take her purse. Maybe she wanted a clean slate. Without any ID. Or credit cards. Or phone." A thump sounded, like a fist hitting a wall. "Which was found in the lake?"

"Besides giving interviews and dining out with other women, David Waverly also stuck to his poker schedule last weekend." I explained my findings from Ramón and the debutantes.

"I'll be."

"I'll be what?"

"Nothing. Just good work." He cleared his throat. "I know William Dixon. Bill also works at Black Pine Group. I shouldn't be showing myself over there. Do you want to handle talking to him?"

"For realsies?" I squealed.

"Why not? Seems like you're pretty good at worming your way into conversations around here."

The door to the phone booth slammed shut, making me jump. I took a deep, soothing breath and another.

"What was that?" said Nash. "And what's with all the heavy breathing?"

"I'm in a phone booth and the door blew shut. I just get a little claustrophobic." I hopped from the bench and turned the handle. The door wouldn't open. "It seems to be locked."

"Locked? How does a phone booth lock?"

"I don't know." I willed my breathing to slow. Would the heavy wood and stained glass allow for air to penetrate? Didn't that happen in elevators? Loss of air? Could you suffocate in a phone booth? Julia Pinkerton did an elevator episode. What had happened? Oh God, I couldn't think. Lack of oxygen was slowing my brain processing.

"Miss Albright, there wouldn't be an outside lock on a tele-phone booth." Nash sounded annoyed. "You locked yourself inside."

"Right. Except there seems to be no lock on this side either." No reply from Nash.

"Are you still there? Is my signal strength gone? I should hang up and call 9-1-1."

"I wouldn't advise calling the police considering they just threatened us with obstruction if we did any more investigating. Where are you?"

"At the club," I whispered. "In an upright wooden coffin."

"Miss Albright, calm down. You're in a public place. Someone will find you. Call the club office to let you out. That phone booth is an antique. The wood's probably swelled or something..."

"Mr. Nash? Are you still there? What's the something?"

"Nothing. I'll call the club and ask somebody to get you out."

"Okay." I took a shallow breath. "Thank you. I'm fine, really. It's silly. But how does a heavy wooden door blow shut? Right? Someone would've had to sneak up from the side and pushed it shut. That's crazy. Why would someone deliberately trap me in a phone booth? My claustrophobia's so well known in Holly-wood, it's almost a joke. You know that old story about me getting accidentally locked in a closet for six hours because the *Kung Fu Kate* director and producers got into an argument? Everyone stormed off set and forgot me..." A tear leaked out and I pinched my thumb skin. "It's really a funny story if you think about it."

"I'll be there in ten minutes. You're not going to run out of air in ten minutes."

Fifteen minutes later, the final screw fell from the hinge and a handyman lifted the door from its frame. I fell out, trying not to gasp, and thudded against Nash's chest.

He patted my back, then peeled me off. "You okay?"

"Totally. I used the time in there to think. You know, maybe it's good to face my fears. Better here than on *Celebrity Fear Factor*, right?" I faked a laugh. "I know, rule one. And two. Sorry about the hug. I'm ready to go back to work and talk to Mr. Dixon."

"Are you sure?" Nash's jaw tightened. "Maybe you need some time off."

"Don't be silly." I forced another chuckle. "It's not like somebody locked me in there."

Nash's lips drew tight.

"Somebody locked me in there?"

He held out his hand.

"Those are pennies."

"It's an easy prank to lock somebody in a room. Shove pennies in the door crack above and below the knob."

"Oh."

He placed a big hand on my shoulder and squeezed. "Why don't I take you home?"

I feigned a smile. "Probably one of the *Albright* crew, trying to be funny. They're staying in the villas."

Nash's face darkened.

"I'll handle it. Don't worry. You've wasted enough time here. Go on and get back to whatever you were doing. I'm off to talk to Mr. Dixon."

Of all people, the *Albright* crew would never lock me in a telephone booth. My contracts had clauses about my claustrophobia. But I didn't want Nash to pull me off the case because of a cruel prank. This was what I got for ignoring "Members Only" signs. Somebody in Black Pine didn't like me. It wasn't like I'd hidden the reason I visited the club this morning. Maybe someone didn't want me working on the Waverly case.

I considered myself warned.

EIGHTEEN

#HotNeandrathals #EauDeDonut

THE GREAT THING ABOUT BEING an actress is that I'm good at pretending. For example, at this moment, I pretended someone hadn't locked me in a phone booth, causing me to take stock of my life. While hyperventilating. But I learned something valuable from my life inventory. I could not back down from this investigation.

And not because I didn't have any non-acting job prospects. Or because Vicki scared me more than the threat of imprisonment.

A woman could be dead. A woman I had lost. Vicki wanted me to think about my responsibilities. To find Sarah Waverly was my responsibility. And I might have made an enemy because I took that responsibility seriously.

In a weird way, it was nice to know someone took me seriously. Even if they might be my nemesis.

Speaking of nemeses, the Black Pine Group receptionist looked the opposite of thrilled to see me. Again.

"Hey there," I said. "Today I'd like to speak to Mr. Dixon."

"Why?" The why hinted at "are you planning on sleeping with all the men in my office?"

"Maybe I want to open a thingy. Or take over a thingy."

"He's our CFO."

"Perfect." I wasn't quite sure what the CFO did. We only used CEOs in scripts. All the evil businessmen were CEOs. "I'm sure he won't mind speaking to me."

"I'm sure you'd like to think so," she said but picked up the phone. A few terse words later, she set the phone down. "You're going to have to wait."

"No problem. I'll hang with you," I said, relishing the annoyance flashing across her face. "You probably knew Sarah Waverly, since she came in here every day. I'm sorry to hear about her disappearance. What do you think happened?"

"It's pretty strange she disappeared on the day you showed up in here asking questions, that's what I think."

"I see."

"And I think it's extremely inappropriate for you to continue to—" Her mouth snapped shut and her gaze fixed over my shoulder.

I turned to smile at William Dixon, but instead, Ed Sweeney stood behind me, pursing his lips and shaking his head.

"Now, now, Elaine," said Ed. "We're very happy Maizie Albright continues to grace us with her gorgeous presence. If you're not a fan, that's your prerogative, but how anyone couldn't love Julia Pinkerton, even without the cheer skirt, I don't know."

I rolled my eyes and waved a hand to dismiss his flirting, but secretly I gloated. Turning my back on Elaine the Office Defender, I thanked Ed Sweeney and gave him an appreciative smile. The one used in that Japanese pickle commercial.

Ed placed a hand on the small of my back and ushered me toward his office. "Now my dear, it's lovely to see you again. What can we do for you? I hope you came in to tell me you've decided to leave Nash Security to become the next Mrs. Sweeney."

Giggling, I gave him an "oh, you" and found myself seated in the sailboat office. "Actually, I'm here to see William Dixon."

Ed Sweeney dropped in his office chair, crossed an ankle over his knee, and leaned back. "Why do you need Bill? He's busy today. I heard him grumbling about something earlier. Besides, I'm much more charming."

How do I say, "I'm questioning everyone who knows David Waverly to get their opinion on the odds of David killing his wife," and not sound tacky?

"Don't look so glum. Maybe I can help."

"I wanted to ask Mr. Dixon a few questions about David

Waverly. I know they play poker together. I guess you do, too. And Jolene."

"With Sarah missing, David looks a little suspect now. Is that where your line of inquiry is headed? Nash Security is still on the case, whether David likes it or not?"

"Not officially," I hedged.

"Is Nash worried about Chapter Eleven? I heard some of his clients walked after David's interviews. The press sure loves Waverly now. Though I can't tell if they sympathize with David or are circling him like turkey buzzards, hoping to catch him when he goes down. Cold bastards."

"What do you think happened?"

"What do I think about David's part in Sarah's disappearance? Do I think David killed her?"

"I know you're friends. It would be difficult to think that of a friend. But you said you thought he treated her badly."

"Offing your wife and taking her for granted are very different." Ed ducked his head. "Sorry to be so harsh. I never thought David would hurt Sarah. Physically, anyway. I figured she got tired of David, found out about him spying on her, and took off. Now I'm not sure. I heard her phone was found in the lake."

"Did David or Sarah have any enemies? Someone else who might have harmed or kidnapped her?"

"Kidnapping? Wouldn't there be a ransom? Unless David's keeping that secret. Maybe he doesn't want the police involved. That'd be something."

The door popped open and I turned in my chair. An older man with the typical Black Pine golf tan walked into the office. He gave me a quick smile but focused on Ed. "If you've got a minute, I need to talk to you about something."

"Have a seat, Bill." Ed gestured to the chair next to mine. "This is Maizie Albright. Maizie, Bill Dixon. Have y'all met?"

"I'm sorry, I can't. We've got an emergency, Ed. The numbers are off..." William glanced at me. "Sorry, ma'am. Ed, I really need to speak to you privately.»

"I understand." I stood. "I'll come back another time. Mr.

Dixon, I'd really like to talk to you."

"Sorry about this," said Ed.

I scooted past William Dixon. As I stepped into the hallway, I heard William's anxious voice. "Where's Waverly? I've been trying to get a hold of him."

The door closed and Elaine appeared, eager to escort me off the premises. No luck on eavesdropping.

I filed the bit I heard under "I" for "interesting."

I'd put Elaine under "I" as well. "Irritating," "irrational," and "impolite."

THE POPULARITY FOR STACKED STONE, glass and timber buildings continued with Sweeney Realty. I parked Lucky, trying to decide how best to approach Jolene. As Maizie or Julia? Normally, I'd defer to Julia, but at the Cove, Jolene had met me as Maizie.

I really felt for those Method actors. Wearing a role off-screen can be really confusing.

Deciding to wing it as best I could, I trotted into the picturesque building. Inside, everything felt homey and modern, all *Southern Living* meets *Architectural Digest*, designed to impress Black Pine's top ten percent. Jolene understood branding and all those things that my publicist Sherry appreciated.

At the receptionist's desk, a skinny girl in an adorable Isaac Mizrahi sheath greeted me. I asked for Jolene and perched my leather butt on a leather couch.

Then held on to keep from sliding off.

Jolene breezed in wearing a tortoise print blouse and black pencil skirt with a deep side split. All business but showing enough leg and curves to encourage non-business thoughts. Jolene was one smart cookie.

"Maizie Albright, how nice to see you again. I wish I'd known you were going to call."

I returned her apprehensive smile and *Gone with the Wind* dialogue. "I do declare that's the prettiest blouse I've seen in some time."

"Come on back to my office." She sashayed forth, expecting me to follow.

Which I did, of course.

Her office looked slick and modern, all glass, leather, and stainless steel. Which seemed more suited for men, but that's sexist, so I focused on the very feminine redhead sitting behind the desk and tried not to feel intimidated.

Women like Jolene scared me. Probably because I was raised by a scary woman. Although my previous therapist (a woman) felt it had more to do with my absent father, therefore creating my need to please men more than women since women don't have penises.

Yeah, made no sense to me either. I prefer not to think about penises at all if I can help it.

"Are you looking for your own place?" Jolene tapped a mouse on her desk, summoning a site with luxury house listings on the oversized computer screen. "I've been getting to know your mother real well, Maizie. And while she's been looking at homes, I've learned a lot about you. What an interesting life you've led."

"Isn't that nice?" I spoke through the smile frozen on my lips. Why was Vicki looking at houses? "Then you probably know I'll be living with my father for a while."

"Mercy, yes." She trilled a snicker into a laugh. "Judge's orders, right? I suppose at this point, you don't have the assets for a house, anyway. If it's not real estate, what can I help you with?"

Oh no. She. Didn't. Even.

Really, Vicki? Reveal my assets and my probation details to Nash's friggin' EX-WIFE? Why was I surprised? Vicki had warned me things would get worse. But how would she know the extent of this humiliation?

Mothers.

Before my thoughts completely derailed, I blurted, "I know you're friends with the Waverlys. You must be upset about the news surrounding Sarah. I wanted to hear your ideas on the subject."

Jolene's smirk faltered. After a moment's consideration, she sank back into her desk chair and rocked it with the toe of her Kate Spade pump. "So that's why you're here. Listen, I don't know what you and Wyatt think you're doing, but the police are handling this now. If I were you, I'd find another agency to do your research or whatever it is you're doing."

"Mostly billing, but occasionally I get out to do surveillance and interviews."

Her brows drew together and she frowned. "Seriously, Wyatt Nash is bad news. I know you're mad at Vicki, but aren't you a little old for the rebellious teenager role?"

"Is that what Vicki told you?" I couldn't stop the heat from speeding up my neck and licking my cheeks. "What I do for a career isn't anybody's business."

"You forget, as half owner of Nash Security Solutions, it is my business." She tipped her chair back and gazed at the vaulted ceiling. "What is it about Wyatt that makes us girls stupid? The man is positively Neanderthal. I was young and yes, Good Lord, he had that bad boy sexy thing going for him. But still, what's your excuse? You're from Beverly Hills where hot men are a dime a dozen. I'm from Black Pine where we fish from a much smaller pond."

"I don't know what you mean." I could feel my flush intensify. "You play poker with David Waverly. I just wanted to know how you felt about him. In relation to his wife's disappearance."

"How I feel about David Waverly?" Jolene laughed, lifted her toe, and let the chair drop back in place. "Come on, Maizie. You're not here about David. You want to know about Wyatt. It's all over your face. You think I haven't been keeping tabs on you and him? Wyatt's in deep shit. Any person with half a brain would have taken their paycheck and hightailed it out of there. You're not even on the payroll. So, either you're really dumb or you're thinking with something other than your brain."

And damn, if she didn't cut her eyes to my leather clad vajayjay. My ears felt hot enough to burn a hole through Lucky's helmet. I straightened in the chair, raised my chin, and gave her a full-on Julia Pinkerton stink eye.

Because I didn't really know what else to do.

«Are you covering for David Waverly?" I said in my very best snotty teenage Julia tones. "Or are you jealous of my relationship with Nash?"

The air temperature dropped about fifteen hundred degrees. Oh shizzles, I thought. That was stupid. I might have totally screwed Nash out of his company. I don't even have a relationship with Nash. And she's right, I'm not even on the payroll. Yet. And thanks to me, I might never be.

Jolene leaned forward to splay her hands against the cool glass on her desk. "Let me offer you some advice. Sign that contract with Albright Productions before your ten days run out. Some folks around here might be smitten with the whole cute celebrity thing, not to mention all the T and A you flash around town, but I know there's a judge in California waiting for you to screw up again. And I also know you can't afford a cushy California prison. Your momma is tired of bailing you out and your daddy's got too much pride."

She leaned back in her chair and smiled. "So will we see you on *All is Albright* next year? I'm helping the producers scout location shots. Between the taxes and beautiful scenery, I think Black Pine could be a big studio draw. I figure *AIA* is just the beginning."

Dollar signs might as well have flashed in her eyes.

"I've got some advice for you, Jolene," I said. "If you think you've gotten into Vicki's pocket, think again. She doesn't make friends, only business associates. And she only shares personal details if she thinks it will forward her goals. If you use that information in a way that pisses her off, God help you."

I stood and strode to the door. "Blood's thicker than water, even with Vicki. As my manager, she'll do anything to get me back on *Albright*. But I'm still her daughter. That woman would do anything for me."

Unless it messed with Vicki's production plans, but I wasn't going to tell Jolene that. Vicki really believed there was no such thing as bad publicity, including my butt landing in prison.

I RETURNED TO NASH SECURITY SOLUTIONS with some reluctance. Truthfully, mostly I returned for the donuts. Jolene's observations had embarrassed me and while I privately enjoyed my costar-crush on Nash, I certainly didn't want anyone else to know about it. Particularly Nash.

However, I was more troubled by what Jolene didn't reveal. She successfully got me out of her office without giving me any information on David Waverly or the sale of Nash Security Solutions. I'd learned that A, Jolene knew all my business, and B, Nash was an irresistible Neanderthal.

Hello, knew B already.

Sweeney Realty had been a big old bust. Although I now had a suspect for my phone booth prank. Little Miss Jolene could've easily spied me at the club while visiting with the *Albright* gang. Vicki did say she had a meeting at the club.

Unless it wasn't a prank.

As I yanked off my helmet, I spied a tall, black van idling on the opposite side of the street. Tired of the charade, I jogged across the street and knocked on the window.

One tinted window rolled down. Before I could glance inside, a giant lens rose to center my face. The light flashed, the shutter whirred, and the van roared off.

I recognized the snickers behind that camera. Vicki was forcing the *Albright* camera crew to stalk me.

Maybe not forcing so much as paying the *Albright* crew to stalk me.

My suspicions confirmed I trudged back across the street to Nash Security. After eating a donut (or three), I hauled myself up the wooden stairs and through the old-timey door of Nash Security Solutions. The front room was empty. The door to the back office closed. I hesitated, then knocked on the glass.

The door swung open. Nash stood in the doorway, shirtless and gripping unbuttoned slacks that threatened to fall off his lean hips. We stood inches apart, gaping at one another for a long, heated moment. The mighty shoulders flexed and he half-turned. I got a shot of rippling back muscles and a sexy Jessica Rabbit tattoo on one powerful deltoid.

Holy Honey-Bunny. Donuts no longer trumped nudity.

Nash snatched the old Armani shirt off his desk and glanced back at me. "Criminy, I thought you were Lamar."

As he shrugged the shirt on, Nash's slacks slipped lower. He wore faded, black Hugo Boss boxer briefs. I wouldn't have known except Hugo Boss puts their name in giant capital letters on the elastic band, which was centered between Nash's bellybutton and No Man's Land. Like a tiny, black and white billboard.

I peeled my eyes off Hugo Boss and centered them on Nash's face.

"We've got to stop meeting like this." Nash forced an embarrassed chuckle and zipped his pants. His scowl reappeared as I continued my idiot gawk from the open doorway. "What's the matter? You've never seen a man in his drawers before? I've not seen you speechless for this long. Don't I measure up to Giulio Whatshisface?"

I was pretty sure Nash measured up to Giulio Whatshisface. Up. Over. Beyond.

"Nothing's wrong. I'm used to naked men. On set." Good Lord, he's going to think I did do porn. "Wardrobe changes. Not that you're naked. You've got on pants. Sort of. I mean, your underwear was right there. Not that I looked. But Hugo Boss is very... boss."

My face heated with what felt like the fire of ten million suns.

He snorted, then turned toward a filing cabinet. Yanking open drawer O-S, he grabbed a pair of jeans, and in the drawer marked H-N, a t-shirt. He tossed the t-shirt and jeans on his desk and slipped out of the Armani before turning back toward me. Where I still stood in the doorway gaping like one of Daddy's wall-mounted trout.

I snapped shut my mouth and backed into the doorframe.

"You're still here? Miss Albright, you're not a sex addict, are you? Is voyeurism one of your many rehab issues?"

"God, no. I mean, I was considered an addiction patient. Treatment covers everything. Drugs, alcohol, food, shopping. Sex. Just in case we swapped addictions. So, like, therapy included a healthy sex class. Not that I needed it. Well, I supposed everyone needs healthy sex. Class."

"Healthy sex?" He quirked an eyebrow.

Oh. My. God. Why could I not shut up? Or leave?

He sauntered to the door and stopped before reaching me. Poised on the edge of what my bodyguard used to call my personal space box. The Paul Newmans studied me for a long second.

I gripped the molding behind me and tried not to squirm. Or talk. Or look at his well-defined pecs.

Placing a big palm on the frame above my head, he leaned in. Spicy aftershave wafted around me, jerking the chain on my libido.

I hiked in a deep breath, hoping to find my center, which had been lost about the time Nash had flashed the Hugo Boss.

As my chest rose, his eyes dropped. He slanted a long look over my figure, paused on the dip of lace in the front of my Tortoise Jeans camisole, and returned to meet my gape. "Rule number three, Miss Albright. Probably not a good idea for me to hear about your sex...treatment classes."

"Right, TMI." I tried to blink but my eyelashes had fused to my upper lids. My mouth was also dry. I ran my tongue over my lips, trying to wet them, and tasted powdered sugar.

Oh, craptastic. Did I have powdered sugar all over my face? He was going to think I was a cokehead.

Nash's eyes flickered again, this time stopping on my sugared lips. He rested there for a beat, considering my mouth or the powdered sugar or the alleged cocaine. The hand above my head clenched the door frame. Closing his eyes, he took a deep breath. Nash opened his eyes. The brilliant blue accosted me. "You smell like donuts."

I opened my mouth to admit my feeding frenzy but stopped when his finger landed on my lips.

"It's okay," he whispered. "It's not a crime to like donuts. Take it easy, kid."

"How did you know—"

His phone rang, breaking the moment. Nash whipped toward the desk, slipping on his t-shirt, and reached for the phone.

I continued to grip the doorframe, trying to prevent my body from slithering down the molding into a puddle on the floor. How could I take it easy when he just said the most romantic line in the history of my life? For years eating donuts WAS a crime in MaizieLand. A crime of passion.

"Are you kidding me?" Nash's voice had gone from polite drawl to enthusiastic. "Where'd they find it?"

I shook off my libido, checked my face for powdered sugar, and sought out a chair in which to slump.

Nash scribbled on a notepad, adding three exclamation marks. The excitement must indicate the police had found Sarah Waverly's body. Knowing that David Waverly had threatened to sue meant Nash needed to prove his allegations. Hard to prove that David Waverly was a suspect in his wife's murder when she had literally disappeared.

Nash dropped his cell phone on the desk, sat on the edge, and folded his arms. His expression could be described as triumphant. Almost gloating. "That was Lamar. His buddy on Black Pine PD's keeping him informed."

"They found Sarah Waverly."

He shook his head. "Found a suitcase with her old clothes in it. Someone had tossed it in a trashcan in the alley that runs behind Black Pine Boulevard."

"The street that has all those big Victorians? I love those old houses." I stopped, realizing I was about to segue off into a meaningless tangent on period homes.

"Anyway, a homeowner saw it in her garbage can and hauled it out because she doesn't like other folks using her bin. She looked inside the suitcase and saw Sarah's clothes. There's a women's shelter nearby and she was going to take it there but wanted to report the illegal use of her garbage to the police first. A patrol officer showed to take her report and remembered the missing suitcase from the Waverly case."

"Illegal use of her garbage?"

"Dumping trash on her property." Nash waved away my concern. "It's a break. Someone wanted it to look like Sarah Waverly was leaving by packing that suitcase."

"And it couldn't have been Sarah because she wouldn't pack her Goodwill clothes." I glanced at his dated designer shirt, still lying on the desk. "Not that there's anything wrong with Goodwill. It's a great place to find vintage."

"I hope they get that bastard. He had a wife who brought him lunch every day and he treated her like dirt." Nash's focus had turned inward, and I wondered once again if Sarah Waverly had meant more to Nash than a victim.

"I just hope they find Sarah." I couldn't bring myself to say, Sarah's body.

"What did you learn today? Did Bill Dixon know if David was going to rendezvous with anyone on his boat?" Nash stroked his chin. "It's still possible he hid her body that morning. He could have taken her to a cove and dragged her body into one of the marshes."

"Ed Sweeney can't believe Waverly would do anything to Sarah. He reluctantly called Waverly a bully, though."

"I thought you were going to talk to Bill Dixon."

"Mr. Dixon was busy with some number problem at the office, so I hung out with Ed instead."

"You and Ed are getting along real well, aren't you?" Nash scowled and pushed off the desk. "I'm headed out to see if I can't learn more about the suitcase."

"Do you want me to go with you?" I hopped from my chair.

"Why don't you stay and handle the phone." He waved a hand toward the old IBM office phone that hadn't rung once in my proximity. "Just in case a client calls or something. Lamar showed you how to do the computer stuff?"

I nodded and pinched my thumb skin.

He turned from me, as if embarrassed, and bundled up the Armani. "I've got a stain on this. I'll take it with me."

"Okay." I watched him practically run out the door.

If he had asked me to take care of his dry cleaning, I probably would have cried. And still done it.

God, I was lame when it came to men.

Jolene Sweeney was right. Wyatt Nash did make me stupid.

NINETEEN

#stupidisastupiddoes #InquityPits

WYATT NASH MIGHT MAKE ME stupid, but lucky for me, stupid was nothing new. I checked the little pad where Nash had made his triple exclamation point, underlined note. Besides punctuation, he had also written 620 Black Pine Boulevard. An interesting place to visit, given that all my other clues had taken me to the other side of town.

Black Pine Boulevard was virtually behind the Dixie Kreme building. Virtually meaning six blocks from our little downtown square. Six blocks that I could walk, saving my butt and thighs from Lucky distress.

After a quickie database search for a name to match the address, I swung out the Dixie Kreme door. Six scorching blocks later, I approached the home of Madeline Talmadge. The lavender Queen Anne had a wraparound veranda with pink and purple accents. Adorbs.

Madeline Talmadge also wore lavender with pink and purple accents. Instead of a wraparound veranda, she had wrapped herself in sweaters. Also adorbs. But not helpful in the cooling off department. Particularly after walking a sweltering six blocks while wearing leather pants.

"My dear, you look like you're going to melt," said Madeline after finding out I had heard about her garbage dilemma. "You are just dripping."

"Excuse me, ma'am." I found a tissue in my backpack and dabbed at my face. The paper ripped and glued to my forehead.

Madeline leaned forward to whisper. "You're not going through the change, are you? I remember mine. Positively miserable. I used to stand in a bucket of ice water with the fridge door open."

Now I had a new worry. It seemed my twenty-five years of age could be mistaken for fifty. Afraid Madeline might start quizzing me about my cycles, I segued. "Mrs. Talmadge, I understand the police took the suitcase you found. Did you get a chance to see what was inside?"

"Mercy, yes. Ladies' clothing. A few suits. Silk. Very nice but one had a stain. Some lovely blouses. Two pairs of cropped slacks. Not my size. A windbreaker with a ripped pocket and boating shoes with a loose sole."

"I see you were thorough."

Madeline's pale cheeks turned rosy. Her glance skittered sideways. "There was also a watch. A nice metal watch. No jewels or anything fancy. Just plain. It had an inscription. I didn't think it was appropriate to throw such a nice, thoughtful gift away."

"Did you keep this watch by chance? And not give it to the police? Can I see it?"

She reached within her fuzzy purple swaddling and pulled out a slim, stainless steel and mother of pearl Michele Watches. No wonder Madeline had sticky fingers. True, no diamonds, but someone had thrown down close to a grand for this watch. I turned it over and squinted at the inscription. "My SS Sarah." Considering Sarah had no recent history of two-timing, this watch must have been from David.

"Apology jewelry," I said, handing back the watch. "And he didn't even get her diamonds. No wonder she tossed it in with the Goodwill."

"Do you know the owner?" Madeline slipped the watch between the folds of her sweaters. "I suppose you should let them know I have it. But if it was meant for Goodwill, maybe she doesn't really want it?"

"Who wants to wear apology jewelry? It's a constant reminder that your husband screws around. There's a reason she tossed it. I say give it to Goodwill."

Madeline wrung her thin hands. "I always give my clothes to

the battered women's shelter. It's behind my house, although the location is supposed to be a secret. Don't tell."

"Okay."

"I suppose I should give the watch to them? Maybe that's where the suitcase was meant to go, but they couldn't find the right house."

Madeline did not want to give up that watch. Who was I to tell her no? It would serve David Waverly right if Madeline kept the thousand dollar watch David had given to the wife he had murdered. Allegedly.

"Maybe you have something else you can give the shelter?" I offered.

With glee, Madeline popped into the house and returned with three garbage bags of mothball-scented items. Not exactly a fair trade, but Madeline was, you know, old. She pointed out the direction of the secret shelter.

I cut through Madeline's drive to the alley where her garbage had been violated, trudged down the alley, and around to the next street. Three houses down stood an unassuming Victorian. No sign it was a secret shelter other than multiple vehicles lined the drive and the shades had been pulled tight on all the windows. I climbed up the porch stairs and rang the bell.

A moment later, a woman peeped out from behind the chain lock. "Do you need help?" she said.

"No, a neighbor wanted to give you these bags of clothes."

The woman glanced at the garbage bags. "Madeline Talmadge?" I nodded.

"Thank you." Eyes still on the bags, the woman chewed her lip.

"You don't want Madeline's clothes," I said. "I understand. They're kind of old and musty."

"It's really sweet of her..."

"Probably depressing for your ladies to wear vintage polyester. They've already been through a lot. And one bag is crocheted potholders. I guess there's not much you can do with that."

The woman gazed at me in relief. "So you wouldn't mind taking them with you? But tell Madeline we appreciate her thinking of us."

Like a rejected Santa, I heaved the bags over my shoulder, jogged down the steps, and trudged down the street. In the alley, I dumped the bags on the ground and leaned against a fence.

The sun's heat beat inside my head with a similar intensity to vodka mixed with club music. Sweat had pooled in the cups of my Cosabella bra. My leather pants felt like shrink-wrap and my Golden Goose sneakers squelched when I walked. I thought about carrying the heavy bags six blocks to the Dixie Kreme building. The idea made me light-headed, so I closed my eyes and prayed for a garbage truck.

In the distance, I heard the rumble of a motor idling on the street, then the screech of tires turning into the alley. I opened one eye, squinting into the dazzle of sunlight. An older car pulled into the alley. No garbage truck. I kicked the bags closer and edged against the fence, giving the vehicle plenty of room.

The rusted-out Honda idled for a second, then accelerated into the narrow lane. After slamming into a plastic garbage can, it didn't slow. The plastic lid sailed over the back fence and trash rained on the gravel drive.

The hells?

I grabbed Madeline's trash bags and ran down the alley. At Madeline's house, I tossed the bags over the gate and reached over to pull back the sliding bolt.

The Honda gunned its motor.

I abandoned the gate and galloped toward the street.

The car plowed into Madeline's metal trash bin with a deafening crash.

Sunlight had masked the driver. Was this one of Madeline's elderly neighbors whose license needed to be revoked? Or—the alternative made me ill, not that getting run over by a leaden foot, glaucoma-impaired driver wasn't bad enough—had David Waverly heard about the suitcase and had seen me asking Madeline questions? Was he looking to cover up his crime with a hit and run?

Holy Friggin' Shizzolis.

At the corner, I cut a quick left toward Black Pine Boulevard. The side street didn't have a sidewalk. My chest felt like it would implode, but Black Pine Boulevard was only one block away. One long block. I hoofed along the fenced-in yard of a big Greek revival.

Damn, these historic homes had massive yards.

Behind me, the Honda swerved into the street. A renewed burst of speed lifted my feet, almost like I could hear Jerry threatening me with an extra fifty squats if I didn't "move my cheeseburger and side of fries a hell of a lot faster."

Or like a car was about to mow me down.

My arms pumped and my leather-clad thighs squeaked.

The Honda sped up.

The scent of burning oil filled my lungs. I could feel the heat pouring off its hood. Black Pine Boulevard was still twenty yards ahead.

The bumper grazed me.

I flew forward, my arms spiraling. I stumbled but righted.

Ahead, a black van pulled to the corner and stopped. Behind me, the Honda's brakes squealed.

I waved and screamed at the van. The side door flew open and Al poked his head out, camera in hand.

Wheels screeched on pavement.

I spun around.

The Honda reversed down the street, past the drive, and peeled into the alley. Exhaust fumes and gravel dust exploded behind it.

I didn't even consider chasing the car. I leaned over with my hands on my knees, trying to catch my breath. After a minute of heavy panting, I tottered to Al and the camera crew.

"Did you get any film of that car?" I wheezed.

"Dammit, no. Were you doing a chase scene?"

"Tell me you saw the driver. Or got a license plate?"

Al shook his head. "Is the scene over?"

I looked behind me. The street stood empty, save for a rolling garbage can lid. "I guess so."

"Damn." The side door slammed shut and a second later, the

van pulled away.

I thought about the garbage bags now lying in Madeline's back yard and the six blocks back to Dixie Kreme, then tried out the new swear words I had learned from Nash.

Al deserved every last one of them. But Vicki deserved them more.

AFTER SWEATING WITH BAGS OF oldies, I climbed into Nash's recliner, unzipped my pants, and waited for my skin to return to room temperature. Then I used Nash's bat phone to call LA HAIR for backup. If more cars sought to mow me down, I needed someone more dependable than Al watching my ass.

"Girl, I thought you were fixing to stay on the down low?" said Rhonda. "I can't look at Facebook without seeing your face plastered all over my feed.»

Tiffany joined in on the extension. "Way to stay out of the limelight, Not-Teenage Detective."

"I screwed up. I was trying to clear Nash's name and it backfired."

"Well, good news is you're trending," said Rhonda.

"That was not my intent. Listen, things are getting real. For reals. I could use some help."

"What's up?"

I decided not to mention the recent threats—phone booths, cars, Jolene—in favor of saving their friendship. In my experience, exposing your troubles was the quickest way to lose friends. "I've turned my investigations toward Mr. Waverly, our chief suspect. And I wondered if you girls wanted to go on a mission with me?"

"What'd you have in mind?" said Tiffany.

"Meet me at the Cove tonight. We're going to put the screws to that bartender, Alex. The one that dissed you. He owes me, too. Big time."

"That's my kind of party."

I could imagine Tiffany's smile. It looked like the evil grin on the puppet from *Saw*.

A T THE DEERNOSE ABODE, I readied myself to meet Tiffany and Rhonda at the Cove. I needed dirt to break David Waverly's fishing alibi. If he met a woman on the lake like Bethann Bergh suspected, then we knew he wasn't tossing Sarah's body overboard.

And if there was no lake rendezvous?

Then David Waverly had a very bad alibi for the morning his wife vanished. Nash would happily comb through all the marshy goo along the lake's hidden banks looking for evidence.

And I'd eagerly search Black Pine for an old, green Honda that had my sweat stains on its bumper. Although, where David Waverly would have gotten that car was a puzzle. And why he didn't actually run me over, another mystery. I had no illusions of track star abilities. That car could have splattered me in the alley—but didn't. Had it been toying with me? Had Al's van prevented the driver from squashing me or had the driver planned on giving me a warning instead? If the driver wasn't David, had my detecting skills been noted by Sarah's kidnapper?

I must be on the right track if someone wanted to kill me.

That idea was both terrifying and thrilling.

Light from the Cove's patio and the decked-out yachts shimmered against the lake's mirrored surface. For a Tuesday night, the restaurant seemed busy, but the *Albright* crew made for a full house. Lucky's motor died near the tennis courts, which seemed as good a place as any to park, particularly when you didn't want to be seen riding a dirt bike.

Shallow, yes, but going to the Cove meant wading among the shallow.

Tonight, I dressed for the cameras, tired of looking like I had been voted off *Survivor*. Vicki taught me to use fashion as a weapon, and I needed off-the-rack armor. I had assembled myself in an A.L.C. crepe jumpsuit. The black number had tapered ankles which meant the pants wouldn't get sucked into Lucky's engine (which had become my most recent fear). There was the issue of a V-neck cut midway to my belly, but I had the miracle of Fixomull, my stylist's favorite boob lift tape. Also beneficial for its intended use as a surgical bandage in case Lucky's engine did burn my legs.

After swapping out my sneakers for some sweet Giuseppe Zanotti t-straps, I strutted to the restaurant. Alex, Cove bartender and Vicki minion, was not in the fireplace bar. Neither were Rhonda and Tiffany. I traipsed toward the fairy-lighted patio and paused in the doorway.

The patio had been doused in *All is Albright* crew like Axe Body Spray. Lounging and drinking, they waited for something to happen. Something as in me, signing a contract that would keep them in their current financial states. Or not.

As I stood in the patio door, their eyes cut to mine. Amid their smiles and waves, I sensed an upsurge in the deep-rooted anxiety felt by all industry insiders. One that helped to maintain a luxurious lifestyle for Los Angeles health professionals.

And a luxurious lifestyle for the industry's addiction pushers. Including the Cove's own Alex. I set my brain to Julia and my sea glass greens to stun.

On cue, Tiffany and Rhonda flanked my left and right. Just like *Kung Fu Kate's* posse right before the final battle at the end of every episode. Except Kate's posse didn't wear net shirts or strapless dresses. I would not be the only one worried about slippage tonight. *Charlie's Angels* for realsies.

My body hummed with electric anticipation and residual sexual frustration. "There he is. The narc."

"I've been looking forward to this all day," said Tiffany.

"Can I get another mai tai first?" asked Rhonda.

We marched to the bar, our eyes on Alex. Who had his eyes on the blonde at a nearby table.

Vicki.

"Frigtacular," I mumbled. "I can't shake her. She's going to interfere with my missions until she breaks me."

Vicki's famous platinum waves kissed the back of her Donna Karan wrap dress. She gave me a brief glance over her shoulder and returned to chatting with Al, the cameraman.

He snapped a picture of my open-mouthed gape, then resumed

their conversation.

"Don't let her distract you, Maizie," said Rhonda. "You can do this."

We stopped at the bar. Pumped for the mission, I leaned forward and placed a hand on the bartender's arm. "Can I talk to you for a minute? In private?"

Alex struggled to keep his vision north of my neck. "I have to keep an eye on the bar."

"Don't look like it's the bar you're eyeing," said Tiffany. She glanced at Rhonda. "Does he look busy to you?"

"I think you better talk to the girl," said Rhonda. "You owe her. Because of you, *OK!* reported Maizie's delivering Giulio's baby live during sweeps week."

I felt my knees buckle and Rhonda grabbed my elbow.

"Move it or we tell your boss that you've been nipping the Absolut during office hours," said Tiffany.

"I don't drink vodka." His eyes cut to the glass of Coke sitting next to the cash register.

"Whatever. We don't play," said Rhonda. "Maizie needs some information from you."

Alex rolled his eyes and pointed toward the servers' entrance to the kitchen. He waved a waiter over and stalked toward the kitchen door.

After an exchange of raised eyebrows, fist pumps, and goofy smiles, we followed.

Inside the kitchen door, Alex ushered us into a pantry.

I hesitated then followed. The phone booth had been much smaller. And less stocked with people and carbs.

Alex glanced at my belly skimming V-neck and softened his irritation. "Hey, Maizie. You aren't still mad at me, are you?"

"Why would I be mad? For selling me out for a Benji? Happens to me all the time. Next time, hold out for more. Vicki always lowballs the first offer."

"Oh snap," said Rhonda.

"You going to help out our girl?" Tiffany slitted her electric blue lined eyes. "She needs some dirt on a club member. David

Waverly."

"We're not allowed to talk about members," said Alex.

"You're also not allowed to sell out customers." Tiffany cracked her knuckles. "So you make another exception."

I hoped Tiffany never joined the mob.

Alex sighed. "What do you want to know?"

"You worked the inside bar on Saturday night. David Waverly had a drink with a woman. Who?"

Alex stared at the mayonnaise jars on the upper shelf. "Redhead. You talked to her the other night. Has the real estate company."

I blinked. David Waverly had met with Jolene the weekend his wife disappeared? Why did that feel hinky? They saw each other at poker Sunday night. What was with the private meeting? Just chatting about selling Nash Security? Maybe Jolene was trying to cover her ass, in case Nash blew the sale.

"Do you think they're having an affair?" I asked.

Alex shrugged. "Everyone knows David Waverly will screw anything not nailed down."

"Eew," said Rhonda.

"Interesting," I said. Jolene could have been using David. He had money and reeked of corporate power. Jolene probably went in for that sort of thing. But would she go along with getting rid of his wife?

"I need to know if he met anyone on Friday morning," I continued. "He took the boat out and I heard that's where he does his hookups. How does that work?"

"If the lady has her own boat, they dock out at the Bourne place and one of them climbs aboard the other." Alex waggled his eyebrows.

"Eew," said Rhonda.

"Why do rich people have to be so complicated?" said Tiffany. "Can't they do it in a sleazy motel or a car like everyone else?"

Alex shrugged. "Why would you when you have a tricked-out boat with a bed?"

"Eew," said Rhonda.

"What is this Bourne place?" I asked.

"The Bournes don't use their dock anymore. They're elderly. The house is up on a ridge overlooking the lake with steps leading down to the dock. At one time, they had put in a nice patio and a small beach by their dock. They allowed club members to use it."

"Do the Bournes know club members are using it for hookups?" I wrinkled my nose. "Those poor people."

"I heard the Bournes were swingers back in the day." Alex smirked. "Maybe they're passing the torch."

"What is wrong with Black Pine?" I shuddered. "I thought this kind of thing was exclusive to LA."

"It's not geographic," said Tiffany. "It's money."

"I had money and didn't act like that."

"You did a bunch of other stupid stuff, though," said Rhonda. "You didn't give yourself enough time to get to swinging."

"Are we done here?" said Alex. "People are going to wonder what I'm doing in the pantry with three women."

We got out of the closet.

Leaving Alex to his bar, the girls and I found an empty table on the patio. We ordered three waters with lemon and a mai tai. Then handed over twenty-three dollars and a tip.

"It's too expensive to drink here," said Tiffany. "Why don't you come out with us?"

"I think I should visit the Bournes before it gets too late," I said. "They might have seen something last Friday."

Tiffany shook her head. "Putting the screws to Alex was fun, but count me out on the Bournes. Elderly swingers give me the creeps."

I sank my chin into my palm. "I don't really want to visit them either. I'm totally grossed out over the lack of morals in Black Pine. Thank God DeerNose hasn't fallen into this pit of iniquity."

"DeerNose banks on clean, country living," said Tiffany. "That's their edge."

I winced at her cynicism. "Judge Ellis sent me here to get away from the 'depravity of the young, moneyed culture of Beverly Hills.' Little did he know he sent the lamb to the slaughter."

"The moneyed culture in Black Pine is not young," said Rhonda. "You'll do okay."

TWENTY

#SwingerMiss #PimpMyCareer

RHONDA AND TIFFANY LEFT TO find more affordable libations. I borrowed Alex's cell phone to call Nash.

"Don't drive to the Bournes on that scooter. I'll pick you up at the Cove."

My heart accelerated. "You want to question them together?"

"I want to question them and I don't want you following me. Those old mountain roads are crap and barely wide enough for two vehicles. Someone comes speeding down one and they'll squash you like a bug."

Nash worried about my safety. My toes curled inside the Zanotti's.

"Last thing I need is a headline saying, 'Nash Security Solutions Sends Actress to Her Death.' I've already got a similar headline with Sarah Waverly."

Just for that, I didn't tell him the Bournes were swingers.

We hung up. I hammered my fingers on the bar, wondering what was wrong with me that I could be attracted to someone so irritating. Irresistible Neanderthal, my ass. More like costar crushing. I had serious issues and needed a new therapist. But first I needed a paycheck to pay said therapist.

"Baby."

I sucked in a breath, then let it out to keep my Fixomull from ripping.

Giulio strode up the patio steps from the cart path. He wore Armani, per ushe. A painted-on polo that grappled his biceps and hinted at his daily ab workouts. With those damn skinny jeans.

However, he was too silly for me to stay angry. The baby stunt had to have been Vicki's idea. Giulio was paid to act, not think.

The locals watched the proceedings with unconcealed interest as did the *Albright* crew. The patio hummed with boozed anticipation. Al grabbed his camera.

Using a stage voice to project his admiration of my Zanottis, Giulio paced across the patio.

I dodged his open embrace.

He parried with a shoulder hug.

We bumped chests and noses.

He countered my double cheek kiss with a longer lip lock. Fake shutter whirs abounded. Al's Canon DSLR hummed.

I lost all my NARS Orgasm. Truthfully, I let him. My lips had been frustrated ever since the powdered sugar debacle at Nash's office. And Giulio was that good.

Glancing down into my décolletage, Giulio whispered, "Watch the nip slip, my darling. I heard your tape rip."

With Giulio's hard body to block the cameras, I adjusted the girls then gently pushed him away. "Thanks."

"Anytime." He gave me a lazy, Italian smile. "You know I have the quick eye for this sort of thing."

"Of course you do. Listen, I've got to go. Nash is picking me up so we can question some swingers."

"Darling, do you mean the detective work? It is so sexy when you say, 'question some swingers.' Very hard-boiled, you know? It has that noir edge. I think it will be our best season yet."

"Giulio, you know I'm not doing the show. You're making it hard on the crew if you continue to let them think they'll be staying in Black Pine."

"But darling, we are staying in Black Pine this season."

"Sweetie." I patted his chiseled cheek bone, stroking the bare scant of stubble Giulio spent much time maintaining. "Don't worry. You won't be stuck in Black Pine. As long as I can solve this case for Nash, I am not signing. You will be going back to LA very soon."

"Let me explain. But I need a drink. You have the minute, don't you, my darling?" Giulio wrapped an arm around my waist and guided me to the bar. Within seconds, I held a seltzer with lime and he a Campari. His fingers trailed against my hip. I sucked in my stomach and tried not to think about fried pickles.

Giulio slid a sloe-eyed glance across the patio. I didn't have to look to know where it landed. "Your *madre*," he paused and lowered his voice. "Vicki. She says whether you sign or not is irrelevant."

"What do you mean?"

"The other producers agree it is cheaper to film in Black Pine, Georgia."

I set my glass on the bar and gripped his shoulders. "Please don't tell me she's moving the crew and cast to Black Pine permanently."

"Then I won't tell you." His hand glided from my hip to my waist, forcing me to tighten my withering abs, which automatically plumped out my chest. Giulio noticed and smiled. "Let me 'question the swingers' with you darling. I want to be your bad cop. That jumpsuit is exquisite. I'm not dressed properly, but maybe Costume has a leather jacket I can borrow. The pairing will look fabulous."

"No bad cop. And no photograph." I removed his hands from my waist. Then relaxed my stomach and thought about ordering the fried Vidalia onion blossom. But Giulio would expense it and I didn't want Vicki signing off on my trans-fat charges. "Why is she doing this?"

Giulio leaned against the bar and sipped his Campari cocktail. "It's much cheaper to film here. We are professionals. We will adjust."

"I won't adjust if she stays."

"I'd adjust your eating habits," said Vicki from behind my shoulder. "Your cleavage has grown and soon no amount of tape can help you there."

"Unbelievable." I swore under my breath. "How do you keep doing that?"

"I know, her breasts are fabulous," said Giulio. "But Vicki's right. You cannot get fat, darling. You know how the camera packs on the pounds. Unless it's a baby bump. We can work with that."

Taking courage, I turned to face Vicki. "It doesn't matter because I no longer need to be in front of a camera."

She zipped a finger across an iPad. A photo of me riding Lucky flashed across the screen. Knees and elbows jutted stork-like. Neck lost within my hunched shoulders. In the wind, the Tortoise Jeans camisole had plastered against my skin, revealing the belly rim squeezed out by the leather pants. The wedge of Lucky's seat betwixt my bubble crack was nothing to admire, either.

"I'm sorry, dear, but you can't hide from the camera."

I choked on seltzer. "Is that online or in your photo stream?"

"What does it matter if you're no longer in front of the camera?"

«You have Al and his camera crew following me around town, taping me. I'll press harassment charges."

"So press." Vicki shrugged. "You don't care about us anymore, so I'm sure you don't care what happens to Al if he has stalking charges on his record. His ex-wife will be thrilled. Something to show the judge when she sues for full custody of his kids."

Giulio whistled.

"You are diabolical," I whispered.

"When are you going to grow up, Maizie? A lot of people are dependent on this show. Not just the cast and crew, but the network. Sponsors are lined up. For God sakes, it's only been a few weeks since we presented the next season proposal at the Lincoln Center upfronts."

"It's not my fault you agreed to another season without asking me."

"As your manager, I felt I could answer for you. If you weren't dealing with another legal catastrophe, I would have gotten you to sign that contract earlier." Vicki's eyes narrowed. "Have your identity crisis, but you're not screwing us over. Have you ever heard of a network suing a producer? It's always the other way around."

"I'm not having an identity crisis." Except for all the Julia Pinkerton channeling. Which meant I might be having an identity crisis.

"Maizie, you know I don't play softball. But I made an exception since you are," she shot a look at Giulio, who had the brains to look away, "my daughter. I gave you several opportunities to sign a new contract. I could have helped you in your latest disaster. No more."

There was that Space Mountain star room feeling again.

"You're going to be on the show whether you like it or not. Belly bulge and all."

Oh. My. God. The black van was going to follow me everywhere. Nash would never let me out of the office. If there was an office to let me out of.

"But Vicki, darling," said Giulio. "If Maizie continues to look like this, the media will eat her alive."

"The sponsors will hate it, but the network will love all the press. Following a girl pretending to be a detective is a lot more interesting than following around a has-been student who dates drug dealers."

"You are a genius," said Giulio. "What is my part? Maizie will not let me seduce her."

"I'm considering different roles for you, but don't worry Giulio. Your paycheck is safe."

"How many times do I have to tell you, I can't legally work in the industry anymore?" My voice climbed from frustration toward panic.

Giulio slipped an arm around my waist and raised my hand to his lips. "Don't worry, darling. If the filming is candid, you don't need a contract. The judge can't complain."

"Which means I'm filmed without getting paid?"

"Miss Albright." Nash's voice floated over my shoulder. "If you're done schmoozing, the Bournes are waiting."

I spun around, horrified at what Nash might have heard.

He stood with his arms folded, that hard-edged look returned.

"And you are?" said Vicki.

"Leaving," I said. "You need to leave. We need to leave. Go. Now."

"Darling," said Giulio. "Introduce us. Is this your private dick? He's so..."

"Don't," I pleaded.

"Manly."

I looked at Nash. I had never seen disgust so plainly visible on a man's face before.

Giulio flashed a razor-edged smile between his symmetrical dimples. "Dick? Is that not the right word? I'm sorry, my English is not always so good, darling."

Vicki trailed a long look over Nash, then handed him a card. "We need to talk."

Nash arched a brow. "Do you have security needs?"

"Jolene Sweeney has informed me about your predicament. I've come to the conclusion that we can help each other. That one," Vicki flicked a look at me, "needs a salary to keep her out of the California penal system. It'll be cheaper to keep you afloat and Maizie accessible."

"No," said Nash.

"Think about it. I've got no interest in your business. Only what Maizie does for it. Or for you, if that's the case." The glance she tossed between us made me want to consume the Cove's entire fried menu, shrivel up, and die. In that order. "Work her how you want, I'll cover the cost and keep you in business."

"Are you her pimp?" asked Nash.

During the whole Oliver scandal, when I stood in court and let a judge give me a very public tongue-lashing, I thought I had lost all my pride. But no. This was pretty much it. The pinnacle of my humiliation.

"Ma'am." Nash nodded and slipped the business card into his shirt pocket. Then he grabbed my arm and marched my Zanottis out of the restaurant.

B Y THE TIME WE ARRIVED at the Bournes, we still hadn't talked. I spent the entire ride pinching my thumb skin and wondering why Nash had hauled me into his truck instead of leaving me at the Cove. No explanation. No questions. No sarcastic quips. He kept his eyes on the road, his mouth shut, and his expression grim. I knew he regretted his decision to let me help in the investigation. Therefore, for once, I was glad he didn't attempt conversation.

I kept my mouth shut, too. And I had stuff to tell him. About his ex-wife in particular.

The Bournes' ivy-covered brick box and crumbling circular drive screamed mid-century money pit. Nature had taken over the yard service. Oaks and pines yawned over the long ranch's peaked roof.

Nash stared at the house for a long second, thumped his hand on the steering wheel, and slid out of the truck without comment.

I scrambled out the passenger door and traipsed across the weedy, cracked cement in my Zanottis, trying not to break an ankle.

At the door, Nash glanced at me, glared at my shoes, and rang the bell.

A withered, little man wearing a faded corduroy suit answered the door. Not having any previous experience with swingers, his attire surprised me. Rather than leather sleeve patches, I expected something more along the lines of an ascot and silk robe.

I've got to stop judging people by their clothes.

"Mr. Bourne," said Nash. "I'm from Nash Security Solutions. I spoke to your wife on the phone."

Mr. Bourne raised a hand to his ear. A high pitched whine rent the night air.

Nash winced.

Somewhere nearby, a dog howled.

"Speak up," said Mr. Bourne, then yelled over his shoulder, "Marie, I need you."

Behind Mr. Bourne, a rhythmic shuffle thump preceded the

appearance of a woman in a zippered velour robe, clutching a walker. She blinked behind oversized glasses, lenses thicker than my ankles. "Are you Officer Nash?" she shouted.

Nash paused, seeming to consider the correction. "Yes, ma'am," he yelled.

Mr. Bourne stuck his finger in his ear and the sonic screech of his hearing aid pierced the air again.

"Stop that, Jefferson." Mrs. Bourne swatted his arm. Behind her mega-prescriptions, she blinked and squinted at me. "Come in. We're about to have our dessert. You're here about our dock, aren't you? We have all the boats recorded."

Nash and I glanced at each other and followed them inside.

In the foyer, watercolor paintings of yachts covered a large wall, almost hiding the flocked wallpaper. We stopped to examine the paintings, but Mr. Bourne pointed down the hall.

"This way," he shouted. "She's got more."

His wife had already disappeared behind the giant wall, the tennis-balled walker whispering across the parquet.

Mr. Bourne held the edge of the wall to step down into the room and I hurried to grab his arm.

He grinned appreciatively and dug his arm into my ribcage. "Thank you, honey."

A piece of tape popped. I held my breath to keep my chest from moving. We tread across the matted shag carpet, my steps mincing more to stop the chest avalanche than to meet Mr. Bourne's gait. Mrs. Bourne and Nash had crossed the room to a set of French doors that exited onto a screened porch. With his leather patched elbow slicing across the Fixomull strips, Mr. Bourne and I shuffled toward the door.

He didn't hear the tear, but judging by his smile, he might have felt it.

Released from bondage, half of my upper body jiggled in rejoice. I clamped my free arm across my chest and prayed Mrs. Bourne's myopia was catching.

Inside the porch, I moved toward the screened windows for covert wardrobe malfunction adjustments. Below us, outdoor lighting lit a long wooden dock and adjoining boathouse. A flagstone patio with a vine covered pergola looked romantically inviting. It depressed me to think the club members used the Bournes' retreat for illicit liaisons. It depressed me more to think the Bournes were okay with that. They seemed grandparently.

Mr. Bourne grabbed a bottle of Jim Bean and splashed bourbon in four glasses. Mrs. Bourne sank on a wrought iron chair and waved her hand at a Wedgwood plate of cookies. Oreos. Nutter Butters. Lorna Doones. Oh, my.

"Will you join us?" she asked.

I smiled and reached, felt the slide of skin against crepe, and slapped my arms across my chest. "No, thank you."

Nash stood before an easel, examining a half-painted watercolor of another yacht. A large magnifying glass had been clamped on the easel, enlarging a photo of the subject. "I take it you paint the boats you see on the lake."

Mrs. Bourne nodded her head and twisted apart an Oreo. "It's my hobby. But I can't see them anymore, so Jefferson uses the digital thingy to snap a shot and print it. Technology is wonderful."

I glanced at the Nikon sitting on the table, not too different from the professional camera Al used for stills.

Mr. Bourne pointed into the living room where a desk held a slick inkjet printer and an Apple Mac Pro desktop. The Bournes might not have updated their house since 1972, but they stayed on top of technological trends better than my hipster friends.

"How often do you take pictures?" Nash accentuated his words in loud, crisp tones, but I could tell he was getting excited.

"Every day," said Mrs. Bourne, crunching into a Nutter Butter.

"Wonderful." Nash's face revealed happy thoughts of crime scenes and evidence bags.

My face probably revealed happy thoughts of Nutter Butters. I licked my lips. "Do you have a photo from last Friday?"

Mr. Bourne held out a glass of bourbon to me. "Drink?"

I shook my head, focusing on Mrs. Bourne, who now attacked a Lorna Doone.

"Oh, we toss the photos," she said. "What would we do with

thousands of pictures of the Black Pine Club yachts? There're so many, we bought a shredder."

Nash winced at "shredder" and reached for the Jim Bean offered by Mr. Bourne.

"Did you paint any boats last Friday?" I asked, hoping to cheer Nash. "The *Playbuoy* might have come out this way. Did you see it? Maybe docked on your landing? With another boat?"

"Jefferson," shouted Mrs. Bourne. "Take them to the latest wall."

Mr. Bourne stuck his finger in his ear. The shrill decibel rent our eardrums.

"Have mercy, Jefferson. Get a new battery. The wall. Friday last," she hollered. Snagging another Oreo, she glanced at us. "I'd take you myself, but I can't see worth a damn. I won't know which painting is which."

This time, I didn't offer Jefferson my arm, afraid for the damage his sharp elbows might do to my right side. I plodded after Mr. Bourne. Nash plodded after me. Mr. Bourne led us through the living room and down the front hall to a bedroom. I stopped in the doorway. I'm always hesitant about entering strange bedrooms. Especially in rumored swinger abodes.

Behind me, Nash pressed close and leaned into my ear. I could sense the look he cast over my shoulder, and I squeezed my arms tightly across the V-neck.

"Miss Albright."

I waited for the cutting remark about the inappropriateness of my attire. His breath tickled my neck, but the pause ripped at my nerves. "Yes, Mr. Nash?"

A sigh dusted my shoulders, causing shivers in all sorts of places. "David Waverly is at large. He left the house this morning but didn't show up for work. Never came home. I got a call from my friend after I talked to you on the phone. They have an APB out on him, but no one's seen him today."

"He ran?" Still clutching my chest, I spun around and teetered in the heels.

Nash grabbed my elbows until I steadied.

"Why didn't you tell me in the truck?" I asked.

"I was thinking."

"So why'd you agree to come here?"

"Because it's a good lead."

A thrill of pride stole through me, but I didn't want to get ahead of myself. "You were disappointed they shredded the photos."

"The pictures might still be on the memory card. That's evidence. We can get a time record for Friday. Who knows, they might have captured Waverly doing something."

I grabbed his arms. "Thank you for believing in me."

He scowled. "It's not about believing in you. You got a good lead. We're following it."

Embarrassed, I released his arms and found Julia's confidence. "Anyway, I appreciate the chance."

The scowl melted and his eyes dropped.

I followed his look to my V-neck.

Oh. My. God.

"I appreciate the chance, too," he said, admiringly. "Is that tape?"

I slapped my arms over my chest.

His eyes slid up to meet my heated face. "Tape's tricky. You might need help getting it off."

O.M.G.

"Baby oil."

"Baby oil?" I formed the words while lewd images filled my brain. I had spent too much time among the licentious Black Piners. Plus, my time in Hollywood didn't help.

"Heard it works wonders for getting tape off. Good luck."

"Thanks." The heat coiling in my nether regions fizzled, cooled, and iced.

"Anytime."

I turned and walked into the bedroom. "Huh."

"What's the matter?"

"Black Pine decorating habits astound me." The entire room had been wallpapered in psychedelic flowers and covered in boat paintings. Mr. Bourne leaned over a canvas hung at shin height between a closet door and a dressing table with a yellow flounced skirt.

"What'd you expect? A jungle room? We're not in Hollywood." Nash stood close, speaking in hushed tones that did crazy things to my skin.

"I believe you're thinking of Graceland." I peeked over my shoulder, wishing my heart would quit with the costar crushing. I strode to the chenille covered twin bed where Mr. Bourne had laid the painting of the boat.

Actually, a painting of two boats. One behind the other, lined up like toys along the long dock. The birds-eye-view of dappled colors also showed two people on the dock. One appeared to be tying off the second boat. The other person, a redhead in a green bikini, stood with her hands on her hips. A good likeness even with the medium's mottled, soft-edges.

"Isn't she talented?" Mr. Bourne eyed his wife's painting with pride.

"Are you sure that's from last Friday morning?" hollered Nash into Mr. Bourne's ear.

"Oh, yes." He flipped the painting over, where the time and date had been printed carefully with a sharpie on the back of the canvas. "Marie likes to paint. I like to record. Plus, I couldn't forget that redhead. I took a lot of pictures of that bikini."

"Shit," said Nash.

But Mr. Bourne hadn't heard, too caught up in admiring his wife's painting of Jolene's bikini.

TWENTY-ONE

#Swingshift #BikinisAhoy

MORE APPROPRIATELY DRESSED, I RETURNED to Nash Security Solutions the next morning. The media had abandoned their Dixie Kreme recon, but the black van still trolled for pictures.

I could imagine the new show. They already had tons of footage from college graduation and Oliver's arrest to build onto the next season. Now they'd have shots of me walking into the office. Cut to Giulio and my "sexy neighbor," Bethann, gossiping about the cheating spouse I watched. Cut to me riding Lucky to a surveillance opportunity, edited to catch me falling asleep or scarfing donuts. Cut to Vicki planning the takeover of Nash Security Solutions. Cut to me walking down the side of a highway after falling from a tree. Cut to Nash looking pissed. Then me getting kicked out of Daddy's house.

Great TV.

I had three more days to get that W-4 sent to Judge Ellis. Three days to publicly extricate Nash's name from the case and keep his office from folding. Three days to figure out what had happened to Sarah Waverly.

Essentially three days to save two lives and remake my own.

No pressure.

I wondered if Nash would consider letting Vicki buy Jolene's share. Which meant I'd work for Vicki again. What kind of contract would she make me sign as a PI assistant? Would it have weight clauses and nip and tuck stipulations? Would I be released after my two-year apprenticeship?

Would I end my life in a twin burial plot next to Vicki, too afraid to ever leave her, even in death?

I'd already tried the typical child star revolt. She used that to launch the *Albright* show. And here we were again. Vicki prepared to spin my latest disaster into a new story beat for my life's teledrama.

And me not strong enough to stop her.

This was the thought that had brought on the extra helping of Carol Lynn's cheesy bacon tater skillet.

I don't think that food combination is even legal in California.

Inside Nash's office, Lamar lounged while Nash paced. I found my place on the couch and joined in the think-fest.

"Nash gave Black Pine police the painting and the Bourne's memory card," explained Lamar.

"Did you get in trouble?"

"An anonymous drop-off," said Nash. "Although they'll figure it out when they talk to the Bournes. I've got to work quickly. But that's not the problem. They're going to question Jolene."

"Yikes," I said.

Lamar nodded. "Nash'll be lucky if Jolene doesn't shoot him. She's tried that once before."

Nash flicked an irritated look at Lamar. "She missed."

"Do you think Jolene could be involved?" I asked Lamar, but I meant it for Nash. "She also met David on Saturday night at the Cove. They had a drink together in the bar."

"Jolene would need a strong motive for accessory or aiding and abetting, much less murder. She's one who would weigh the consequences."

Ignoring us, Nash paced to set his gaze out the window. "Jolene didn't do anything."

"I hope feelings aren't clouding your judgement," said Lamar.

I sucked in my breath. Feelings for Jolene? Or for Sarah Waverly?

Julia Pinkerton rolled her teenage eyes at those self-absorbed questions.

I made a mental note to mark the conscious thought of subconscious subtext for my next therapy appointment and directed my attention toward more important considerations. "What did the police find out, Lamar?"

"Atlanta police found the Corvette in Hartsfield-Jackson's long term parking yesterday. They're waiting to see if Waverly checked on a flight," said Lamar. "Black Pine PD did a good job getting the word out."

"Wow. Did Waverly have a plane ticket?"

"Don't know. The police are waiting on the warrant to look at the flight logs. And to look in the Corvette."

"How long until they know?"

"The flight logs? That's a whole lot of Homeland Security red tape. The vehicle warrant shouldn't take much time unless airport parking falls under Homeland Security, too."

"Waverly could've skipped," said Nash. "But not because he's on the lam. The bastard probably ran out of adjectives to describe me and wanted a vacation from all the interviews."

"You don't think he killed Sarah?" said Lamar. "Want to elucidate us on your newest deduction?"

Nash turned to lean against the window. "Docking at the Bournes to dump a body? Even if Waverly and Jolene didn't know about the Bourne peepshow, why risk it?"

I had wondered that myself. "Plus, that means Waverly and Jolene had planned on killing Sarah. I always thought Sarah's murder would be second degree. Like they fought and in his anger David Waverly accidentally killed his wife, then hid it. Why would he plan a murder for the morning he knew I'd be watching Sarah?"

"Unless he thought you might flake out. No offense, but you are an actress," said Lamar. "But Nash, you must have more than that. Stop keeping everything so close to your vest."

"I checked the DVR recording of the minicam I had planted in the Waverly driveway," said Nash. "Waverly left his house in the Corvette same time as usual yesterday morning. But the night before, a taxi parked on their street. Drove real slow, like it was parking nearby. Maybe someone else is involved."

"That could be anything," said Lamar. "One of the neighbors coming home from the airport."

"Around midnight?"

"Coming home drunk from the Cove, then."

"On a Monday night?" said Nash. "I don't like it."

"Can't we ask Platinum Ridge's security about the taxi?" I asked. "They keep records and have a video camera on their booth."

"Doubt if they'd tell you," said Lamar. "They'd keep the records confidential for the home owners' privacy."

"I'll try anyway."

"This is what it boils down to," said Nash. "Waverly has a sketchy alibi for the morning his wife disappeared. Yesterday he took off. The police will be looking for him, but my name is still linked to this case."

"What if she was kidnapped?" I said. "And there was a ransom but Waverly didn't tell anybody? Yesterday at Black Pine Group, William Dixon said the numbers were off. What if Waverly took money from Black Pine Group to pay the ransom?"

"And slipped off to the airport to bring the money?" said Lamar. "Could be."

"Then where is Waverly?" said Nash.

"We need to find him," I said. "If we can solve this, the media will make you a hero."

"The media's blackened my name thanks to Waverly. I don't want anything to do with the media."

"Then kiss your business goodbye." Julia's snark was better for making a point. "Whether you like it or not, the media will follow this case. They can spin a story any which way. Nobody knows that better than me. We solve this and Nash Security Solutions is back on the map."

NASH LEFT TO MEET JOLENE at the police station. He called it damage control, but Lamar exchanged a look with me that spoke of something else.

I set that look aside and thought about how I could help with the case. Mr. Deevers, Platinum Ridge's night security guard, had said Community Management's Mark Jacobs—as opposed to

Marc Jacobs—kept the subdivision's vehicle reports and security videos. I should at least try to get a look at the taxi. Speaking as someone without any investigative training (still), it seemed like a good lead.

Two women ran the Community Management Office: Debby and Jessica. It was hard to switch on Julia Pinkerton because Debby and Jessica wanted Maizie Albright. Not only did they have copies of my photos from the *AJC* and the *Black Pine Gazette*, they also had Sharpies and Instagram and lots of squealing.

I signed the photos of Giulio clenching my butt and smiled for two snapshots and one group selfie. And then, at their request, told them my rehab story about meeting the singer from Atomic, who's real name is Chad, and how he wrote the song, "Sorry Daughter," about me.

Of course, I didn't tell Debby and Jessica about Chad and his wife's codependency or Chad's father giving Chad his first bong hit when he was only eight. When Chad isn't stoned out of his mind, he's actually a nice guy. Just loose with the tongue while song writing. Which he does stoned.

"So what are the chances of *All is Albright* filming in Black Pine?" asked Debby.

"I have no idea," I said.

"We know a realtor we can recommend if you or anyone from the show is looking for housing in our communities," said Jessica. "We have premium rentals, too."

"Who's your realtor?" I had a feeling she was going to say...

"Jolene Sweeney."

"Would you like to look at our community maps?" asked Debby.

"That's okay. I'm interested in speaking to Mark Jacobs," I hesitated. "Do you know if Jolene sold the Waverlys their house?"

Jessica tapped her chin with her French manicure. "Probably."

"Does Jolene live in Platinum Ridge?"

"I'll just say, Platinum Ridge is for the Who's Who of Black Pine. Unless you're an original. Then you might live in the historic district. Except of course, if someone's like your daddy..."

"A 'Who's Who' who wants a lot of property for hunting and

fishing."

"Exactly," said Debby, relieved to get past any awkwardness for a potential client. "Everyone knows Boomer Spayberry is not an in-town person. And we respect that."

Which meant Daddy and his deer pee were better off back in the woods. Although the club wouldn't mind his money and name.

"Back to Jolene Sweeney. She seems successful."

They bobbed their heads.

"She could sell a bulldog to a Gator fan," said Jessica.

I didn't get the analogy, but I got her drift. "I guess she and David Waverly probably had a lot in common. He's pretty successful at"—I still had no clue what he did—"making money. You heard about his wife, Sarah, disappearing? Do you think she might have taken off? Because of? You know? Jolene?"

"Jolene?" Debby raised her eyebrows at Jessica.

"You didn't hear anything like that?"

They shook their heads.

Great, I had started an unfounded rumor. "Can I talk to Mark Jacobs now?"

We walked into the map room which featured a scale model of Black Pine including the mountain, lake, and wooded hills encompassing Daddy's acreage. They even had a tiny factory set in the adjoining DeerNose property woods. With a gravel parking lot with teeny cars. And bitty boats on the lake. Adorbs.

I walked around the glass-cased model. On the surrounding walls, Community Management subdivision maps had been hung in elegant frames. Photographs of featured homes and subdivision amenities clustered around the maps. I found Platinum Ridge and studied the parallel streets that snaked up the side of the mountain. There was only one way in and out of Platinum Ridge—at the guard house—unless one wanted to scale a fence and drop into the surrounding woods.

Or fall over a wall into the adjoining subdivision, Echo Ridge. After climbing a tree while being chased by a dog.

A moment later, Mark Jacobs appeared. Very different from

Marc Jacobs. Mark was stocky, although the Community Management polo and pleated Dockers did him no favors. He could have used some tips from Marc.

"Look, Mark," squealed Debby. "It's Maizie Albright. She needs to see how our security works. Maybe for a role. Isn't that exciting?"

"You're my appointment?" Mark Jacobs did not look excited to meet me. He looked annoyed.

I seemed to have that effect on some Black Pine men.

"Come on," he grunted, clomping toward the offices in the back.

I scurried behind him, focusing on recreating Julia's moxie. We entered a room with more maps pinned to the wall along with a rack of clipboards and an open security box of keys. He settled behind his desk and leaned back in his chair. I lowered myself across from him in the only other chair. Between us sat a ginormous monitor for his computer, stacks of *Guns & Ammo* magazines, and a bag of pork rinds. I scooted my chair to the right so I could see him. Evidently, Mark Jacobs did not often entertain in his office.

"What's all this about?" Mark Jacobs liked to get to the point. Which was fine with me.

"I'm actually here representing a private investigation firm." I flashed him the business card I'd taken from Nash's desk. "One of our clients lives in Platinum Ridge. We'd like to see your logs and video footage from this week."

"Why?"

"We're tracking a missing person."

"Who?"

I thought for a minute. "Someone related to our client."

"This isn't about that Waverly business? Because I already spoke to the police."

"I'm not looking for Sarah Waverly." Which was not a lie. I was looking for her husband.

"Why hasn't the police contacted me about this one?"

"They probably will. Soon. And I'll let them know how compliant you were." I shot him my *Maxim* smile.

Mark Jacobs frowned and massaged his chin curtain.

I scooted forward in my chair. "Mr. Jacobs. A missing person. Can you imagine? How awful? Timeliness is so important, you know. Please. I just want to see who left in a taxi on Monday night."

"Our homeowners pay a lot of money to guard their privacy." Mark Jacobs steepled his hands on his belly and rocked in his chair for a good twenty seconds.

I got the feeling Mark Jacobs didn't like to put out extra effort. I also got the feeling he was waiting for something. And then it dawned on me. He was in need of some palm greasing. And I had no money. Well, I did have some money, but with no credit card, I wasn't willing to part with the cash.

"An autographed photo of me can get around one hundred dollars on Ebay. Especially when I've recently been in the news."

Twenty minutes later Mark Jacobs took a picture of me signing the photo we had shot and printed on glossy paper using Debby's photo printer. I signed a print for Debby and Jessica, too. Which they planned to hang in the reception room. Hopefully, Daddy would never have reason to enter Community Management.

Our photo shoot over, I ran my finger down the log of vehicle entries for Platinum Ridge. While I eyeballed the video footage on his computer, Mark Jacobs admired the cheesecake image of me twisting my t-shirt and chewing on a pen.

It could have been worse.

The log book made it a lot easier to race through a lot of dead time. Two taxis had entered Platinum Ridge on Monday, one at four-thirty in the afternoon and one at eleven forty-six in the evening. I found the night time footage of the taxi pulling through the security gates. The back seat looked empty. The guard had written a Granite Curve address, but it was across the street from the Waverlys.

"I guess Lamar was right," I said.

"Who's Lamar?" Mark Jacobs looked up from his phone where he had been entering his eBay information.

"I'll check to see who the taxi picked up anyway."

Mark rolled his eyes and returned to his thumb typing.

I forwarded the footage six minutes. The taxi reappeared at the gates. As it pulled through, I paused the film. The cab driver had his window open. Behind him, the fare had leaned forward, his attention on something blocked by the seat. Judging by the glow, it was probably his phone. And because of the light, I managed to see the shock of white hair and lean, chiseled face of Ed Sweeney.

"Whoa," I said.

"What?" Mark had finished his eBay form and now thumbed through collectible liquor bottles.

"Eddie's got some 'splaining to do," I said in my best Ricky Riccardo voice.

Mark rolled his eyes entirely too much.

"Let me check the next morning," I said and sped the footage forward.

At eight forty-five the next morning, Waverly's Corvette pulled up to the security gates, waited for them to open, then zoomed through. Because the camera had been mounted on the rear of the security booth, I had a perfect shot of the Corvette's driver. Who, I thought, made an obvious attempt to avoid the camera.

"The hells?"

"Can you stop with the speaking out loud?"

"I can't help it. It's an honest reaction. Look at this still." I pointed to the driver. "Do you recognize this man?"

"Hard to tell." Mark squinted at the screen. "He's turned like he's looking in the backseat. Plus there's the hat, glasses, and big windbreaker."

"He stays like that until the gates open and then pulls forward. Who does that? I think it's hinky."

"Hinky?"

I sighed. "Can I get a print of this picture?"

Mark Jacobs glanced at the eBay screen on his phone and flicked his gaze back to me. "Sign the pen you chewed."

"Are you kidding me? That's disgusting. Nobody is going to buy a chewed pen."

"Not according to eBay."

"This country is in a deplorable state."

"Actually, you're really popular in North Korea."

WHILE DEBBY AND JESSICA HUNG the non-cheesecake photo of me behind their desk, I used their phone to call Nash.

"Ed Sweeney visited David Waverly the night before," I said. "The cab picked him up across the street."

"He could have given them the wrong address." I could hear Nash tapping his finger against the phone. "I wonder why he didn't drive."

"I can ask."

"I forgot how cozy you are with Ed Sweeney, Miss Albright. By all means, ask."

"I'm not cozy with Ed Sweeney."

"More cozy than me. Particularly since he's heading the sale of my business."

"Cheer up. With all the bad press, Ed doesn't think it'll sell."

"Because I lost all the clients that would go with the sale." Nash cleared his throat. "Anything else, Miss Albright?"

"I don't think David Waverly was driving the Corvette."

"What?"

"I have a still from the security footage. You should look at it. The police, too."

"Bring it here."

"Did I do good?"

No finger tapping, but also no comment.

"Please don't make 'no praise' a rule," I begged. "This information might cost me a weird relationship with a communist dictator."

"I don't even know what that means." Nash chuckled. "But you did good, kid."

TWENTY-TWO

#RestingBFace #BahamaBankroll

NASH WAS NOT AT THE office. I dropped off the photos and aimed Lucky toward Black Pine Group. I could understand why Nash disliked Ed Sweeney. Not just because Ed headed the corporate buyout of Nash Security. That was business, after all. Ed was Jolene's uncle. Relationships with the relatives of ex-spouses could be tricky and in towns like Black Pine, it was hard to avoid them. According to Remi, Vicki's kin had a habit of hitting Daddy up for money. By staying in California, Vicki had dodged any Spayberrys looking for celebrity freebies. As the child of a bitter divorce, I learned to dance between families.

I could pirouette between Nash and Ed Sweeney, too. No problemo.

Vehicles filled Black Pine Group's parking lot, although David Waverly's Corvette was noticeably absent. I hurried through the big glass doors. The office seemed businessy quiet, per ushe. Even Elaine, the receptionist, wore her normal glare. Elaine had what my publicist, Sherry, called RBF. «Resting bitch face.»

Sherry felt everyone should smile big. All. The. Time. Her favorite saying was "fake it until you make it." Because I had spent most of my childhood in LA, I had thought she had meant boobs.

I smoothed my beaded Saint Laurent t-shirt, pasted on a Sherry-worthy big smile, and strode to the reception desk. "Hi, Elaine. I'm here to see Ed again."

Elaine folded her hands over her keypad. "He's not available. Everyone else is busy."

"He's not here or he's not available?"

Elaine smirked.

Behind Elaine, a woman in a dark suit and knotted Hermès scarf popped through an office door and ran-walked down the hall. Two men in ties followed, also run-walking.

Elaine spun in her chair to watch them, leaving me free to gawk the office sprint.

The woman yanked open the door to a conference room and the trio hurried inside. Another office door banged open and two more businessy types rushed out, their arms heavy with copier boxes filled with binders. They hammered on the door to the conference room with elbows and toes until the door opened.

"What's going on?" I asked.

Elaine twisted back to face me. "I can't say. And I wouldn't anyway. You need to leave."

The Hermés-scarf woman slipped out of the room, poked her head into reception, and spoke in a quick staccato that still managed a Georgia drawl. "Elaine, honey, can I borrow you for a minute?" She unstaccatoed. "I'm sorry, ma'am. We're not taking appointments today."

Elaine pushed from her desk. "I'm sure you can see your own way to the door, Miss Albright." She hurried toward the woman. The door closed behind them.

Shizzles. Was Ed here or not?

I leaned over the reception desk, tapped the space bar on her keypad, and swiveled the monitor toward me. The BPG screensaver slid away, revealing Candy Crush. I minimized the game, checked Elaine's other open windows, and found the scheduler. Under Ed Sweeney's name, the entire day had been blocked off for "vacation." I clicked on his vacation tab and learned Ed had taken two weeks.

Zoinkies, what a coinkydink.

Clicking on a tab showed Ed had scheduled the trip six months ago. "Savannah-Nassau Regatta. Limited contact."

The thrill of discovery petered out. Ed sailed often. No surprise there. I glanced at the closed conference room door, knowing Elaine and her upside down smile would be back soon. But why had Ed gone to David's two days before his vacation?

I escaped out of the "vacation" note box. Clicked on Monday's schedule. Ed's Mercedes had gone to the shop. Elaine had written, "Dealer pick up. Request rental." Again, nothing headline worthy. Ed must have skipped the rental to hang out at his friend's house, then taxied home. Designated driver stuff. Sarah was gone. Ed probably offered David consolation before he left on vacation, knowing they would toss back a few. They were poker and office buddies, after all.

Returning the screen to Candy Crush, I swiveled the monitor back. I still hadn't talked to William Dixon. The trip might not be wasted. As I reached for the monitor to check William Dixon's schedule, the BPG's front door opened. Ushering in a hellstorm.

Jolene. In her post-interrogation garb. I didn't know Lily Pulitzer sold yoga outfits. Adorbs. However, the visible anger didn't match. Lilly has a much happier vibe. Jolene should have gone with Helmut Lang.

"What are you doing here?" Jolene strode forward, each step marked by a finger jab. "I told you to drop this nonsense. Do you know what you did?"

I thought over the various things I had done. Reporting a painting had gotten her in the most trouble, but I didn't want to take a chance on saying the wrong thing. "I heard you had to speak to the police. I hope it went well."

"You hope it went well?"

I nodded, focusing on summoning Julia, and edged around Elaine's desk.

"I warned you." Jolene paced toward me, forcing me around the desk. "I told Wyatt I'm going to sue him. He knows I mean it because I've done it before."

"Jolene, please. I understand you want to sell your half of the business, but sue him? We're trying to figure out what happened to Sarah Waverly. It's not personal."

"Getting questioned by the police is personal, Maizie. Very personal. Kind of like how you'll feel when you end up in a California prison."

"Totally get that." We had rounded the desk and I backed toward the hallway of offices. Where was Julia when I needed her? "I guess you must be really worried about David Waverly."

"What are you implying?"

I stopped before the office door interring Elaine and the rest of BPG. "No one knows where David Waverly's gone. And you two seemed...friendly. You saw him Friday on the boat, Saturday at the cove, and Sunday for poker, right?"

Jolene's blue eyes glittered. The same way a shark's fin glitters as it pushes out of the water and hits the sunlight.

The door behind me opened, revealing a packed house. Standing room only in the BPG conference room. Everyone but David Waverly and Ed Sweeney.

William Dixon strode through the door and closed it behind him. "What's going on out here? Is there a problem?"

Jolene's mouth pursed. "Bill, I want to talk about David."

Ignoring Jolene, William glanced at me. "Can I help you?"

"I was looking for Ed."

He turned back to Jolene. "About David. Can you wait in my office?"

"Sure, Bill." Jolene leaned toward me and muttered, "We're not finished. Good luck with your next probation meeting." The implied threat in her eyes promised bad luck in my next probation meeting.

That woman might be scarier than Vicki.

Dixon watched Jolene sashay down the hall, then turned to me. "Ed's on vacation. You were in his office yesterday, waiting to talk to me?"

"That's right. About David Waverly, actually."

"You were working for David. You and Wyatt Nash." Dixon's voice dropped and he stepped closer. "In fact, Waverly had employed Nash for the last month."

I nodded and scooted back a step.

He pushed forward. I slid back. We tangoed toward the lobby.

"Are you still working for Waverly?"

"Not really." I hedged, unsure of where this conversation

headed. "Aren't you friends with David? I heard he didn't show up for work yesterday. Any idea where we went?"

Dixon's stern features darkened. "Tell me what you know about the money."

My butt collided with the reception desk. "What money?"

"The Black Pine Group funds. How can you be investigating Waverly's wife and not notice what's going on in his bank accounts?"

"Um." Note to self: ask Nash about bank accounts.

Dixon edged closer, looming over me. "If you and Wyatt Nash are any kind of detectives, you'll find those funds."

"Um?" I had run out of words and room. I slid along the desk until my butt touched air.

His finger shot out and stopped three millimeters from my throat. "You think we don't know people? You find our money or I'm making some calls."

"People?"

"People." He peppered the final word with a look that would make an evil villain flinch.

I flinched, too. Then got the hells out.

I SPENT ABOUT THIRTY SECONDS LOOKING for Lucky when it occurred to me to look for Nash's Silverado instead.

"Really?" I said. "It's still daylight. Not that I don't appreciate a lift. I swear the helmet is a million degrees. Luckily, my trainer Jerry says sweat is good for—"

"Is Ed Sweeney inside?"

I shook my head. "He's on vacation."

"Get in." Nash jerked his head at the passenger door. "There's been a development."

I hurried around the truck and clambered inside. Before I could get my seatbelt on, Nash peeled out of the parking lot. The quick swing threw me against his shoulder. I pushed away, rubbing my nose.

"I have some developments, too," I said. "You won't believe

what William Dixon told me."

"David Waverly is dead."

"Oh." My head fell against the seat back.

"Lamar's buddy on the force said Fulton cops got around the vehicle warrant by bringing in a K9 unit. The K9 smelled the body in the trunk."

"Wow."

Nash cut me a sharp glance. "Are you okay?"

"Sure." I turned to look out my window and pinched my thumb skin. "Where are we going?"

"You said Ed Sweeney was in that taxi Monday night. He didn't mention it when you talked to him Tuesday. He's the last person who saw Waverly alive, that we know of. We're headed to his house before the police figure it out."

"He's not home. He put in for a vacation six months ago for a sailing trip."

"Dammit." Nash swerved the truck into a parking lot, spinning the wheel. The Silverado fishtailed and slammed to a stop facing the road.

I slowly eased forward in my seat, pulling the seatbelt from its tight cinch.

The black Sprinter van drove past the parking lot and whipped into a Mrs. Winter's Chicken across the street.

I hoped Al didn't have a boom mike especially made for picking up conversations in trucks. Knowing Vicki, she'd probably find it a worthy investment.

Grabbing his phone out of the console, Nash looked at me. "Are you sure about this? You just talked to him yesterday. He doesn't mention going to Waverly's the night before and doesn't mention he's leaving on vacation the next day. That's pretty damn hinky."

"We didn't have much time to talk. I went in to speak to Dixon and he had an emergency that interrupted our meeting. And now I know what that was all about. And it's important."

"First things first. Let me see if I can talk to Ed."

"Did you tell the police about the taxi?"

"And get accused of obstruction again? They have a tip to check the Community Management security footage. They'll figure it out. We need to get to Ed first before he's sitting in an interview room and waiting on charges."

"You don't think he could have murdered David Waverly? Should we be talking to a possible killer who stashes people in Corvettes?" I realized my voice had gone all high and reedy, but I couldn't help it.

"Are you going to hyperventilate?" Nash placed a hand on the back of my neck and squeezed. "Maybe you should lean over."

That hand worked better than Prozac. I took a deep breath. "I'm fine."

"Listen, I saw the pictures you left at the office. That wasn't Ed in the Corvette Wednesday morning. We know Ed went home in a taxi on Tuesday. Someone else, trying to look like David Waverly, was driving the Corvette the next morning." He slipped his hand off my neck and clamped it on the steering wheel. "That was solid investigative work."

"Thanks."

"I'm still not sure if Ed Sweeney is involved. That's why I want to talk to him." He thumbed through his phone's contacts. "You can wait in the truck."

"No, I can handle it," I said quickly. "If Ed's on a murderous rampage, he's only been charming to me."

"Ted Bundy was also charming."

"I thought you were trying to help me feel better." I took a deep breath and let it out slowly. "Before you talk to Ed, you should hear what William Dixon told me. We might have a motive." I repeated my encounter with Dixon.

"Holy shit." Nash started the Silverado.

"Where are we going?"

"Back to the office. I can't think here and we need a plan. I didn't notice anything in the Waverly bank accounts, but I want to look again."

He had used "we." If I wasn't dealing with the realities of embezzlement and murder, I would have broken rule number two and hugged him.

TWENTY-THREE

#thetroublewithtears
#ConfessionsofaJuliaPinkertonWannabe

"WHAT PEOPLE?" NASH WAS GOING to wear a rut in his office floor. Lucky for him they knew how to make strong floors back in the day. "What did Dixon mean by people?"

"I don't know." I squirmed on the couch, pulled a balled pair of socks from behind a cushion, and discreetly shoved them back.

"We don't have 'people' in Black Pine. If that's the 'people' he's talking about."

"I don't know what 'people' you're talking about either."

"You're telling me Julia Pinkerton never did a gangster episode?"

"Like the mob? I did a 'gangsta' episode where Julia infiltrated a gang to convince a teen who was a talented spoken word poet to resist the pressure to become a thug and—" I stopped at his look. "I know. Rule one."

"Did Dixon really say, 'our money?'" continued Nash. "Does he mean 'our money' or BPG's money? If it's 'our money,' who is our?"

"Some or all of the poker buddies? Ed Sweeney, Dixon, and Jolene?"

Rubbing his mouth and shaking his head, Nash turned to make another pass in his rut.

"Three out of the four work at Black Pine Group and Jolene has certainly been busy there, trying to get your business sold." She also seemed crafty enough but Nash seemed touchy on the subject of Jolene, so I kept that thought to myself. "William Dixon was hostile. Actually, the only one who's been forthcoming in that group is Ed Sweeney."

Nash snorted.

"Ed made the plans six months ago. And why would he go on a scheduled vacation when all this blew up? They'd know his plans. If I had schemed to double-cross my friends, I wouldn't take off. I'd wait it out to not look suspicious."

Nash stopped, shoved his hands in his pockets, and rocked back on his heels. "We don't know why Ed Sweeney visited David Waverly Monday night. Except his vehicle was in the shop."

"But now we know Waverly and maybe others had embezzled from the Black Pine Group. The loss was flagged on Tuesday, judging by the way Dixon acted when I spoke to Ed at their office. Do you think Ed could have figured it out before Dixon and went home with David to talk to him?"

"This is a mare's nest." Nash stopped at the tall window and peered out into the street. "I need to get us clear of this mess and the sooner the better. I can't see waiting on police procedures if there's a possible mob angle, even with the threat of obstruction charges. And then there's Jolene. She knows we turned in those photos of her and Waverly on the Bournes' dock. With Waverly dead, she's sure to get hauled in for questioning again. Probably made Black Pine PD's suspect list."

I drew out the words slowly, "Jolene said she might sue."

"She threatened to castrate me. She promised to sue. If she's not involved, I better find proof."

"Wow." I took her prison promises more seriously. "Did you find out why she met Waverly?"

"Jolene said they visited privately to talk about my buyout." He glared at the window. "In a bikini."

"It was a nice day."

"Don't worry. Waverly isn't her type. But she's the type who would use the bikini to distract him. Sarah was taken while Waverly and Jolene were on the lake. Jolene likely met with Waverly to persuade him to relax until the buyout went through."

I wasn't worried about Jolene and Waverly, but now I felt a

teeny worried about Jolene and Nash. He had major post-relationship codependent complications. I focused on keeping my voice neutral. "Okay."

Nash scowled and pivoted to face me. "Let's regroup. At least one other person was partnered with Waverly in the embezzlement. Maybe something went sour and the partner needed to threaten Waverly and therefore kidnapped Sarah. That could be why he was cagey about reporting her disappearance. He obviously didn't deliver whatever they wanted and they killed him."

"It certainly sheds a different light on things."

"Ed's still our best lead since he's the last known person to see Waverly alive."

"He must be involved."

"I don't think he's smart enough to pull this off. He's a great salesman, but he's kind of soft."

"Soft?"

"The kind of guy who takes a couple weeks off every few months to go sailing." Nash's lip curled.

No wonder he had such disgust for my previous lifestyle. In Nash's book, taking a vacation made you soft. But then, my parents held a similar attitude toward work.

"Someone who plans a kidnapping is going to be more hard-edged than Ed Sweeney," he continued. "Devious. Organized. Patient enough to wait for the opportunity to grab her. Ed's an instant gratification sort of guy."

"They waited until you weren't watching Sarah. But why would David have you watch her in the first place?"

"Exactly. Why have me watch a woman who is plainly not having an affair? David didn't have any evidence except a 'feeling.' And he was so desperate, he'd take an inexperienced actress watching her over no one." Nash slammed his fist into his palm. "That sumbitch must have known Sarah could be taken. He got himself and his wife killed."

I drew my breath in. "Sarah's dead?"

"Kidnapping's a felony case. They wouldn't risk keeping her alive. What would be the point now that Waverly is dead?"

"Oh."

"You look funny again." He moved to the couch and stood over me. "Are you going to cry?"

"No." I sniffled and pinched my thumb skin. "Of course not. I knew she could be dead."

A fat tear rolled off my cheek and splashed onto my lap. I pinched harder and two more tears ran down my nose.

"Hey." Nash dropped to a crouch and rested his hands on either side of my legs. "Don't cry. Maybe Sarah's not dead."

"I'm not crying." I rubbed my eyes. "Private investigators don't cry. Julia Pinkerton never cried. Except for the time that lab monkey died in 'Dirty Monkey Business.' But do you have a tissue?" A hiccuping sob broke and I clamped a hand over my mouth.

"Come on, now." Nash leaned forward and patted my shoulder. "Don't worry. I'm not giving up. I've got to see this through."

"Me, too," I whimpered. "I lost Sarah Waverly. If it wasn't for me, she wouldn't be dead."

"Maizie, don't say that."

"It's true. I may as well have killed her myself." I tried a calming breath and it turned into a jerking wail that opened the tear-pressured floodgates.

Sighing, Nash scooted onto the couch and wrapped an arm around my shoulders.

I cried harder.

He pulled me closer, fitted my head under his chin, and hugged me against him.

I clutched his Scorpions t-shirt in my fist and bawled. Heaving, jerky sobs that soaked his shirt and bloated my face into what would look like a blotchy, pink orb.

"I think we were duped. It's not your fault. Please don't cry." Slow, soft circles caressed my back.

"It's just so horrible." I pulled in a lurching breath. "Sarah and David Waverly are dead. If I didn't suck at everything, I might have seen who had taken her."

"You don't suck at everything." He relaxed the grip on my shoulder to smooth the damp hair away from my face. "I let you follow her when I knew you had no clue how to do a proper surveillance. Besides, you have a lot of ideas. You're pretty good at this."

I peeled my face from his shirt and blinked up at him through spiky lashes.

"You are."

Nash had read my mind. And the Paul Newmans had lost their cool edge. They looked soft and unfocused, the blue dazzling in my tear-stained sight.

He stroked a finger across my cheek, caught a tear, and wiped it on his t-shirt. "You're more than a pretty face. Must be hard for some folks to see that."

"Thank you," I said, feeling ashamed and awkward and not pretty. A fresh bout of tears approached. I ducked my head against his chest. "It's not really me, though. Julia's smart. I just try to think like her."

"Darlin', look at me." Nash ran his thumb along the curve of my jaw and cradled my chin in his palm. The thumb traced the edges of my swollen bottom lip. "Don't talk like that. Julia Pinkerton is a character. Writers gave her thoughts."

"I'm sorry." I sniffled. "It does sound a little schizo. I don't hear voices or anything. I just try to channel what I think she'd do. When I say channel, I mean—"

His thumb pressed against my lips. "Maizie."

"Muh?"

"I meant the ideas are yours. Not Julia Pinkerton's."

O.M.G. That was even better than the donut line. Nash could write a Nicholas Sparks movie.

His thumb lifted and my lips felt unbearably cool. For a long, slow second, his gaze remained fixed on my mouth. The big palm slid off my chin to cup my cheek. His fingers dug into my hair.

I pulled in a breath and tightened my grip on his t-shirt.

This was the big moment. I didn't look fabulous. A sticky film of snot and tears covered my face. But Nash didn't care. He thought better of me than anyone I'd ever known. Even my parents. Which wasn't saying much. But still. He preferred me to Julia

Pinkerton.

All my misgivings about costar/boss love issues fell away.

Arching against his chest, I tipped my head back. My tear-dampened hair slid across my shoulders and trickled down my back. I licked my lips and parted them. Which felt sexy. And practical, as I was unable to breathe through my nose.

Nash leaned forward. His breath skated across my face. His hand slipped from my hair.

I waited for it to land on my boob, the usual man-hand resting place.

Instead, his arm dropped from my shoulders. "Feeling better?"

I snapped my head down, ramming my chin into his shoulder. He barked an "ouch" and I scooted away.

O.M.G. I was the dumbest girl alive. No amount of Julia Pinkerton channeling could help me. Why would he want to kiss me when Sarah Waverly could be dead? Could I be more insensitive?

Clearing his throat, he slid to the other end of the couch. "Ready? We need to do some research to find Ed Sweeney. He's not answering his phone."

I took a hearty sniff, swiped a forearm across my face, and hopped from the couch. "He's sailing for the Bahamas from Savannah at Magnolia Marina. *A Little Nauti*. That's his boat."

"Good work, Miss Albright." The hard glint to his eyes had returned.

"I saw the photos in his office." I gritted my teeth in an effort to smile. "Excuse me for a moment while I step into the bathroom."

"Sure. Fine." Nash rose from the couch and strode into his office. "Let me see if I can talk to someone at Magnolia Marina."

I lunged for the hall door. We were back to Miss Albright. A new bout of tears threatened to gut me. Now that I was already puffy, I might as well let them fly.

THE BATHROOM WAS LOCATED DOWN the old-timey hall from Nash's office. Like a tiny version of Nash's office, it consisted of two rooms. The front held the sink and a small chest of drawers where I had snooped and found Nash's Acqua di Selva aftershave as well as other toiletries. The back room had a poky stall shower and the toilet. More clues that told me Nash lived in his office and not in the home he had most likely lost to Jolene in their divorce wars.

Jolene had done a doozy on Nash. Which made me wonder if she had done a doozy on David Waverly as well. She was shady and devious, revealed by her quick friendship with Vicki and horrible treatment of Nash. She loved money, shown in her totally rad taste in clothes and office design. Jolene probably bought Nash's classic designer duds back in their marriage days, evident by their wear and tear. And she was willing to debase herself, as evidenced by the bikini meeting. How far off could she be from kidnapping, extortion, and embezzlement? Even murder?

She was evil. I'd even bet her bikini meeting had nothing to do with the buyout and everything to do with the fact that she was putting the screws to Waverly. Maybe the poker buddies had partnered in an embezzlement caper. But Jolene got greedy. Probably hired a hit man. Jolene had the hit man kidnap Sarah while she and David launched their respective yachts. They'd docked at the Bournes. Jolene had sidetracked Waverly with her bikini, then lowered the boom.

"I've just kidnapped your wife. Give me all the money or else Sarah gets it," I said in Jolene's snarky drawl.

Splashing cold water on my face, I blotted it dry and drew out my makeup bag.

"No, please Jolene," I continued in David Waverly's voice while pulling out my Bobbi Brown Creamy Concealer. "I'll do anything you want. As long as you're in that bikini."

Squinting my eyes—bright green from crying and made greener from the splotchy red—I replied as Jolene. "Transfer all the money to my account in the..." I considered the possibilities. Vicki kept money in the Bahamas. She said offshore money in the Caymans was passé, everyone did the Bahamas now. Unless you had Panama money. Besides, the Bahamas seemed popular with Black Pine's glitterati.

"The Bahamas. Give me proof you've done as I asked at the Cove Saturday night. Then I might let Sarah live. Remember, I'll be watching you all weekend."

"It's already in the Bahamas' bank, Jolene." My David Waverly impression was not great, but I was on a roll. "As poker buddies and cheating spouses, we've been planning this forever. I used your ex-husband to watch my wife. Because I hired a PI, everyone will think she ran away with her pretend lover and at the same time make Nash look like an idiot. Ha."

My maniacal laughter also needed work. But I might have figured out what had happened to Sarah. Even if Nash wouldn't appreciate the thought of his ex-wife popping off the Waverlys.

Outside the wooden door, the floorboards creaked.

Great, Nash probably heard me talking to myself.

"Just a minute," I called and turned on the sink faucet to drown my Jolene/David dialogue.

I tossed my bronzer brush into my makeup bag and slipped into the toilet room. A few minutes later, I pushed open the powder room door. The room was dark. I hesitated in the doorway, using the light from the toilet room to see into the small space. My makeup bag lay on the sink top, undisturbed. The water still ran.

Weird.

I glanced at the light, wondering if a bulb had blown, and stepped toward the sink to turn off the faucet.

The toilet room door swung closed, throwing the room into darkness. I fumbled for the light.

A body slipped behind me, clamping a hand over my mouth.

My fingers dug into the hand and the barrel of a gun rammed my ribs. My hands flew away and into the air. I drew in a shuddering breath and tasted antibacterial soap.

The old hide-behind-the-door trick. They did it a million times on *Julia Pinkerton*. And *Kung Fu Kate*. Why hadn't I seen this coming?

"This is your last warning." The voice was low and throaty, obviously disguised. The gun jabbed into my back. "Get Nash to drop the case or I *will* kill you."

Thank God my bladder had been recently emptied.

The pistol pulled away my ribs. "I'll be watching you."

I tried to let out a breath but the hand on my mouth tightened.

The gun slammed into my skull. A skyrocket burst inside my head and I slumped to the ground like a spent roman candle tube.

TWENTY-FOUR

#hitandrunholla #assinhand

B RIGHT LIGHT WOKE ME, BUT I refused to open my eyes. My head throbbed, my body ached, and for a moment I feared Vicki had slipped me in for a surprise nip and tuck. But the voice I heard sounded like Nash, whom I doubted would accompany me to a surgical procedure. He also sounded gentle and concerned, which also didn't fit with the little I knew of Nash. Had Lucky and I been in a smash-up? My brain chased that thought, but hitting a wall of pain, I came up short.

"Maizie. Hon, are you with me?"

A memory swelled against the wall of pain. A gun had been pressed against my ribs.

"Oh my God, I've been shot," I cried. "In the head? How am I not dead? How am I talking?"

"Hush." A hand pressed against my forehead, cool and calming. "You haven't been shot. You're going to be fine."

I opened one eye.

He crouched over me, the icy blue eyes squinting and the scar standing stark white against his tanned skin. No self-tanner needed on this one. He probably didn't use SPF. My thoughts ping-ponged between pain and bronzers.

I shut the eye to find focus.

"Don't move, Maizie. Just lie still a moment and let me check you out."

His hands slipped across my face to the back of my neck and a whopping fireball of agony slammed into me. Followed by the realization that I lay on the floor of the bathroom in the Dixie

Kreme building. I squeezed my eyelids, determined to lie still, but the idea of a bathroom floor was too disgusting. My t-shirt was beaded silk and I couldn't stand for a Saint Laurent to lay in the grime of a Nash's dubious cleaning skills.

I jackknifed and vaulted to my feet. A wave of dizziness and nausea slammed into me. My palms hit the wall and I slid to a crouch, hanging my head between my legs.

"What part of 'lie still so I can check you out' didn't you understand?" Nash snarled.

"The floor is dirty."

"Who cares? You might have a concussion."

"This top is fifteen hundred dollars. Do you think I can afford dry cleaning right now?"

"Criminy." His big palm glided up my back to rest between my shoulder blades. "You've got a goose-egg the size of Detroit on the back of your head. What happened?"

"Oh God." I panted between words, trying to deal with the roiling bitterness in my stomach that was only slightly less awful than the pain in my head. "Someone was in here."

"What?" His head swiveled toward the open doorway.

"They had a gun. They threatened to kill me if I didn't get you to drop the case. Then they must have hit me on the head."

"Shit." Nash rubbed a circle between my shoulders. "I didn't see anyone. They've probably left by now."

The shoulder rubbing helped my stomach. I eased my head up and rested my forearms on my thighs.

"I'll take you to the hospital." At my look, he added, "I'm sure Boomer would pay to get your head checked."

"I don't want him to pay. And I don't want to go to the hospital. We need to talk to Ed Sweeney."

"No. You're done."

I slid my back up the bathroom wall and tried a hard stare. My vision wobbled, but no worse than the time I went clubbing with the Lohan entourage. "I'm fine. I just need some ibuprofen."

"Hell, no. Maizie, you've been bludgeoned by a flippin' unknown assailant. I'll take you to a hospital, the police station, or Boomer

Spayberry's house, but I will not let you—"

"I've had concussions before. They won't give me a prescription and I'll spend the entire day at the hospital. And guess who will find me there? Paparazzi love chasing ambulances more than lawyers." I narrowed my eyes. "And they'll find out I was bludgeoned by an unknown assailant in the Nash Security Solutions' bathroom."

"Are you threatening blackmail?" His scar stretched and throbbed against the firming of his jaw.

"No, I'm only pointing out facts." I took a deep breath and pushed off the wall. "We must be getting close if they're taking a risk like this. You could've come out of the office at any time and seen them."

"Dammit. This deal's gotten too dangerous. We don't even know who hit you."

"The only person who couldn't have done it was Ed Sweeney." I rubbed the back of my neck, wishing for the return of Nash's comforting hand and gentle voice. "Ed's sailing."

"His boat's still docked in Savannah. But he's not answering his phone."

"Then I guess we need to go to Savannah to talk to him."

"Not we. Me."

"You're going to leave me in Black Pine with my assailant? I didn't stop you from dropping the case. That means they'll try to kill me."

Whatever Nash felt about me, I knew he was protective. He'd have to take me with him to Savannah.

I WAS WRONG.

When Nash told me, I should "stay put in the office with the doors locked until he got back" and I told him, I wouldn't "wait for someone to shoot down the door" and I'd "rather take my chances following him to Savannah on Lucky," the man picked me up, threw me over his shoulder, and carried me to his truck.

While I kicked and hollered about Neanderthal tactics and

the effects of a sudden blood rush to my aching head, the black Sprinter van across the street slid open their door to take film.

More pictures of me with a man's hand on my ass. And this time, my butt was next to the man's face. Even better, the man flipped off the camera crew as he jogged down the steps of the Dixie Kreme building. In fact, his right hand tightened the clench on my butt as he drew out the middle left finger for the cameras.

Nash really needed better PR awareness. Particularly when they were hired by Vicki. That bit would probably make the cut for the new season's trailer.

Twenty minutes later, my butt and aching head could be found in my DeerNose bedroom. Remi hung upside down on the bed, grinning, while I hammered on the door, spending more voice time on "unfair treatment of women" and "unethical use of brute force."

"Baby girl." Boomer Spayberry had taken a position on the other side of the door. Probably relaxed in a chair with a gun on his lap while thumbing through his phone. "Nash said some attention you received today could land you in legal trouble and serious harm. It'd be for your own benefit to stay home while he's out of town."

"Daddy, this is the twenty-first century. You're acting like it's the Wild West or something. Not that I've ever done a western—"

I stopped myself from breaking rule one. Then realized I had started applying Nash's rules to my family. "This is ridiculous. Nash thinks he's protecting me when all he's done is shown this person I wasn't able to prevent Nash from dropping the case. They're still going to want to—"

I shut up before the words "kill me" fell on Boomer's ears. Not that Daddy was listening.

"You've been in the news too much, girl. If Nash wants to do some undercover work out of town, he doesn't need your baggage tagging along. He knows those reporters won't cross my property line. I've threatened them with lead in their backside."

I leaned against the door. Nash knew the DeerNose cabin's security system. He had let Boomer think I needed to be protected from paparazzi to protect me from my attacker.

A chair scraped against the pine floors. "I'm headed back to DeerNose HQ, but I told Carol Lynn you're to stay here until I give the say-so. She agrees you need a break from the press, too. And to make you feel better, she's fixing y'all chicken and dumplings for lunch."

"I hate chicken and dumplin's." Remi flipped backward off the bed and slid underneath.

"And Remi. You will eat your momma's food. If I hear you've fed those damn dogs your lunch again, I'm going to tan your backside."

Boomer's boots clunked down the hall. A few seconds later, a door banged.

Remi poked her head out. "I'm getting out of here. You coming?"

"You're running from lunch? How can anyone not like chicken and dumplings?" I said the words before the implication hit me. "What do you mean you're getting out? The house is alarmed. Isn't it?"

Remi scrunched her nose. "I know a way out. No cameras neither."

I gaped. If I was going to defy a killer, I didn't want to hide in my father's house. If Remi could get out, a killer could get in. I was putting my family in danger.

And that was something Julia Pinkerton would never do.

Nor Maizie Albright.

"Remi, if I can get you out of lunch, will you promise to keep the alarm on and not leave the house?"

Remi hopped to her feet. "How're you going to get me out of lunch?"

"I learned a thing or two when I didn't feel like studying with my tutor."

She cocked her head.

"It's like homeschool for actors. I also need you to show me how to sneak out."

"Are you taking me with y'all?"

"Absolutely not. I need you to stay in the cabin." I fisted my hands on my hips. "But I'm going to teach you how to heat a thermometer. If you're sick, you can lay in bed and not eat your lunch. How about that?"

She narrowed her eyes. "I also want a Happy Meal."

"I don't have time to get you a—" I shrugged. "Fine. I, of all people, understand forbidden fruit. You're crazy to want a Happy Meal over Carol Lynn's cooking, but I get it."

"No fruit. I want French fries." She spat on her palm and held out her hand. "Shake on it, sister."

R EMI WAS AS GOOD AS her spit-slimed palm. Thirty seconds later I had talked (begged) the LA HAIR girls into borrowing a car. Remi showed me her route for sneaking out of the cabin and I made a mental note to add an alarm to the doggy door.

I walked Lucky to the road and made a big production of driving away to lure my stalker from the Spayberry cabin. I drove to McDonald's, returned to the cabin to sneak Remi her Happy Meal, and made a bigger production of driving away before heading to LA HAIR.

I couldn't tell if my stalker still stalked, but the *Albright* van caught on pretty quick.

Inside LA HAIR, Rhonda and Tiffany stood before the reception desk, purses strapped to their fronts. One quilted paisley and big enough to hide a rocket launcher. The other a combination of faux fur, studs, and leather fringe. Also big enough to carry a substantial weapon. Knowing Tiffany, she probably did. They also had roll-on suitcases. Pink zebra stripes. Black with a torn pocket and missing a wheel.

I eyed the suitcases and purses, then the women. Rhonda's sausage curls had been replaced by an up-do that looked like a giant donut. Tiffany's blue ombre shag hadn't changed, but her eyeliner appeared fresh and plentiful.

"Are you girls going somewhere?" I asked.

"Road trip," Rhonda squealed. She rushed forward to hug me and bounced us in a circle. "I'm so excited. I love Savannah."

"Wait a minute." I disentangled myself from Rhonda. "I'm not taking you to Savannah. I just need to borrow a car."

"I'm not letting you drive my Firebird to Savannah." Tiffany reached inside her faux fur and leather trimmed missile silo and looped a key holder around her wrist. Plastic cards, charms, and a pink-jeweled pepper spray mister rattled against her arm. "Besides, we want to watch when you tell that detective to go to hell."

"I'm not even sure if it's a good idea to chase after Nash to Savannah. I know it's not a good idea to take you two. I don't want to put you in danger."

Tiffany cocked a brow.

"David Waverly is dead."

Grabbing her black roll-on, Tiffany grabbed my arm and walked us to the back door. "Now I know you need us. I thought it was bad, but shit's really going to hit the fan now."

"What do you mean?"

"You need some cover." Rhonda shoved an orange and silver cheetah print cap on my head and handed me a pair of over-sized tortoiseshell sunglasses. "Tiff and I've been talking. You need some protection from the paparazzi."

"She means we've been watching E! online and we don't think you have a clue about the shit storm that's about to swallow you whole," said Tiffany. "Did you know reporters are staking out the courthouse?"

My stomach dropped. "What courthouse?"

"Beverly Hills. Hoping to catch your judge and ask him about your involvement with a missing woman in Black Pine, Georgia."

Rhonda hooted. "They said Black Pine on the news. They showed Black Pine Mountain, Black Pine Lake, and the Deer-Nose factory. We're famous."

"Oh, God." My knees buckled.

Tiffany jerked me to standing. "You need help, girl. TMZ got an anonymous tip you were involved in Sarah Waverly's murder. The tipper claimed because you wanted to work for Nash, you bungled a case and got the wife killed."

"Holy crap. I'm going to lose my probation." I shook off Tiffany's arm and swung to face them. "Jolene."

"Jolene?" said Rhonda. "What do you mean Jolene? Is that some kind of code word?"

"No. Nash's ex-wife, Jolene Sweeney. You met her that first night at the Cove."

"The skinny bitch, Rhon," Tiffany mumbled past the cigarette dangling from her lips. "Realtor."

"Jolene threatened to get me sent to a So Cal pen. And she promised to sink Nash. And castrate him."

"Oh my stars," said Rhonda. "Did she also kill David Waverly?"

"That's a good question, Rhonda. Maybe. And maybe she had Sarah Waverly murdered." I skipped the part about hitting me on the head and threatening to kill me.

Rhonda rounded her eyes at Tiffany.

"Anyway, that's why Nash went to Savannah without me. Ed Sweeney's getting ready to sail off on a vacation. He was the last known person to talk to David Waverly. Waverly and somebody else embezzled from their company. We think Ed knows something and is using the vacation as an excuse to cool it."

"Jolene Sweeney is Nash's ex-wife," said Tiffany. "And this Ed and this Jolene are also related?"

I nodded.

"And Jolene knew David Waverly, too?"

"Jolene spent the morning Sarah Waverly disappeared entertaining Waverly in a bikini. Then met with him at the Cove the following night." I quoted Nash, "It's a mare's nest."

"Shit, girl," said Tiffany. "That ain't a mare's nest, it's a flippin' fire ant hill."

"It gets better. Jolene, David, Ed, and Bill Dixon are poker buddies at the Club. Three of them work at Black Pine Group where there's now money missing."

"We need to get you out of here," said Rhonda. "A road trip is the perfect excuse."

We walked past the line of hair stations. At the sinks, Shelly raised a soapy hand to wave. Rhonda yanked opened the back door and Tiffany pushed me through. The afternoon sunshine heated the broken blacktop in the rear of the strip mall. Tiffany unlocked a maroon sedan trimmed with gold. Rhonda called shotgun and I climbed into the backseat next to a large box with the word "Shithead" written on it.

"Sorry about the box," said Tiffany. "It's my ex-husband's crap he hasn't picked up. I keep meaning to set it on fire and throw it in his yard and haven't gotten around to it."

"I thought you were going to rub the box with meat and chuck it in the backyard for his pit bull to chew on," said Rhonda. "I like the fire idea better. It's got more flair. And the neighbors will see it."

"That's what I thought, too," said Tiffany.

I stopped worrying about endangering my new friends and started worrying about my new friends endangering my stalker.

TWENTY-FIVE

#RoadTrip #MarinaMayhem

THE DRIVE TO SAVANNAH SHOULD have taken about four-and-a-half hours. Instead, it took just over three. Tiffany kept her steely gaze on the road, cursing the left lane huggers as she whipped the Firebird around semis and minivans.

Rhonda DJ'd. Loudly. Consistently. And mostly pop country.

Gripping Shithead's box to keep it from banging into my shoulder, I swallowed Motrin and reflected on us dying in a horrific accident as a remedy for the pain in my head. Also useful for distracting myself from obsessing over the gun-toting stalker who caused the pain in my head. In between distressing thoughts, I checked for tails. Tails other than the black Sprinter van that occasionally sped alongside with a camera glued to its window.

Vicki had me followed. No reason to make my friends self-conscious because I had an overbearing mother. Just like when I was sixteen. Even the threat of death by a murderous kidnapper couldn't get me to stand up to my mother.

I switched back to focusing on the pain in my head.

"Here we go, ladies," called Tiffany.

The exit for Savannah approached. Rhonda turned down the music and we peered out the window, oohing and awing.

Spanish moss dripped from the spreading branches of oak trees. The clapboard houses and brick buildings aged as we drew closer to the water. Palmetto palms and flowering plants grew along the road until they gave way to reedy marshes. Same state but a totally different view from the mountain and lake vista of Black Pine.

"So, what's the plan, Grownup Teen Detective?" asked Tiffany.

"Besides driving 300 miles to stick it to the man?"

"Head to the marina. We'll look for Nash's truck and Ed's boat to make sure they're there."

"You think Nash is going to let you waltz in and hang out with him?"

"No." My stomach rolled at the thought of what Nash might do. Possibly toss me into the Savannah River. "We're staying clear of Nash. I just want to know where he is. I want to talk to Ed Sweeney by myself if he's still there."

"What do you hope to learn from Ed that Nash doesn't already know?"

"I want to know what he and David Waverly talked about that night. Also what Ed knows about Black Pine Group's missing money and if David Waverly was connected. I think Ed will be more forthcoming with me than Nash. Unless Nash has already scared him off."

"Nash's probably scared him off," said Rhonda. "That guy is scary."

"Nash scary?" I said. "Crabby, yes. Scary, not so much."

Rhonda and Tiffany exchanged a look.

"You've got a thing for him, don't you?" said Tiffany.

"What? Nash? Thing? No."

"She does, Tiff," said Rhonda. "She gots it bad. For reals."

"That's crazy. He's my boss. Sort of. And anyway, he's not interested."

"How do you know?" Rhonda turned and peered at me around her headrest. "Tiff, something happened. I can tell by the way she's not looking at me."

"Nothing happened." Nothing except embarrassing myself over and over again with "I think Nash is going to kiss me" incidents. What was I, fifteen?

"What'd you think, Rhon?" asked Tiffany.

"Remember when I asked if you had done it with Shithead?" said Rhonda. "Not the last time, but after the second time you left him? And you wouldn't answer me because you had a makeup hookup?"

"Thanks for reminding me. I blame Cinco de Mayo tequila. "

"Maizie's got that same look in her eye whenever we talk about her boss."

"What look?" My face heated. "I'm an actress. I've got lots of looks. You're probably getting my looks mixed up."

"Sure, Maizie," said Tiffany. "By the way, isn't that Nash's vehicle up ahead?"

"It is?" I shot forward in my seat. "Where?"

Tiffany and Rhonda looked at each other and snort laughed.

"Very funny," I said. "I'm sure the Waverlys appreciate the humor, too. But wait, they can't because they've been murdered and my *boss* and I are trying to figure out who killed them."

That shut down the giggling.

I leaned back and rolled down my window. Fresh salt air washed over my skin, cooling my heated cheeks and ebbing my headache.

"We're sorry," said Rhonda. "We're just teasing."

"I'm sorry, too," I said. "It's nice to have friends who'll give me a hard time and not report it to the tabloids."

"Aw," said Rhonda. "After you talk to Ed Sweeney, maybe we can have a couple Coronas before heading back to Black Pine. Get us some shrimp and grits. Or a Po Boy and some fried oysters. We could go to the Crab Shack!"

My stomach gurgled. "That's a totally awesome idea."

We crossed another marsh and turned onto a smaller road lined with trees. Large, sprawling mansions peeked between vegetation. The road ended at the entrance to Magnolia Marina.

Tiffany pulled over next to the Magnolia Marina sign. "Okay chief, what's the plan?"

The Sprinter van drove past us to find parking.

"Check on the vehicles first. Nash has a Silverado. And see if any are Pine County plates. Look for rentals. Ed would've driven his rental down here."

"Aye, aye."

We crawled through the crowded lot, checking plates.

"There's a rental." Rhonda nodded at a Navigator. "Black Pine plates. Must be Ed Sweeney's."

"I don't see Nash's truck." A wave of relief washed over me. Followed by a wave of anxiety. "Let's find Ed's boat. Maybe he's still here."

We parked and strolled through the parking lot. On the muggy island, my Belstaff motorcycle boots felt clunky and my jeans sticky. Music poured out of the marina's waterfront bar. Cups and people lined the open railings.

"Wow. That's a big party for a Wednesday night," I said.

"You're in Savannah, girl." Rhonda bounced. "That's what I'm talking about. Savannah knows how to have fun."

"How long is this questioning thing going to take?" asked Tiffany, her eyes on the party.

"Help me find Ed's boat and I'll take it from there. You two can hang out at the bar. Maybe watch the parking lot for suspicious peeps. Like Jolene. Especially Jolene. And ignore anyone from that big, black van that's been following us."

"I love being tailed by the paparazzi," said Rhonda.

I didn't have the heart to tell her it wasn't paparazzi. I also didn't have the heart to say she and Tiffany might make the next season of *All is Albright* as extras. Unpaid extras.

We sauntered on the dock and surveyed the pier. Forty-foot sailboats, luxury speedboats, and catamarans filled this harbor.

"These boats make Black Pine Lake yachters look like amateurs," said Tiffany.

"This is going to take a while to find your boat." Rhonda glanced back at Magnolia Marina's bar. "I need to tee-tee."

"And after four hours in the car, I need a drink," said Tiffany. "We'll be back in a minute."

I waved them off, traipsed toward the boardwalk, and began my diligent search for Ed's sailboat. Each dock had an adorable brass lantern hanging from a post, lighting the dock number but not much else. Some yachts had festive party lights, providing me illumination. Most were unlit. At the end of the second pier, the forty-plus-foot *A Little Nauti* bobbed, tall, dark, and silent. With a quick glance around, I scooted closer to the boat, then braved a shout for Ed.

No response.

I waited another moment, considered boarding, and glanced toward the marina. It made more sense to find Ed in the marina restaurant than hanging out alone on his dark boat. He was on vacation. Charming Ed probably sat at the bar with a martini in one hand and his attention on a woman. Maybe his other hand, too.

A thump caused me to turn back toward the boat.

"Hello?" I called. "Ed? It's Maizie."

Nothing. The water sloshed and a neighboring boat butted against the pier.

I shivered and hurried to the boardwalk. Questioning Ed at a party sounded a lot better than waiting for him to return to a dark and desolate sailboat.

BACK AT THE BAR, I waded through a room full of "Shuck it" shirts and more swishy, maxi dresses. Surprisingly, no Paul Newman eyes hid in the crowd, waiting to pounce on me with the "I told you to hide from the homicidal stalker at home" lecture. I found Tiffany and Rhonda parked at the bar. Spotting me, they waved a mai tai and a Corona.

"Have you seen Ed?" I asked.

"You forget, we don't know Ed." Tiffany jerked her chin at the bartender. "But we met Patrick. Say hey, Patrick."

A young, grinning ginger pushed a beer toward me. "Don't I know you? Are you a member?"

"We're with Ed Sweeney. Nice to meet you, Patrick." I stood on my toes to look over the crowd. "Girls, give me some news. Have you seen Nash? Or Jolene?"

"No and no," said Rhonda. "Did you find the sailboat?"

I nodded. "Nobody's home. I'm going to search the bar. This place is packed."

"Who are you looking for?" asked Patrick. "If they're a regular, I probably know them."

I turned toward him. "Ed Sweeney. He sails *A Little Nauti*. He might have been with another guy. Big. Shredded, but not bulky. A scar on his chin. Brilliant blue eyes and sometimes when he smiles, he shows a dimple. It's really heart stopping. But he rarely smiles so I've doubt you've seen the dimple."

"No, you don't have a thing for him at all," said Tiffany.

"I know Ed Sweeney," said Patrick. "I saw him earlier, actually."

"When was this?"

"Couple hours ago."

"Thanks." I chewed my lip. "Ed could have gone out to dinner in Savannah."

"I thought we saw his car," said Tiffany. "The rental."

"Maybe he left with Nash. I should go hang out near the parking lot and wait for him to get back."

"Don't forget we have two lots," said Patrick. "Other one's on the far end of the harbor, near the slip. Not many people park there unless they're using the slip, but you might check it anyway."

"Girls, I'm going to check this other parking lot. Thoroughness is key in an investigation."

"Right." Rhonda's mai tai disappeared through a straw with a powerful squelch. "Let's go."

Tiffany handed Patrick her bottle and wiped her lips on the back of her hand. "Later."

I shot Patrick with my finger and signature catch phrase.

Charlie's Angels we weren't.

But Patrick didn't know that.

THE SECOND PARKING LOT ANCHORED the far end of Magnolia's piers. A wide boat slip gave the yachters access to the water. And as Patrick guessed, the parking lot here was empty. Save for a BMW and a Silverado truck.

The parking lot was surrounded by trees, obscuring the already murky security lighting and making the scene Savannah Spooky. We hid behind the bathroom at the far end of the parking lot. The bathroom smelled like a Febrezed monkey house, making it hard to think. And breathe.

"I should have checked to see if there was another parking lot right away. Nash was here the whole time."

"Nash hasn't seen you yet," said Rhonda. "No way is that guy going to let you skulk around the marina detecting on your own."

"No kidding," said Tiffany. "That man'd be all over you like white on rice. Probably toss you over his shoulder and throw you in the bed of his pickup."

An extraordinary image flooded my mind, beginning with the memory of me bouncing against Nash's back, his hand tightening over my bottom.

Rhonda poked me. "You're doing it again. Focus, Maizie."

"You're right." I took a deep Ujjayi yoga breath. Inhaling Febrezed monkey house did wonders for shaking off my Nash crushing. Unfortunately, my focus moved from plans of action to hurling. I fought off my shudders and stepped away from the building. "I guess we should check on the BMW."

We slid out from behind the bathroom and tiptoe-ran toward the vehicles. At the sedan, I squatted behind its trunk and squinted up at the Silverado.

"No one's in the truck," I whispered. "Thank goodness."

"This is another rental." Rhonda pointed at the sticker in the window of the BMW.

"Fulton County plates, though," I said. "Where's Fulton County?"

"Atlanta," said Tiffany. "That could be anybody."

"It's weird Nash would park right next to this car in an empty lot." I peered into the sedan's back window. "Everyone keeps their cars so clean here."

Rhonda edged around the car to the passenger window. "There's a coffee mug in the cup holder. It's a Black Pine Club mug. I'd know that little crest anywhere. The golf club sticking out of the lake always looks like the Loch Ness monster to me."

"But the Black Pine rental's in the other lot," said Tiffany. "One has to be Ed Sweeney's."

"Who else from Black Pine would be down here?" said Rhonda. "Except for us. And Nash. Why would they rent a car?"

"My friggin' gun-toting stalker. A good stalker would rent a car to better stalk." I backed away from the BMW and bumped against Nash's Silverado. "They must have followed Nash down here."

"Gun-toting stalker? Girl." Rhonda's hand flew off the vehicle to her throat. "Do you think they got Nash?"

I leaned over, supporting my heavy head with my hands. "I need to find Nash and Ed Sweeney. The stalker told me to get Nash to drop the case. If he's down here talking to Ed Sweeney, he obviously did not drop the case."

Rhonda rubbed my back. "It's gonna be okay, Maizie."

"It's not going to be okay," said Tiffany.

I looked up.

Tiffany stood on her toes, looking into the Silverado's window.

"Why is it not going to be okay, Tiffany?"

"Because there's a dead guy in Nash's truck."

TWENTY-SIX

#WeekendAtEd's #HandyCam

"ED SWEENEY HAS A BULLET hole in his head." I couldn't turn off my babbling mechanism. "Someone shot Ed Sweeney in the head. In Nash's truck. He's never going to get the blood out of those seats."

"Stop saying that," moaned Rhonda. "We need to call an ambulance."

"An ambulance ain't going to help this guy," said Tiffany. "I think Maizie's in shock. Her eyes are bigger than her head and she's even whiter than usual."

"I'm in shock, too," said Rhonda. "I'm never drinking a mai tai again. It's not feeling so good."

"No puking near the crime scene, Rhon," said Tiffany. "The cops get testy about that."

I didn't want to know how Tiffany had come across this information, but it did snap me out of my shock. "You're right. This is a crime scene."

"You want my phone for the police?" Tiffany pulled a flip phone covered in rhinestones from her purse.

"You guys should get out of here. Go back to the bar. Or get a hotel room. Just go. But stay where there's a crowd. Like, run through the marina park as fast as you can. Zigzag run," I babbled. "Why didn't we drive over here?"

I didn't want to utter the obvious, but someone with a gun was shooting people in the head. I knew my attacker was packing heat and I let Rhonda and Tiffany talk me into a road trip. How could I be so irresponsible? If Tiffany or Rhonda got hurt, I would never forgive myself. Even Renata the wonder therapist couldn't help me with that one.

"You come with us, Maizie," said Rhonda. "There's a crazy person on the loose."

I shook my head.

"This is not an episode of *Julia Pinkerton*," said Tiffany. "Call the flippin' cops."

"Right," I drew out the word. "Except Ed Sweeney's in Nash's truck. And Nash is missing. And Nash is a suspect in the Waverly case. So...this looks pretty bad for Nash."

"You're protecting Wyatt Nash?" Tiffany swore. "You're an even bigger idiot than I thought. This is just like what's-his-name all over again."

"This is not like Oliver. Once I knew Oliver was selling Oxy, I told the police everything I knew."

"Because you were arrested as an accessory to a drug dealer."

"Tiffany, this is no longer David Waverly trying to make Nash look incompetent. Someone's trying to frame Nash for murder. Why else would Ed be dead in Nash's truck? Isn't that a little obvious in body placement?"

"Whose body placement are you really worried about? Dead Ed's? Or your boss? On top of you?"

"Calm down," said Rhonda. "Tiffany, you get so ugly when you're stressed."

"I can't help it," snapped Tiffany. "I'm freaking out about the dead guy in the truck."

"You're right. We should call the cops." My voice edged toward Valley. "But could you like do it? Like when you've reached safety? I've got to find Nash. And maybe give me a minute to do that?"

"Lord, help me, but I may kill you myself," said Tiffany. "Maizie, someone at this marina is shooting folks. Just wait for the police like a normal person."

I drew myself up and riveted Tiffany with my best Beverly Hills I'm-a-star-and-you-can-suck-it look. "My partner is in trouble, Tiffany. And he's in trouble because of me. I lost Sarah Waverly. David Waverly is dead. I might've gotten Ed Sweeney killed. Now is the not the time for me to act like a normal person."

∞

ARMED WITH TIFFANY'S BEJEWELED CAN of pepper spray and a giant wrench from Shithead's box, I headed back to *A Little Nauti*. Tiffany and Rhonda waited in the marina bar, keeping an eye out for any criminal Black Piners. And Nash. And Jolene Sweeney. Although I found it hard to believe she would shoot her own uncle. But I was going to give her the benefit of the doubt on that one. Sometimes the benefit of the doubt can save your life.

I hoped.

Near the water, the marina dimmed to the fuzzy glow of little brass lanterns. I crept toward the docks, pepper spray in hand, wrench at the ready in the pocket of my Simon Miller jeans.

I had kept a brave face for the girls. In theory, I wanted to help Nash. I did feel responsible. I wanted to save him if he needed saving. But in reality, I felt about as useful as olfactories the day after a rhinoplasty. And scared witless. My plan was to locate Nash, who probably watched Ed's boat, not realizing Ed was actually dead in his truck. Then let Nash handle the crazy person with a gun.

"But why kill Ed?" I thought. The motive had to be tied to the missing money stolen by David Waverly.

By whom? Someone had to have been partnered with David in embezzling BPG's money. Someone who had kidnapped Sarah. And murdered them both. Which meant they had access to David's secret embezzlement bank account.

I wanted to slap myself in the head. Sarah knew her kidnapper. Of course, she had left the Prada in the Porsche. She hadn't realized she'd be going anywhere. Sarah had probably gotten into the kidnapper's vehicle for a quick chat and had been shanghaied. The kidnapper had tossed Sarah's phone in the lake and snatched a suitcase with some handy, already bagged clothes from the house, dumping them along the way. No one would know Sarah was snatched. Just that she had disappeared.

And if the phone and suitcase were found, it would look like David Waverly had done in his own wife. And obviously, David couldn't admit to what had happened to the police unless he also wanted to face embezzlement charges.

Ed Sweeney had to die because he had been at David Waverly's house the night David was murdered. Ed might have seen the killer that night and not even known it. Had David brought anyone else home from work besides Ed?

"Wait a minute," I muttered, "the Stingray doesn't have a backseat. The murderer had either waited for David to get home or arrived later. Either way, they wouldn't have known Ed was visiting since Ed's car was in the shop."

Why didn't I examine all the vehicles entering Platinum Ridge that day? There had been a taxi earlier but I hadn't checked the footage. That was not thorough. That was me trying to get away from skeevy Mark Jacobs and his plot to sell chewed pens.

My stalker was brilliant. They had disguised themselves as David Waverly and driven out of Platinum Ridge the next day, leaving David's car and body at the airport and getting away by renting another car.

Who was it? Jolene? William Dixon? Someone else?

"At least I can cross off Ed Sweeney," I thought miserably.

Fear helped clarify my thoughts. But not make me sharp enough to solidify a good plan to find Nash and escape from our bloodthirsty embezzler.

"Okay, Maizie, time to think like Julia. How many times did she sneak around a marina with a killer on the loose?"

Julia had plenty of experience with wharfs. From human trafficking to underground fight rings, wharfs made for a popular setting with the writers. But marinas? I could only think of one episode, filmed on the *Queen Mary* for Julia's prom. That's where she learned of her basketball star boyfriend's drug habits. She had captured his dealer on the docks. Stabbed him in the carotid with her corsage pin.

And still managed to not get arterial spray on her dress, which meant she could get back to prom and be crowned queen without a cleanup.

Behind me, the party continued in the bar. Down at the docks, the lapping water and creaking boats sounded eerie. A chill broke across my flesh, despite the humidity. I was glad I was not at a wharf. This ritzy marina club was scary enough in the dark.

Where could Nash be? There weren't many places to hide other than the yachts. Could he be on some boat, watching *A Little Nauti* for Ed Sweeney? I hoped whoever killed Ed was only interested in select murders, not a full-on marina bloodbath.

That thought combined with the salty, dead fish aroma and the vision of Ed Sweeney's body had me leaning over the pier, heaving up road trip snacks.

Something heavy hit the wooden dock with a thump I could feel through my boots. I whipped around, brandishing the wrench and pepper spray. "Nash?"

Near a picnic area at the far end of the boardwalk, stood a man strapped and swaddled in equipment. A telescopic rig rose from a base hooked to his waist with a thick belt and shoulder straps. Curling wires, jutting handles, and small black boxes covered the contraption.

Al with a Steadicam.

From this distance, he looked like a walking Mars probe. Al had knocked into an Adirondack chair. In his defense, it was dark and he had been focusing on the shot of me yakking.

I shoved the wrench back in my pocket and rushed to Al.

"What are you doing here?" I whispered.

Al grinned. "Hey, Maizie. Sorry, but you know how Vicki likes the grisly stuff."

"There's been a serious crime," I said. "You need to leave."

"What kind of crime?" Al's eyes widened and he tightened his grip on the Gimbal control handle. "Did you do it? Or help with it?"

"No. I'm trying to prevent the crimes, not assist in them. There's been a murder."

"Whoa. Cool."

"Not cool, Al. Totally not cool. Pack up your equipment and get back to Black Pine."

"Maizie, you know your mom would never let me do that. I've

got to keep filming."

"She will when you have to turn over all your film as evidence in a murder case. And no way will you get those reels back for years and years. Maybe never. You know how long felony cases take at trial."

Al's grin fled. "Damn, you're right. I was waiting for Joe and the sound equipment when I saw you. He's grabbing us some beers."

"Have your beers in the bar far away from here. But keep your eye out for anything suspect. If you see Wyatt Nash, the private investigator, tell him I'm looking for him."

"You're really serious about this detective stuff, aren't you?" Al rested his hand on the monitor. "You're really growing up."

I wanted to beam, but I didn't feel grown up. I felt like a bumbling idiot.

"Who got murdered?" asked Al. "Wait, don't tell me. Better not to know anything. I don't want to get involved in a trial."

"You might not have a choice if the cops arrive and find a camera crew." I eyed his monitor and thought about what might be on his camera. "Al, how long have you been filming tonight?"

∞

INSIDE THE SPRINTER, WE USED Al's monitor to play back his most recent footage. I watched myself get hauled out of the Nash Security Solutions office on Nash's shoulder—glutes workouts were in my future— sneak out of the DeerNose property, drive through McDonald's on Lucky, and climb into Tiffany's Firebird. The Sprinter Van had a few shots of me crammed in the back seat on the drive to Savannah but with no microphone to pick up our conversation, those scenes were a dud. They picked up again after spying me on the docks, lost me at the bar, and found me again barfing off the side of the boardwalk.

Al had no idea I'd been attacked in the bathroom nor that I was in any danger. The *Albright* crew didn't know David Waverly had been found in the trunk of his car, let alone that Ed Sweeney had been killed.

Without the facts, I had made for an entertaining Inspector Clouseau. I didn't enlighten Al. Clouseau was better than the alternative, a series spinoff Vicki would likely name *Albright Undercover*. Giulio would love the costumes. Probably a lot of leather.

"Did you see anyone follow me to the marina? Maybe a rental car?" I focused on the tiny screen, watching the dock footage B-roll and concentrating on the background.

"No." Al peered over my shoulder. "Why would someone be following you?"

I thought for a minute, not wanting to implicate myself with a murderer. "Crazy stalker fan."

"Oh." Al sounded disappointed by the banality. "No one followed you on the road. I would have noticed because I was looking for anything remotely interesting."

"They must have driven to Savannah after leaving me in the bathroom," I muttered. "I helped Remi dupe Carol Lynn for nothing."

"What?"

"Hang on." I paused the film and rewound. "There's Nash. When was this shot?" The blip showed Nash loping along the boardwalk, checking over his shoulder.

"That investigator doesn't do a whole lot, but Vicki wants some footage of him anyway."

"You mean Nash doesn't act like an idiot on-screen. You better get a good lawyer. Black Pine people are litigation happy and I can guarantee Nash won't give you permission to show him on a reality show."

"We'll mosaic his face out," Al said, but without confidence. Vicki probably didn't mention that little fact. "Let's see. This was right after we arrived. I think you girls were in the marina gift shop. I was shooting B-roll.»

"Nash looks like he's headed to *A Little Nauti*. But I didn't see him there earlier. Did you catch him leaving at all?"

"Nope. I took that from the van and stayed put until you disappeared into the bar."

"Nash's got to be on one of those boats."
I just hoped he was still alive.

TWENTY-SEVEN

#TieMeTapeMe #KneeFetish

ILEFT AL AND JOE AND snuck toward the dark docks with my wrench and pink pepper spray. I sped past the neighboring vessels toward *A Little Nauti*. If Nash wasn't on board, I'd have to check the other yachts, one by one. And if that didn't work, I'd run back to the bar to find Tiffany and Rhonda.

No blue lights had flooded the parking lot yet. I didn't know if that meant Tiffany and Rhonda were giving me some lead time to find Nash or if an unmarked car had arrived to investigate Ed's death. Given the exclusivity of the marina, I suspected the local police wouldn't want to advertise their presence. But I figured they'd immediately crime scene tape his boat.

No tape.

I boarded.

Stepping over the stern, I tread across the polished wood deck toward the companionway. "Nash?" I whispered. "Nash are you here? The police are coming."

The last bit I said more loudly. I had not forgotten about the gun toting, kidnapping, murderous embezzler. Who, I hoped, had decided to take a beat somewhere other than the marina.

"So it's important you get off Ed's boat before the police get here. Which will be any second."

I tried the companionway door. It turned easily. Then remembered the rule about fingerprints on dead people's doorknobs. My fingerprints were already in the California law enforcement database. Super easy to trace.

"Frig." I had some wiping to do on my way off the boat.

I stole down the ladder's short flight of steps and entered a spacious galley, decorated in glossy wood with a lounging area and bitty kitchen. No Nash. But luckily, no crazed shooter either.

At the end of the room was a door. And behind me, next to the stairway, another door.

These door decisions always ended badly in the movies.

I listened for bumps in the night. And for the sound of bullets leaving guns. Proceeded to door number one. The master bedroom in the bow. No Nash. But a lovely queen sized bed and more wood paneling. After checking the head and closets—Ed liked Henri Lloyd, Mauri Pro, and Helly Hanson with the occasional Tommy Bahama—I scooted toward the stern.

Door number two was locked. I jiggled and chewed a thumbnail. Now was not the time to fear the worst—my boss laid out with a bullet in his brain, like the owner of this beautiful sailboat—but I feared the worst. I had to get inside that room.

"Nash," I called through the door. "Are you in there?"

Thumping inside told me Nash was alive.

Thumping above told me someone had just boarded.

The thumping in my chest told me I had better hurry the hell up.

"Nash," I whispered. "Someone's here. Hang on."

The stainless steel latch had a keyhole, one that looked the size of a file cabinet key. Julia Pinkerton had a set of lock picks she kept in her backpack. Maizie Albright didn't come equipped with anything useful other than a wrench and pink pepper spray. I spun toward the little kitchen and jerked open drawers, looking for tiny keys. Ice pick? Fork? Fish knife? I stuck the fish knife in my back pocket where it joined the wrench. Why didn't Ed keep lobster picks? Didn't they do lobster in Savannah?

The sounds of bumping and scuffling from the deck grew louder.

I flew around the cabin, dithering between my search for lock picking devices and wanting to hide. A teeny map area had been built into a recess near the master bedroom. A small table had inlaid wood to look like a nautical compass, and there were round holes for rolled charts, built-in shelves, and cabinets. I skimmed the cubbies. Radio, books, laptop, and a GPS. Not a paperclip or bobby pin to be found.

More clunking and thudding sounded from above.

Below the table lay three tackle boxes. None had paperclips, but they did have plenty of fishhooks and pliers. Careful of the barbs, I snatched a handful of fishhooks and ran back to the cabin door. My first attempt at lock picking met with failure. The pliers straightened the second hook with precious minutes wasted trying to hold the damn thing down with my boot. I shoved the makeshift pick into the lock.

Julia Pinkerton made lock picking look easy. Lock picking is not easy.

Sweat beaded the nape of my neck. My palms grew sticky. I felt a tiny tumbler give. I wiped my forehead with my arm and continued with the wiggling and jiggling.

The boat lurched.

The fishhook flew out of the hole.

My body fell sideways into the wall and I slid to the floor, landing my knee on a fishhook. The barb ripped through five hundred dollar jeans and embedded into my skin. I pulled my entire bottom lip into my mouth, bit down to keep from screaming, and tried, for about twenty agonizing seconds, to rip out the hook. Blinking back tears, I gave my knee over to its new accessory, found my fishhook pick, and jammed it back into the hole.

Tumbler two gave.

I tore a nail pulling on the latch and stumbled into the bedroom, ready to free my costar.

I mean boss.

A bed filled the room. Wall-to-wall. On the bed, facedown, lay Nash. His hands thickly bound in duct tape. Crossed over his nicely shaped bum.

I only noticed because of the duct-taped hands.

He shot me a hard look over a shoulder, showing me duct tape covered his mouth. And more encircled his ankles, knees, and elbows.

This kidnapper really liked duct tape.

I did the finger over the lips sign—unnecessary considering the duct tape—and brandished the fish knife. Then climbed on the bed and reluctantly shut the door.

"Nash," I whispered. "Someone's up there doing something to the boat."

He nodded and jerked his chin up, pushing his mouth toward me.

I grabbed a corner of the duct tape and ripped.

His eyes squeezed shut and he clamped down hard on his bottom lip.

I knew the feeling. Blood still trickled down my leg from the damn fishhook.

"What are you doing here?" he whispered. "Of all the dumbass things to do. I told you to stay at Boomer's."

This was not the reaction I anticipated. I ignored his complaints, grabbed the fish knife, and went to work sawing his feet apart.

"Get my hands," he said. "Hurry it up."

I stopped sawing. "Maybe you don't know this, but Ed Sweeney is dead. I found him shot in the head in your truck."

"Dammit."

"That's all you have to say? Dammit? Ed Sweeney's dead. In your truck."

He glanced over his shoulder. "I'll grieve Ed Sweeney after you get the tape off, Miss Albright. We have a more pressing issue above deck."

I turned my back to him, straddled his legs, and resumed cutting. His feet split apart, and I moved backward to work at his knees.

Fingers tickled my butt, then stroked one cheek.

I looked over my shoulder and shot him a "really?" look.

"I was trying to feel what's in your pocket. It's digging into my thighs."

"Shithead's big wrench." I accosted him with one of Julia's fierce glares, pulled the wrench from my pocket followed by its companion pepper spray and the pliers. "I have a fish knife, a wrench, and pepper spray. And a fishhook stuck in my knee. That's what I'm using to save you."

An abashed smile crept over his hard edges. "I'm sorry. Thanks for breaking in and cutting me free."

"You're welcome. And later you can thank Tiffany and Rhonda. They gave me a ride to the marina."

"If we get off the boat, I will." His head dropped back to the nautical bedspread.

I turned back to the duct tape, sawing faster. His knees pulled apart, and I flipped around to cut his elbows and hands free.

"Hurry," he said. "That's the engine turning on."

"Engine? This is a sailboat. They have engines? Don't they use sails? Why is an engine turning on?"

"Don't panic. Just focus on the tape."

"Not panicking," I said in a panicked voice. I dropped the knife against his thighs, picked it up, and gouged him in the elbow with the point.

"You're doing fine. And you're not heavy at all."

"Gee, thanks."

"I'm being literal. I know you worry about that kind of thing. Just relax."

"Relax?"

"It's okay. She won't come below yet. She has to maneuver out of the marina first, then down the river. We've got time, considering."

"Out of the marina? We're going out to sea?"

I jerked the knife up, catching the point in the thick tape and rent a hole. Wiggling the knife through the hole, the seam split.

Nash flexed his biceps and wrenched his hands apart.

The tape tore, the boat jerked left, and I fell across Nash's back.

He flipped over, pinning me under him on the bed. We lay there for a long moment, his hard muscles evident against my cushioning. I tried not to think of my lack of recent workouts. Nor my breasts squished against his firm chest. Or our other parts tangled together. On a wall-to-wall bed.

Pushing up on his elbows, Nash hovered over me. "Don't be

scared. I've been considering all the options while I lay here. She caught me by surprise just like she did you."

"The old 'hide behind the door' trick? Is your head okay?"

"It's hard enough." He tried out a smile, but couldn't quite make it work. "I feel like an idiot."

"Me, too. But I usually do." I gazed into the pale blue eyes. "The police are coming. But we're getting away. What happens if we're out at sea?"

"The police will call the coast guard. It'll be okay. Breathe."

My deep breath caused my chest to swell against his.

He ducked his head to watch.

I quickly expelled, but the air caught on the ball of misery stuck in my throat. "I was really worried about you." I blinked to keep the tears from my eyes. "I thought you might have been shot like Ed Sweeney."

"At the time there were too many people around for her to shoot me. Probably planned on doing it out on the open water and dumping me over. Where's my truck?"

"Near the boat slip. In an empty parking lot."

"She must've had Ed move my truck then shot him there. Poor bastard. He thought they were going to escape to the Bahamas together. She's been siphoning BPG's money away for a long time with Ed's help."

"Nash." The idea of him getting shot and dumped into the ocean caused larger tears to well. "The police are going to think you killed Ed Sweeney. And you'll be dead and dumped in the ocean."

"The police are smarter than that." He rolled over and rose to sit next to me. He gently wiped a tear from my cheek and rubbed it between his fingers. "No tears, darlin'."

I nodded and grabbed my thumb skin for a hard pinch.

He watched my hands then contemplated my prone form. A faint smile touched his lips, softening his features. "How'd you get away from Boomer?"

"I crawled through a doggy door."

He flinched.

"You're surprised I fit, I know. The pack wouldn't take turns, so Daddy put in an oversized flap. I barely made it through with all I've been eating— Sorry. TMI."

"I wasn't thinking about you fitting in the doggy door. It was the fact you'd crawl through it to get out." He gathered my hands in his. "I don't know if I should kiss you or kill you for being here."

"Are you serious?"

"What do you think?"

I didn't want to think. Either one could be fatal. Well, one was definitely fatal. I changed the subject. "What are we going to do about Jolene?"

"I don't know."

"Shouldn't we come up with a plan?"

"First things first." His gaze roamed over my hair spilling across the pillow, down my body to where our hands were clasped, and back to my face. "Which knee?"

Was he into knees? That was a little weird. Still, heat zipped through me, despite our current circumstances. I blamed it on the wall-to-wall bed. "What do you mean?"

"Which knee has the fishhook in it? We don't have a lot of time, but I can get it out. You'll be gimping about otherwise and that's no good."

"My left one."

His hands found the tear in my jeans, then ripped the hole wider. Grabbing the pliers, he cast me a long look. "It's really important you don't scream."

I felt my stomach lurch into my throat. Before I could say anything, Nash had grasped the bend in the fishhook with the pliers, pressed it against my skin, yanked up and away. I gasped but felt little pain.

"Good girl. Can't tell you how many fishhooks I've pulled out in my time. The only one I'd taken off a gal was Jolene. She screamed like a banshee." Nash reached toward the pillow beneath my head, ripped off a strip of the case, and held it against my knee to stem the blood. Turning back to look at me, his eyebrow quirked. "Anyone ever say you look a little like Jolene?"

That was not what I wanted to hear. Particularly after fishhook surgery.

"I thought you were just like her. At first anyway. Spoiled rich girls. Princess types." He ripped off another strip of the pillow case, looped it around my knee through the tear in my jeans, and tied it over the fishhook wound. "You know, expensive taste. High maintenance. Sex as a weapon. Nuclear weapon. But you're not exactly a Jolene."

I gulped. "Jolene's a regular Mata Hari, isn't she?"

A genuine smile lit his face, followed by a dreamy gaze that traveled to the ceiling. "She is. Lord, she tied me up in knots. If I ever had an Achilles Heel, it was goddamn Jolene Sweeney."

Definitely what I didn't want to hear. Sliding back on my elbows, I pushed to sitting. "I'll do it if you can't."

His eyes swept back to mine and he tightened the grasp on my knee. "Do what?"

"Stop her. But you'll need to get her gun. I don't think I could beat anyone with a wrench."

Confusion bit into his eyes.

Jolene Sweeney had done a number on him. Enough so he felt helpless to stop our ruthless shanghaier.

"Sorry to be cold, but it is self-defense," I explained. "She's already murdered three people. I'd rather you and I weren't number four and five."

Nash snorted then scooted forward. He grasped my hand and pulled me down the length of the bed. "Maizie, Jolene didn't murder anyone."

Poor, poor Nash. My wounded bird had been crippled by a true femme fatale. I couldn't help myself. I reached to stroke his stubbled cheek. "I'm sorry, Nash. It must be hard to hear this about your ex-wife."

A harsh laugh tore through him.

I dropped my hand. "What's so funny?"

"Jolene's not navigating this boat."

"What do you mean? Who's up there?"

"I thought you knew. Sarah Waverly."

TWENTY-EIGHT

#peppersprazed #SavannahShanghai

NASH ROOTED AROUND THE CABIN for weapons, while I thought about the woman piloting this ship of doom. Sarah Waverly had faked her disappearance. I couldn't get over it. All this time I had worried about Sarah, then feared for Sarah, then grieved Sarah. Whereas she had been stealing from Black Pine Group and pinning her probable death on her husband. With Ed Sweeney. Who she murdered. And loosely framed Nash for it. Whom she also planned to murder.

What a bitch.

"Flare gun," muttered Nash, handing me a plastic orange pistol. "Hold this."

"How are we going to stop her?"

"We aren't doing anything. You're going to stay down here. Sarah doesn't know you're on board. I'm going to disarm her, then tie her up."

"With what? Fishing lines?"

"Duct tape." Triumphant, he held up a silver roll. "What's good for the gander."

"Was she your gander?" I couldn't stop myself. "I mean, it seemed like you were kind of sweet on Sarah at one time. David Waverly thought so, too."

"Miss Albright, your questions seem a mite irrelevant in light of our circumstances." An eyebrow quirked. "You also sound jealous."

"This is not a jealousy thing. Sarah played Ed Sweeney. Did she play you, too?"

With serious eyes, he winked. "Wouldn't you like to know."

I did want to know. But it was a mite irrelevant. "So while I'm down here what should I be doing? Radioing for help?"

"Do you know how to use an SSB radio? Marine single sideband?"

I shook my head.

"Me, either. If you don't know what you're doing, it's hard to find a frequency. Different bands have different ranges. It's not like dialing 9-1-1. You can play with it if you want, but you'll probably be wasting your time."

"You're very discouraging."

"I'm just being realistic. The flare gun will have quicker results this close to shore. People will see the flare, report it, and the Coast Guard will investigate. Particularly if the police already know about us. Wish I could find more flares, though."

"So you're going to disarm Sarah, tie her up, then shoot the flare gun? Do you know how to pilot this boat?"

"I can figure out how to shut off the engine. Maybe even drop the anchor. And you're going to lock yourself in one of the cabins. With your pepper spray."

"You don't trust me. I saved you. Let me help. I'm sure I can shoot a flare gun."

He cupped my chin and tipped it up. "You're worth a lot more than me, Miss Albright. It's better if I know you're safe down here. It'll be harder to subdue her if I'm worried about you getting hurt."

"I'm not worth any more than you," I protested. "If we're being realistic, I'd make a better sacrificial lamb. Sarah Waverly could have shot me in your bathroom or run me down in Madeline's alley. But she didn't. Not to brag, but my murder would get major press and she'd have a harder time escaping."

The Paul Newmans glinted and his hand slid off my chin to caress my cheek. "Not happening, Maizie."

"I'm serious, Nash. Sarah's cold blooded. I saw what she did to Ed. That engraved Michele Watches was probably from him and she threw it out like trash. She left her own husband in the trunk of a car. She's a lot more likely to shoot you than me. Sarah probably thinks I can't do anything to stop her. I'd have the element of surprise."

"And how would you stop her?"

"I still have some *Kung Fu Kate* moves. And my Tae Bo."

"Exactly why you're going to lock yourself in a cabin and wait for me." His hand slid to the nape of my neck and he leaned in.

Nash-might-kiss-me déjà vu flooded me. I clutched the flare gun in one hand and tilted my face up. The arctic blues met my sea glass greens, then dropped to my mouth. I flicked a tongue, moistening my dry lips, and heard Nash's quick intake of breath.

He stepped into my personal space box, cradling the nape of my neck. The hand holding the duct tape ran light fingers down my bare arm.

"Wish me luck, darlin'." His breath whispered across my cheek.

"I could use it."

"Vicki taught me that you make your own luck." I reached a hand between us and raised it toward his face.

Then sprayed him with pepper spray, grabbed the duct tape, and ran up the galley steps.

I truly was Vicki's daughter.

∞

I PAUSED AT THE COMPANIONWAY DOOR, barely able to hear the rush of water over the engine. Ambient light brightened the night, and I breathed a sigh. We were still on a river or in one of Savannah's many channels.

The port lights on either side of the door kept me hidden but lit Sarah, some ten feet away. Leaning slightly to one side with her gaze trained on the distant sea and her hand on the steering helm, she looked like a Ralph Lauren ad. Particularly as there was no handgun in sight, which would not be Ralph Lauren-ish.

I glanced back to where Nash writhed on the floor, then cracked the door.

There was no sneaking up behind her. I could dart out, but

would have to maneuver around the cockpit table. The giant steering wheel stood between us, too. Not much room for a crescent kick or a Tiger-Crane combination.

I had been totally serious about my *Kung Fu Kate* moves.

With Sarah Waverly's positioning, there wasn't much chance of surprising her, except she wasn't expecting Maizie Albright. If Nash rushed out the doorway, she would shoot and be done with him, save the dumping of his body. However, there was a teeny possibility I could distract her. If I could lure her out from behind the big steering wheel, I could pepper spray her, pin her down, and duct tape the bejeezus out of her.

I felt pleased to have a plan. Another Vicki moment.

If only I was certain the plan would work. Which wasn't very Vicki of me.

Water ran in the galley sink. Nash washing his eyes. I had better hurry before Nash dragged me down the galley stairs and tied me up with the duct tape.

The cockpit table looked promising. Sarah had left the hinged sides down creating a small, low blind. Shoving the flare gun into the back of my jeans, I pushed the door open a bit wider and crawled on the deck. With my eyes on Sarah, I moved hand-over-hand, feeling the fishhook hole with every drag of my knee. Her concentration on steering the channel meant she didn't notice my deck crawl.

Her shoes gave me my opening line.

I popped up next to the table, tossing the duct tape behind her GPS screen. "Are those Sperry's?"

Startled, Sarah blinked at me, her hands still gripping the ship's wheel.

"I mean, I've never seen plaid Sperry's. Aren't they cute? Not that I've spent much time researching boat shoes. I don't spend much time on boats. I kind of found myself on this one by accident. A Goldilocks moment, right? I was looking for Ed Sweeney. Didn't see him downstairs. I mean, below deck. Like I said, I don't really know anything about boats. Or should I call this a ship?"

I moved forward as I chattered, allowing the babble to flow

over my lips in typical Maizie fashion. Julia would have cut to the chase, announcing the gig was up in the snarkiest voice possible. Then shoot the flare gun, aiming just above her head to temporarily blind her. *Kung Fu Kate* would have done some kind of flip from the side bench to the stern, ending in a praying mantis hook. Maizie Albright babbled about shoes. But it was working. Sarah looked confused.

"I know you're totally surprised to see me. Imagine my shock when you started the engine on this thing. I didn't even know sailboats had engines." I waved and gave her my best red carpet smile. "I'm Maizie Albright. I used to be on TV. Most recently on *All is Albright*. I quit that show, but they're still filming me. Very frustrating. Anyway, I've been on *Entertainment Tonight* and *Extra* a lot lately, although I don't know if you've had time to watch. You were featured a bit, too. At least, that's what I heard. I haven't watched TV in forever."

"What?" Sarah narrowed her eyes. "Where's Wyatt Nash?"

"He's kind of incapacitated at the moment." True, although he wasn't tied up like Sarah thought. "It seems like you're in a hurry to get out of town, but could you drop me off somewhere before you head out to...Where are you going? Is it the Bahamas?"

She didn't answer but took one hand from the steering wheel and slipped it into her jacket pocket.

I continued my prattle, slowly moving toward Sarah. "I figured the Bahamas because that's where Ed sails. This is his boat isn't it, Sarah?"

"I'm a co-owner." Her tone was clipped, but I believed it. Sarah didn't seem one to leave paperwork to chance.

"I heard you used to sail with Ed before you and David moved to Black Pine." Thank you Bethann Bergh, Burlesque Wannabe and Queen Gossip of Platinum Ridge, for that bit of info. "You almost left David ten years ago. For Ed? Are you his SS Sarah? Is that when you two bought this boat? Not judging. It seemed like your marriage had some issues. I know about David's own boating rendezvous. That must have been rough to live with."

Sarah remained silent, but pieces of her plan began to fit together.

I continued my chatter, waiting for my chance to pounce.

"Did you hide out in the women's shelter when you went missing? That was smart. Nobody would ask questions or report you. They probably let you borrow the rusty car, too. I guess Ed picked you up at Black Pine Club and left you at the shelter. We found the suitcase you tossed near the shelter. He must have dropped your phone in the lake, too. I thought you'd been kidnapped."

She angled her head, studying me. Her hand remained in the jacket pocket. As long as it stayed there, I didn't mind as much. Who would blow a hole in a J Crew windbreaker? You'd burn the crap out of your hand and your jacket.

"Like I said, I was looking for Ed Sweeney. And Nash. Found Nash. And now I found you. What a shocker."

I could tell Sarah wasn't sure if I knew about the murders or the embezzling, only that we'd been looking for her. She was trying to figure out what to do with me. I could almost see the gears whirring in her brain. I wondered if she had an "If Maizie Shows Up On My Boat" Plan B.

"I'm kind of stuck going to the Bahamas with you, unless you can dock somewhere? These clothes are like so not Bahamas."

I sounded like I was channeling Paris. Or Buffy. Or, oh my god, Kim.

"Cut the crap." She pulled the gun from her pocket, but with her free hand on the ship's wheel, she had a disadvantage. "What are you really doing here?"

"Whoa, Sarah. Chill. Here's the thing. The Coast Guard should be here any minute looking for this boat. If they drive up, or whatever, and see you with a gun, what are they going to think?"

"Listen, you idiot." Sarah's frosty voice chipped at my nerves. "I've spent an enormous amount of time and effort planning the next stage of my life. I have come too far to let you stop me now. I'd advise you to cooperate. When we reach Green Turtle Cay, I'll decide what to do. Cause me trouble before then and I'll kill both of you. You know I will."

I knew she would.

TWENTY-NINE

#chatterboxed #tBacktrouble

SARAH WAS AN EXCELLENT MULTITASKER, I'll give her that. With one hand, she steered the channel. With the other, she held the gun.

A Glock by the look of it. Maybe a Sig Sauer. I wasn't sure. Gun labels weren't as easy to identify as clothing labels. Whatever it was, it looked dangerous.

Her eyes would zoom from the winding channel to laser back to me. She had me empty my pockets—goodbye wrench, fish knife, and pepper spray—and stand before the big steering wheel, which looked nothing like the wooden kind that pirates employed. This one was metal and bigger than a bike wheel, with only three gleaming spokes for a sleeker, Mercedes star-type look.

If I were Jackie Chan, I would thrust-kick through the wheel, turning my foot as it hit her chest, and knock her over the low transom wall.

But I wasn't Jackie Chan. *Kung Fu Kate* had the help of green screens and harnesses for that kind of move. But I had to do something before Nash regained his sight and charged up the companionway.

Although my pepper spray had been confiscated, my unbuttoned Simon Miller jeans and billowy Saint Laurent tee had concealed the flare gun shoved down my pants. I needed a distraction to retrieve the flare gun. And I needed Sarah not to point a real gun at me for best use of said flare gun. Which meant getting Sarah out from behind the steering wheel and into the slightly roomier cockpit area. Where I might be able to employ my few but surprisingly adept martial arts moves.

"I have to know, did you really bring David lunch every day?" Chitchat as a pressure point. I could annoy her into moving around the steering helm, giving me more room to operate.

She flashed me a hard look then averted her eyes to the dark channel.

"But why, when you must have hated him? Every morning? That's like a total waste of time, unless you were doing something else. Stringing along Ed?"

I snapped my fingers. "The BPG accounts. I bet BPG had daily passwords. My accounting firm does that, too. Very frustrating for Vicki who wants access at all times. Bringing David lunch gave you an excuse to get the password so you could shift the money a little at a time. With your accounting background, that must have been the easy part. I guess they noticed when you took a larger chunk before taking off. To make David look suspicious?"

"Good Lord, do you ever shut up?" She flipped open a storage locker and rooted inside before slamming it. "Come over here and take the helm."

Oh frigizzle, I thought. She was supposed to come to *my* side, not the other way around. Come on, Maizie, think of something. "I don't know how to steer a ship."

"Stay in the middle of the channel," she barked. "Run us aground and I'll shoot you."

"But..."

"Shut up." She motioned with the pistol. "Hurry it up. I need to find my duct tape."

I slipped alongside to face her, hoping she didn't immediately look on the cockpit table for the tape. The flare gun was still secured inside my thong strap. Where I hoped it wouldn't go off.

"Take the wheel."

"What if there's a rock? Or another boat? Or a dolphin? Is it dolphins or porpoises? Honestly, I don't know the difference. I'd hate to run over either one. I hit a squirrel once. That was awful. I couldn't handle hitting a dolphin." I waved a hand at the channel where dolphins possibly lurked. The other hand swung behind my back, ready to yank the flare gun from its elastic bondage. "I heard there's a lot of dolphin activity around here and sometimes they swim up the rivers. And this water's super dark."

"Lord, you're an idiot. David insisted on watching that stupid show so he could ogle you in that ridiculous cheer outfit. I hated it then and I hate you now." She raised the handgun to center it on my chest. "Get your hands on that wheel."

Now we were both behind the wheel with no room to maneuver. One wrong move and I'd be shot at point blank range. Or I'd fall over the stern's folding transom wall into the river. Or both.

"To be honest, I wasn't crazy about the cheer outfit either." My hand dug inside my jeans for the flare gun, but the thong had caught itself around the handle.

"Hands on the wheel," snapped Sarah, flicking her finger against the safety.

My hand flew out of my pants and latched onto the steering wheel. I had the most epic wedgie in the history of wedgies and a weapon lost somewhere in my butt crack. If I were shot, it might relieve me of my discomfort, but I'd never live down the humiliation.

And I'd be dead.

The cabin door burst open and Nash rushed out. In two long strides he reached the stern. His hand shot through the steering wheel.

My hands flew off the wheel.

Grabbing Sarah's arm, he twisted. She spun toward him, jerking the muzzle off my chest and toward the bow.

One shot rang out. A portlight exploded.

Sarah grabbed for the handgun with her free hand.

He reached through the opening, gripping her elbow. With his other hand, he reached around the wheel for Sarah's neck. Nash was stronger, but she rammed her body against the steering wheel, using it for leverage.

In the dim light, I could see his puffy, red eyes, no hint of the marvelous blue, and tears streamed in constant rivulets down his cheeks. I hadn't counted on him attacking Sarah half-blind.

Sarah fought with a ferocious desperation, utilizing Nash's awkward stance as an advantage. She pushed against the wheel, ramming the spoke against his arm.

Nash grunted and his hand lost its grip on her elbow. His other closed on her neck.

Sarah hopped back, jerking out of his reach, and swung the gun between them. The muzzle smacked against the hub of the wheel.

Just as I feared, Nash would be shot. My heart accelerated in my throat. I couldn't kick with the damn flare gun tied up in my thong. I didn't have time to consider what Julia Pinkerton would do. I lunged at Sarah, throwing my heavier self at her. Knocking her sideways, we both fell to the teak deck.

She rolled.

I flopped on top, spreading my arms and legs wide, like a massive starfish. Somewhere beneath me was a pistol. I reverse planked, pushing my torso into Sarah, trying to pin her with my body.

Sarah was lithe and wiry, a sailing and ladies' golf master. Wriggling beneath me, her muscles corded and flexed, like the sinewy rippling of Madonna's arms. Sarah probably lifted weights at the gym to make her more sea-hearty.

No longer gym fit, I couldn't wrestle Sarah and win. But I could use youth and voluptuous shaping to my advantage.

I could squash her.

Heaving myself into a pushup that would make Trainer Jerry proud, I dropped one hundred forty-plus pounds on top of Sarah. My forehead slammed into her nose. I heard a crunch and a grunt, followed by a clatter and a shot.

The reverb of the gun blast shuddered through me. My vision spotted, my ears rang, and I felt a heavy thud hit the decking. Sarah lay limp beneath me. I rolled to one side, squinting into the dim light.

The gun lay near my hip.

And Nash lay on the floor of the deck.

Oh God.

I had accidentally shot my boss.

This was much worse than a California prison sentence.

THIRTY

#HighSeasEscape #ShotintheDark

"NASH. NASH?" I SCRAMBLED TO sitting and glanced at Sarah. Blood trickled from her nose. Her eyes were closed and her body still. My body slam had worked. Too well.

Without thinking, I snagged the gun with two fingers and flung it over the side of the boat. I turned and looked at Nash. His body was also still, eyes also closed. And still puffy and red. Sliding across the decking on my knees, I scooted to his side and bent over him.

"Nash. Can you hear me?"

He didn't move.

"Please don't be dead." I planted a small kiss on his forehead. Still warm. My fingers skimmed the contours of his tough but secretly lovable face, then felt behind his head and neck.

"No head trauma, thank God." Splaying my hands across his chest, I ran them over his shoulders and down his sides, searching for a wound. My hands glided over the hard planes and indentations, feeling for the hint of blood or worse. The man had abs of steel. How did he do that? I was pretty sure he didn't have a gym membership. And his arms. Hard, packed muscle. Solid biceps without flexing. I knew an actor who paid a hefty price for implants that couldn't compare to these guns.

I ran my hands back to his chest, relieved at the steady thumping beneath my palm. Wasn't that a good sign?

"Lower," he croaked.

"Nash," I cried. My hands lay on his flat belly, mere centimeters from the button on his fly. I shot a look at his face. "Lower?"

A slit of fierce blue appeared in the puffy red eyelids. "My foot. She shot me in the foot. Get my boot off."

"O.M.G." Exhaling, I slid toward his feet. A singed hole had torn through the side of his left boot. Blood oozed from the hole, darkening the leather. I rested my hands on either side of his ankle and leaned over his foot. The sole had ripped and burst. More blood oozed inside the jagged tear. "The bullet went clean through. But you're bleeding pretty bad."

"I know."

"Hang on." I hopped up and grabbed the duct tape from the cockpit table. Winding the tape around the ripped boot, I cinched it tighter with each circle. "I'm leaving your boot on to exact more pressure. No time to find a tourniquet. Just lie still, okay? I'm going to shoot the flare and get help."

He nodded, staring at the underside of the cockpit table.

"I'm sorry about the pepper spray. But I didn't want you to get shot. I just knew you would. And it scared me into action."

He flicked a glance at me, his lips twisting into a thin line. The white scar pulsed on his chin beneath the grinding of his jaw.

"I guess you got shot anyway. But if you had stayed below, you wouldn't have." My point was lost somewhere in his anger. "I couldn't bear it if Sarah had killed you."

"Too bad," drawled the voice behind me. "Because I'm going to do it anyway. I'll put you out of your agony soon after I get rid of him."

THIRTY-ONE

#flaregunfollies #sugarshakershakeup

I PIVOTED ON MY KNEES TO face Sarah. Blood had smeared beneath her nose and the bridge looked puffy. I had broken her nose.

Ironic, considering the start of my failed detective career.

She stood above me, holding a wicked-looking folding knife. Small enough to keep in her pocket, but gleaming sharp and half-serrated for all sorts of nautical jobs.

Like gutting fish or stabbing humans.

"Just stay where you are." Snatching the duct tape from the deck, Sarah slipped it over her left wrist.

"You should put some ice on that nose before your eyes blacken," I responded without thinking. "Or mashed banana. Totally worked."

In reply, she stomped on Nash's foot.

His howl made my hair stand on end. I leaped to shove her away from Nash. The knife point whipped across my torso, slicing my silk Saint Laurent. Tiny beads and sequins flew across the deck.

My Barney's personal shopper would have slapped her.

"Sit down," barked Sarah, pointing the knife at my chest.

I sat.

Beside me, Nash drug himself to lean against the cockpit table leg. Beads of sweat dotted his brow and his scar stood stark against his jaw. "You're facing double homicide, kidnapping, and embezzlement."

"Don't forget assault," I said. "And battery. Deadly force? And can I charge damages for my Saint Laurent? What do you think?"

Nash's puffy eyes flashed me a grim look.

I quieted.

"You're not going to make it to Nassau," he said. "Give it up, Sarah."

She responded by kicking his foot.

The curses he screamed at her would have made a pirate blush.

Sarah's swollen nose burned crimson against her pale cheeks. "As long as I get rid of the evidence, I don't see a problem. No one knows I'm alive but you. Ed and I already registered *A Little Nauti* under my new identity." She brandished the knife, gave me a mean smile, then shook the duct tape bracelet down her arm. "Now where's the gun? Obviously, you don't have it on you."

"I threw it overboard."

I felt Nash's disapproval before I heard his low growl.

"Flare gun?" Sarah ripped off a piece of duct tape.

I shrugged.

"You told the detective you had a flare gun. Lift your shirt."

I flipped the hem up.

She caught my hem with the knife blade and poked the tip into my skin. "Higher."

"Close your eyes," I hissed at Nash and raised my shirt past my bra.

Sarah peered over my shoulder and down my back.

For once, I felt glad for the wedgie. Thanks to all the kneeling, the flare gun had slid into the seat of my pants. As long as I didn't have to ride a horse, it would remain hidden.

"For an actress, I thought you'd be more fit." She pulled off a length of duct tape.

I dropped my shirt, feeling a hot flash of humiliation tear up my spine to burn my neck and cheeks. Bad enough to expose yourself while kneeling in jeans—not a flattering pose, unless you arch your back like a swimsuit model—but in front of Nash, it was downright mortifying.

And insulting someone while threatening them? Total salt in the wound stuff. Instead of facing death, I could've signed with Vicki for this sort of thing.

With more force and excitement than necessary, she slapped a piece of duct tape over my mouth, grazing my cheek with the knife blade.

I needed another distraction to retrieve the flare gun before she busied herself duct taping me into a cocoon. No room for *Kung Fu Kate* moves with Nash's long legs and bloody foot taking up most of the available floor space. Not to mention the flare gun lodged in my pants.

The boat slowed and the engine whined, distracting Sarah. She glanced over her shoulder and muttered a curse. *A Little Nauti* bumped against something below surface, tilted, and righted. "Damn it, we're motoring starboard."

With Sarah distracted, the boat's pause gave me my exit cue. Pushing to my feet, I stumbled toward the cabin door, hopping like a cowboy saddled too long. The flare gun had caught in the crotch of my jeans, pointing down one leg hole. I unzipped my Simon Millers while reaching for the door. I'd grab another fish knife, then retrieve the flare gun.

Footsteps slapped the deck.

Leaving my fly open, I yanked on the companionway door.

Sarah slammed a hand on the door. "Where do you think you're going?"

"Mowm m Mem."

"Get back here." She shoved me away from the door, then pulled at her duct tape bracelet. "We'll see how well you swim with your legs and arms tied."

I staggered two steps and fell over Nash's legs.

"Maizie," he muttered, "just jump ship. You can swim to shore."

I wanted to tell him I wouldn't leave him. No way. No how. Sarah was going down. No one shoots my boss and gets away with it. I would have also liked to mention my hidden surprise. But I'd have to rip the duct tape off to speak clearly and my hands had busied themselves with the effort of reaching into my jeans for the unsaid flare gun.

"What in the hell are you doing?" he whispered as I flopped against his legs. "Move it, Maizie. Get off the boat."

"Get up," said Sarah. "And you, detective. Don't move." She rammed her cute Sperry into his boot.

His thighs tensed, then jerked against the floor. His chest shook with the effort not to scream.

I pushed off the deck and carefully stepped over Nash's shuddering body. My jeans' fly flapped against my hip and my teal whale tail peeked beneath the torn Saint Laurent. The flare gun had slipped into my right leg, wedged against my inner thigh. As I turned my back to Sarah, I stuck a hand down my pants.

Classic fits and I still couldn't retrieve a damn gun. Of course, if I had worn skinny jeans the gun never would have made it down my back in the first place.

Sarah grabbed my arm, jerking it from my pants, and spun me toward her.

"Did you know there are a lot of sharks off this coast? And plenty of gators nearby." She sliced my arm from wrist to elbow. "We're not far from the Wassaw Sound. It'll be deep enough to dump you. This should help the predators find their dinner."

The pain appeared with the line of red dots down my arm. A wave of dizziness smacked me. Pulling my focus off my bleeding arm, I glanced over Sarah's shoulder. A sprawling live oak with a zillion knobby knees stretched into the river. The boat's diagonal trajectory set us on a course for ramming into that old tree.

Within my duct tape gag, I shouted and pointed at the giant speed bump in our path to ruin.

Still gripping my arm, she glanced behind her. "Shit."

I pushed down my jeans with my free hand and prayed Nash wouldn't notice my exposed left cheek.

Nash pulled in an astounded breath.

He noticed.

"I've got to straighten us out." Sarah whipped back to face me. "What are you doing?"

I needed both hands to peel down the jeans. Or someone else's hands. Ripping at the duct tape covering my mouth, I felt my skin give like the worst facial peel ever.

She yanked on my arm, pulling me toward the stern. "Come on.

You're coming with me."

"Nash, my jeans," I said. "Rip them off."

Nash's hands stretched toward my waist.

I dug my boots into the slippery deck, pulling against Sarah's tug.

The knife flashed before my face and pushed against my throat. "What are you doing?" snarled Sarah. Below us, the boat stuttered again, scraping against the channel debris. "The helm. Go. Before my keel catches."

The knife point pierced my skin.

The hells, I thought, this is it. This is where I get my throat cut. Just like in Season 2, Episode 4: "The Road Not Taken." Julia had tracked her runaway sister to skid row and a junkie had pulled a knife. But thanks to Julia's father's friend, an ex-Israeli commando, she surprised the junkie with her Krav Maga skills.

"It's going to take more than a knife to get your point across," I recited, using scene blocking muscle memory. I twisted my shoulder back and my hand shot between us. I grabbed Sarah's knife wrist. Trying for a left hook, I slammed my fist against her cheek. Unfortunately, my muscle memory remembered stage combat and not actual Krav Maga. The landed punch was more of a slap.

"God Almighty." Below me, Nash steadied me with one hand and shimmied my jeans past my hips. A hand plunged between my thighs.

I grabbed for Sarah's right shoulder.

Sarah ducked away from my shoulder clutch and jabbed her knee into my exposed groin.

My hand flew off her wrist. I doubled over, trapping Nash's hand between my thighs.

An echoey screech marked the slow grind of branches grating the ship's hull. The boat shuddered again.

I fell into Nash's lap, tangling his arm beneath me.

Sarah grabbed the cushioned bench as *A Little Nauti* lurched. Gasping, she glanced from our buffoonery to the looming tree. Cut and run was written all over her face. Or maybe stab and run.

I crawled forward, feeling the smooth edge of plastic and the rough graze of his hand glide across my skin past my rolled waistband. I continued to crawl, scrambling over Nash's legs toward Sarah. Grabbing an ankle, I yanked.

She slid off the bench, kicking her Sperry's and slashing with the knife.

Behind us, a crack burst the air, whizzed past our heads, and red streaked the sky.

While Sarah glanced up, I hurtled forward. Heaving myself against Sarah's right shoulder, I wedged her arm against the cockpit bench, trapping her knife hand away from my body.

"Sarah, this is done," I said, gripping her wrist. "And you know it. Just give up already."

"No," she cried out, pummeling my side with her left fist. "I had a plan."

"God, you're lucky Jerry made me take that chick boxing class." I held my breath as she socked me with a light kidney punch. Holding her wrist with my right, I cracked my left elbow against her hand. The knife clattered to the floor. "Nash. Help."

"On it." He crawled toward us and reached for the blade. "I'll take over."

"Not with your shot up foot," I grunted.

Beneath me, Sarah writhed and pummeled my back. I slapped, scratched, and kicked like I was on a *Real Housewives* reunion episode. Rearing back, I readied to rebreak her nose with my forehead.

Sarah shot up, kicking her feet at my head, and clambered on the bench.

Avoiding the plaid Sperrys, I fell back and thudded against Nash.

Scrambling from the bench, Sarah grabbed the rail and jumped into the stern. She spun the wheel, but the sprawling root system had snatched her sailboat and the tide shoved us against the giant tree.

The engine whined, then bellowed. We pitched sideways. A sickening crack ended Sarah's high seas escape. She spun and jumped over the low transom gate, splashing into the murky water below.

I reached above Nash to grab the bench. Hands tightened

around my waist and pulled me back to the deck.

"Let her go," Nash whispered in my ear.

"What?" I slipped my hand off the seat to turn and face Nash. "We can't let her go."

"She's headed into a swamp. How far do you think she'll get?"

"What if she comes back to attack us?"

"She doesn't have any weapons. This boat is good as sunk. What would be the point?"

"But—" My lip trembled. "I fought so hard. I can't let her go now."

"I know you did, kid." Nash scooted to rest his back against the bench, then slipped his arm around my shoulder. "The Coast Guard will see the flare. They'll be here any minute."

"Why is it taking so long? Shouldn't they have been looking for Ed's boat?»

"When we don't appear in the sound, they'll send a cutter up river." He leaned against me and kissed the side of my head. "You did good. We should patch you up. How's that arm?"

I ignored the stinging cut on my arm and the bruises I could feel forming on my back. "How can you say I did good? You've got a bullet hole through your foot and Sarah Waverly got away."

"We're alive and she's alive but soon to be captured. If you hadn't found me, I'd be dead. Even though I was pretty sore about that pepper spray."

A cool breeze dusted my bare thighs. The Simon Millers were still rolled halfway down my hips. Thank God for bikini waxes. I lifted my butt and quickly scooted the jeans up my hips.

"Now that's a real shame," said Nash. "Seeing your sugar shaker was the highlight of this whole ordeal. I've never seen a bare-assed girl fight. That's one for the bucket list."

O.M.G. Sarah Waverly hadn't killed me, but I would still die of humiliation.

"Rip them off, Nash," he cried in a high falsetto and snort laughed.

"Shut up."

"What was that about the knife getting a point across?"

"I was using Julia Pinkerton self-defense. Saying the line helps me remember."

"Maizie, you're a real pistol."

I sniffed. "I am?"

"Sure enough." The hand on my shoulder slipped to my waist. Tipping his head back, he rested his cheek against my hair and sighed. "You'll be all right."

What did that mean? You'll do all right as an investigator? Or you'll be all right without me? I gave up thinking and turned to face him. "Nash."

"Yes, ma'am?" A lazy smile slid from scar to dimple, but the sky blue eyes appeared weary. And still red from the pepper spray.

Heat licked my cheeks. Here I was, still the selfish, spoiled brat worried about my future career while this man had been pepper sprayed, shot, and his business almost destroyed by my hand. "Never mind."

"Don't hold back on me now." His hand grazed my cheek. Tucking a tendril of hair behind my ear, he winked. "I hear the rumbling of a motor boat. That'll be the cavalry. If you've got something on your chest, better spill it. In a minute, we'll be tied up with the police."

The sexiest wink ever.

I no longer thought about my career, but I certainly wasn't going to spill the thoughts speeding through my head after that wink. "How's your foot? Do you want me to cut off the tape and redress it? There's probably a first aid kit below deck. Maybe you need something for the pain? I'm sure Ed kept—"

Nash's finger pressed against my lips.

"I'll let EMS handle getting the tape off. You were a little rough with that fish knife last time." Another wink and the finger traced my bottom lip. "I can think of other things that'd help keep my mind off my foot."

I sighed.

His fingers stole to the back of my neck and his palm slid to cup my head. "Did I ever tell you that I like green thongs?"

"No." I pressed against his side. "Too bad my thong is teal."

He sighed.

Waves sloshed against the hull. A bright light swept across the river and halted on our boat.

Backlit, his face was thrown in shadow, but I could still see his lips purse. "When you broke into that cabin, I'd never been so glad or so furious to see anyone in my life."

"You mostly seemed furious." My hand had crept behind his neck. I laid the other flat on his chest, happy to feel the rapid-fire thumping of the heart beneath.

His fingers tangled in my hair. "You don't listen to me."

"I do listen, I just don't always do what you say."

"You're inexperienced. I know better. Dammit, Maizie, you were almost killed today."

"So were you." My breath caught in my throat as his hand skimmed beneath my destroyed Saint Laurent and found the bottom edge of my bra.

His fingers dug into my scalp and guided my head toward his. "Doesn't count."

"Counted enough for me."

"Hush."

Our foreheads touched. He held my gaze, then flicked a glance past me. Drawing back, he stared over my shoulder.

"Nash." I gathered his t-shirt into my hand and tried to yank his attention back. But the roar of a powerboat engine grew and the boat rocked, bumping us against the oak's jutting tree roots and low hanging branches. The engine slowed. I held tight as *A Little Nauti* bobbed in the sloshing waves.

"Dammit." Nash's hands flew off my body.

"What?" I reluctantly peeled my fingers from his t-shirt and glanced over my shoulder.

A spotlight zoomed on our deck huddle. Turning fully, I raised my hand to my eyes and squinted past the light. Our would-be rescuers didn't wear Coast Guard or Chatham County Sheriff uniforms. They wore jeans and t-shirts and looked a lot like Al's camera team. Except for the man in classic Breton stripes, chinos, and sailor cap.

Giulio. Jumping, waving, and shouting, "Ahoy, my beautiful mateys."

I swiveled back to Nash. His look was unreadable, his features grim. Thrusting his hands beneath my bottom, he shoved me to my feet.

I stumbled to standing, then turned to face him.

"Nash."

One eyebrow lifted and he flicked a hand toward the boat. "Your fans await."

THIRTY-TWO

#ByeFelicia #PaulNewmanEyes

I WAITED TWO DAYS. NOT SO much waited, because waiting implies sitting around. I spent two days going over police statements and getting tetanus shots. Sometimes with Nash, but mostly alone. Together, we were as awkward as eleven-year-olds at a school dance. He called me Miss Albright. I stuck with Mr. Nash. No slick glances filled with passionate regret. No brushing of fingertips as we passed in the hall. No "see you when this mess is done and we can get back to work." Nothing.

Not. A. Thing.

Lamar brought me donuts. Carol Lynn made me hushpuppies, fritters, and homemade fried pickles. Remi gave me her Happy Meal toy. Then took it back. Tiffany and Rhonda delivered a "Shuck it" t-shirt along with hugs and incriminating photos from their all-night party in Savannah. Daddy drove me back and forth to the police station. And Giulio offered me sex.

Which I turned down.

But by the third day, my job hunting time had run out. I was ready to beg, borrow, or steal.

Mostly beg.

I had to give Judge Ellis some evidence I was working or risk his wrath. I heard through the grapevine (Giulio) that Jolene Sweeney's *TMZ* leak about my failed investigative attempt had yet to be cleared up while Sarah Waverly's crimes were still under investigation.

Sarah had been caught in the swamp, soaked to the bone and hanging from a tree after getting bit by a turtle.

I secretly hoped she got some weird turtle disease. Unless it got her out of her prison sentence.

For my "begging for a W-4" scene, I wore Valentino. A red, crepe sheath that hid my extra curves and hit me mid-thigh. With little Dolce & Gabbana slides that I slipped on after dismounting from Lucky.

Glancing up at the Dixie Kreme building, I took a deep, refreshing breath of donut air and marched up the stairs to the Nash Security Solutions office. I paused at the door, decided to skip the knock, and strode through. From the recliner, Lamar opened one eye and smiled, then opened both eyes and gave the Valentino a once over.

"Is he in?" I said.

"Oh, he's in, all right."

"Is he dressed?"

"I believe so." Lamar noticed my hesitation. "Just go on in. If you wait, you might miss your chance."

I blew out my breath, grabbed the old-timey knob, and yanked the door wide. Then halted my go-get-her stride and almost dropped my bag.

Felt like old times.

Nash was indeed dressed, in another huggy t-shirt and jeans, with his Aircast boot propped on his desk. The other foot hid beneath his desk, evidenced by the bouncing of his chair and the sound of his heel hammering the wood floor in a staccato sure to annoy his guests.

The hammering stopped. "Miss Albright. I wasn't expecting you."

I took a small step back, glanced again at the two women seated in his office, and straightened my shoulders. Jolene and Vicki. Yay.

"I won't be a minute," I said. "You see, I need—"

"A new wardrobe?" said Vicki, barely looking up from her phone. "Really, Maizie. Valentino at ten in the morning? In Black Pine?"

Jolene smirked. "Does Valentino make orange jumpsuits?"

"Mostly red and white, I think," I said, then got her point.

"Don't worry about claustrophobia in jail, Maizie," she said. "There'll be bars on your room. Unless you get solitary."

"Shut it down, Jolene," barked Nash.

Ignoring Jolene and her incriminating statements hinting at the phone booth escapade, I sidled next to the desk and leaned toward Nash for a whisper. "Excuse me, Mr. Nash, but if I could see you for a tiny, quick second? Out in the other office? If we could talk, I'll totally get out of the way."

"I'm not going anywhere." Nash pointed at his foot. "Get on with it."

"Of course." I avoided his gaze by reaching into my Tod's tote for the W-4 form I had downloaded and the time sheet I had prepared. I dropped the papers on his desk and slid them before him. "It's about the work I've done for you."

"We were just talking about that," said Vicki.

A leaden ball of anxiety lodged in the pit of my gut. Turning to face the women, I leaned a hip against the desk for moral and physical support. "Oh?"

"Black Pine Group has dropped the sale of Nash Security Solutions." Vicki clicked off her phone and cut her eyes toward Jolene.

"I'm sorry about your uncle," I said. "I liked Ed."

Jolene narrowed her eyes. "I'm sure you did."

"Rein it in, Jolene," said Nash.

"I've offered to buy out Jolene's half of the company." Vicki brushed invisible lint off her Donna Karan linen skirt. "But only if we could film you working."

Shizzles.

"But I don't want you working with Nash." Jolene arched a brow. "Not to be ugly, but I don't like you. At all. In fact, I pretty much hate your guts."

Double Shizzles.

"Don't be spiteful," said Vicki. "You don't have to like Maizie. This is business. There's no room for liking in business. What are you worried about? That she'll sleep with him?"

"Vicki," I gasped.

"Really, Maizie." Vicki rolled her eyes. "Don't be such a prude.

It'd be better for ratings if you did. Or at least acted like it."

Jolene set her lips to pout and folded her arms over her jersey wrap dress.

"I don't know why y'all are here. It's like this has nothing to do with me." Nash's voice rose. «Even if it's my own damn business you're talking about."

"Half yours," said Jolene.

"The working half." He pushed back in his chair and the cast thudded to the floor with a bang.

I winced.

Nash slammed his fist on the desk. "Dammit, Jolene, I'll hire whoever the hell I want. And I'll sleep with whoever the hell I want."

My eyes flew to the open office door.

Outside, Lamar had lowered the recliner's footrest and had turned in the chair to watch us. He winked at me.

Mortified, I switched my gaze to the ceiling.

"That being said, Miss Vicki," continued Nash. "I do not have relations with my assistants. And I will not have your silly show compromising my investigations. I'm currently exploring other financial backers to buy out Jolene's half."

No relations with assistants. My eyes dropped from the ceiling to the floor.

"You can't get another backer without my permission," said Jolene.

"I've got prints of David Waverly and you in a green bikini that'd say otherwise."

Now it was Jolene's turn to match the Valentino red. "That's flippin' blackmail, Wyatt."

"You're bluffing," said Vicki, who had no issues with blackmail. She reached into her Dior bag, pulled out a credit card, and set it on the desk. "No camera on you or your clients. We mosaic out all products and addresses. Just a few cameos of Maizie doing whatever as filler. The rest we'll film with the cast."

My fate signed, sealed, and delivered. I had survived a beat-down and near-shooting by a calculating killer, yet still cowered in Vicki's shadow. Hadn't I had my "wax-on-wax-off" moment?

"No way." I pushed off my desk lean. "Nash's right. This business is about privacy and security."

Vicki's eyebrows rose a half centimeter.

"I appreciate what you've done for me, Vicki, but you can't interfere anymore. You could have endangered the lives of Al and his crew. Not to mention gotten them involved in a murder one case."

Not quite on the same level as the prom queen speech from *Mean Girls*. But I wasn't crying or using a rising intonation to reveal my cowardice. Yay me.

"If you're worried about how *you* endangered the crew, there is a simpler solution," said Vicki. "I'll even give you a bonus. One that would get Mr. Nash out of hock. Think about it. You could be part-owner instead of a mere assistant."

She glanced at the Black card sitting on the desk. Our eyes followed. "Maizie Albright" had been inscribed on the bottom left.

My fingers itched to stroke that fifteen-digit code.

"We didn't discuss this," said Jolene.

"Why would I have discussed this with you?" Vicki turned to me. "You could play detective when you're not on the show. I'd schedule breaks, real breaks, so not to interfere with the investigation business. We wouldn't film Mr. Nash or his…" She smirked. "Exploits."

I could feel Nash studying me.

Instead of Nash, I stared at the card.

Just to have the ability to buy out Jolene. That'd be sweet.

Not to mention writing my own W-4.

We could hire someone else to do the billing.

To afford a vehicle with four wheels! Maybe get my blue Jag back.

Don't even think about the shopping, I told myself. But I did. Couldn't help it.

But I'd still work for Vicki. We'd still be Manager and Daughter. I'd be "playing detective."

I picked up the card, checked the security code, and forced

myself to forget the four-digit number. "Don't you want me to try to become successful on my own?"

"Really, Maizie." A line flickered in her forehead despite the injections. "I've seen your successes. As Kate. As Julia. Even on *All is Albright*. Your Teen Choice Award for Choice TV Actress is sitting in my living room."

"Not as my manager. That Teen Choice Award is yours as much as it is mine. I meant, as my…you know," I braced myself not to fumble the words, "my mom."

She cut her eyes away. "You're not taking this seriously. This season is locked in. I have to film you."

Okay, that hurt.

"Then I've got no choice." I doled out Hollywood's—and Black Pine's—favorite threat. "I'll sue you if you try to film me again. Or Nash. Or anything to do with his investigations. No joke."

"Like you could afford a lawyer," said Jolene.

"I have friends willing to help me. Support me," I amended. My new friends couldn't help me with legal funds. "And considering Vicki's assets and my celebrity status, I don't think it'll be a problem getting a float on the retainer."

I paused, hoping Vicki would capitulate, realizing our relationship as mother and daughter was at stake. "Is that what you want for us? A legal battle?"

"Don't be ridiculous." But she didn't move from the door. She waited for something. And stared at my hand. Like she thought I wasn't cold sober serious.

Glancing at my hand, I saw I still gripped the Black card.

She thought I wasn't cold sober serious.

"This is for real, Vicki." With great triumph—and internal remorse—I held the credit card before me and attempted to rip it.

Damn Titanium.

Jolene snickered.

I slammed the card into Nash's metal bin and kicked the trashcan. Looking up, I narrowed my eyes at Vicki. "In conclusion, I don't want to sue. But I will."

"We'll see," she said and sailed out the door, Chanel No. 5 trailing in her wake.

Okay, not the big climatic scene I was hoping for. More like a *Mommy Dearest* ending.

Small victories.

Jolene stood to follow but turned in the doorway. "I want to know these other backers, Nash, or I'm selling to Vicki Albright."

Nash nodded, watching her fingers skim across her jersey-wrapped hip.

"I can make your life hell if I don't get what I want." Jolene smiled her best malicious smile.

Nash wisely kept his mouth shut, but his eyes remained glued to the fingertip that skimmed the length of her thigh.

"You, too, Maizie," said Jolene. "Your so-called new life? Hell. On. Earth." She spun and slammed the front door.

I jumped and slid off the desk. "Is she for real?»

Of course, she was serious. She had already gotten me in trouble with Judge Ellis. Trouble I could save myself from if Nash would sign the W-4. But if I could stand up to Vicki, I could deal with Jolene.

Hopefully.

Nash collapsed into his chair and pointed at the form on his desk. "'Maizie Marlin Albright.' Marlin? That's your middle name?"

"Family name." Sort of. Daddy had snuck his other favorite hunting rifle on my birth certificate while Vicki enjoyed post-delivery Percocet. "About the job..."

"Are you really going to sue your mother?" Nash heaved his booted leg on his desk and leaned back in his chair. "That took guts to say it to her. Did you mean it?"

I twisted the handle on my Tod's tote. "I can't afford a lawyer and she'll probably countersue or something." I looked up. "But if that's what it takes, then yes."

"You should be proud of yourself."

"I guess," I said. "I'd be prouder if you'd say you'd hire me to train under you."

He smirked, then glanced toward the front office. "What'd you say, Lamar? I'm putting you in charge of hiring."

"I said I'd be a silent partner, Nash." Lamar stepped into the office and leaned against the door. "I have another business to run. One that gets me up before dawn. And actually pays my bills."

"Never known you to be silent about anything, Lamar."

"And never known you to be a tease. Tell the girl she has the job."

I sucked in a breath. My dream had been realized.

Maizie Albright, Adult Detective.

Which sounded a bit like porn. I'd have to work on the title.

I squealed and hugged Lamar. Rounding on Nash, I looped my arms around his neck and squeezed.

"Rule number two, Miss Albright," he gasped. "Investigators don't hug."

"You didn't mind on the boat," I whispered.

"We'll work on the rules," he said and gave me a stunning Paul Newman wink.

THANK YOU FOR READING 15 MINUTES

When I began to imagine Maizie Albright, I was inspired by the for-real tv and movie business growing in and around my hometown in Georgia. The sets for *The Walking Dead, Drop Dead Diva*, and numerous movies like *Sweet Home Alabama* plus the US location for Pinewood Studios were all a stone's throw away. And then my family moved to Nagoya, Japan, and I got to play reality star when we appeared on HGTV's *House Hunters International* "Living for the Weekend in Nagoya" episode. There's my 15 MINUTES of fame! I hope you enjoyed Maizie's adventures. I had a lot of fun writing them.

Want more Maizie Albright? Her next adventures, 16 MILLIMETERS and NC-17, are coming soon! **Read on for previews in the Maizie Albright Star Detective and the Cherry Tucker Mystery series.**

If you'd like to be alerted of my new releases, please sign up for my book newsletter and to be automatically entered in my quarterly subscriber drawing plus entered for my signed book drawing at each new release (http://smarturl.it/LarissasBookNews or go to the link on my website at larissareinhart.com).

And finally, you can help others by writing a review. Your five minutes of time is greatly appreciated by me and other readers!

Feel free to visit my website: http://larissareinhart.com/
or friend me on social media:
https://www.facebook.com/larissareinhartwriter
http://instagram.com/larissareinhart\
https://twitter.com/LarissaReinhart
http://pinterest.com/LarissaReinhart/
http://smarturl.it/LarissaGoodreads

Thank you!
xoxo

Larissa

16 MILLIMETERS

A MAIZIE ALBRIGHT STAR DETECTIVE MYSTERY #2

MAIZIE ALBRIGHT
Star Detective

IN CONTINUING HER CAREER-MAKEOVER QUEST as a for-real detective, ex-teen and reality star Maizie Albright has a big learning curve to overcome. A sleuthing background starring in a TV show— *Julia Pinkerton, Teen Detective*—does not cut the real life mustard. It doesn't even buy her lunch, let alone extra condiments. Her chosen mentor, Wyatt Nash of Nash Security Solutions, is not a willing teacher. He'd rather stick Maizie with a safe desk job and handle the security solution-ing himself. But Maizie's got other plans to help Nash. First, win Nash's trust. Second, his heart.

Wait, not his heart. His respect. His hearty respect.

So when a major movie producer needs a babysitter for his hot mess starlet, Maizie eagerly takes the job. But when her starlet appears dead, and then not dead, Maizie's got more than an actress to watch and a missing corpse to find. Body doubles, dead bodies, and hot bodies abound when the big screen, small screen, and silent screams collide. Maizie's on the job, on the skids, and on thin ice, hunting a killer who may be a celebrity stalker. And Maizie just might be the next celebrity who gets snuffed.

PORTRAIT OF A DEAD GUY

A CHERRY TUCKER MYSTERY #1

IN HALO, GEORGIA, FOLKS KNOW Cherry Tucker as big in mouth, small in stature, and able to sketch a portrait faster than buckshot rips from a ten gauge -- but commissions are scarce. So when the well-heeled Branson family wants to memorialize their murdered son in a coffin portrait, Cherry scrambles to win their patronage from her small town rival. As the clock ticks toward the deadline, Cherry faces more trouble than just a controversial subject. Between ex-boyfriends, her flaky family, an illegal gambling ring, and outwitting a killer on a spree, Cherry finds herself painted into a corner she'll be lucky to survive.

★ Winner of the Dixie Kane Memorial Award ★ Nominated for the Daphne du Maurier Award and the Emily Award ★

☉☉

KEEP READING FOR THE SNEAK PEEK OF

PORTRAIT OF A DEAD GUY

PORTRAIT of a DEAD GUY

A Cherry Tucker Mystery

LARISSA REINHART

ONE

IN A SMALL TOWN, THERE is a thin gray line between personal freedom and public ruin. Everyone knows your business without even trying. Folks act polite all the while remembering every stupid thing you've done in your life. Not to mention getting tied to all the dumbass stuff your relations — even those dead or gone — have done. We forgive but don't forget.

I thought the name Cherry Tucker carried some respectability as an artist in my hometown of Halo. I actually chose to live in rural Georgia. I could have sought a loft apartment in Atlanta where people appreciate your talent to paint nudes in classical poses, but I like my town and most of the three thousand or so people that live in it. Even though most of Halo wouldn't know a Picasso from a plate of spaghetti. Still, it's a nice town full of nice people and a lot cheaper to live in than Atlanta.

Halo citizens might buy their living room art from the guy who hawks motel overstock in front of the Winn-Dixie, but they also love personalized mementos. Portraits of their kids and their dogs, architectural photos of their homes and gardens, poster"-size photos of their trips to Daytona and Disney World. God bless them. That's my specialty, portraits. But at this point, I'd paint the side of a barn to make some money. I'm this close from working the night shift at the Waffle House. And if I had to wear one of those starchy, brown uniforms day after day, a little part of my soul would die.

Actually a big part of my soul would die, because I'd shoot myself first.

When I heard the highfalutin Bransons wanted to commission a portrait of Dustin, their recently deceased thug son, I hightailed it to Cooper's Funeral Home. I assumed they hadn't called me for the commission yet because the shock of Dustin's murder rendered them senseless. After all, what kind of crazy called for a portrait of their murdered boy? But then, important members of a small community could get away with little eccentricities. I was in no position to judge. I needed the money.

After Dustin's death made the paper three days ago, there'd been a lot of teeth sucking and head shaking in town, but no surprise at Dustin's untimely demise from questionable circumstances. It was going to be that or the State Pen. Dustin had been a criminal in the making for twenty-seven years.

Not that I'd share my observations with the Bransons. Good customer service is important for starving artists if we want to get over that whole starving thing.

As if to remind me, my stomach responded with a sound similar to a lawnmower hitting a chunk of wood. Luckily, the metallic knocking in the long-suffering Datsun engine of my pickup drowned out the hunger rumblings of my tummy. My poor truck shuddered into Cooper's Funeral Home parking lot in a flurry of flaking yellow paint, jerking and gasping in what sounded like a death rattle. However, I needed her to hang on. After a couple big commissions, hopefully the Datsun could go to the big junkyard in the sky. My little yellow workhorse deserved to rest in peace.

I entered the Victorian monstrosity that is Cooper's, leaving my portfolio case in the truck. I made a quick scan of the lobby and headed toward the first viewing room on the right. A sizable group of Bransons huddled in a corner. Sporadic groupings of flower arrangements sat around the narrow room, though the viewing didn't actually start until tomorrow.

A plump woman in her early fifties, hair colored and high-lighted sunshine blonde, spun around in kitten heel mules and pulled me into her considerable soft chest. Wanda Branson, step-mother to the deceased, was a hugger. As a kid, I spent many a Sunday School smothered in Miss Wanda's loving arms.

"Cherry!" She rocked me into a deeper hug. "What are you doing here? It's so nice to see you. You can't believe how hard these past few days have been for us."

Wanda began sobbing. I continued to rock with her, patting her back while I eased my face out of the ample bosom.

"I'm glad I can help." The turquoise and salmon print silk top muffled my voice. I extricated myself and patted her arm. "It was a shock to hear about Dustin's passing. I remember him from high school."

I remembered him, all right. I remembered hiding from the already notorious Dustin as a freshman and all through high school. Of course, that's water under the bridge now, since he's dead and all.

"It's so sweet of you to come."

"Now Miss Wanda, why don't we find you a place to sit? You tell me exactly what you want, and I'll take notes. How about the lobby? There are some chairs out there. Or outside? It's a beautiful morning and the fresh air might be nice."

"I'm not sure what you mean," said Wanda. "Tell you what I want?"

"For the portrait. Dustin's portrait."

"Is there a problem?" An older gentleman in a golf shirt and khaki slacks eyed me while running a hand through his thinning salt and pepper hair. John Branson, locally known as JB, strode to his wife's side. "You're Cherry Tucker, Ed Ballard's granddaughter, right?"

I nodded, whipping out a business card. He glanced at it and looked me over. I had the feeling JB wasn't expecting this little bitty girl with flyaway blonde hair and cornflower blue eyes. My local customers find my appearance disappointing. I think they expected me to return from art school looking as if I walked out of 1920s' bohemian Paris wearing black, slouchy clothes and a ridiculous beret. I like color and a little bling myself. However, I toned it down for this occasion and chose jeans and a soft orange tee with sequins circling the collar.

"Yes sir," I said, shaking his hand. "I got here as soon as I could. I'm sorry about Dustin."

"Why exactly did you come?" JB spoke calmly but with distaste, as if he held something bitter on his tongue. Probably the idea of me painting his dead son.

"To do the portrait, of course. I figured the sooner I got here, the sooner I could get started. I am pretty fast. You probably heard about my time in high school as a Six Flags Quick Sketch artist. But time is money, the way I look at it.

You'll want your painting sooner than later."

"Cherry, honey, I think there's been some kind of misunderstanding." Wanda looped her arm around JB's elbow. "JB's niece Shawna is doing the painting."

"Shawna Branson?" I would have keeled over if I hadn't been at Cooper's and worried someone might pop me in a coffin. Shawna was a smooth-talking Amazonian poacher who wrestled me for the last piece of cake at a church picnic some fifteen years ago. Although she was three heads taller, my scrappy tenacity and love of sugar helped me win. Shawna marked that day as a challenge to defeat me at every turn. In high school, she stole my leather jacket, slept with my boyfriend, and brown-nosed my teachers. She didn't even go to my school. And now she was after my commission.

"She's driving over from Line Creek today," Wanda said. "You know, she got her degree from Georgia Southern and started a business. She's very busy, but she thinks she can make the time for us."

"I've seen her work," I said. "Lots of hearts, polka dots, and those curlicue letters you monogram on everything."

"Oh yes," said Wanda, showing her fondness for curlicue letters. "She's very talented."

"But ma'am. Can she paint a portrait? I have credentials. I'm a graduate of SCAD, Savannah College of Art and Design. I'm formally trained on mixing color, using light, creating perspective, not to mention the hours spent with live models. I can do curlicue. But don't you want more than curlicue?"

Wanda relaxed her grip on JB's arm. Her eyes wandered to the floral arrangements, considering.

"I have the skill and the eye for portraiture," I continued. "And this is Dustin's final portrait. Don't you want an expert to handle his precious memory?"

"She does have a point, J.B," Wanda conceded.

JB grunted. "The whole idea is damn foolish."

Wanda blushed and fidgeted with JB's sleeve.

"The Victorians used to wear a cameo pin with a lock of their deceased's hair in it," I said, glad to reference my last minute research as I defended her. "It was considered a memorial. When photography became popular, some propped up the dead for one last picture."

"Exactly. Besides, this is a painting not a photograph," said Wanda. "It's been harder as Dustin got older. I wanted to be closer to him. JB did, too, in his way. And then Dustin was taken before his time."

I detected an eye roll from JB. Money wasn't the issue. Propriety needled him. Wanda loved to spend JB's money, and he encouraged her. JB's problem wasn't that Wanda was flashy; she just shopped above her raising. Which can have unfortunate results. Like hiring someone to paint her dead stepson.

"A somber representation of your son could be com- forting," I said. Not that I believed it for a minute.

"Do you need the work, honey?" Wanda asked. "I want to do a memory box. You know, pick up one of those frames at the Crafty Corner for his mementos. You could do that."

"I'll do the memory box," I said. "I've done some flag cases, so a memory box will be no problem. But I really think you should reconsider Shawna for the painting."

"Now lookee here," said JB. "Shawna's my niece."

"Let me get my portfolio," I said. Pictures speak louder than words, and it looked like JB needed more convincing.

I dashed out of the viewing room and took a deep breath to regain some composure. I couldn't let Shawna Branson steal my commission. The Bransons needed this portrait done right. Who knows what kind of paint slaughter Shawna would commit. As far as I was concerned, she could keep her curlicue business as long as she left the real art to me.

M Y BRIGHT YELLOW PICKUP GLOWED like a radiant bea-
con in the sea of black, silver, and white cars. I opened the
driver door with a yank, cursing a patch of rust growing around
the lock. Standing on my toes, I reached for the portfolio bag on
the passenger side. The stretch tipped me off my toes and splayed
me flat across the bench.

"I recognize this truck," a lazy voice floated behind me. "And
the view. Doesn't look like much's changed either way in ten
years."

I gasped and crawled out.

Luke Harper, Dustin's stepbrother.

I had forgotten that twig on the Branson family tree. More like
snapped it from my memory. His lanky stance blocked the open
truck door. One hand splayed against my side window. His other
wrist lay propped over the top of my door. Within the cage of
Luke's arms, we examined each other. Fondness didn't dwell in
my eyes. I'm never sure what dwelled in his.

Luke drove me crazy in ways I didn't appreciate. He knew how
to push buttons that switched me from tough to soft, smart to
dumb. Beautiful men were my kryptonite. Local gossip said my
mother had the same problem. My poor sister, Casey, was just as
inflicted. We would have been better off inheriting a squinty eye
or a duck walk.

"Hello, Luke Harper." I tried not to sound snide. Drawing up
to my fullest five foot and a half inches, I cocked a hip in casual
belligerence.

"How's it going, Cherry?" A glint of light sparked his smoky
eyes, and I expected it corresponded with a certain memory of
a nineteen-year-old me wearing a pair of red cowboy boots and
not much else. "You hanging out at funeral homes now? Never
took you for a necrophiliac."

This time I gave Luke my best what-the-hell redneck glare.
Crossing my arms, I took a tiny step forward in the trapped space.
He stared at me with a faint smile tugging the corners of his

mouth. If I could paint those gorgeous curls and long sideburns — which will never happen, by the way — I would use a rich, raw umber with burnt sienna highlights. For his eyes, I'd mix Prussian blue and a teensy Napthal red. However, he would call his hair "plain old dark brown" and eyes "gray." But, what does he know? Not much about art, I can tell you that.

"I thought you were in Afghanistan or Alabama," I said. "What are you doing back?"

"Discharged. You still mad at me? It's been a while."

"Mad? I barely remember the last time I saw you." I wasn't really lying. My last memory wasn't of seeing him, but seeing the piece of trash in his truck. And by piece of trash, I mean the kind with boobs.

"You were pretty mad at the time. And I know you and your grudges."

"I've got more to do than think about something that happened when I was barely out of high school."

"Are you going to hold my youthful indiscretions against me now?" He smiled. "I'm only in town for a short time. You know I can only take Halo in small doses."

"If you're not sticking around, I can't see how my opinion of you matters. Not like you asked me about your sudden decision to join the Army and clear out of dodge."

"That's what you're mad about?"

Dear God, men are clueless. Why He didn't sharpen them up a bit has to be one of life's greatest mysteries.

"There are a number of things you did. But I'm not about to print you out a list."

"We had some good times, too."

"Which you sabotaged with your idiocy."

"You're one to talk," he mumbled.

I took another step forward, but Luke didn't move. His eyes roamed from my face to my boots. My irritation grew. "Do you mind? I need to get back to Cooper's. I'm working." I shoved him out of the way, dragging my unwieldy portfolio bag behind me.

"Just trying to put my finger on what about you changed."

I clamped my mouth shut as an unwelcome blush crept up the back of my neck.

"I know," he continued. "Your boots are plain old brown. Where're those red cowboy boots?"

I stomped toward the funeral home. "At home with my Backstreet Boys albums. I don't have time to play catch up with you. I've got stuff to do."

"How about playing catch up later, then?" I glanced back to see a glimmer of a smile. "Don't you think it'd be fun to stroll down memory lane? Does everybody still hang out at Red's?" The sunlight played with the auburn highlights in his dark curls and the tips of his long, black eyelashes.

Lord, why does he have to be so good looking? It was incredibly unfair how easily beauty weakened me. Gave suffering for art a whole new meaning.

"It was seven years ago," I said before I could stop myself.

"What?"

"Not ten years," I corrected. "But a lot has happened in seven."

"I bet."

I found Wanda shredding a tissue in the viewing room, watching JB bark orders at the assorted non-nuclear Bransons who then cowed and scurried as if he were the king of Forks County. He owned many businesses that supported most of the Branson clan, including the big Ford dealership, but he had actually inherited the Branson patrilineal power seat. Ironically, the two Bransons who never bowed to JB were his son, Dustin, and stepson, Luke. And that was where the similarities between Dustin and Luke stopped.

Luke and Dustin were never close. Luke loved his mother and put up with Dustin when she remarried. However, Luke got out of Halo as soon as possible. Couldn't blame him, with a cold stepfather and a mother pouring her attention into rehabilitating an emerging sociopath. But poor Wanda had her hands full.

Made me wonder, though. With Dustin out of the picture, was there now more room for Luke? Interesting that Luke left the

Army right when his stepbrother got offed.

Hating that ugly thought, I hurried over to Wanda. "I just ran into Luke," I said, giving her shoulder a quick hug. "I'm glad to see he's here to help you through this."

"Yes, it is a blessing. Served his time, you know, and of course, he won't tell me his plans yet. But that's Luke. Doesn't like to worry me."

"Keeps his cards pretty close to his chest, does he?"

"Look at him," Wanda waved at her son. "I've never been able to tell what he's thinking. Just like his father, God bless him. Maybe it was losing his daddy so young. He just keeps everything clammed up inside."

Spotting his mother's wave, Luke wandered into the viewing room. He had always been a wiry guy, displaying his strength in high school on the wrestling team and fighting behind the Highway 19 Quik Stop with the other boys carrying boulder-size chips on their shoulder. He still seemed dangerous, yet more settled and confident. There was no softness about him. Luke was all hard edges.

"Oh, I don't know," I murmured. "I lost my daddy young, too, but I've always been an open book."

"Well, boys and girls are different," said Wanda.

"Don't I know it." I swung one palm to my hip but waved my other in casual deference to Luke's arrival. "Let's go sit, and you can take a look at my portfolio. While you're looking at my samples, I'll sketch some ideas I have for Dustin."

"What's this?" Luke asked. "Ideas for Dustin?"

"I'm having Dustin's portrait done," Wanda explained. "I'll hang it next to the painting of him as a child. That one's thirty-by-forty. I'd like them to be the same size."

Holy cow, that's a big picture of a dead guy, I thought, but nodded my head as if it was the most reasonable idea in the world.

"That's downright morbid." Although he directed the statement to his mother, the accusation lay at my feet. "I swear you haven't changed Cherry, with all the nutty art stuff."

I felt like telling Luke, this is your mother's crazy notion, not mine. Instead I responded in my most proper aren't-you-an-idiot drawl, "Your momma is just dealing with this horrible tragedy the best she can, God bless her. It's a memorial."

"A memorial for Dustin? You don't know what Dustin was mixed up in, Mom. Death doesn't turn a sinner into a saint. God knows you tried your best. More than his own father."

"Come on, Miss Wanda," I tugged on her arm. Between Luke and Shawna, I was going to lose this commission. "I'll get you a cup of tea and you can look at my paintings. It'll get your mind off things for a minute, anyway. I've got a real cute one of Snug, Terrell Jacob's Coonhound."

Wanda beckoned JB and they conferred for a moment. With a shrug he followed her out of the viewing room.

Luke shoved his hands in his pockets. "You spent all that money on art school to paint pictures of dogs?"

"I spent all that money on art school to become a professional artist," I said. "It's early days yet. For now, I take what I can get."

"Including painting the departed?"

"You ever heard of a still life?" I shot back and stalked out of the viewing room, swinging my portfolio bag behind me.

I followed Wanda and JB into a little room crowded with a table and chairs. Unzipping the large bag, I pulled out a binder of photographs of my college works and a sheaf of plastic-encased photos of my newer stuff. Snug the dog, a horse named Conquering Hero, and a half-dozen kid portraits. I much preferred animals to children as subjects, something you don't learn in school. Getting a four-year-old to sit still is damn near impossible. However, you take a well-trained dog in the right pose, and you've got the perfect model. Snug the Coonhound sat better than most people. We had an easy working relationship, what with Snug's deferential silence.

No need for forced conversation with that subject. Of course with this job, I couldn't expect any conversation either. I could make do with photographs.

But first I needed to get the job.

"I don't know why you're wasting my time looking at pictures," said JB. He tossed the portraits of Snug and Hero on the table.

"This one is just beautiful, Cherry," said Wanda, hold- ing up a Sargent inspired painting. The model wore a sheet draped like a toga, but the effect was tasteful with wonderful folds to show depth and shadow.

"I'm glad you pointed out that one. Don't you love the light on her face? You might not be able to tell, but that's not an oil paint- ing. I had a tight schedule, so I used acrylics. They dry quickly and I didn't have to varnish the painting immediately. Someone mentioned you displaying the portrait at the funeral service? Oils wouldn't dry fast enough to get the painting done without mess- ing up the color."

"I was fixing on making a photo display for the service when I realized we didn't have many of Dustin after he passed a certain age." Wanda's face colored and she cast her eyes away from JB. "I've just been in a tizzy, not knowing what to do with myself and not sleeping. That's when I got the idea for the memory box. Started gathering stuff Dustin left in his old room. Then I remembered the family portraits we had done at our wedding and thought maybe a new painting would be a nice tribute."

"Let her have what she needs," said JB. "A picture's not bringing him back, but if it makes Wanda feel better, she can have it."

"I totally agree, sir," I said. "That's why you should let me have the honor of painting this portrait. You can see what quality I can produce. You don't want a final memorial done by an amateur."

"What about Shawna?" he said, eyeing me. "Although Shawna did set a pretty hefty price for painting my son."

I squirmed, caught between a rock and a rattlesnake. JB would sell out his niece for a cheaper price. But probably wouldn't help me underbid her, either.

"A portrait lasts for generations." I began with my salesman pitch. "My paintings are heirloom quality and will be around long after..." Since the subject was dead, I stopped before my mouth ate my foot. "Anyway, a portrait is priceless."

"Priceless? You talking free?" JB leaned back in his chair.

"Of course a professional artist would base the price on other

"Tell you what." JB leaned forward, hands flat on the table. "I'll give you a shot. I want Wanda to be happy after what all she's endured with Dustin. He was my son and I owe her that."

"Yes, sir," I said, although my skin still prickled from the word formaldehyde.

"But," he said, "you got to have the painting done for the funeral. The whole she-bang. Wanda can choose between you and Shawna, so you better make it good. She likes quality. After the funeral, I'm done. Wanda can hang up his picture and look at it all she wants, but I'm putting this whole blasted deal out of my mind. I'm paying off his creditors right and left, dealing with folks' complaints, and living through the embarrassment of the way he went. Do you know what they are saying about him?"

I knew, but I sure wasn't going to say. Folks thought a bad drug deal or payback from a robbery ring. Or someone just got tired of Dustin's mouth and went postal on him. Hard to say with Dustin. There were so many crimes to choose from.

"I'll work up a contract," I said. "Thank you for this opportunity. I'll get cracking right away and I'll also do the memory box."

"We'll have Cooper set out the body for you then." JB didn't smile but I did see a flash of teeth. "Got to admire your tenacity, Cherry. I hate to say it, but stories I heard about your family made me question your reliability."

A shot of heat worked its way from my toes to my scalp. People always bring up my family's history over the years, but it never got any easier.

"My reputation is important to me. I am judged by my own actions as well as those that surround me. You know how people like to talk."

"Yes, sir."

He looked at me evenly. "I'm glad we agree on this issue. As a businesswoman, you have your own reputation to protect and a lot of history to overcome."

A million comebacks crossed my mind, but none were appropriate for a bereaved father sitting in a funeral home with a large check that could have my name on it. I swallowed my pride and tried not to choke. "I'll bring that contract by tomorrow."

He had better keep his end of the bargain, because after that humiliation, I sure as hell wasn't working for free.

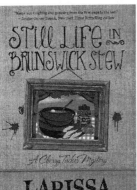

STILL LIFE IN
BRUNSWICK STEW

A Cherry Tucker Mystery

LARISSA
REINHART

HIJACK IN
ABSTRACT

A Cherry Tucker Mystery

LARISSA
REINHART

DEATH IN
PERSPECTIVE

A Cherry Tucker Mystery

LARISSA
REINHART

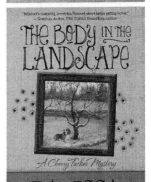

THE BODY IN THE
LANDSCAPE

A Cherry Tucker Mystery

LARISSA
REINHART

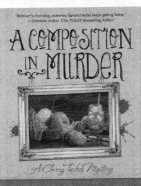

A COMPOSITION
IN MURDER

A Cherry Tucker Mystery

LARISSA
REINHART

HEARTACHE
MOTEL

THREE
INTERCONNECTED
MYSTERY
NOVELLAS

*Terri L. Austin, Larissa Reinhart
and LynDee Walker*

A 2015 Georgia Author of the Year Best Mystery finalist, Larissa writes the Cherry Tucker Mystery and Maizie Albright Star Detective series. The first in the Cherry Tucker series, *Portrait of a Dead Guy*, is a 2012 Daphne du Maurier finalist, 2012 The Emily finalist, and 2011 Dixie Kane Memorial winner. She loves books, food, and travel in any and all combinations.

Her family and Cairn Terrier, Biscuit, live in Nagoya, Japan, but they still call Georgia home. You can see them on HGTV's *House Hunters International* "Living for the Weekend in Nagoya" episode. Visit her website, find her chatting on Facebook, Instagram, and Goodreads, and sign up for her newsletter.

If you enjoy her books, please leave a review or tell a friend. She sends you virtual hugs and undying gratitude for your support! An honest review from a reader is the best gift you can give an author.

Made in the USA
Lexington, KY
01 February 2017